SONG OF MOONRISE

A LITTLE RED RIDING HOOD RETELLING

THE SINGER TALES
BOOK 4

DEBORAH GRACE WHITE

LUMINANT PUBLICATIONS

SONG OF MOONRISE: A LITTLE RED RIDING HOOD RETELLING

By Deborah Grace White

For Annabeth
Walk lightly and joyfully where others fear to tread.

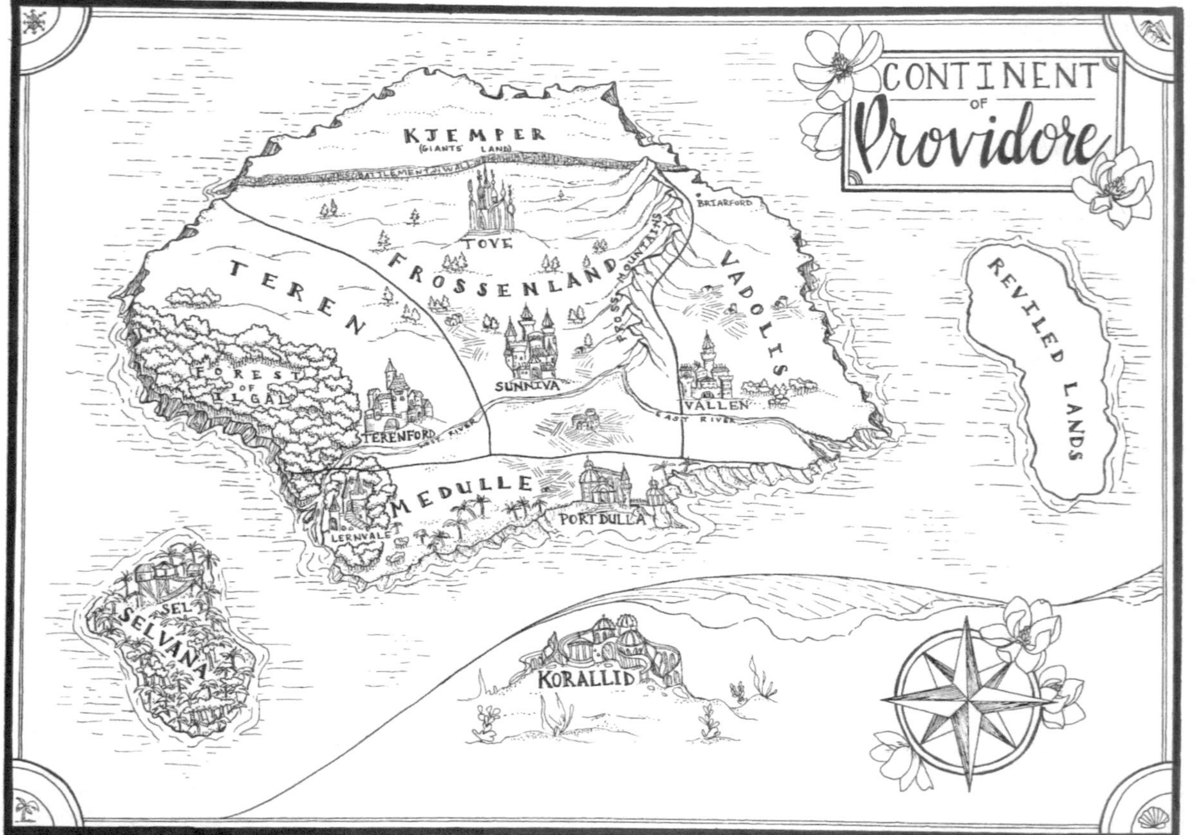

CONTINENT OF Providore
KJEMPER
(GIANTS' LAND)
BATTLEMENT WALL
TOVE
FROSSENLAND
BRIARFORD
VADOLIS
FROSS MOUNTAINS
TEREN
FOREST OF ILGAL
SUNNIVA
VALLEN
EAST RIVER
TERENFORD
WEST RIVER
MEDULLE
PORTDULLA
LERNVALE
REVILED LANDS
SEL SELVANA
KORALLID

Emmett

Emmett stood with his back to the castle's outer wall, the damp of the mossy stone seeping through his tunic. The night was still, nothing interrupting his musings except the muted sounds of the forest's nightlife. And those he didn't mind. Dangerous though he knew the Forest of Ilgal could be, he'd never found it frightening, not even in the darkness. It was the most beautiful part of his kingdom, and it was a crime that the family came so rarely to the forest-encircled castle at Lernvale in recent years. When Emmett had been a child, they'd come at least once a year to enjoy the change in scenery from their home in the castle at Port Dulla, Medulle's seaside capital city. But it had been five years since their last visit, and even this one had been undertaken reluctantly.

Hopefully all that was about to change.

Emmett gripped the rucksack he carried more tightly, sliding it further over his shoulder. He was impatient to begin, and Farrin was late. It was tempting to leave without his brother, but he told himself to give it five more minutes. Afraid or not, it would be wise to have backup when venturing into the Forest of Ilgal in the middle of the night.

Plus Farrin would never forgive him if Emmett left him out after all their scheming.

A noise made Emmett turn his head, but it wasn't Farrin. It was just an owl swooping through a low-hanging branch nearby. The nearest trees were only a stone's throw away, but the area immediately outside the castle wall was kept clear, allowing the scene to be gently illuminated by the moonlight. Emmett cast a glance up at the sky, noting that the moon was at its fullest.

Beautiful.

"A little late for a prince to be out alone in the woods, isn't it?"

The sinister, high-pitched whine of a voice didn't fool Emmett for a moment. He turned, unimpressed, to see Farrin creeping through the darkness from the direction of the normally locked side gate Emmett had spent the afternoon loosening.

"Hypocrite," Emmett grunted without heat, in reference to his little brother's accusation.

Farrin grinned at him, letting the hood of his dark cloak fall back. It revealed a face very similar to Emmett's, although sunlight would have shown that the disordered waves framing Farrin's face were tawny, whereas Emmett's were a dark brown.

"Ah, but I'm not the heir," Farrin said, speaking in his normal voice now. "And I'm therefore expendable enough to wander at will through the most dangerous corners of the forest."

"You wish," said Emmett dryly. "You're late, Farrin. We'd better hurry if we want to be out of sight before the next patrol."

"Lead on," said Farrin amicably.

Emmett struck straight out across the small grassy band that surrounded the castle, plunging into the trees without hesitation. He didn't know exactly where they were going, but he had enough of a general idea to make a start.

"Based on what you're carrying, I assume you got it?" Farrin's question brought Emmett's eyes around to him. It was darker under the shelter of the trees, but he could still see his brother gesturing at his rucksack.

"I did," Emmett confirmed. "With any luck, we'll be able to make a solid start tonight." Glancing ahead at his brother's projected path, he jutted his chin out in an indication. "Watch out—low branch ahead."

"Seriously, Emmett?" Farrin asked, his tone long-suffering. "It's like you can't help yourself. You'd better watch it, or getting old will make you insufferable."

"Getting old?" Emmett scoffed. "I'm nineteen, not ninety."

"And I'm seventeen, not seven." Farrin's response was mild. "I don't exactly need to be told how to walk through the forest. But your overbearing sense of responsibility doesn't know how to deal with someone who doesn't need looking after."

"That's ridiculous," said Emmett impatiently, irked by being called overbearing. The criticism was uncomfortably reminiscent of the frustrations the brothers had often shared regarding their father in recent years, and it unsettled him to be on the receiving end. "If I was such a responsible old man, would I be doing this?" He half lifted his rucksack with one hand, rattling it. "In case you've forgotten, this whole thing was my idea."

"Believe me, I haven't forgotten," said Farrin, stifling a yawn for effect. "I'd be happily asleep right now if you didn't drag me out here."

Emmett snorted. "Who's the old man now? And don't give me that nonsense. You've been as eager about the idea as I have. If you're going to try to convince me that I could've left you behind—"

Farrin cut him off with a laugh. "No, you couldn't have.

You're right, I'm itching for some action as much as you are." He cast a look over his shoulder, his grin a little too eager for Emmett's peace of mind. "Besides, I'd much rather be out here in the dangerous woods with you than back at the castle if Father found out you'd gone out here, and what you're planning to do. He'd have our heads if he knew we were going to actually wield magic. He'd certainly never let us visit Lernvale again. We'd be locked up back home in the capital for the next decade."

"Well, if it works, there's no reason he needs to know," Emmett said, his conscience prickling uneasily at him. "If the magic dissipates enough to make a difference, others will report it back to him. There'll be no reason to connect it to us at all."

Farrin cast a thoughtful look at Emmett, the expression revealed by a sliver of moonlight that slanted through the branches. "That really is your motivation, isn't it?" he said. "At first I thought dissipating the concentration of magic was just your excuse for an adventure. But you really do want to reclaim Ilgal for normal use, don't you?"

"Of course I do!" said Emmett. "I love this forest. The locals are already starting to report greater health problems. If the magic continues to build at the rate it's going now, it'll be uninhabitable in a generation. We'll end up like Selvana, with the magic so thick that the ground becomes deadly."

"That's a stretch," said Farrin.

He was clearly unconvinced by this mention of the island kingdom to the southwest, but Emmett felt sobered by Selvana's example. The island had been cut off from the mainland for all of living memory due to the deadliness of the wild magic that had overrun it. If magic was truly gathering strength in the Forest of Ilgal at the rate rumor said, what was to stop them going the same way?

"Even if things are as dire as that," Farrin went on, "the forest makes up such a small portion of our kingdom. And it's the least populated area. It wouldn't be the end of the world if humans had to stay out of it. We don't have the same problem anywhere else in Medulle."

Emmett frowned as he picked his way carefully through a thick patch of undergrowth, picturing in his mind the map of their kingdom. Medulle took up the entire southern coastline of the continent of Providore, and his brother was right that the Forest of Ilgal occupied only a small slice at the kingdom's western edge. But it was a slice very dear to his heart.

"How can we be sure it won't spread across the whole kingdom?" he challenged. "And even if it is contained to Ilgal, I imagine it would feel like the end of the world to the Medullans who live in the forest. Not to mention the Terenans."

"Yes, Teren has more at stake here, really," Farrin acknowledged. He paused to watch a rabbit scurry frantically into the undergrowth at their approach. "Given the forest covers half their kingdom, they should really be the ones trying to fix it." He sent his brother a grin. "Maybe we should have invited Otto along."

Emmett gave a grunt. "Not likely. Prince Otto has as much sense in his head as that rabbit."

Farrin laughed. "He's young. Give him a few years, and he'll probably be as serious and responsible as you are. Comes with being crown prince, probably." He gave his brother a playful shove. "At least you've got me to lighten you up. Poor Otto doesn't have any siblings. Or even a mother to soften things. Just him and King Ryker—must be a lonely existence."

"Actually, I heard some gossip from the servants this morning," Emmett commented. "Apparently King Ryker has been courting someone. It's caused quite a stir in Teren, because she's a commoner."

"Really?" Farrin sounded intrigued. "So Otto might have a stepmother soon."

"And, more to the point, King Ryker will be too distracted with his own affairs to worry about the growing crisis in Ilgal," Emmett said. "He'll probably do nothing until it's too late."

Farrin shook his head. "And the weight of the world is back on your shoulders. It's quite impressive, really, how you've managed to make Teren's problems your responsibility, as well as our own kingdom's problems."

"No I haven't," said Emmett, irritated. "The two kingdoms just have a shared interest, that's all. You sound ridiculous, Farrin, prosing on about my supposed insufferable responsibility when we're sneaking into the forest at night."

Farrin didn't respond to his brother's admittedly belligerent tone, just giving his head another shake. "You really don't see it, do you? You want to throw off the restrictions of our position as much as I do, but it's like you can't—like your sense of duty physically prevents you. I can't decide if you're incredibly noble or just absolutely absurd for framing this stunt as some kind of necessary heroics to save two kingdoms."

Emmett just rolled his eyes, unable to take that type of criticism seriously from his carefree little brother.

"Let me know when you decide." They'd just entered a moonlit clearing, and he came to a stop, reaching into his rucksack. The item he extracted was a small metal cylinder, twice as long as his hand. A strip of gold ran its length, glinting in the moonlight.

"Is that it?" Farrin asked eagerly, leaning in for a closer look. "The detector or whatever it's called?"

Emmett nodded.

"And we can really use it, even though we're not singers?"

Emmett nodded again. "It's not designed for singers. We don't have to wield magic to use it. It's powered by mined magic, intended for use by the elves. It directs them to where the magic is most concentrated, so they know where it's best to start mining." He cast a rueful look around the dark, silent forest. "Although I suppose that's no great issue in Ilgal these days. Probably anywhere they go is rich with magic for them to mine."

He looked at his brother, frowning a little at the undisguised excitement on Farrin's face. He'd tried to explain the risks when he shared his plan, but he still felt like the younger prince didn't fully understand the gravity of their illicit undertaking.

"About what you said earlier, Farrin," he said. "We're not going to *wield* the magic. You know as well as I do that only singers can do that. None of the devices I've acquired can give us that capacity. We're just going to release it."

"Yes, yes, I know," said Farrin impatiently. He gestured at the gold-embellished cylinder. "Let's see it in action."

Emmett raised the item, rubbing the heel of his hand along the gold strip a few times, letting the warmth of his skin soak into it.

"The elf said it would be easy," he said, feeling a little foolish. "He said that it would just show us where—"

He broke off as his brother gasped, his own eyes widening at the sudden glow in the ground directly in front of him. Nothing visible had changed about the device in his hand, but when his gaze followed the direction the cylinder was pointing, he saw a golden light pulsing faintly, as if from underneath the soil.

"Is that the magic?" Farrin asked eagerly.

"Must be," Emmett said.

He swung the device slowly around, watching in fascination as the glow faded from the previous spot, following the direction of the detector. He angled it up a little, aiming for the trees on the other side of the clearing, and saw that the glow was brighter under their canopy. Clearly the magic was more concentrated in that direction.

"Come on," he said, shouldering the rucksack again and pushing on deeper into the forest.

Farrin followed him, and the two brothers made their way between tree trunks until they hit a spot where the glow was so bright Emmett had to squint.

"That boulder," he said, lowering the object. "Let's start there. Looks like a lot of magic concentrated."

"All right," said Farrin obligingly. "I still don't really understand how it works, but I'll follow your lead."

Emmett grunted as he fished around in his rucksack. "I don't really know, either," he admitted. "But the elf who sold me this —not the same one who had the detector—explained the basics."

"He didn't know who you were, did he?" Farrin asked, his forehead creasing.

Emmett gave him a look. "Do you really think there's any chance I was *less* cautious than you think I should be? Of course I did everything I could to obscure my identity. If anyone found out the *crown prince* was trying to mine magic..."

"I thought you said we were just going to release it," Farrin pointed out.

"Yes, but who'd believe that if they learned I'd acquired mining tools and asked about how to extract magic from the ground?" Emmett said dryly.

"I sure wouldn't." Farrin's voice was cheerful, and Emmett couldn't help a chuckle, even as he rolled his eyes.

"I'm confident he didn't know who I was, anyway. He wouldn't have sold it to me if he did, given it's so highly illegal to provide magic-mining tools to humans. Now remember," he added, as he inserted the chisel—modified through the use of mined magic in a way he didn't at all comprehend—into the boulder in question. "It can apparently be quite danger—"

The word was cut off abruptly as the rock split in two with a deafening crack, sending a bird fluttering out of a nearby tree in alarm. Both princes were thrown backward by the rush of magic they could neither see nor sense. Emmett hit a tree trunk so hard the breath was knocked out of him. He slid down onto the grass, and for a moment he could only gasp, slumped over and disoriented.

"Em! Em, are you all right?" Farrin's alarmed voice gave Emmett the kickstart he needed. With an effort, he struggled to his feet, wincing at the bruise already blooming on his hip, and blinking rapidly to try to clear his vision.

"I'm all right," he assured his brother, giving his head a little shake. "The elf did say it could be dangerous. I guess we should have taken more precautions."

"Do you think it worked though?" Farrin asked, bouncing on the balls of his feet in a way that suggested he'd fallen more fortuitously.

"Good question." Emmett fumbled with his rucksack, his ears still ringing as he pulled out the detector. He pointed it at the rock and saw, with great excitement, that only the faintest shimmer of golden light was visible on it now. The inferno of earlier was gone, the magic presumably having dissipated into the air.

"It worked!" he cried, forgetting his injuries in his excitement. His eyes met Farrin's, and they broke into grins.

"Let's go again," Farrin said.

A part of Emmett—the part that was still radiating pain from the first attempt—knew it wasn't wise to press on when they had no real idea what they were doing. Especially if there was a chance he was putting Farrin in danger. But the thrill of success was intoxicating, and it was hard to be concerned for

Farrin when he was not only so eager but clearly unhurt. Perhaps just a few more releases. Then Emmett could do some research during the day, and the following night they could come more prepared to protect themselves.

The next two attempts yielded a similar result, except that they were smarter about their own placement, lying on the ground rather than leaning over the site of the magic. Not being a singer, Emmett couldn't feel magic, but he guessed it must be washing over him rather than knocking him down, because he sustained no further injuries.

If the area had been heavily populated, their carelessness would probably have revealed their activities. But none of Ilgal was heavily populated by humans anymore, and this particular section was close to the castle, and therefore any human habitation had been strongly discouraged for decades. As for the animals, they had more sense than the princes, and stayed well away from the unpredictable releases of magic.

"We should probably head back," Emmett said, realizing just how deep they'd moved into the forest. "We need to be back in our rooms before dawn if we want to keep our heads."

"But that last one was paltry," Farrin complained. "I don't think it would have even knocked me over, and my ears didn't ring at all." He grinned at his brother. "One more, come on. How often do we get the chance to manipulate magic in any way at all?"

Emmett grunted, but he couldn't stop the smile spreading over his own face. He was getting as big a thrill out of the exercise as his brother was. And, best of all, it was actually working! If he kept at this, he might be able to reclaim the forest. Why hadn't this been attempted before now? Sure, raw magic was dangerous, but risks were necessary in the face of threats like the one the wild magic posed to the forest.

"All right," he said, lifting up the detector. "One more. Whoa! Look at that."

He'd swung the implement in a slow circle, and when it pointed slightly to his left, it revealed a powerful glow between the trees.

"That's a lot of magic," Farrin said, already moving forward. "Let's check it out."

They wended quickly between the trunks, their eyes fixed on the brightening glow. If the first cache they'd released had been an inferno, this was an out-of-control wildfire, leading them in a clear path through the trees. By the time they found themselves in a small clearing, at the center of which was a flattened rock, Emmett could barely see anything through the slits he'd had to narrow his eyes into. The light was blinding. This wasn't like the other points of magic they'd found. This was a hundred times more potent.

"What is this place?" he asked uneasily. "What's going on here? It doesn't seem like a natural concentration, does it?" He lowered the detector, and the glow faded, leaving an ordinary looking clearing.

"I don't see why not," said Farrin. "All the others were, weren't they? The magic has just gathered more strongly here. Maybe it's some kind of source point or something. Is that how it works?"

"Honestly, I have no idea," said Emmett helplessly. He bit his lip, frowning as he inspected the quiet clearing. To the eye, it looked innocuous. Some instinct, however, was warning him that something was amiss. "I'm not sure if we should try to release this one. It might be too big for us."

"You're probably right," said Farrin regretfully. "Shame, though. If there was a way to safely do it, it would probably achieve more than everything else we've done tonight put together."

It was true. Emmett frowned as he glanced around the clearing, the detector dangling in one hand and the mining tool in the other. Was there a way to do it without risking their safety? He stepped forward, thinking himself still outside the circle of the intense magic. He knew he wouldn't be able to feel it, not being a singer, but he couldn't help trying to assess the magic. He knelt, laying a hand to the ground and willing his senses to get some concept of the scale of what they were facing.

What he failed to realize was that the gesture would put the enchanted mining tool in contact with the ground. On the previous occasions he'd swung it intentionally into rock, so it didn't even occur to him that having it rest on the ground would activate whatever magic-extracting enchantment was constructed into it.

But apparently that was exactly what it did.

This time there was no loud crack, but even without it, and without the ability to sense magic, Emmett could tell. The ground rumbled angrily, and he could feel something furious and powerful gathering at the center of the clearing, preparing to surge. Emmett's eyes flew to his brother, horrified, and he saw that Farrin had sensed it, too. It wasn't like the other times, with a quick and invisible explosion followed by an instant release. Something terrible was about to erupt.

There was no time for thought. Emmett dropped the items in his hand, springing up and launching himself at his brother. All his focus was on protecting Farrin from whatever disaster he'd just unleashed. He was on Farrin in a moment. Emmett was larger and stronger, and before Farrin could make a sound, Emmett had seized his shoulders and thrown him bodily behind a nearby tree, causing the younger prince to hit the ground hard.

Emmett barely had time to turn before the invisible eruption broke. A powerful rushing sound filled the clearing, and something slammed into him with enough force to send him to his knees. Some instinct told him that it wasn't like the raw, unmolded magic he'd released at the other sites. This power felt targeted, almost like it was alive. Whatever it was seized hold of him, lifting him bodily from the ground before slamming him back down.

Unable to so much as cry out, Emmett could comprehend nothing but the pain that blossomed in every nerve, the sensation so violent he felt like his body was being stretched and torn.

Then, in a second, it was over. He found himself lying with his head pressed against the grass, confusion making his head spin, and his body still so discomposed from the memory of the pain that it felt unfamiliar. A low whine—the sound more animal than human—brought his head up. Farrin! Where was his brother? What had happened to Farrin? Unease swept over him. For that matter, what had happened to Emmett?

He cast his eyes frantically along the tree line, relieved to see Farrin picking himself up off the ground, looking dazed but not hurt. Emmett tried to call out to him, but only another whine emerged. Emmett stilled, a horrible fear racing over him as he realized that the first whine had come from him as well. He didn't dare move, his mind too terrified by what he might discover.

"Emmett?" Farrin called, stumbling into the quiet clearing. "Emmett, where are you? Emmett!"

Emmett tried to struggle to his feet, but something was horrifyingly wrong with his body. Before he could make sense of what he was feeling, Farrin's eyes found him, widening in fear.

"Get back!" cried the younger prince, pulling out his sword and extending it toward Emmett with a hand that wasn't quite steady. "Stay back!"

Emmett stared in bemusement at his brother's pale face,

unable to make sense of any of it. Farrin turning on him was more incomprehensible than all the rest.

"EMMETT?!" Farrin screamed, his blade still extended toward Emmett's prone form while his eyes scanned the area. "EMMETT, WHERE ARE YOU?"

Confused as he still was, it was clear to Emmett that his brother couldn't recognize him. With an effort, he pushed himself onto all fours, trying to get his strangely rebellious body under control. He wasn't in any pain, but something had clearly been damaged. Something significant, given how bizarrely his body was responding to his directions.

"No, stay back!" Farrin cried in response to this movement, although the younger man was the one to step back. His voice dropped to a mutter as he again scanned the area. "Emmett, where *are* you?"

Still on all fours, but for some reason reluctant to fully stand, Emmett took a tentative step forward. How could he make Farrin see it was him?

His advance didn't have the desired effect. After a moment's pause, Farrin turned abruptly, plunging into the trees and sprinting through the darkness. He was quickly lost to Emmett's sight, but his trajectory was still clear, given how well Emmett could both hear and smell him.

Smell him? The thought rattled Emmett as he realized that his nose was indeed twitching as it inhaled Farrin's scent. He'd never thought of his brother as having a particular scent before. At last, he allowed his eyes to stray down his body, and another frantic whine escaped him without his permission.

His familiar limbs were gone, replaced with four sinewy legs, covered in sleek fur, its precise color impossible to tell in the moonlight. An ear twitched, and Emmett tried instinctively to lift his hand to feel his face. A paw came up, but it wasn't able to properly feel anything. Not that he really needed it. His other senses were catching up, and the bizarre movements of his body were starting to make sense. Miraculously, his mind was unaffected, but his body, it seemed, had been completely transformed.

He was a wolf.

And, judging by how high his head was from the ground, even on all fours, an unnaturally large one. He knew wolves roamed the forest—although not usually in this area so much as deeper in, across the border to Teren—but he'd certainly never seen one so big.

For a moment panic washed over him, threatening to cripple him completely. While his human mind was unable to master a single thought, however, his new form continued to take in information. He could still faintly hear Farrin's frantic flight in the distance, and the scent of the fleeing prey was tugging at him, urging him to follow.

Abandoning the attempt to find answers, Emmett took off through the woods, following his brother. He stumbled as he tried to adjust to his uneven, loping gait, but he still covered the ground at a reasonable rate. It was quickly clear that Farrin was heading back to the castle, probably to get help, and Emmett's instinct in this nightmare was also to run toward home and family.

He had no idea what would await him when he got there, or whether the catastrophe he'd unleashed was reversible. He had no clear thoughts in his mind as he crashed through the forest under the light of the full moon, only a tangle of fear and regret.

He and Farrin had messed with something they should never have touched, something much too powerful for them.

And there might be no one and nothing that could save him from paying a terrible price.

FOUR YEARS LATER...

CHAPTER ONE

Rosa

"Your Highness! You forgot your shawl!"

Rosa heard the words, but she didn't pause. Instead, she increased her pace, hoping that for once her lady-in-waiting would abandon her usual dogged persistence.

She should have known better.

"Princess Rosa! Your Highness, you really *must* be appropriately covered for this chill—"

"All right," said Rosa, turning abruptly to face the middle-aged woman who'd hurried after her. The admonishment had been loud enough to catch the attention of everyone in the vicinity, and Rosa knew that rebuffing her lady-in-waiting's attention would only gain her even more unwanted attention.

The amount of fuss made around a princess was absolutely unbelievable. She had no idea how princesses who were born into the role put up with it. At least she'd had fifteen blissfully status-free years to enjoy before her title was thrust on her.

She took the offered shawl from her companion, her patience worn too thin to be as polite as she knew she should be.

"I'll wear it if you insist, but it really isn't cold. I'm perfectly fine without it."

The other woman pursed her lips disapprovingly. "Forgive me, Your Highness, but it's my job to be the judge of that, not yours. And I disagree."

Her eyes roamed over Rosa's dark hair, and the line between her brows deepened. Rosa wasn't surprised. She'd risen early to evade the ministrations of her maids, pulling her hair into two simple braids as she often did. She could feel that they'd mostly come loose now. It didn't bother her in the slightest.

"Well, I'd best go," said Rosa quickly, before the older woman could begin a lecture on the hairstyles appropriate to a lady of Rosa's station. "My mother is expecting me."

The mention of the queen had a magical effect, causing Rosa's lady-in-waiting to draw back respectfully, dipping into a half-curtsy as she figuratively released her charge. Of course she would be horrified to be the reason a monarch was kept waiting.

Rosa hid a smirk as she hurried down the open walkway, the wind tugging at the dark strands of her hair. There were some advantages to her mother's absurdly dramatic leap in station. And given the staggering number of disadvantages that also came with it, she had no qualms whatsoever about squeezing every ounce of benefit possible.

True to what she'd told her minder, Rosa felt no discomfort from the cool breeze. She might not be overly fond of royal life, but one thing she liked very much about the castle in Terenford —Teren's capital—was the openness of the design. It wasn't a stuffy building, and both the original architects and the current decorators did an excellent job of making even the inside feel light and breezy. Best of all, most of the main connecting corridors were mirrored by open walkways that ran along the same path outdoors. Apparently it made security difficult, given how many exits and entrances the castle boasted, but in Rosa's eyes, that was a small price to pay for the fact that she could usually make her way around the castle out of doors.

A figure approached under the covered walkway, his eyes lowered and his features pinched in thought. Rosa recognized him as one of the king's advisors, one for whom she felt little warmth. She tried to move inconspicuously, eager to avoid interaction, but unfortunately he glanced up as he drew near.

"Your Highness."

As always, he seemed surprised to see her, as if her presence in the castle was an anomaly he struggled to make sense of. It was the one topic on which he and Rosa were essentially aligned, and one might have supposed it would form a point of connection between them.

It didn't.

Rosa suppressed a sigh as she dipped her head, keeping her expression pleasant.

"Leonhard."

She was braced for mind-numbing small talk, but to her relief the advisor said nothing further, merely bending in a stiff half-bow before sweeping off down the walkway.

Dismissing him from her mind, Rosa continued toward the royal wing before taking advantage of one of the many entrances to duck back inside the building. When she reached the private sitting room to which she'd been directed, she rapped once for form's sake then let herself in.

"Ah, Rosa, there you are," said her mother brightly, rising from the chair in which she'd been seated. "Thank you for coming so quickly."

"It is my honor and duty to do as I'm commanded, Your Majesty," said Rosa meekly.

Her mother gave her a look, unimpressed, and Rosa couldn't stop the grin that broke free of her formal expression. "Sorry, should I have curtsied as well?"

She swept into a curtsy that was—if she said so herself—perfect. She'd resented the hours spent with her tutor perfecting the skill, but she had to admit she enjoyed feeling so graceful.

"Don't start with me, Rosa," said her mother crisply. "I've already covered for you with the head groom this morning, and I'm not in the mood for more dramatics."

"He is quite dramatic when he gets worked up, isn't he?" Rosa said, plopping ungracefully onto a settee. "He's a good soul at heart, and not nearly as obsessed with protocol as most of the servants, but he gets ridiculous over Otto's horses."

The door opened, but Rosa didn't bother looking around to see who'd entered the room. Judging by the fact that her mother kept scolding her, it wasn't anyone she had to be formal for.

"It's not ridiculous to object to unauthorized use of the crown prince's personal horse," said Queen Ada tartly.

"Been riding Bullion again, Rosa?" The cheerful voice from behind her told Rosa that her stepbrother had joined them. "I really don't mind, Mama," he said, directing the words to his stepmother this time. "Rosa can handle her seat on any horse in our stables. I've told the head groom as much, but he's determined to be offended on my behalf if anyone other than me rides Bullion."

"Naturally," Rosa said solemnly, letting her head fall back over the arm of the settee so she was looking at the prince upside down. "My common-born posterior ought not to rest upon the very saddle graced by the rear of the future king."

"Ugh," laughed Otto, tweaking the end of one of her braids as he strolled past her. "In that kind of humor, are we?"

"Yes, and I can't for the life of me figure out why," said the queen crisply. "I've barely spoken a word to provoke you."

Rosa let out a sigh that was half groan. "I'm sorry, Mama," she said. "But I'm not in this mood for no reason. Castle gossip has gone ahead of you. As it turns out, I'm perfectly aware of what you want to speak with me about."

Her mother lowered herself into a chair, her expression resigned. "I see. And I take it you're intending to be difficult again."

"Again?" Rosa said, outraged. "When have I been difficult before? I endured the visit from Prince Matthias very meekly!"

Otto snorted, shoving Rosa's legs so that she went back into a sitting position, making room for him to join her on the settee. "I don't think I've ever seen you do anything meekly."

Rosa grinned at him. "I meant relatively speaking. I refrained from telling him to his face that whatever scheming anyone else might do, I have no intention of marrying him and moving so far from my forest to live in his wasteland. And I think that kind of restraint was positively heroic."

"I don't think you could call Vadolis a wasteland," said Otto fairly. "It's a very pleasant and fertile kingdom. Besides," he added without heat, "I don't believe he wanted to marry you at all."

"He did display excellent sense," Rosa agreed magnanimously. "I can only hope all your other friends will be as obliging." She cast a dark look at her mother. "But I doubt it."

"I see rumor truly has gone ahead of me," said the queen with a sigh. "I should have spoken to you earlier."

"What rumor?" Otto asked, straightening. "What do my friends have to do with Rosa?"

"She wants me to marry one of them," Rosa informed him. "She's planning some kind of a ball where I can select one, or be selected by one, or something like that."

"As usual, gossip isn't entirely accurate," her mother said dryly. "That's not what I was going to propose at all. But I did hope that we could make an extra effort this summer to give you a chance to get to know the more eligible options from among the court." She nodded at her stepson. "Many of whom are Otto's friends, as you said."

"I don't know, Mama," said Otto, sounding uneasy. "I don't know how they'd take me trying to foist Rosa onto them."

The queen's brows drew together, and she looked on the point of taking offense, but Rosa didn't feel insulted in the least.

"Thank you, Otto," she said emphatically. "Someone's talking sense. Mama, no self-respecting noble wants to marry *me*. Any that do only care about my title, and let's be honest, it's not mine at all."

"Of course it's yours," her mother said impatiently, but Rosa shook her head.

"Your marriage made you queen, and you're excellent at your role, Mama. But *I* didn't marry royalty! And I'm not a child, who needs to fall under your protection."

"You were when Ryker and I married," her mother pointed out.

"I was fifteen," protested Rosa. "Nearly fully grown. There's really no reason any title at all should have been conferred on me."

"Nice try," said Otto, around a mouthful of grapes he'd grabbed from the table in front of them. "But that's not how it works."

"Otto is perfectly right, as I know you know," the queen chimed in.

Rosa scowled. "Fine, so maybe there's nothing I can do about being a princess. But why do I have to be subjected to a parade of potential suitors? I don't see what the rush is for me to be married."

"You're nineteen," her mother reminded her.

"So's Otto, and I don't see anyone pressuring him to find a bride," said Rosa hotly.

"That's also not how it works," Otto informed her comfortably.

"Of course it's not," said the queen, standing. "Rosa, I know you find being a princess frustrating at times. But that's what you are. And part of that means marrying according to your station. I've heard you when you say you don't want to move away from Terenford. That's why I'm proposing that we find a suitor who lives here in the city."

"I don't mind moving away from Terenford," said Rosa. "I just didn't want to move to Vadolis. I'd be happy to move back to the forest tomorrow."

"Don't be absurd," said her mother, her calm flickering for a moment.

Realizing she'd touched a nerve, Rosa fell silent. She wished her mother wasn't so uncomfortable to remember Rosa's early years, when they'd lived in the forest with her father. Before his death, they'd lived much simpler lives. It was only after he was gone that they moved to the capital, so her mother could find work to support them both. Rosa had few memories of her father, but she did remember their forest home with great fondness. She'd loved it as much as he had. Her mother, evidently, hadn't felt quite the same way, and she always closed up if Rosa spoke of those years.

It was a shame. Rosa couldn't help but feel that it would be healthier—and less painful—for them both if they could reminisce freely about their old life.

"I will organize a small event to kick off the summer season," her mother said, already moving toward the door. "We will invite a few appropriate young men." She fixed her daughter with a stern look. "I expect you to cooperate, Rosa. It's not as though anyone is forcing you into anything unpleasant. The least you can do is keep an open mind."

With those words she swept from the room, leaving Rosa to let out another groan.

"So arduous, isn't it, this opulent lifestyle?" Otto said, selecting another bunch of grapes.

Rosa batted half-heartedly at his hand, watching morosely as he pulled the grapes from their stems. Her expression grew thoughtful as she examined his face.

"You know it's not about you or your father, right?"

He nodded, his smile unruffled. "I know."

"I like my new family," Rosa persevered. "I just don't like my new status." She let her head fall back against the settee. "I feel like a bird in a cage."

"That's a bit grandiose," said Otto, shoving all of the grapes into his mouth at once. "A field mouse in a cage, maybe."

"Watch it," Rosa growled, giving him a playful shove that made him lose his balance and lurch sideways across the settee.

He chuckled, righting himself so as to better throw a grape at her. "Did you really use my saddle when you rode Bullion?" he asked.

Rosa nodded, a smirk in her eyes. "I think the groom was more scandalized by that than by me taking your horse."

Otto shook his head, a grin spreading over his face. "No doubt. I'll say this for you, sis. You certainly make life more interesting around here." A wistful look came into his eyes. "We hadn't felt much like a family for a long time when you and your mother came along."

Rosa squeezed his arm, digging her nails in slightly to make the gesture playful. She knew the death of his mother was a more painful topic for him than her own bereavement. He'd certainly been much more eager than she had to embrace his new family in the early months. She felt ashamed now of how long it had taken her to warm up to him and his father.

"You're a hopeless romantic at heart, aren't you?" she teased him.

He shot her a look that was both rueful and a little sad. "You say that like it's a bad thing."

"I suppose it isn't," Rosa said fairly. She had no doubt Otto would sweep some starry-eyed courtier's daughter off her feet when the time came, and probably be quite sickeningly sweet about the whole thing. She released his arm and leaned back again. "Well, we're a family now, at any rate. And I'm only too delighted to be able to provide more family drama than you know what to do with."

"Hardly," scoffed Otto. "You're easy enough to handle." He tossed another grape, which bounced off her forehead. "But I'm not bullying any of my friends into proposing to you, not for anything. I value their good opinion too highly."

"Thank the stars above for that," grinned Rosa. She rose to her feet. "Now that my mother's request for my exalted company has given me an excuse to shake my usual retinue, I think I should make the most of it. We're even on the right side of the castle to slip straight into the forest."

Otto frowned at her. "You're going to sneak off into the woods alone again? Is that really wise? Haven't you heard all the reports about increased wolf sightings right across Ilgal?"

Rosa waved a dismissive hand. "Wolves are nothing new in the forest. They don't worry me. If you know how to be smart, you can generally avoid them."

"Generally?" Otto repeated darkly. He bit his lip. "I do worry about your health, though, Rosa. Everyone says the magic of the forest is growing oppressive. Do you truly not feel the pressure they all talk about?"

"City-dwellers talk about it," Rosa corrected. "Those who live in the forest don't feel a thing. And I suppose I'm in there often enough to be acclimatized, because I truly don't. Either that, or it's all just gossip and has no basis in truth."

Otto didn't look convinced. "You know it's not just gossip. The Academy of Song regularly sends its best experts to monitor the levels, and they all say that it's growing dangerous for non-singers."

Rosa just shrugged, and Otto made one last attempt.

"What about the rumor that the recent wolf sightings aren't normal wolves? People are muttering that they're some kind of supersized monster wolves."

This time Rosa actually snorted aloud. "That's exactly the type of nonsense scaremongering I'd expect from city-dwellers who are too timid to set foot under the trees. Those legends have been bandied about since before I was born, and you don't see them slowing any of the forest-dwellers down. Because legends is all they are. Wolves are wolves. There are no super-sized monster ones."

She plucked her shawl from her shoulders, frowning distastefully at it before dropping it in a heap on the settee she'd just vacated.

"It'll take more than wolves and rumors to keep me from visiting my grandmother," she said decisively. "It's been too long, and she'll be wondering what's become of me."

"Yes," said Otto dryly. "She must be sick with worry at the thought of you wasting away in your fancy castle." He shook his head. "You know I think it's nice that you keep contact with your father's family, but is a forest cottage really so much more appealing than all this?" He waved a hand at the richly furnished room.

Rosa grinned, amused by his description of her grandparents' home. "Why don't you come with me and find out?"

"I'd rather not," said Otto frankly. A long-suffering look

crossed his features. "Although I suppose I should, to make sure you don't run into trouble."

"Offer rescinded," said Rosa flatly. "If I wanted a guard to accompany me, I wouldn't have spent years learning how to lose mine."

"Well, if you don't need my company, I'll decline to trek through the forest for hours," said Otto comfortably. He settled back, taking full possession of the settee with his arms folded behind his head. "I suppose you'll despise me for it, but I confess I enjoy living in luxury."

"I don't despise you," Rosa reassured him. "It's natural to be loyal to how we were raised, I think." She made her way to the window, hiking her skirts up with a practiced action as she unlocked the casement. "Besides," she threw a cheeky grin over her shoulder, "I don't mind the luxury part of it myself, in spite of my affection for Granny's *forest cottage*. Be a dear and lock the window behind me, won't you?"

CHAPTER TWO

Rosa

Rosa didn't stay to see whether Otto obeyed her flippant command, climbing onto the windowsill and dropping noiselessly to the ground beyond.

It was an escape route she'd used before, and the short trip through the gardens to the outer wall was accomplished in a moment. With practiced stealth she made her way up the stairs to the battlements that ran along the top of the wall. It wasn't an especially high wall, but high enough she couldn't just jump down into the undergrowth on the other side. And although the castle sat right on the forest edge of the capital city, the trees had most regrettably been cleared in the immediate vicinity of the wall.

Security measures. One of the burdens of royal status.

Glancing around to make sure no guard was in sight, Rosa slipped the sash from around her waist. It took a minute, as it was wrapped around her many times. She'd received a few odd looks for her habit of wearing the apparently bulky sash, but it had its uses. She looped it around the stone in front of her, tying a fairly loose knot. She secured it more firmly around her waist, grasping hold of it right below the knot around the battlement. She then climbed over the top of the wall and lowered herself rapidly down, arms straining as she grumbled to herself about her restrictive skirts. The sash wasn't long enough to get her all the way to the ground. But she was far enough down that when she reached the end and let go with her hands—so that her weight fell suddenly onto the loose knot above and caused it to give way—she was uninjured by the inevitable tumble into the bracken below.

It was an imprecise method, trusting a fair bit to luck for her knot to hold until the appropriate moment, but it had only failed her once. The resultant broken leg and towering scold from her mother had all been part of the adventure as far as Rosa was concerned. Her only true regret was that her recovery had prevented her from sneaking into the forest for many weeks. Otto had been very sweet about helping her around and bringing her things. Now she thought about it, that forced time in the castle was when she'd finally started to warm up to her stepbrother and stepfather, and begun to accept the new family she'd been catapulted into by her mother's whirlwind romance and marriage.

The point being, it had all worked out for the best, and there was absolutely no reason to consider Rosa's method of exiting the castle to be inappropriate in any way.

No reason at all.

It was all ridiculous, she reflected, picking pine needles out of her hair as she hurried into the shelter of the trees and out of sight of the wall. Any other resident of Terenford could stroll out the city gates and into the forest anytime they liked. It wasn't as though the area was forbidden.

Back when she'd been a lowly commoner, she'd imagined that elevated status came with a great deal of freedom.

Blissful ignorance.

The section of forest was familiar, and it took her very little time to reach the main forest road that led due west from the city all the way to the coast. Somewhere it forked, a southern branch providing an alternative route south toward West River and the border with the neighboring kingdom of Medulle. But given there was a better road further east, the one through the forest was little used, except by locals. In any event, her grandparents' house was on the Terenan side of the border, although not by a great distance.

In spite of the superstitions of many residents of Terenford, the forest wasn't a dark and terrifying domain of lawlessness. The road that cut through this section was wide and well-maintained, and it took Rosa less than an hour to reach the dirt track that wound off through the trees toward her paternal grandparents' home. And, as she'd told Otto, she felt no sign of the pressure that the magic supposedly created for outsiders who strayed in.

There was a skip in her step as she neared the familiar gate. She knew the forest was teeming with life, but any nearby woodland creatures were keeping out of sight. She thought of Otto's warnings and scoffed under her breath. The only wolf she caught sight of was the one formed from burnished metal on the gate of her grandparents' property. She passed through the open entrance, picking up her pace.

This path was even better maintained than the public one, and it was an easy few minutes' walk before the building came into view. Once again Rosa chuckled internally at her stepbrother's expense. What had he called her grandmother's house? A forest cottage?

The imposing manor loomed into sight, its stone walls tastefully covered with creeping ivy, and its sweeping carriageway meticulously maintained. Maybe if Otto overcame his distaste for the forest enough to accompany her one of these days, he'd see for himself just how primitive her grandparents' lives *weren't*. But until then, she would continue to take private amusement from his misconceptions.

Rosa hadn't made it far up the carriageway before she was hailed by a middle-aged man who'd worked at the manor for as long as she could remember. She returned a cheerful greeting, asking after her grandparents.

"Oh your Grandpa is out back on the plantation, but I think the boss is in the library," the man told her obligingly, resting a huge ax on his shoulder as he spoke.

Rosa's eyes lingered on the weapon. They must be felling a section of the groves. Rosa's paternal grandparents produced the finest timber in Teren. At least in her completely objective opinion.

With a thanks, Rosa let herself in through the manor's front doors. She made for the library, knowing full well whom she would find there. Her grandfather was well liked and respected by all at the manor, but there was no doubt whatsoever who was meant by *the boss*. Rosa's grandmother had inherited the property from her own parents, and she'd been running the operation since well before Rosa was born.

Rosa glanced around fondly as she entered the library. The manor boasted one of the kingdom's finest private collections of documents—at least, excluding those held by members of the nobility. It had already been extensive when her grandparents married, and her grandfather had dedicated a considerable amount of time to expanding it. He loved the quiet peace of the room of knowledge, and had instilled a love for it in Rosa, too.

In her childhood, she'd whiled away many an inclement afternoon reading by the big, mullioned window that looked out on a forest view. The trees came closest to the dwelling on that part of the building.

It wasn't hard to find her grandmother among the shelves—she just had to follow the sound of disgruntled muttering.

"...know I returned it here last time. Where has that fool of a woman put it now?"

"Insulting your hardworking and long-suffering house-keeper again, Granny?" Rosa asked cheerfully, by way of announcing her presence.

Her grandmother looked up as casually as if her now-royal granddaughter lived in the manor rather than being an increasingly infrequent visitor. "Hardworking, maybe," she snorted. "But hardly long-suffering. She scolded me this morning for letting my tea go cold. My own tea! The cheek of it."

Rosa chuckled as she embraced the elderly woman. She knew her grandmother had a soft spot for the housekeeper, who was even older than her, and had been with the family all her life. Their feud was decades old, but only surface deep.

"What are you wearing, child?" Granny scolded, her brow furrowing as she took in Rosa's gown.

"I know it's silly," Rosa sighed. "Believe it or not, it's one of my simplest gowns."

"No, no, I'm not talking about the quality of the dress," said Granny. She cast a dismissive eye over the costly fabric, wearing her own simple brown garment as grandly as a queen. "Although it's a waste of perfectly good gold, I'm sure. I meant what are they thinking to send you out without so much as a shawl? It's colder in the woods than in that city of yours. No doubt they waste lumber on fires all year round in that castle you've been banished to, but out here we feel the weather."

Rosa rolled her eyes, as if she was still a ten-year-old, being scolded by Granny for stealing apples from the orchard on one of her visits, or by her mother for climbing trees in a good frock.

Granny never scolded her for climbing trees.

"You're all as bad as each other," she informed her grandmother. "My *lady-in-waiting* insisted I needed to wear a shawl, but I'm not in the least cold. In fact," she admitted unashamedly, "I discarded it purely as an act of totally pointless defiance."

"Did you now?" Her grandmother eyed her. "Sounds like your usual pigheadedness." Her wrinkled face suddenly split into a grin. "That's my girl."

Rosa grinned back. "Now what book are you looking for?"

"An encyclopedia on wolf behavior," her grandmother said. "Your grandfather, darling dolt that he is, has fallen for some tall tale from one of the workers. The man is convinced he was hunted by a wolf a few days ago. Nonsense, of course. Quite apart from the fact that it's not physically possible for wolves to grow anywhere near the size this man is claiming, wolves don't hunt at noontime. Need that encyclopedia to prove him wrong."

"Proving Grampy wrong, your favorite pastime," Rosa said impudently. She reached over her grandmother's head. "I think this is the one you want. And I feel compelled to add in your housekeeper's defense that it's stored right where it should be."

"Aha!" A victorious light entered Granny's eyes as she seized the book from Rosa's hand. She disregarded the other comment completely. "Now he'll have to listen."

"I doubt it," laughed Rosa. "Now let's get you out of here before you disrupt Grampy's beautifully organized system any further."

She knew exactly how the scene would play out, but she took great pleasure a couple of hours later from watching the confrontation anyway. Just as Rosa had expected, her grandfather listened with fond good humor while his wife pointed out the passages Rosa had helped her identify, then said, "Yes dear, of course, dear," with a relaxed expression that told Rosa he wasn't in the least convinced, but had no interest in arguing with his wife.

His refusal to be baited infuriated Granny, but she also

couldn't quite keep the sparkle from her eyes as she glared at her husband. She'd take it on as her personal challenge to persuade him, Rosa had no doubt.

"So this fear-mongering about giant wolves is affecting you out here, is it?" Rosa asked shortly afterward, as the maligned housekeeper plied her with food. "I thought it was only a city-dwellers' superstition."

"Fear-mongering is the term for it," her grandmother scoffed. "Those legends were very popular bedtime stories when I was a small child. I've no idea what's made them resurface now. As if we don't know how to deal with wolves out here." Her frown deepened. "Wolves don't trouble us—it's that stepfather of yours with his nonsensical rumblings that I'm worried about."

"Our sovereign deserves a little more respect, love," said Rosa's grandfather mildly. "And I don't think he can be blamed for any of it."

"Any of what?" Rosa demanded. "What rumblings are you talking about? I hadn't heard about any trouble between King Ryker and anyone out here."

"That's because there is no trouble," said her grandfather firmly. "Your grandmother is leaping ahead of herself. Your step-father's done nothing but communicate honestly, and he can hardly be faulted for that."

"I'll give him honest communication," muttered Granny.

"You already have, dearest," her husband reminded her. "I don't think anyone would accuse you of speaking in riddles in the reply you gave that poor messenger."

"Well, if the man *was* going to complain about this mythical pressure on his chest, acting as if he was dying when there was absolutely nothing wrong with him, then—"

"What messenger?" Rosa interrupted, bewildered.

"It's nothing of concern," her grandfather said. "Just routine communication regarding the increasing potency of the magic out here, and its impact on forest life—and very courteous, I thought it."

"Hah!" Granny clearly didn't share his view. "Say what you like—there's trouble coming, you mark my words."

Rosa frowned, dissatisfied by the vague answers. It was no secret to anyone in the region that magic had been growing steadily wilder in the forest for many years. The lush ground was too fertile, and magic thrived unchecked. It was the same principle that made the continent's frozen northern wastes as empty of magic as they were barren.

Not being a singer—one of those humans born with the ability to sing and, through songcraft, to harness the power that emanated from the land—Rosa couldn't sense the magic building in the Forest of Ilgal. But, in spite of her light words to Otto, she didn't fully dismiss the reports claiming that most outsiders who entered the forest felt increasingly heavy pressure on their chests. They claimed the magic was trying to crush them. And although forest-dwellers might be more acclimatized, if it grew out of hand, only singers would truly be immune. Or so the experts claimed.

The thought worried Rosa considerably on her grandparents' behalf, but she'd thus far followed Granny's lead in assuming the reports to be greatly exaggerated. Granny always claimed that the problem belonged mainly to the deeper parts of the forest. It was alarming to think it was already beginning to affect her grandparents, who lived so close to its edge.

"What did the king say about it?" she pressed, still troubled by her grandmother's curt mention of her stepfather. From what Rosa knew of King Ryker, he was a fair king and a reasonable man. Her grandmother was sometimes a little stiff in speaking of him—only natural when discussing the man who'd married her son's widow—but she'd never had any real criticism to level at him before.

Her grandfather shook his head. "We can discuss all that later." He glanced out the window. "Wolves might not trouble us in here, but you'd best be heading back before their more traditional hunting hour, Rosie."

"I don't think wolves will hunt me on the public road, Grampy," Rosa said with a smile. "The forest isn't that wild yet, unchecked magic or not."

"All the same," he said. "It'd set my old mind at ease."

"Well, that is a worthy cause," Rosa said, relinquishing the other matter for the moment. "And you're right anyway, it's probably past time I go. Poor Mama will be worrying. I'll be in for a tremendous scold as it is." It didn't worry her too much. Scold as she might, neither the queen nor the king ever really curbed Rosa's visits to the forest. They seemed to both recognize the importance of her maintaining her relationship with her grandparents.

"Ah, your mother has a good heart, really," Granny said indulgently. "It's just a shame it's too faint for the forest. Thank goodness you're made of sterner stuff, Rosa. Like your father."

"Don't start on all that, love, Rosa needs to go," interjected her husband.

Granny nodded. "True. Rosa, you really will be cold in that silly gown." She brightened. "I have just the thing for you, actually. I've been going through some old chests from my own youth, and I found my favorite cloak. Color still as bright as the day I bought it! I'll fetch it for you."

Deaf to Rosa's protests, she strode from the room with a confident step that belied her age. When she returned with the garment in question, Rosa couldn't help laughing.

"Scarlet, Granny? That's very bold. I imagine you turned heads."

"I did indeed," said her grandmother comfortably. "I was quite dashing in my day, I'll have you know."

"She was," confirmed Rosa's grandfather. "She could have had her pick of the men in Terenford if she'd been willing to live in the city."

Granny made a scornful noise in her throat. "Why would I want to do a thing like that?" She sent her husband a fond look that didn't entirely soften the habitual fierceness of her features. "I knew I had to find a man who had sense enough to fall in love with the forest as well as with me."

Rosa's smile was a little tight. "You succeeded admirably, Granny. And thank you for the cloak. I'll wear it with pride. But now I really must be going."

Her grandmother waved her off with her usual briskness, but her grandfather walked her all the way to the gate, giving her a tighter squeeze than normal when they parted.

"The forest has many paths, Rosie," he told her in his gentle way. "And every person's life leads down a different one. Doesn't mean any are worse than the others."

"Thanks Grampy," said Rosa softly. Neither spoke it aloud, but she was left in no doubt that her grandfather had picked up on her discomfort at the turn of the earlier conversation.

As she hurried down the path toward the main road, she couldn't help but compare her parents' marriage to that of her grandparents. Would her life have been different if her mother had been able to fall in love with the forest when she fell in love with Rosa's father? Was it always inevitable that it would end in unhappiness for Rosa's mother to love one without the other? Not that anyone could have foreseen the tragedy that took her father's life. But Rosa had long fought a niggling discomfort that even before her father's death, her mother hadn't been happy. Had he lived, would she have become bitter instead of bereft? Would Rosa's own love of the forest have injured her relationship with her mother no matter the path their lives took?

They were questions without answers, and there was no point dwelling on them. Pulling her new red cloak around her shoulders, Rosa turned her face toward the city that, while it had become her home, hadn't even begun to capture her heart.

CHAPTER THREE

Emmett

Emmett stood straight, trying to maintain the regal look that had once come so naturally to him. He knew a moment of regret that he couldn't let his guard down even in front of his father, another thing that had once been easier to do. His eyes were fixed on the large portrait hanging behind his father's desk, but he wasn't really looking at the bittersweet image of his own smiling likeness seated in a chair, with his brother Farrin's arm laid across the back of it.

If Farrin was here, Emmett could be honest with him. Farrin would always have his back, no matter what. But Farrin was far away on his new island kingdom, and this wasn't his problem to solve. It was Emmett's.

The door opened, and Emmett's father strode in at last. Emmett straightened his back further, fighting a horrifying and embarrassing urge to scratch behind his ear. That one had been growing more persistent lately, but it would be disastrous to let his father see it. King Johannes already looked agitated, and what Emmett had to say wouldn't make him any happier.

"Emmett, I'm sorry to keep you waiting." In spite of his polite words, the king's tone was clipped.

"Not at all, Father," said Emmett. "I trust the meeting with the Vadolisian elves went well?"

His father grunted. "As well as could be expected. They're as difficult as ever, but that's no surprise. You remember what they were like when we met last month regarding trading licenses for the regional markets. They're still—ah. But of course, you don't remember. You were in Lernvale, weren't you?"

Emmett swallowed. "I believe so."

Bitterness fought with guilt at this reminder of how much of his role as crown prince he was unable to fulfill thanks to his... situation. He'd missed so many important events and critical meetings. At twenty-three, he'd reached an age where he should be increasing his duties and taking some pressure off his father. Instead, he'd been forced to draw back from many of the ones he used to fill. And it was about to get worse.

"Well, never mind that, the elves can wait," his father said curtly. He nodded to someone outside of Emmett's range of sight, and he heard the door click shut. They were alone in the study now, and the grand room suddenly felt as close as a broom cupboard.

"What did you wish to speak with me about?" King Johannes pressed. "Your message said something about departure preparations, but that can't be right, surely. I don't keep track of the timing as closely as I ought, perhaps, but I thought you only arrived back from your last trip to Lernvale a week ago."

"I did," Emmett confirmed. "But unfortunately I'm due to return sooner than you might imagine. I'm afraid it's lasting longer each time. I didn't return to my normal self for almost two weeks this time, and my return to the capital was delayed accordingly."

"Two weeks?" his father demanded. "I thought it was only supposed to go for a week."

"That's how it was at the beginning," Emmett agreed, shifting uncomfortably. He hated discussing his condition with his father almost as much as the older man clearly did. "But it's been steadily lengthening, and recently it's begun to...escalate. Quite dramatically."

"What does that mean?" his father's voice was sharper now, his gaze piercing. "Dramatically in terms of the length of time?"

"Yes," said Emmett quickly. *Among other things*, he added in his mind. But coward though it made him feel, he just couldn't bring himself to tell his father the full extent of it. "That's why I need to speak to you. About my living arrangements."

"Your living arrangements?" the king repeated, his tone far from encouraging. "You're dissatisfied with your accommodations in Lernvale? I realize the castle there isn't as well-equipped as we are here in the capital, but that seems a small price to pay for keeping the populace from becoming aware of your situation."

"It's not that," Emmett said quickly. "I'm well provided for at the castle in Lernvale. And even if I wasn't, I wouldn't suggest staying in the capital during my transformations. I agree that it would be too difficult to keep the truth hidden if I was here, and I certainly have no desire for news to get out."

"So what's the problem?" his father asked suspiciously.

Emmett sighed, relaxing his posture slightly. The itch behind his ear was gone for now, which helped. "It's becoming too impractical to go back and forth. With the nightly transformations happening for up to two weeks at a time, and the journey taking two days each way, I'm spending half my life on the road. I haven't been able to properly support you here for a long time, and I'm only going to become less reliable if the periods of my affliction continue to be unpredictable."

"What exactly are you proposing?" King Johannes was becoming agitated. Emmett didn't really blame him. For a king, having a son and heir who was afflicted as Emmett was must be almost as bad as being childless.

"I think I should settle permanently in Lernvale," he said in a rush.

There was a moment of silence before the king spoke. "Permanently."

The word was repeated not as a question, but as the vocalization of some thought Emmett couldn't fully decipher. Disregarding his father's stormy expression, he pushed on.

"Not permanently as in forever. Only until we can figure out a way to break my curse. I just meant permanently in the sense that I wouldn't move back to Port Dulla in between each transformation period."

His father didn't answer at once, but his brow grew heavier with each passing moment.

"You've been steeling yourself to suggest this for some time, haven't you?" he asked at last. "I've noticed your restlessness."

Emmett said nothing. His father was more perceptive than he'd realized.

"Is it possible this has been your intention all along?" The king's voice was forbidding, and Emmett had to suppress a shiver. He felt like he was a child again, being reprimanded for some youthful misdemeanor. "After all, the whole incident came about through some misguided attempt of yours to reclaim the forest for habitation, didn't it? You wanted to be able to spend more time there."

"What?" The realization of his father's meaning startled Emmett out of his discomfort. "No, Father, of course not. How can you think I planned for *this*? This isn't what I want. I wish I could be here, in the capital, fulfilling my role as I'm supposed to. I don't *want* to banish myself to the forest."

He'd planned to remain calm, but he couldn't help his words becoming more passionate as he saw his father's skepticism.

"Father, I know you hate what I've become. But you can't possibility hate it more than I do. I bitterly regret all of it, but most of all the fact that it causes me to fail in my role every single day. More than anything I wish to do my duty to you and the kingdom, and I can never forgive myself for failing in that."

He ran a hand through his hair, shaking slightly at the intensity of putting these feelings into words. He couldn't even meet his father's eyes.

"I don't want to abandon my duty. I hoped that by being settled in one place, even if it's not the ideal place, I could be more available, not less. I could correspond where helpful, even host meetings for influential parties in the region." He paused. "During daylight hours, of course. And we might have more success in coming up with a plausible reason for a full-time relocation than the increasingly flimsy excuses we're giving everyone for my frequent journeys."

There was a long moment of silence after this speech, and Emmett forced himself to look up at his father's face. The king was regarding him thoughtfully, his forehead furrowed in a habitual expression.

"I think your mother needs to join us before we can continue this conversation," he said abruptly.

King Johannes strode to the door, leaving his son blinking behind him. Those were the last words Emmett had expected to come out of his father's mouth. The king wasn't usually one to involve his wife in decision-making regarding matters of state. But he supposed his own situation was as much a family affair as a kingdom-wide issue.

The king sent a servant in search of Queen Sula, and the two men waited in tense silence. Emmett took a seat at his father's gesture, but it didn't make him feel more relaxed. The whole time he had to fight the urge to pace the room. He couldn't tell if that was the wolf in him, or just normal human nerves. The fact that it was getting hard to tell his two types of instincts apart was...concerning.

When his mother arrived, Emmett rose courteously to his feet.

"Sit down, Emmett, I'm sure you could use the rest," said the queen.

Ominously, she didn't take the seat beside her son, instead going behind the desk to place a hand delicately on the back of her husband's chair. Whatever she was going to say, she wanted it to come with the weight of the crown.

"Is something amiss, Johannes?" she asked Emmett's father.

He cleared his throat. "Emmett has just informed me he wishes to live full-time in Lernvale."

She let out a genteel noise of surprise, and Emmett hastened to clarify.

"It's not exactly that I wish it, Mother. But it seems the most practical course given the situation."

She regarded him shrewdly, and grown man though he was, he found himself fidgeting.

"Is this because of what that healer-singer said last year?" the king asked gruffly. "When he examined you and said that whatever magic is at work could shorten your life?"

Emmett sighed. Somewhat to his own surprise, the blow of that news barely stung anymore. Other considerations were more alarming than the idea of dying young.

"No, it's nothing to do with that. I don't think where I live will make any great difference to my lifespan."

"And the singer was far from certain," said the queen crisply. She shot her husband a glance. "Probably because he was barely given a fraction of the relevant information."

"The whole point is to *conceal* the boy's affliction, Sula," said the king impatiently.

The queen pursed her lips but gave no reply. Instead she

turned her searching gaze back on her son. "Are the changes so bad? Do you really think it will imminently reach the point where you need to be hidden away at all times?"

"Changes?" Emmett asked, with a confusion even he could tell was unconvincing.

"Don't be foolish, Emmett, I'm your mother," the queen informed him. "Did you think I wouldn't notice the changes in your habits, your mannerisms, your food preferences, your way of walking?"

"What are you talking about?" King Johannes demanded, but Emmett winced.

His mother had seen far too much. He should have removed himself from the capital months ago. But he never could have predicted such a rapid escalation in the process he'd been slowly experiencing for four years.

"Not imminently," he said quietly. "But the time will come, and sooner than you might think. I'm afraid that eventually, I might not even transform back between full moons."

For a long moment, there was silence. The king's jaw was locked, the queen's eyes masked as she kept her emotions within. Emmett was forcibly reminded of the two occasions when they'd all believed his brother Farrin to be dead, lost at sea. He felt like he was watching his parents receive that news all over again.

Only now he was the cause of their anguish. It was unendurable.

"If I'm settled in Lernvale, I'll have more time to investigate," he offered.

"What do you hope to find?" his mother asked wearily. "You know we had the matter discreetly researched by Medulle's highest scholars of magic back when you were first afflicted. No one could explain why the magic would do what it did, or how it could be reversed."

"I'm not talking about research, Mother," said Emmett. "I'm talking about investigating. If I can figure out where that magic came from—"

"We know where it came from," his father interrupted in a growl. "The wild magic of the forest is nothing new. The only thing we don't comprehend is how our own sons, fully educated in the dangers of magic, were fools enough to unleash that magic on themselves."

"Peace, Johannes." The queen laid a hand on her husband's arm in response to his steadily rising voice.

"It wasn't just wild magic, Father," Emmett said, taking no offense at the justified rebuke. "There was something else at work in the clearing that night. I'm sure of it. What we unleashed was well beyond the unformed wild magic we encountered elsewhere in the forest."

"It was stronger because you were deeper in the forest," said his father, with the impatience he always showed when Emmett raised the matter.

It was clear to the prince that his father considered the argument an attempt to mitigate Emmett's blame in the situation. But that was far from the truth. Emmett knew perfectly well how much to blame he was for all of it. His lingering suspicion about the magic they'd unleashed wasn't an excuse—it was a search for a solution.

"I called you to join us, Sula, because it occurred to me that Emmett's proposal is entirely contradictory to your own plans for the season."

"What plans?" Emmett asked, his eyes flying to his mother.

She shifted forward, a hint of eagerness in her eyes. "I have many plans for the entertainment of the younger members of court, Emmett. I had hoped to interest you in organizing them."

Emmett stared at her blankly, confused by why she would

hope anything so bizarre. He was grateful when his father came to his rescue.

"Don't draw it out, Sula, just give him the truth." His gaze flicked to Emmett. "The object of all these social events is for you to choose a wife."

"What?" Emmett's mouth fell open. "Choose a wife? Surely that's the last thing on all our minds."

"Far from it," said the king sternly. "Don't be foolish, Emmett."

Emmett stared between his parents, feeling as though he was trapped in a strange dream. He could never before remember his father showing interest in matchmaking, even for his own sons.

"How could I be thinking about marriage with this affliction still hanging over me?" Emmett demanded.

"The affliction is precisely the reason you need to be thinking about marriage," his father told him.

"With respect, Father, I disagree," said Emmett firmly. "What woman would agree to chain herself to a monster?"

"For a crown?" his father said cynically. "Many, I daresay."

"Johannes," scolded the queen. She frowned at her son. "Emmett, you are *not* a monster. And becoming crown princess is hardly some terrible fate."

"Mother," said Emmett disbelievingly. "Have you forgotten that every full moon, I spend the nights roaming around as a—"

"Of course I haven't," she cut him off shortly. "But perhaps your wife wouldn't need to know about that."

"Wouldn't need to know?" Emmett could only stare. Had they both lost their minds? "We'd have to live very separate lives for her not to know. What would even be the point of a marriage so distant?"

"You know the point," said the king, clearly irritated at being forced to spell it out. "You need to produce an heir, Emmett. In ordinary circumstances, I would say you have plenty of time, and twenty-three is too young to be rushing you. But these aren't ordinary circumstances, and it seems you may not have plenty of time."

Emmett's mouth snapping shut was the only sound to break the silence that followed these words. Of course that was his parents' meaning. How had it taken him so long to grasp what they were getting at? They wanted him to secure the succession before the magic that had him in its grip either sent him to an early grave, or rendered him...ineffective.

He supposed it was a natural priority for them to have, but he couldn't get behind it. The idea of trapping some poor girl into marrying him without telling her the truth was unthinkable. He cast his mind over the young noblewomen of his father's court, many of whom had been making their interest clear for years. The idea of unburdening his soul and telling the full truth to any of them was even more unthinkable.

"We have to resolve the curse first," he said. "That's the only way I would consent to a marriage."

"What if we can't resolve it?" his father asked bluntly. The queen made a noise of distress, but King Johannes didn't soften. "The question needs to be considered, Sula. We've left it too long as it is. We need to prepare for the worst."

"I won't deceive a prospective bride," Emmett said stubbornly.

"Perhaps that wouldn't be necessary," the queen suggested. "Perhaps there's someone to whom we could tell—"

"No." The king and prince spoke simultaneously.

"You can't say no to everything we suggest without offering any solutions, Emmett," his mother said impatiently. "Why are you so determined to think of marriage to you as some kind of trap? Even with your...limitations, I daresay most of the girls in the kingdom would be glad to marry you."

"Limitations?" Emmett gave her an incredulous look.

But evidently his father agreed with the queen. "She's right, Emmett. We've managed to conceal the reality from the kingdom for four years. Not all marriages have to be as emotional as your brother's. If you took a wife, I'm sure there would be ways to keep details private from her."

Something prickly passed over Emmett at the image of marriage presented by his father's words. It wasn't what he'd hoped for, especially after witnessing his brother's relationship with the woman who was now his wife. But that wasn't what made Emmett adamant not to yield. For the sake of his duty and his kingdom, he could have swallowed a bloodless marriage if it was only his own desires at stake. But he couldn't in good conscience do what his parents suggested.

"It's not just information I'd be concerned about getting to her," he said gruffly. "It's...well, myself." Unable to meet his father's eye, he looked instead at his mother, a slightly gentler target. "I might be a danger to her."

His mother looked startled. "What do you mean? I thought you were fully in control of your mind even when...you know."

Emmett swallowed. "I was. At the start. And I still am, mostly. But it's changing. I can't deny it any longer. As the other details you mention change, this changes as well. I can't guarantee that it will be safe for a wife to live with me in the months to come."

"But remaining unmarried won't resolve that danger," protested the queen, her face ashen.

"I know," Emmett acknowledged. He fixed his eyes on the wall above his father's head, drawing a deep breath. "That's another reason I proposed moving to Lernvale. If it becomes necessary to restrain me, that will be easier to orchestrate there than here in the capital."

There was a moment of silence, and against his better judgment, Emmett let his eyes flick to his father's face. The king looked truly horrified, unable to maintain his usual stoic front at the idea of his son and heir needing to be restrained like a wild animal.

"I'm sorry, Father," Emmett said, the soft words slipping out unthinkingly. He'd said it all before, and he knew it brought no comfort to either him or his father for him to acknowledge his fault yet again. But he couldn't help it when he saw how stricken the king was by his affliction.

A look of pain crossed King Johannes's features, but he smoothed them out quickly.

"I can see you've given the matter some thought, and you have your reasons for the proposal you've made. Although your presence and assistance in the capital will be sorely missed, I agree it may be best for you to relocate to the castle at Lernvale, at least for the present."

Emmett inclined his head. His father's capitulation was exactly what he'd sought, but it felt like defeat rather than victory.

"As it happens," the king went on, "I've just recently received a missive from King Ryker which may help us."

Emmett looked up inquiringly at this mention of the king of the neighboring kingdom of Teren.

"He is becoming increasingly concerned about the thickening of the wild magic in the Forest of Ilgal. He's exploring concrete actions he can take to find a solution."

"That's excellent," said Emmett in surprise. "Isn't it?"

After all, it had been concern over that issue that had first led him to make his own disastrous attempt at alleviating the problem. Although the results of that endeavor had taken priority over everything else since, he still cared about the fate of the forest he'd loved since he was a child.

His father gave a noncommittal grunt, clearly not as invested in the state of Ilgal. "Reading between the lines, I'd say he's under considerable pressure from his people to do something about it. Not surprising—not only does so much more of Ilgal fall within his borders, but his own capital is right on the forest's doorstep. Naturally the residents of Terenford would be worried."

His hand came to rest on a stack of blank parchment as he continued, as if he was impatient to get Emmett's relocation underway as soon as possible.

"I intended to tell him that I had no immediate plans to take action regarding the part of Ilgal which belongs to us, but fortunately I haven't yet responded to that effect. I will instead inform him that we take the matter seriously as well, and that I'm sending you to Lernvale to take up residence there in an attempt to negotiate a solution together. That should provide a credible reason for your move." He bent a stern look on Emmett. "It hardly needs to be said that you do not have authority to commit us to any action regarding the forest. Any suggestions will be run past me."

"Yes, Father," said Emmett quietly, trying not to show how the words stung.

Perhaps his father could see it anyway, because his voice softened slightly. "You know I value your counsel in all other areas, Emmett. But when it comes to the forest, your judgment has been shown to be unsound."

"It was years ago, Johannes," said the queen wearily. "Don't you think he's learned his lesson?"

The king studied his son for a long moment. "I hope so," he said flatly.

Disheartened, Emmett didn't reply. If, after four years of Emmett's suffering and regret, his father wasn't truly convinced of his contrition over what had happened, it didn't seem likely anything he said or did now would change that.

"You said that I hate what you've become." The king's gruff words surprised Emmett back to attentiveness. "The truth is, Emmett, I'm proud of the man you are, under...all of it. I always have been."

Emmett stared at his father, thrown by the unusual words of praise. But he didn't have long to enjoy the sensation.

"And I wish that could be enough," the king continued. "But with the role we fill, Emmett, we can't afford to just be ourselves and nothing more."

"I know, Father," Emmett said quickly. "I know the kingdom needs me to not be what I am. And I truly do intend to look for answers in Lernvale. I'm not relocating as a means of slowly disappearing."

"I should think not," said the queen briskly. "Moving to Lernvale is a good solution, but it will require regular interactions with the Terenans. If you're sending Emmett to Ilgal in person, King Ryker will surely expect to meet face to face."

The king grunted, looking faintly relieved at this interruption to the moment he and his son had been sharing. "Naturally. I'm sure Emmett can arrange any such meetings for an appropriate time of day or month or whatever is needed." He reached for a quill. "I'll write to Ryker at once, and leave it to you to make preparations for your departure, Emmett."

Emmett nodded, and the queen let out a sigh, looking forlorn. "Perhaps I can come and visit you," she suggested. "Brighten up the tedium."

Emmett sent her a tight smile. "You would be very welcome, Mother."

Her gaze sharpened a little as she studied him. "I haven't given up on the other matter," she warned him.

"Certainly not," King Johannes agreed, his quill already scratching away on the parchment. "The matter of you marrying and producing an heir is only more urgent in light of this new information."

Internally Emmett groaned, but aloud he put up no fight. He didn't intend to budge, but there was nothing to be gained from pushing the point now. His parents would be much less able to badger him about finding a wife when he was living in Lernvale.

He took his leave, striding out of the study and into the empty antechamber beyond. There were no guards—they must be out in the corridor. He'd pushed the door mostly closed behind him when he caught his mother's low voice. Guiltily, he paused, stilling so as to catch her words.

"What are we going to do, Johannes?"

The king gave no answer that Emmett could hear, and after a moment his mother spoke again.

"Perhaps it's time to abandon caution. Perhaps we should make the truth public, put every mind onto the task of finding a solution. Other singers might be able to help where those we've tried have failed. Other scholars might have different answers."

"No." His father's voice was sharp. "Secrecy is paramount. With our only other heir now committed to a different kingdom, we cannot afford the truth about Emmett to be known. The monarchy would be far too vulnerable."

"The monarchy?" There was a defiant note in the queen's voice that she would never use on the king in front of others. "Is the monarchy all you care about, Johannes? We're speaking of our *son*."

His conscience getting the better of him, Emmett eased the door shut. He had no desire to hear more, anyway.

Fueled by his guilt, he threw himself into preparations, all of which went smoothly. Everyone seemed to accept the stated reason for his change of residence. The idea that the crown prince loved the forest and took every opportunity to spend time there had been encouraged for years, so it was probably no surprise to anyone that the king was giving him the task of coordinating with King Ryker regarding Ilgal.

The rumor was based on truth, but it was equally true that Emmett loved his seaside home of Port Dulla. As he stood on the cliffs the morning after his discussion with his parents, he felt a pang of anticipated homesickness. He would miss the capital. He would miss this vista. His eyes passed over the endless expanse of water, thinking of his brother, who'd always loved the ocean to a downright dangerous extent. Farrin was out there, far across the water, in his new home.

Much as he missed his brother, Emmett couldn't bring himself to wish Farrin was with him. The younger prince had sacrificed so much in his attempts to fix Emmett's situation. It had all been as futile as Emmett could have told him it would be, if Farrin had stopped to ask anyone's advice before very nearly throwing his life away. If Farrin was here now, and aware of the escalation in Emmett's affliction, what would stop him from doing the same again?

His new wife might, Emmett reflected, and that was some satisfaction. Whatever became of him, Farrin had every likelihood of a long and happy life. And if the worst came to it, and Emmett died without an heir, perhaps Farrin's second child could one day take the throne of Medulle. Such things weren't unheard of.

The ocean was flat and still, no sign on its surface of the empire Emmett now knew was thriving in its depths. That was another thing he regretted about the need to banish himself to Lernvale. Even after six months, the process of opening diplomatic relations with Emperor Aefic's merfolk remained in its early stages, and there would be many fascinating developments Emmett would miss.

The thought brought his mind to the underwater empire's ambassador to Medulle. He should pay a visit to Princess Estelle before he left Port Dulla. She had a comforting way about her—perhaps spending two years without a voice had made her a good listener. Even though he couldn't tell her the truth of what was happening, he would appreciate the chance to express his mixed emotions regarding his move to the forest.

Within a week, everything was in place. The journey itself was smooth, Emmett and his small retinue making good time. After two days of solid riding along a now incredibly familiar route, Emmett found himself once again under the trees of Ilgal.

When the group emerged in the clearing, Emmett looked up at the castle. The outer walls were covered with moss, but the building itself was in good repair. Better repair than it had been when he'd gotten himself cursed. It was much more inhabited now. The gray turrets were stately, rising above the surrounding trees and yet still seeming to belong among them. But no pennants fluttered cheerfully, and no bustling town surrounded it. It was nothing to the beautiful seaside castle which graced the capital. In fact, it was hard to believe that the castle in Lernvale had once been the primary seat of the monarchs. Apparently a greater area had been cleared around it back then, but that was some eight generations ago. The trees growing outside the narrow band of grass that acted as the castle's border were tall and established, even if they couldn't match the giants deeper in the forest.

In spite of its humbler appearance—or perhaps because of it—Emmett had always been fond of the old castle. But there was no denying that his appreciation of it was marred by all it had come to represent.

Beautiful as it might be, the castle was increasingly becoming his prison. And, to acknowledge the plain truth, it was likely to be his final prison.

CHAPTER FOUR

Rosa

"Otto." Rosa's voice came out muffled from where she'd laid her head across the tablecloth. "I'm hideously bored."

"You'll get over it," her stepbrother told her cheerfully. He flicked one of her braids aside to more easily reach the salt cellar. "Mama will have your hide if you get egg on your gown."

Rosa groaned, lifting her head and leaning back in her chair. He was right. "Where are they, anyway? When was the last time we beat them to breakfast?"

"Father was walking in with me when Mama called him aside for a private word," Otto informed her. "I think they're talking about you. How to tame you."

Rosa ripped a piece of crust from her bread for the express purpose of tossing it at him. "Oi. That's no way to speak of a princess."

Otto grinned around his mouthful. "Oh, so *now* you want to be a princess? You can't have it both ways, Rosa."

"I can, and I shall," Rosa said contrarily. She sighed. She knew her stepbrother's talk of taming her was a joke—mostly—but she didn't doubt her mother and stepfather were speaking of her right now. "They're trying to figure out how to marry me off, more like."

"Maybe," said Otto, unconcerned. "It might not be so bad if they did, Rosa. Maybe you'll marry someone who'll be perfectly happy to let you roam at will."

Rosa snorted, drawing a scandalized look from a serving man who was depositing a fresh basket of bread on the table.

"Not to be insufferable," Otto added, "but it is your own fault you're bored, you know. You wouldn't be under instructions to stay in the castle if you didn't keep sneaking off into the forest. Even I got in trouble for last time, because I didn't stop you, and didn't tell anyone that you'd gone."

Rosa eyed him, lounging comfortably in his seat. She could see no sign of this supposed *trouble*. "But the whole reason I'm annoyed about being kept here is because it means I can't go see my grandparents," she pointed out. "If I stop sneaking off to see them so as to not be restricted to the castle, what have I gained?"

Otto shrugged. "Suit yourself."

"I usually do," grinned Rosa. She let out a breath, blowing a disobedient strand of hair out of her eyes. "I've been very docile for two whole weeks, anyway. I think they're easing off with the scrutiny."

The door opened on the words, and the king and queen entered. Rosa and Otto both straightened in their seats, murmuring greetings as the older couple took their seats. King Ryker waved away a servant with a smile of thanks.

"No fish this morning. I'm expected in a meeting shortly."

"What meeting, Father?" Otto asked, helping himself to wine.

"Leonhard has been asking for some time to meet with the Council of Nobles regarding the magic situation in the forest," the king replied. "I agreed to hear what he has to say, and the

Council is to convene in a quarter of an hour. You should attend, Otto."

"Certainly, Father," the prince agreed readily.

"I would like to attend as well, if I'm welcome," Rosa piped up.

Her stepfather considered her thoughtfully as he accepted a buttered roll from a servant. "Would you?"

She nodded eagerly. "I take a great interest in the forest, after all."

In fact, she'd been meaning to ask about the matter for two weeks, since her last visit to her grandparents, but the king was a busy man. Plus she wasn't sure how to ask about the missive he'd sent to her grandparents without making it appear that they'd been complaining about him, an impression she certainly didn't want to give. This might be an opportunity to discover exactly where the king and his Council of Nobles stood on the matter without saying a word about her grandparents.

"It's not your place, Rosa," said her mother with a touch of impatience. "The Council is not somewhere to push yourself in."

"No, Ada, she's right," the king said. "She does have a vested interest." He gave his stepdaughter a wry smile. "And I know my slow and steady methods frustrate you at times, Rosa. It might be instructive for you to better understand how these decisions are made. You'll see that even a monarch is not free to do exactly as he wishes."

Rosa grinned in response to the sparkle in his eyes. "I knew the benefits of this exalted position had been greatly overstated."

Otto chuckled at that, leaning forward to help himself to one of the still-steaming rolls. "I don't know if I'd say that, Rosa. You're just focusing on the wrong benefits."

Rosa felt elated when she followed Otto up the corridor a

short time later. At least she had something to do with her time. At King Ryker's instruction, the siblings sat against the wall rather than joining the table of nobles. Rosa suspected that Otto would usually sit with the Council and had been sent to sit with her so that she would seem less out of place. She was grateful, both for the king's consideration, and for Otto's cheerful willingness to be demoted for her convenience.

She watched with interest as the nobles filed in. Some of them—including Leonhard—shot bemused looks in her direction, but most ignored her. They were mainly men, although there was one noblewoman among their ranks.

"Who's that?" Rosa whispered to Otto.

"Lady Louisa," he murmured back. "Her husband has a long-held hereditary seat on the Council, but he has a health condition that often prevents him from attending. On those occasions, she takes his place." He shot her a grin. "She's often the most sensible member of the Council."

Rosa returned the expression. "I'm not surprised to hear it."

The king rose to his feet, and the pair fell silent, copying the motion along with everyone else in the room. King Ryker called the meeting to order, then resumed his seat. After a few introductory words outlining the nature of the problem, he invited Leonhard to speak.

The advisor stood, thanking the king for the invitation with far too many words, at least in Rosa's opinion. He was a commoner like her, and he wasn't very old—she doubted he'd reached forty—but he had all the pompous air of an elderly courtier.

"Your Highnesses, My Lords, My Lady," he began. "As His Majesty has so aptly outlined, the issue at hand is the Forest of Ilgal. Specifically, the strengthening of the magic that issues from the forest itself. I understand that the Council has previously discussed the matter, so I assume you are all aware that the magic has grown at an unprecedented rate in the last few years."

Murmurs of assent greeted his words.

"I'm sure I don't need to list all the evil effects of outsiders no longer being able to safely set foot in the forest," Leonhard went on. "The region's trade has been affected, families are being separated, travel has become difficult. And of course we cannot have confidence that the pressure of the wild magic will continue to affect only those unfamiliar with the forest. In fact, the information suggests that in time, no amount of exposure will be enough to allow the human body to withstand the effects of the magic. I have made a study of the properties of magic in its raw form, and it is my view that within the next few decades, the Forest of Ilgal will be rendered uninhabitable to humans."

Rosa frowned. Surely that was overstating the severity of the issue. A glance around the room showed that she wasn't the only one surprised by the strength of the verdict.

"Do you mean to suggest that half our kingdom will become like Selvana?" one of the nobles asked.

Murmurs passed around the room at mention of the island kingdom whose very ground had become lethal, forcing its inhabitants to build their city in the treetops. The jungle-dwelling Selvanans had been cut off from the rest of Providore for generations, and only recently reopened contact.

"I fear so," said Leonhard gravely. "And we know from the Selvanans' experience that their failure to fully understand the threat cost many lives when they first moved to the island. We do not want to make the same mistake. Which is why I propose the evacuation of Ilgal."

"What?"

Rosa's protest was lost amid the reactions of various members of the Council. As far as she knew, none of them lived in the forest, but some of them would certainly have holdings there, and if they had to evacuate all their tenants and employ-ees, their estates would suffer.

"That seems a drastic step," said Lady Louisa mildly.

Leonhard dipped his head in acknowledgment. "I under-stand it may seem that way, My Lady. But the truth is, loss of Terenan life would be more drastic. The safety of our people is surely paramount."

"An excellent point," chimed in a middle-aged nobleman whose name Rosa couldn't remember. "And from what I hear, the forest is growing increasingly dangerous. This is my first sojourn in the capital for some months, and quite apart from the magic issue, I've been astounded by the rise in wolf sightings and attacks during my absence. Surely the timber industry can be sustained without it being necessary for humans to *live* in the forest. Can we not cut the groves closest to the forest's edge?"

"If we did that, the forest edge would be driven leagues from the city in no time," said Lady Louisa impatiently.

"Is that undesirable?" the nobleman asked, his voice bland. "That would presumably reduce the risks from wolves and other predators, as well as from the magic that's growing wild. I mean, magic is plentiful on the plains, and we don't have any problems with it growing wild. I understood it was the terrain that fostered such unnatural magical growth."

"His holdings are along the West River, near the border with Frossenland," Otto murmured helpfully to Rosa.

"So he cares nothing about the forest," she muttered back, her eyes narrowed at the nobleman in question.

"That is the widely accepted view among magical scholars, My Lord," Leonhard said, in response to the nobleman's comment. "The terrain is directly linked to the quantity of magic produced by the land. We see it all over the continent. Jungles and forests are at a high risk of magic growing to an unmanageable volume, fertile pasturelands have a healthy but controllable supply, and the frozen northern regions are as barren of magic as they are of crops."

"Is it possible the increased wolf attacks are a direct result of the magic growing wilder?" someone cut in. "I've heard the magic makes the foliage grow prolifically. Does it have the same effect on the wildlife?"

"Very possibly," said Leonhard gravely. "We know from Selvana's example that the ground eventually becomes deadly to humans. It stands to reason that it would have some effect on animals as well."

"What about the elves?" someone chimed in. "Doesn't it affect them too? They have access to magic—they must be mining a wealth of it with the land so overrun. What help can they give?"

"What help they *can* give is unclear," said the king. "But the simple truth is that there's no help they're willing to give. Ilgal is home to many elves, it's true, but the majority of them—including their main tribal leaders—withdrew deeper into the forest some time ago. They have been unresponsive to attempts to involve them in this process. No elves have the capacity to channel magic like singers have, and their bodies are not adversely affected by the magic in the way humans are, so their incentive to assist is negligible. I think we must conclude that we are on our own when it comes to the magic crisis."

"Does that mean there's no hope of reclaiming the forest?" asked a different member of the Council. "Do we have no choice but to let it go? If that's the case, I can certainly see the benefit of evacuating before we reach crisis point."

No one immediately replied, and Rosa was gripped by alarm. It sounded like madness to her, but even her stepfather was saying nothing, merely listening with a solemn expression.

"Surely not," Rosa burst out, unable to help herself. "Surely no one would actually consider evacuating Ilgal."

Many disapproving eyes turned to hers. Otto hissed a warning under his breath, but she barely heard it. She was too busy staring Leonhard down.

"Your Highness cannot be expected to understand all the many complex layers of this issue," the advisor said frostily. "But I assure you—"

"I understand much better than you think," Rosa said, indignant. "I'm a child of the forest, unlike the rest of you in this room, I'd wager. And I can tell you now that from the perspective of those who make Ilgal their home, evacuating the forest and surrendering it to the magic would not be considered a *solution* to anything. They would see that as a greater evil than the wild magic. It would be the ultimate disaster, which most would do anything necessary to prevent."

Leonhard's eyes were hard as he replied. "Your Highness is mistaken. I was born and grew up in the forest. I am not ignorant of the way of life cherished by those who dwell there. But their lives must take precedence over their homes."

Rosa opened her mouth to retort, but King Ryker chose that moment to clear his throat. At once all eyes were on him, and everyone fell silent. The king's expression was mild, and his gaze wasn't on Rosa, but something about his manner brought her back to herself. Realizing at once that she'd erred, she sank hastily back to her seat, wincing a little at the pained demeanor she could feel rather than see from Otto beside her.

"Thank you everyone for your contributions," King Ryker said. "For many of you, this morning is the first you've heard of Leonhard's proposal. Naturally, time must be taken to consider all aspects of the matter and to examine our options. All perspectives are of assistance in this process." He nodded faintly to Rosa. "And the princess gives a timely reminder that we must consult with the forest-dwelling citizens before any decisions are made. We will discuss these issues further tomorrow."

His tone was a clear dismissal, and the members of the Council filed out. At a gesture from the king, Rosa and Otto remained behind. When the three of them were alone, King Ryker turned to his son and stepdaughter.

"Not the best example of a Council meeting for you to witness, Rosa," he said mildly. "They're not normally as short as that."

"If only they were," Otto said emphatically.

The king smiled at his son's attempt at humor, although the expression was weary.

"I shouldn't have spoken up," Rosa said contritely. "Mama was right, it isn't my place."

"You shouldn't have," her stepfather agreed, although there was no heat in his words. "But it's not just about place, Rosa. It's about having the discernment and the strategy to be effective." He met her eyes kindly. "I know you feel strongly regarding the issue at hand. That's understandable and appropriate. But that doesn't mean it's wise to make your feelings public. There's a way to go about these things—laying everything on the table is often not the most effective approach. More often than not, doing so gives those who disagree with you fuel to work against you."

Rosa sighed. "I don't doubt that you're right," she said. "You're the authority, after all. But it seems a miserable way to live."

Her stepfather chuckled tolerantly. "It's not so terrible, Rosa. Refraining from speaking your thoughts doesn't mean you can't have them. In my head, I'm as free as anyone could wish. Just because I didn't disagree aloud doesn't mean I agree with what was said."

Rosa bit her lip. She'd made the mistake of thinking her stepfather was being easily swayed because he wasn't immediately contradicting. That had been foolish.

"I'm sorry," she said.

Her stepfather smiled, the expression increasing his resemblance to Otto. "All is well, Rosa. Even royals learn best from experience. Kings are no exception, and neither are reluctant princesses, as I'm sure you'll discover more and more with time."

Rosa gave a pained laugh at the accurate description of herself. The king's steward appeared in the doorway at that moment, and he took his leave of them.

"Well, that was much more exciting than your average Council meeting," Otto said cheerfully. "I wish you could come to them all, Rosa, so they could all be controversial and short."

"No you don't," sighed Rosa, interlinking her arm with his and steering them toward the royal wing. "You don't have to try to make me feel better, Otto. You were radiating discomfort while I was putting my worst foot forward. I hope I didn't make you look bad."

"Not at all," he said placidly. "Just yourself, I imagine."

Rosa's forehead creased in a frown. "I wasn't wrong, though," she said. "I mean, of course I had to express contrition to your father—and I meant it," she added quickly. "But between you and me, I think what I said was very reasonable. And it's ridiculous that the plain truth can't just be said."

"Perhaps it is," Otto conceded. "But it's a flavor of ridiculous with which I've been familiar all my life, so it doesn't strike me as especially frustrating."

They reached the royal wing just as the queen was leaving it, and one look at their faces caused her to turn back, waving them into her own rooms.

"What's wrong?" she asked warily. "Were you kicked out of the meeting, Rosa?"

"Of course not," said Rosa with dignity. "The meeting is over."

"Already?" The queen was clearly skeptical.

"Rosa spoke up and contradicted the advisor presenting, and Father brought the meeting to a hasty finish," said Otto matter-of-factly, leaning around his stepmother to see if there were any refreshments on the table.

"Traitor," hissed Rosa, as the queen's face transformed in horror.

"If you think the incident is going to stay a secret around here, you've lost your mind," Otto told her frankly.

Rosa sighed, acknowledging the truth of it. "Yes, I gave my opinion where no one wanted it, but I *was* right."

The queen groaned. "Rosa, I told you it wasn't your place! If only you would listen for once in your life! Can you truly not go a few weeks without creating a scandal that reflects badly on me and your stepfather as well as yourself?"

"Scandal is a bit strong," Rosa protested.

"Honestly, Mama, it wasn't as bad as all that," Otto agreed. "Perhaps Rosa spoke out of turn, but I don't think there's any harm done. Father handled it with his usual tact and confidence, and no one present will think any the worse of him."

"I'm glad to hear you say so," Rosa said, softened by this support. "I acknowledge that I spoke out of turn, and I would hate it to affect how the Council members see their king."

"I'm glad as well," said her mother waspishly. "But I don't have the same optimism that none of them will think the worse of you, Rosa."

"Oh, I don't mind about that," Rosa told her seriously.

"Well, I do," her mother said indignantly. She sighed as she looked her daughter over. "You're not exactly going out of your way to make my task easier, are you?"

"What task?" Rosa asked warily.

"You know what I mean, we've already discussed it," her

mother said in a lofty tone. "But clearly I'd best act quickly, before you damage your chances any further."

Rosa groaned. "Mama, this idea of yours to find me a husband this summer is absurd. Why the rush?"

Her mother continued as if she hadn't spoken. "We talked about hosting a small event to start the season. Evidently it's time for me to make that happen. We'll arrange it for next week."

Rosa opened her mouth to argue, but Otto was uninterested in their squabble.

"It was an interesting point, wasn't it?" he mused. "About the wolves. Do you think the magic could be what's behind these increased wolf attacks? Could it be affecting their behavior?"

"Nonsense," said Rosa tersely. "In spite of what Leonhard said, I've never heard of the strength of a region's magic affecting the animals who live there. It only affects humans because we theoretically have the ability to channel the magic. Of course only singers actually have the capacity to do it, but the rest of us are still susceptible to magic's effects when it grows too powerful. More likely it's the other way around—the silly rumors about giant wolves are making everyone more reactive than necessary regarding the wild magic. They're making the forest out to be some dark, mysterious, terrifying place."

"But could the magic actually be causing giant wolves to appear?" Otto persisted. "Could it be mutating them somehow?"

"Magic doesn't morph creatures from one thing to another without assistance," Rosa told him firmly. "It would have to be worked by a singer, or channeled through a talisman by an elf to do something so bizarre and unnatural. If it's even possible."

Otto frowned at her. "I think you're the one who's blinded, Rosa, not everyone else. You're so determined not to believe that your beloved forest is dangerous that you're willing to ignore all evidence to the contrary. Honestly, I'm just worried about your safety."

"Otto is right," the queen said. "You talk very confidently, Rosa, but let's not forget what happened to Frossenland. The kingdom is without a proper monarch because poor King Eerikki and Prince Herleif weren't immune to being savaged by an enormous wild animal, royal or not. You'd do well to remember that you aren't invincible either."

Rosa willed herself to be patient. "Mama, they were killed by a bear. We don't have bears in Ilgal."

"Bears, wolves...my point still stands," her mother replied with dignity. "Now enough of this gruesome talk. We have more pleasant matters to discuss if we're to host a social event in only a week."

Rosa submitted with as much grace as she could muster, but inside she chafed unbearably. She'd joked that morning that her mother and stepfather were about to let her out of the cage, but it felt as though the opposite were true. Perhaps she would once again be able to get away with visiting her grandparents, but her mother seemed intent on fashioning a much more permanent cage for Rosa.

And, to add insult to injury, she expected Rosa to cheerfully assist in the process. If she'd ever felt the smallest spark of attraction for any of the young noblemen her mother had set her sights on, she might feel differently. But she never had, and the thought of marrying any of them produced nothing but misery.

She submitted for the rest of the day, but her forbearance only caused her inner rebellion to grow. By the time she went to bed, she'd decided on her course of action. The dawn saw Rosa slipping out her own window, her grandmother's red cloak secured around her throat in a sign that spoke more of defiance than any kind of sensible attempt at stealth.

Leaving the city presented no great challenge to her vast experience, and soon she was walking below the trees, cutting across a familiar stretch of woods to reach the road. She would be at her grandparents' house in time to join them for breakfast.

Some part of her knew that sneaking out was foolish, but she couldn't help herself. She felt like a creature in a net, and her every instinct was to get free at the first opportunity.

She was just stepping quietly over a potentially noisy patch of bracken when a sound ahead made her go still. In spite of Otto's accusations, her love for the forest hadn't blinded her to its dangers. She knew that there were creatures about who could do her harm, and although dawn had passed now, it was still early enough that she would be wise to be careful of wolves.

But as she peered warily ahead, her caution turned to confusion. The figure in front of her wasn't a wolf, or any other kind of predatory animal. It was a human.

Rosa moved forward to get a better look, still trying to stay undetected. The man wasn't a wolf, but that didn't mean he wasn't dangerous. The stranger was a young man, probably not much older than her. She wasn't too far from her grandparents' part of the forest, and she'd wondered if he might be one of their workers. But she was fairly certain she'd never seen him before.

As she watched, he stumbled over a mossy log. Although he righted himself quickly, his demeanor as he looked around gave the definite impression that he was lost. Swallowing her caution, Rosa decided to take pity on him. If he turned out to have ill intentions, she could probably outmaneuver him, here in her familiar forest.

"Are you lost, sir?" She stepped out from behind a trunk with the words.

Starting, the man turned around. He took Rosa in with a quick glance, then dipped his head respectfully.

"I beg your pardon. I didn't see you. I hope I haven't disturbed you."

Rosa considered him, surprised. She'd expected to see a vagabond, perhaps even someone nursing the results of a night of inebriation. But although the stranger looked a little disheveled, he was neither a waif nor drunk. He was very well-dressed, his speech refined and his gaze clear and polite.

"I'm not easily disturbed," she assured him lightly.

She let her gaze pass over him again, taking in his closely cropped dark hair, brown eyes, and muscular figure. The dark hair across his chin was light enough that she couldn't tell whether it was intentionally grown, or whether he'd neglected to shave for a few days. Which wasn't to say it was unattractive. She tried to think of a circumstance that would bring a wealthy, possibly noble, man wandering through the forest just after dawn, and came up blank.

She was about to repeat her question about him being lost, but he forestalled her.

"Are you alone out here?" The man's brow furrowed in concern as he glanced around them. "Are you in need of any assistance? I could see you to your destination, if you would permit me."

"I won't permit you," said Rosa, any charitable feelings toward the stranger fleeing at once. "I'm not in the least in need of assistance, and I highly doubt that you could see me to my destination when you appear not to have the faintest idea of where you are, let alone where I'm going."

The man had the grace to look sheepish. "Forgive me. I didn't mean to offend. It's just very early for you to be out alone, and—"

"The same could be said of you," Rosa pointed out. "I was going to offer to help you find your way, but if you're so confident as to attempt to steer me within my own forest, you clearly don't need it. So I'll bid you good morning."

With her best state curtsy—a gesture she'd learned could be more cutting than the choicest words, if used correctly—she swept off in the direction of the road that would lead her to her grandparents' gate.

"Wait!" the stranger called after her, the hint of desperation in his voice causing her to begrudgingly pause. "Do you really live here?"

"I don't think that's any of your business," said Rosa with a sniff. She resumed walking.

"I really didn't mean to offend you," the stranger tried again, his voice raised to reach her in light of her rapid pace. "Can you at least tell me which way is south?"

Rosa sighed, relenting in spite of herself and turning back toward him at last. "That way is south," she said, raising her arm. "But you'd be better off traveling west for a short distance. Then you'll hit the road, and can follow that southward, all the way to the border if you wish."

"Thank you!" The man's words were faint, since Rosa had started walking again before the last words were even out of her mouth.

Her mind was on the bizarre encounter all the way to her grandparents' house. Who could the strange man possibly be, all the way out here alone? If he was heading south instead of east, he presumably wasn't from Terenford.

And he clearly wasn't from the forest. Yet he had the cheek to offer to see her safely through Ilgal's hazards!

Honestly. Everyone was all worked up over wolves, a perfectly natural part of forest life, but they should be worried about insolent men wandering around giving unsolicited aid to perfectly capable travelers who were simply minding their own business.

CHAPTER FIVE

Emmett

Emmett paused at the edge of the trees, closing his eyes for a moment and blocking out the view of the castle walls just ahead. He'd been walking for hours, and in addition to being exhausted, his head was pounding mercilessly. He also felt an uncomfortable pressure in his chest. It wasn't strong enough to be painful, but it was like a constant weight. He couldn't remember feeling it before, and he had no idea what it was.

Even so, those physical discomforts were the least of his problems. He had no doubt there would be a terrible fuss made when he reappeared. And he couldn't for the life of him think what he would tell the flustered servants who must have been fearing the worst after finding his bed empty then hearing nothing from him all day.

It wasn't as though he could tell them that he'd spent the night running wild through the forest on all fours, and been forced to walk home all the way from the neighboring kingdom.

He cast a final glance down himself, making sure there were no lingering signs of his wolf form. He knew there weren't, of course. He'd been upright and human since the sun rose. But it was hard to shake the fear that his affliction was somehow visible on his person. Some part of him, unnervingly deep inside, still *felt* like the wolf.

Telling himself to stop being cowardly, he crossed the cleared band of grass, making his way around the edge of the castle wall to the front gates. The astonishment of the guard on duty told Emmett the state of the household, but the man let his prince through without comment.

The steward wasn't as forbearing, but Emmett deflected all his questions with vague comments about being called away on important business. It was less about the words he used than the tone. When he felt the conversation had gone long enough, he injected a hint of sternness into his voice, and the man let the matter drop. Emmett could only hope the other servants would be as accommodating. He had a sinking feeling this wouldn't be his last nighttime jaunt into the forest.

The night before was mainly a blur, his memories all of motion. The thrill of running fast—impossibly fast—countered with the shame of remembering how eager his wolf senses had been to hunt. He hadn't hunted so much as a rabbit, of course. His human mind had remained enough in control for that. But denying his wolf form some kind of motion was more than he could sustain. From before the change had even occurred, he'd been desperate to run, to *move*. He wasn't even in his wolf form when he snuck out of the castle. But he'd known it was coming.

It was another disheartening example of the acceleration of his affliction. The moon had been waning for days now. The nights should once again be safe for human activities. But the process was lasting longer each time.

Emmett's giant wolf body might have nothing but energy, but his human form felt the full effect of his sleepless night. He spent what remained of the afternoon in his study, attempting to continue his research, but he could barely keep his mind on the parchments he'd collected the day before. After an early dinner, he slipped eagerly into bed, grateful to feel no sign of an approaching transformation. The magic had held him in its grip longer this time, but it seemed to have subsided for now. Until the moon once again began to wax, at least.

When Emmett rose, he felt far from rested, but he intended to waste no more time. He made his way to the small dining parlor he'd claimed for his solitary meals, his nose twitching at the smell of hot food.

Stop it, he told the appendage silently. The last thing he needed was for the already suspicious servants to see his nose twitching.

Emmett sat, his mind straying to the morning before, when he'd come to himself in the forest. He could picture the face of the girl in the red cloak with perfect clarity. It had been a mercy that she'd come upon him then, instead of half an hour earlier when she might have seen his transformation from wolf back to human.

Not that witnessing it could have made her opinion of him too much worse, judging by the angry spark she'd had in her eyes. He couldn't remember the last time he'd offended someone so heartily. Or perhaps most people just hid it better since, unlike the unknown girl, they knew he was a prince.

In his defense, her surprise at his presence had made her hesitate visibly, and he'd mistaken that for uncertainty. Cleary she hadn't been in the least uncertain of herself though, he reflected, his mouth quirking into a smile. She'd put him in his place quickly enough. On reflection, he was glad she hadn't known he was a prince, and not just because it would be humiliating for the crown prince of Medulle to be seen in the state he'd been in. If she'd known his identity, she would likely have been tongue-tied and deferential instead of haughty. And that wouldn't have been nearly as entertaining.

At least the transformation back to human left him with his clothing. That was something to be grateful for. The scene would have been much more memorable, and for vastly different reasons, if his transforming wolf body ripped his human clothes apart, as logic told him it should.

Was this another sign to reinforce the guess he'd formed, that the magic's effect had been targeted and intentional rather than the result of a random burst of power?

It wasn't enough to draw any solid conclusions. Certainly not enough to convince his father.

Emmett's thoughts strayed from the matter, trickling back toward the girl from the forest. She'd called it her forest, but he'd thought most of the inhabitants of Ilgal were common folk, often living in very basic conditions. They were usually tenants of the wealthy estate owners who preferred to live in the city and manage their forest estates from afar. And the girl had been too well dressed and too well spoken to be a forest peasant. Not to mention she'd had the confidence of a queen, not that her antagonism did her any great credit.

There were a few exceptions, he reflected, where estates were held by wealthy commoners who lived on them rather than by distant nobles. Perhaps she belonged to one of those families.

Emmett was barely aware of the food he was putting in his mouth, his mind still on the girl in the red cloak. Between her confident maneuvering of the terrain and her elaborate gown, he couldn't decide if she'd looked at home in the forest or woefully out of place. She'd been striking, in any event. Her pale skin had stood out in the gloom under the trees, the contrast accentuated by her black hair, pulled into two untidy braids that left strands playing around her face. He could picture her haughty expression now, with that straight nose, rather defined jaw, and full lips...

What nonsense was his mind peddling? The girl was nothing more than a chance-met stranger, one whom he would never encounter again. Thinking about her was a waste of his limited time. The most he could do was to hope that she had made it to her destination as safely as she seemed convinced she would, and focus his mind on the urgent matter confronting him.

Unfortunately, that topic was proving no more fruitful. In the weeks since he'd arrived in Lernvale, he'd combed the castle's records and even begun to discreetly interview locals. So far he'd had no success in identifying what type of magic he might have encountered. The only thing of relevance that he'd found had been some tomes regarding magical theory in the castle's records room. They'd confirmed his own observations regarding the importance of the full moon. Apparently, the cycles of the moon were often of significance in magic, affecting such matters as when elves harvested power.

Again, it fit with Emmett's theory that the scene he and Farrin stumbled on that night had been an intentional one, but it proved nothing.

"Ale, Your Highness?"

The question startled Emmett from his thoughts, and he let out a growl before he could stop himself. An actual growl. The poor servant froze, instinctive fear flashing across his face for the briefest moment before he schooled his features. It was all Emmett could do not to hide his face in his hands in mortification.

"I beg your pardon," he said, overdoing the civility in an attempt to cover his wolfish mannerisms. "I didn't see you there."

With a mumbled apology, the servant withdrew, leaving Emmett to his miserable thoughts.

The morning brought no information or amusement to

lighten his mood, but he was gratified after lunch to receive a missive with the Terenan royal seal. He'd sent a dispatch to King Ryker the day before, notifying the Terenan king of his arrival in the region, and expressing the hope that they could meet to discuss the Ilgal crisis soon. The issue of wild magic in the forest might have been merely a front for Emmett's father, but Emmett was genuinely concerned about it and would be glad to know whether King Ryker had come up with any solutions.

But when he broke the seal, the parchment within contained not a letter from King Ryker, but an invitation from Queen Ada.

Emmett stared at the elegant writing. He knew that King Ryker had married again, but he'd never met the new queen. Not that she was new. Emmett had a vague recollection that they'd married not long after he and Farrin fell afoul of the wild magic, meaning it must have been about four years ago. He couldn't be sure. He'd been a little distracted at the time.

He laid the invitation down, not sure how he felt about it. He hadn't come to Lernvale to waste his time on social events. And he wasn't fooled by the description of a "small" gathering. If foreign royalty had been invited, there would be nothing small or informal about it. Still, he had no polite reason to refuse. He knew his mother would be scandalized that he would even consider it. And offending the Terenan royals wasn't likely to help anything.

Glancing down again, Emmett caught sight of a second slip of parchment he'd missed the first time. He picked it up, scanning the note from King Ryker quickly. That was more like it. The king expressed the hope that Emmett would be able to attend the event, inviting him to arrive at the castle earlier in the afternoon so that they could speak about the Ilgal crisis first.

Emmett squinted absently out the window, trying to calculate the days. The event was still the better part of a week away. He'd felt no hint of the change the night before, and he wouldn't be in danger again for at least a fortnight. He should be safe to attend.

He scratched out a hasty reply to send back with the messenger. After all, it was a confined life in the castle in Lernvale. It wouldn't hurt to have something to look forward to.

Emmett left earlier than necessary on the day in question, eager to maximize any time for discussion with King Ryker. It was convenient traveling as a human, he reflected as he climbed into a carriage. The journey would be faster this way, and he wouldn't have to walk home disoriented and with no sleep.

He knew the carriage ride would take several hours, and ordinarily he would have preferred to take the faster approach of riding. But given he was to attend a ball after he met with King Ryker, it had been necessary to dress accordingly, and he'd known a couple hours' hard riding would have done his formal wear no favors.

Once he cleared Lernvale, a well-kept road led him north along the edge of the forest, then, after he crossed the border and left his own kingdom, the road turned east to travel along the West River. At this point the thoroughfare became wider and more heavily trafficked, continuing along the edge of the waterway until he crossed the river at the broad, shallow ford for which Teren's capital city was named.

Terenford's wall rose up before Emmett, looking solid but not imposing in the cheerful afternoon sunshine. He'd been to Terenford once when he was a child, but his recollections of the city weren't strong, and he looked around with interest. It appeared to be a prosperous city. Having carried him through the gates located at the city's southern edge, the carriage continued westward, eventually reaching the royal castle. Its turrets and towers rose a little above the surrounding buildings, but like the city wall it gave an impression of stability without being intimidating. If Emmett's sense of both direction and distance had served him accurately, the castle was right at the city's western edge, meaning the Forest of Ilgal must start just beyond its wall.

Unsurprisingly, the neighborhood surrounding the castle showed all the signs of affluence, but even the outer sections of the city were mostly clean and well-kept. Evidently King Ryker's capital prospered.

On arrival at the castle, Emmett was received deferentially by the king's steward, who invited the visiting prince to follow him. As they walked through the building, Emmett took note of how pleasant and open it was. Outdoor walkways seemed to mirror the corridors, and Emmett found himself wishing he could be traversing those instead.

Soon enough, the steward bowed Emmett into what appeared to be a study. Emmett had expected King Ryker, but the royal who greeted him was much younger. Younger than Emmett, in fact.

"Welcome, Prince Emmett." The tall young man rose and extended his hand. "I imagine you don't recognize me, given how many years it's been since we met. I'm Otto."

Emmett smiled, accepting the offered handshake and seating himself as gestured. "Of course, Prince Otto. You're right, I didn't know you on sight, but I do remember you."

Otto grimaced. "I don't doubt it. The last time you were here, I think I drove you and your brother to distraction with following you everywhere you went."

Emmett chuckled. "We were only children then."

"True," Otto agreed, sinking into the chair behind the desk. "And please, feel free to call me Otto. My father will join us shortly. He is currently occupied in a meeting he can't postpone, and he asked me to begin discussions without him."

Emmett nodded slowly to cover his surprise. He hadn't reckoned on treating with the young prince, but he supposed it was natural enough. In his mind Otto was still a child, but the evidence of his eyes told him that time had moved more quickly than he realized. Otto was a man now and, as Teren's crown prince, Emmett's natural counterpart.

"I understand you're to stay for the ball afterward?" Otto's eyes flicked over Emmett's garb with the question.

Emmett nodded, and Otto's already friendly face broke into a smile.

"That's excellent news. Mama will be especially pleased to have you grace us with your company."

As he gave the polite reply, Emmett noted the warmth of the prince's reference to his stepmother. Clearly the rumors at the time, that the king's second marriage would prove detrimental to the king's heir, had been unfounded.

Otto was still making the expected inquiries after Emmett's family and journey to Lernvale when the door opened, and King Ryker entered. Both princes stood, greeting the older man respectfully.

"Prince Emmett," said the Terenan king. "You're very welcome. I appreciate you traveling all this way to discuss the crisis in Ilgal. And attend the queen's ball, of course," he added as an afterthought.

"I was delighted to receive your invitation, Your Majesty," Emmett said. "And to speak frankly, I'm pleased to hear you refer to the growing magic as a crisis. I've been concerned for years that we're not acting decisively enough to prevent the situation from growing worse."

"Have you?" The king took the seat behind the desk, Otto having shifted to sit between his father and Emmett. "I wasn't aware that you took an interest in the matter."

"I do," Emmett said. "I've always been very attached to the forest, and although it's only a small number of Medullans who live under its trees, the matter is no less grave for those few.

Their livelihoods are on the line. Possibly their very lives if we take Selvana as an example, and as you must be aware, my brother's marriage has brought the Selvanan situation to our attention in Medulle."

"Indeed," the king said.

Emmett noticed Otto watching him with interest. If he had to guess, he would say the younger prince was pleased with how seriously Emmett was taking the matter.

"Selvana's experience is a large part of why my people are so concerned about Ilgal, I think," King Ryker said. "We're all aware that the magic grew so wild that the whole island was overrun. And the forest is right on the doorstep of our capital." He gestured out the window. "Terenford is an old and well-established city. There's no question of moving the capital to another location in the kingdom, as your ancestors did generations ago. And many would lose everything if this city became uninhabitable due to wild magic."

"I can imagine," Emmett agreed gravely. "I assume you've been exploring options to ease the growth of the magic? Do you..." He hesitated, pushing down the sharp memory that assaulted him. "Do you know of any way to safely vent the magic that's building in the ground?"

King Ryker looked thoughtful. "Vent the magic. That's an interesting way of putting it. I had hoped for a way to stem the flow of the magic, but unfortunately our leading expert assures me it's not possible. He says that magic will continue to build in the forest, do what we might to prevent it, and that it will eventually claim the lives of those who live there. Already we are seeing the effects. There's been a sharp increase in the number of forest-dwellers coming to the city for medical treatment. And health issues seem to be appearing younger and younger, especially those to do with breathing, or the function of the heart. That's among the residents. Outsiders who go into the forest are affected in a more measurable way. Most complain of a constant, uncomfortable pressure on their chest, which eases as soon as they leave the forest. What the long-term effects of prolonged exposure might be, we can't predict."

Emmett frowned, remembering the pressure he'd felt during his last expedition into the forest. He'd assumed it to be a new aftereffect of his transformation, but that apparently wasn't so. It had been exactly as the king described.

"The situation is certainly dire," he agreed. "What's this expert's suggestion?"

"He has advised me to evacuate Ilgal as soon as possible," the king said heavily.

"Evacuate?" Emmett's eyes flew to Otto, startled. The other prince looked as somber as his father. Clearly they understood that what they were proposing was no small matter. "Surely that's premature."

"My advisor believes that we would be wise to act before there is loss of human life. Better too early than too late, as he argues."

"But how will evacuating the forest help stop the spread of the magic?" Emmett demanded.

King Ryker settled back in his chair, indicating with a subtle glance that his son was clear to step into the conversation. Emmett felt a flash of envy as Otto leaned forward to engage. His father had once trusted him in that way. No longer.

"Evacuating the forest won't do anything to stop the magic's growth," Otto acknowledged. "The hope is that experiments regarding the magic can more safely be conducted when there are no people in harm's way. Failing a solution, our expert also suggests that it may be possible to set up a magical barrier of some kind, cutting Ilgal off from the rest of the kingdom and preventing the magic from growing wild over its border and onto the plains."

"Cutting the forest off?" Emmett repeated, not trying to hide his disapproval. "Who is this advisor?"

"His name is Leonhard," said King Ryker. "He comes from a very influential family here in Terenford. The family lived in Ilgal previously, but have made the capital their home for many years now."

Emmett's brow creased in thought. "Forgive me if the question seems impertinent, Your Majesty—I don't mean to doubt you—but what makes this man an expert on wild magic?"

"He has made magic his study for many years," said King Ryker. "Others in his family are singers, so he grew up around magic. Although he is not a singer himself, he has studied theoretical magic under the academy's theory program since he was a child. And of course his origins in Ilgal give him an insight into forest life."

Emmett said nothing, troubled by the information that someone so well-informed and connected with the issue truly believed that evacuating the forest was necessary. Had things really escalated to that point already?

"If I may be bold, Your Majesty, are you inclined to follow this Leonhard's advice?" he asked.

King Ryker sighed. "I don't know. I'm reluctant to take such drastic action. Ilgal represents a significant portion of my kingdom, home to many of my subjects. Evacuating the whole forest is not something that could be undertaken lightly. Frankly, I'm not sure it would even be possible to fully clear it. But the problem seems to be the worst in the region near the capital, and that's what's created such unease within the city. Part of that unease is created by the recent wolf attacks, of course, but it all amounts to the same thing."

"Wolf attacks?" Emmett repeated, starting in his chair. He immediately chastised himself for the telling reaction, but neither father nor son seemed to have taken much note of it.

"That's right," Otto said. "Well, more sightings than actual attacks, but rumors tend to conflate the two. Wolves have always been a part of forest life in Ilgal, but if reports are to be believed, the wolves are more numerous, more aggressive, and substantially larger than they used to be. There's a great deal of speculation about whether the change might be linked to the growing magic."

"If there really is a change," said the king, frowning thoughtfully. "It's hard to discern how much is truth and how much rumor."

Emmett said nothing, mortified beyond words. His recollections of his episodes spent as a wolf were becoming hazier with each passing occasion. It was entirely possible that he'd encountered humans numerous times without realizing it. He hadn't attacked anyone, of course. He was confident of that. But he agreed with Prince Otto that sightings could easily become attacks once they'd passed through the rumor mill. The idea that his presence in the region was escalating the fear over the Ilgal crisis was distressing. But what could he do? He couldn't explain to the Terenan king why the increased sightings of wolves—overlarge ones—were in fact nothing to worry about.

"In any event, evacuating the portion of Ilgal nearest the capital, to allow our singers to attempt to create some kind of barrier between the city and the forest, is a possibility I cannot dismiss out of hand," King Ryker went on. "But I have no plans to do it imminently."

"Thank you for honoring me with this confidence," Emmett said, hoping his face wasn't as pale as it felt. "I will certainly recount our conversation to my father. He will be interested to know the information provided by your advisor, as he continues to seek input from our own experts."

King Ryker's gaze was shrewd as he studied Emmett's face.

"What is your view on the matter, Prince Emmett? Speaking entirely unofficially."

Emmett took a moment, drawing in a long breath and releasing it before answering. "I don't have enough information to speak for my kingdom," he said. *Or the authority*, he added in his head—he had no intention of humiliating himself by admitting that aloud. "But if you want my personal opinion, I would be very reluctant to see Medulle's portion of Ilgal either evacuated or cut off from the rest of the kingdom. I feel certain there's a better solution. In fact, I don't see the evacuation of the forest as a solution at all—more like a new problem of its own."

"That's very much what Rosa said," Otto commented. "My stepsister," he explained, in response to Emmett's inquiring look.

Emmett nodded absently. He'd forgotten that King Ryker's new wife had come with a daughter of her own. The child must be perceptive if she was engaged enough with matters of state to have an opinion on the Ilgal crisis.

"Well, we can discuss the matter more as events unfold," said King Ryker, standing. Both princes did the same. "For now, Otto and I must retire to prepare for tonight's event." He smiled at his guest. "We're delighted you are able to join us, Prince Emmett."

"You're welcome to pass the time in my receiving room," Otto offered. "You'll be comfortable there, and I can have refreshments sent."

"You're very kind," Emmett said. "But if I'm permitted, I think I'll wander the gardens." He didn't say so, of course, but in recent times, he was finding pastries and light sandwiches less and less appealing. And he doubted that the prince would order undercooked meat to be served as an afternoon refreshment.

Released, he took his leave, crossing the corridor and exiting at the nearest door. The gardens were just as pleasant as they'd looked, and the time passed quickly. He was curious to see just how close the forest was to the city wall, but he resisted the urge to leave the grounds and explore. He'd probably be back in Ilgal soon enough, whether he wanted to be or not.

His hosts obviously hadn't lost sight of his location, because when it was time for the gala to begin, a servant appeared to lead him to a place of honor. Prince Otto immediately found him, and did an excellent job of making him feel welcome and at ease as servants brought trays of food past.

Emmett didn't hate balls, but he'd never especially enjoyed the idle conversation and coquettish glances that characterized such evenings. He'd hoped for a little less notice in Teren, but his identity had clearly become known, because he was attracting plenty of notice from various young women whose faces told him plainly that they knew he was a prince.

He was scanning the crowd idly, wondering whether he might be able to avoid dancing without causing offense, when his eyes latched on a dark-haired figure whom he'd seen before. He made a soft noise of surprise. The girl from the forest! A glance at her elaborate gown told him that he hadn't been wrong about her wealth, but if she was invited to a royal ball at the castle, it seemed unlikely she belonged to a family of forest-dwelling commoners, however wealthy.

Otto was currently engaged in conversation with a young nobleman of his own age, and Emmett took the opportunity to slip away. He felt strangely nervous as he crossed the room, although why he should feel intimidated by this girl he couldn't explain. She had seen him in a somewhat disheveled state, of course, but that wasn't it. He was just curious to know who she was.

The girl had her back to him when he reached her, and he cleared his throat before addressing her.

"I beg your pardon, but I believe we've met before."

She turned, her confusion turning to surprise before settling quickly into the irritation she'd shown at their last meeting.

"Yes, I believe we have," she said shortly.

Emmett waited for her to say more, but she didn't, and his attention was claimed by a well-dressed young man with a pompous air that didn't match his youth.

"I, on the other hand, do not appear to have the pleasure of your acquaintance."

Emmett pulled his eyes from the forest girl, studying the young man dispassionately. A minor noble, he would guess. The man's dress was overstated, and his manner exaggerated. In Emmett's experience, those with greater actual status felt less need to advertise it with their every move.

"I believe you're right," he said, injecting the tiniest hint of haughtiness into his tone. "I'm Prince Emmett of Medulle. And you are?"

Emmett felt the start of surprise from the girl beside him, but he kept his gaze on the nobleman. Clearly taken aback by Emmett's status, the man stumbled over his own introduction, his name forgotten the moment Emmett heard it.

He caught a movement from another young man standing on the girl's other side, and a glance showed that the stranger seemed amused by the other man's discomposure. Emmett looked from the two young men to the girl who'd brought him across the room. He hadn't even taken note of her companions as he approached her, but she gave every appearance of a young lady beset by unwelcome attention. Although in defense of the amused man, he seemed to be hanging back, not showing any great interest in whatever conversation she'd been having with the pompous one.

The discomposed nobleman quickly excused himself, leaving Emmett free to turn to the girl again. She was wearing a finely embroidered emerald gown that highlighted her dark hair and brought out a hint of green in her eyes which he hadn't noticed in the forest.

But his attempt to speak to her was once again thwarted as the other young man spoke up.

"I am Lord Montague," he said cheerfully. "Son of the Earl of Linley. And I'm honored to have the opportunity to introduce myself." He seemed undeterred by Emmett's distraction. The prince had already forgotten the nobleman's name and rank. "It seems you need no introduction to Princess Rosa, however, Your Highness," the nobleman finished.

"Princess Rosa?" Emmett was startled into replying, his gaze passing between the nobleman and the princess. This girl whom he'd encountered roaming through the forest alone just after dawn was the king's stepdaughter? The one Prince Otto had mentioned? His memory of his lessons on foreign royalty had failed him when he pictured her as a child.

"And you're Prince Emmett," the princess said, her expression thoughtful. "I'll confess, I didn't guess that."

Emmett eyed her, not sure what was behind her veiled eyes. The nobleman, still seeming faintly amused, took his leave. A quick glance showed Emmett that he was joining Prince Otto across the room. Apparently he was a friend of the prince.

"If you're expecting me to thank you, you'll be disappointed," Princess Rosa said, her voice turning waspish as soon as they were alone. "I didn't need you to rescue me in the forest the other day, and I didn't need you to rescue me just now. I'm perfectly capable of handling myself both on my grandparents' land and in my stepfather's ballroom."

Emmett blinked, confused. "I'm sure you are," he said, with stiff politeness. "Although I'm glad to see you made it home safely on that previous occasion."

"You can't help yourself, can you?" the princess said, exasperated. She looked over him, her eyes narrowed. "I suppose you being a prince explains your mistaken belief that it's your job to solve everyone else's problems."

Emmett raised an eyebrow, goaded in spite of his better judgment. "And I suppose you not being raised a princess explains your inability to conform to the basic level of politeness expected in a royal ballroom."

He immediately regretted the rude words, but to his surprise, the princess grinned. "You clearly meant that as an insult, but it's the first sensible thing you've said to me." She gestured around the room. "I belong where we first met much better than I fit in here."

Emmett eyed her, pursing his lips to keep his thoughts inside.

"Go on," she said tartly. "Whatever it is you're thinking, just say it."

"I was thinking that the forest setting didn't lead to any noticeable increase in your manners." The words burst from Emmett, leaving him horrified. As a prince, his control was usually unparalleled in social situations. What had pulled down his usual barriers? Was his human self becoming as wild as his wolf self threatened to be?

Princess Rosa looked like she wasn't sure whether to be angry or amused. "If I wasn't polite, I think I was justified. Did you expect the deference shown to a prince when you were wandering our forest like a vagabond?"

"Much like yourself?" Emmett asked, his attempt at a polite tone somehow only making the words seem more insolent. He pushed on nevertheless, more curious for answers than ever. "What were you doing out there all alone, Princess?"

She raised an eyebrow. "A question I should be asking you. You had even less reason to be there, considering we were in the Terenan part of the forest. What brings a foreign prince wandering through the trees alone at that hour?"

Emmett bit his tongue, wishing he'd been more guarded. Then again, he had the impression that no amount of polite deflection would have discouraged Princess Rosa from speaking her mind, and asking this very obvious question.

Unexpectedly, he was saved from having to reply as the princess's eyes slid over his shoulder and her mouth fell open in a soft groan. "Oh no. Now we're in trouble. No, don't turn!" she chastised, as Emmett made to glance backward. She fixed him with a pained look. "It's probably useless appealing to your humanity, but if you have any decency, please pretend that I've been perfectly polite and proper and we're having a boring, royal ballroom-appropriate conversation."

Emmett raised an eyebrow, unable to resist a quip. "You're asking for my help? I thought you didn't need rescuing."

Princess Rosa glared at him, once again looking torn between irritation and humor.

"You might not need rescuing, but I'm feeling distinctly alarmed at being stalked by an unknown danger," Emmett went on lightly, not giving her a chance to answer. "What terror is coming toward us?"

Princess Rosa let out a gusty sigh. "Her Royal Majesty Queen Ada, of course. My mother."

CHAPTER SIX

Rosa

Rosa's mother descended on the pair, her voluminous skirts swishing impressively.

Prince Emmett turned as the queen drew alongside Rosa, the prince dipping into a stately bow. He was every inch the proper royal.

"Your Majesty, I'm greatly indebted to you for your kind invitation to tonight's delightful event."

Rosa had to refrain from rolling her eyes at the formality which she always found exaggerated. Remembering that he had the power to sink her into disgrace with her mother, however, she refrained.

"Prince Emmett," her mother said warmly. "I'm delighted you were able to come. And I apologize for failing to welcome you properly. I've only just now learned that you were not ensconced with His Majesty all afternoon as I supposed, but were left to wander without escort. Please allow me to apologize."

"Not at all," said Prince Emmett politely. "I thoroughly enjoyed exploring the gardens."

"Prince Emmett likes wandering without escort," Rosa

muttered, quietly enough that her mother wouldn't catch the words. Judging by the twitching muscle in the prince's jaw, he had, however.

"Rosa, my dear." The slight edge of warning in the queen's voice told Rosa that her mother had heard her mumbling, even if the meaning had been indistinguishable. "I'm glad to see you've made the acquaintance of our guest."

"Yes, we've been having a very interesting conversation," Rosa said brightly. She knew it made no sense to speak provocatively when she was the one who asked Emmett to keep their discussion to himself. But it was almost irresistible to bait the stoic-faced prince. It was fascinating to watch that muscle jump.

"I hope you can be persuaded to do more than just converse," the queen said meaningfully.

"Mama!" gasped Rosa. Knowing the purpose of tonight's ball, she'd had no doubt what her mother would be thinking the moment she saw her daughter speaking with the foreign prince. But she was horrified that the older woman would display her marital aspirations so openly.

This time it was the queen's turn to hide a twinkle of amusement, turning to Prince Emmett. "I trust that you enjoy dancing, Your Highness. I believe the musicians are about to begin."

"I would be delighted, if Princess Rosa would honor me," said Emmett promptly, surprising Rosa a little.

She let out a breath, agreeing without much thought. She was too focused on her relief that her mother had been hunting for a vicarious dance invitation rather than an instant proposal.

Before she knew it, she'd taken Prince Emmett's arm and allowed him to lead her into the open space in the middle of the room that was quickly filling up with couples. She peered up at her partner, unable to read his expression.

"*Do* you enjoy dancing?" she asked him suspiciously.

Prince Emmett's face remained inscrutable. "Sometimes, sometimes not. It depends primarily on the partner."

Rosa narrowed her eyes, and the prince cracked a smile.

"But it was clear what the queen expected of me, and I'm not one to shirk my duty."

"That much I could tell," Rosa said shortly.

The music had begun, and they moved apart as the dance required. Rosa couldn't tell whether the prince was irritated by the queen's scheming or not, and she squirmed at the thought that her own words and conduct might be reflecting badly on her mother. Her voice was a little stiff when they came back together.

"I suppose you'll say my mother was too forward on account of 'not being raised a princess'," she said shortly, repeating his earlier words. "But—"

"Not at all," Prince Emmett cut her off quickly. "Her Majesty was very gracious, and her manners are all one would expect from the most regal of hostesses."

Rosa studied him. He seemed sincere, and she relaxed slightly. "Mama is good at being queen," she acknowledged. "You'd think she was born to the role." Unlike herself. Her face froze as she looked at her companion in sudden suspicion. "Hold on. You can't be the younger prince, because he recently got married and moved to Selvana. Does that mean you're the elder one?"

"That's right," said Prince Emmett, seeming bemused.

Rosa couldn't help letting out a groan, but fortunately her reaction was softened by the dance once again pulling them apart.

"Oh dear," she muttered, to the consternation of her temporary partner.

Her mother was going to be uncomfortably determined if she thought there was a chance Rosa could become a future queen. Her mother might have chosen that life, but Rosa couldn't for the life of her think why the older woman would imagine Rosa wished to make the same choice. She hadn't exactly made a secret of her feelings regarding royal status.

She and Prince Emmett were once again brought together, and Rosa found it difficult to recapture her earlier dismissive attitude. She knew there was no foundation to her mother's hopes, and no reason to let them bother her. But somehow, having given this foreign prince the identity of potential suitor in her mind made her feel ill-at-ease around him.

She was overly conscious of the touch of his hands, and of how tall and strong his frame was. His dark beard, while still short, was more carefully groomed than when she'd last seen him, but it retained a somewhat rugged look that seemed out of keeping with the stiff and formal manner he projected.

Distracted by her thoughts, she stumbled in the dance. She knew only the briefest moment of embarrassment, because Emmett's strong arms held her so steady she was fairly certain no one else would have even noticed her slip. She looked up, their gazes locking for a moment, and found herself surprised by the intensity in his dark eyes. What business did a stiff, proper prince have in possessing such fervent eyes?

Unnerved, she pulled away as soon as the musicians wound down, thanking him for the dance with distant politeness. He responded in kind, and they parted ways immediately, no doubt disappointing her mother.

Rosa made her way to her stepbrother's side with single-minded purpose, dodging any potential dance partners on the way.

"Rosa, everything all right?" Otto asked, the moment she joined him.

"Of course," she said lightly. "But you're stuck with me for the rest of the night, Otto. Mama can scold me all she likes in the morning, but I don't intend to dance with the parade of suitors she's coaxed along tonight. I have too high a regard for myself."

A low chuckle brought her attention to Otto's friend, Lord Montague. He was the one who'd witnessed Prince Emmett putting down that pompous baronet's son's pretensions—masterfully, Rosa had to admit.

"I suppose there'd be no use asking you to dance then, Your Highness."

Rosa grinned at him. "None whatsoever. Consider yourself free."

"Oh, he knows," Otto said comfortably. "I've told Monty and the others that in spite of the barrage of social events coming, none of them are to feel the slightest bit of pressure to court you."

Rosa's grin grew. She liked Otto's close friends, and Monty was no exception. He was a notorious charmer, but he'd never tried anything of the kind on her, probably because of her relationship to Otto. In fact, one of the chief qualities of the group at large was that they treated her much like a fellow conspirator, and not at all like a marriage prospect. The more peripheral of Otto's acquaintances were another matter entirely, as the baronet's son had demonstrated earlier.

"Now we've established that I'm disinterested when it comes to claiming you as a dance partner," Monty said, "I hope you'll let me tell you that you look very beautiful tonight, Princess Rosa."

"I suppose I'll allow it," Rosa said, tickled. "It would be very out of character if you didn't say *something* flirtatious." She smoothed the folds of her gown. "This is the first time I've worn this dress, and I'm very happy with how it came out."

"So you should be," Otto declared staunchly, and his friend nodded in good-natured agreement. "Are you sure you don't want to be out there dancing and breaking hearts? I see at least four men looking hopefully your way."

"Don't catch anyone's eye, Otto, whatever you do!" Rosa declared, alarmed. Her stepbrother laughed, and she narrowed her eyes at him. "This is terribly unfair. We're the same age. Why can't Mama focus on marrying *you* off?"

Otto laughed again. "The irony is I probably wouldn't mind," he said, surprising Rosa with the hint of wistfulness in his voice.

"Surely you don't want every hopeful girl in the court paraded past you to compete for your favor," she protested. "Or to be pressured to accept someone before you're ready."

"I suppose not," Otto acknowledged. "I want to choose my own wife, of course. But I think it's nice that Mama wants you to be happy."

Rosa remained silent. Internally, she couldn't help reflecting that being married was not synonymous with being happy. She knew from her own memories that her mother had been unhappy and lonely as a widow, and that marriage had made her very happy. But that didn't mean that Rosa was in need of the same service. She wasn't against getting married one day— in fact, she fully intended to fall in love eventually. But she was perfectly content with her current state.

Or at least she would be, if she didn't have to be a cosseted royal.

The ball continued into the early hours of the morning, but Rosa noted that Prince Emmett departed not long after midnight. She wasn't allowed the same license, and in spite of her bold claims, she did find herself obliged to dance with numerous other partners in the remaining hours of the ball. Several of them were very flattering, and all of them openly admiring. None made cutting remarks about her manners, or unsettled her with the intensity of their eyes.

When Rosa finally retired to bed, she took some time to still herself enough for sleep. And even then her dreams were far from restful.

The prince and princess both slept late the morning after the ball, and by the time they emerged, their parents were already enjoying a light luncheon.

"Good morning—or afternoon," Rosa greeted her mother and stepfather. She kissed her mother's head in greeting before sinking into a chair beside her. "Who knew standing around in a ballroom could be so exhausting? And it gets so hot in there. Surely there's some way to use magic to cool it down?" She eyed her stepfather. "Couldn't the royal coffers afford to pay some singers for the purpose?"

"Probably," Otto answered for his father. "But it's not considered good practice to use magic for frivolities. At least not for royals."

"Why not?" Rosa demanded. "We use talismans for security around the castle, don't we? And I know I've heard you talk about intelligence agents using them."

The king cleared his throat, something in his face reminding Rosa of the listening servants. She grimaced apologetically. This was why the king didn't usually share state secrets with her.

"That's different," Otto explained helpfully. "Refusing to use magic for security purposes would be foolish. But using it for luxuries is starting down an entirely different path. None of the royals in Providore want to end up like the Reviled Lands."

"Certainly not," said the queen emphatically. "Mixing royal responsibilities with magical power brings more risk than reward."

"If you say so," said Rosa. "I still think the ballroom was hot, though." She smiled at her mother. "Not that it stopped me from enjoying the event, or anyone else, from what I saw."

The queen returned the smile indulgently. "I think the ball was a great success. I was delighted with how many guests accepted the invitation."

"It was a beautifully organized event, Ada," the king agreed warmly. "And the meeting with Prince Emmett beforehand went as well as can be expected. It was good to make the initial contact, anyway."

Rosa made a disgruntled noise in her throat at this mention of the foreign prince. Otto was the only one who caught it, and he threw her an amused glance.

"Well, the captain of my guard is waiting for me," King Ryker said cheerfully. He kissed his wife and smiled at his son and stepdaughter. "Enjoy your meal."

As soon as he'd left the room, the queen turned to Rosa, her tone enthusiastic. "You and Prince Emmett seemed to make an impression on each other last night, Rosa."

Rosa snorted, drawing a reproving look from her mother. "Making an impression doesn't necessarily mean a good impression."

"I hope you weren't rude to him," her mother said, sounding alarmed now. "This is his first visit to Teren since his childhood. I know your stepfather wished to make him feel especially welcome, as did I."

Rosa opened her mouth to contradict her mother, then closed it. She knew that Prince Emmett had been in their kingdom prior to the ball, and very recently. Her eyes passed to Otto, cheerfully buttering bread, and she bit her lip. She would love to know what her stepbrother made of the information that she'd encountered Prince Emmett wandering alone, apparently lost, in Ilgal only days before. But, although she could give no reason for it whatsoever, she felt a strange desire to protect the prince's secret. Hopefully he wasn't up to anything nefarious, or she might be betraying her kingdom by remaining silent.

"I'm sure he felt sufficiently welcome, Mama," she said noncommittally, her eyes still on her stepbrother. "Did the meeting truly go well, Otto?" The question held a touch of nervousness.

Otto shrugged. "I thought so. He seemed genuinely interested, and had sensible things to say. I think he'll be an ally in finding a solution."

Rosa raised an eyebrow. "I'm sure he had nothing but sensible things to say. Princes are invariably sensible, aren't they?"

"Why do you say that like it's a bad thing?" Otto asked accusingly.

"I don't know." Rosa rolled her shoulders, feeling a disproportionate irritation when she thought about the proper prince. She remembered his words about being glad she'd made it home safely, and her eyes narrowed. "I just don't know how anyone can stand to be so serious all the time, so prim and proper," she said. "He thought himself very chivalrous, I'm sure, sailing across the room to rescue me from that fool, Lord Ian."

"I saw Lord Ian leave early," said her mother, frowning at this mention of the baronet's son. "He didn't look at all pleased after he'd been talking to you, Rosa."

"I can't imagine what he would have had to be pleased about," said Rosa fairly.

Her mother's frown deepened. "Rosa, the whole aim of these balls is for you to find a suitable husband. Why you insist on offending everyone eligible, I will never understand."

"That may be your aim, Mama, but it's not mine," said Rosa firmly. "And I really didn't do anything to offend Lord Ian. Prince Emmett did that, and frankly, he was perfectly in the right. Except that it wasn't his place to come to my rescue," she amended quickly, catching her own inconsistency and feeling irked by it.

"I agree with Rosa on this one, Mama," said Otto firmly. "Lord Ian is a ridiculous person." He regarded his stepsister. "I think you're being unfair to Prince Emmett, though. I know you like to tease anyone with any sense of responsibility, but I can't believe he did anything to earn your disapproval. Honestly, I've always looked up to him."

Rosa didn't immediately answer. Whether he would still hold that view if he knew about their encounter in the forest, she couldn't guess, but she still found herself inexplicably reluctant to recount it. Certainly not in front of her mother, who had never found out about that particular unsanctioned outing. She'd counted herself very lucky to avoid the scold she'd thought inevitable, and she didn't intend to expose her antics now.

"Did you discuss the evacuation proposal in the meeting?" she asked. "What did he think about that?"

"He was unequivocally against it," Otto said. "He said he's always been very attached to the forest. I remember when the Medullan royal family used to make regular visits to Lernvale, when the princes were children. But they stopped, probably because the magic was growing too wild and the forest was becoming less safe."

"Huh." Begrudgingly, Rosa had to admit she was impressed. "Well, his love of the forest is his only likable quality, then."

"You only need one," chimed in her mother encouragingly.

Rosa groaned, her irritation doubled by the grin on Otto's face. Her stepbrother had more impudence in him, however. The queen excused herself soon after, and Otto immediately leaned forward.

"Prince Emmett does have at least *one* other likable quality, though, doesn't he?" he asked, his tone making it clear the question was a trap.

"I have no idea what you mean," Rosa said loftily.

Otto's grin grew. "Well, the general consensus is that both of the Medullan princes are dishearteningly handsome."

"Dishearteningly?" Rosa asked, amused.

Otto nodded. "It's a lot for us poor other princes to compete with. But that's not the point. The point is that you can't fool me into thinking you're oblivious to Prince Emmett's charms. I saw you gazing into his eyes when you two danced."

"I did not *gaze* into anything!" Rosa cried, the protest almost a shriek. She certainly wouldn't have gotten away with it if her mother had been in the room.

"Whatever you say, sis," Otto smirked. "Are you honestly going to sit there and claim that you didn't find Prince Emmett at all attractive?"

Rosa sighed. "I suppose he is physically attractive, by general standards," she said, resentful. "But honestly, good looks are wasted on someone so stiff and responsible."

"If you say so," said Otto, maddeningly smug.

Rosa just rolled her eyes as she pushed herself to her feet.

"Where are you going?" Otto asked, eyeing her warily.

"I'm going to see my grandparents," said Rosa. "They'll want to hear all about the ball."

"Rosa," Otto protested.

"Don't start," she told him sternly. "If you think I'd rather sit around here listening to you and mother singing the praises of Prince Emmett and Lord Ian of all people, you must have lost your wits."

"I never said anything good about Lord Ian in my life," said Otto, affronted.

Rosa just chuckled, moving toward the door that led from the dining room into the gardens. If she left that way, and circled around carefully rather than returning to her room first, her lady-in-waiting and maids would assume she was still eating. She'd worn a shawl especially, and if she looped it over her head, she could probably leave the city through the western gate without attracting any undue notice.

Twenty minutes later, she was walking cheerfully down the forest road, humming to herself. It was a fine day, and her spirits always lifted when she got out of the city and into the fresh air. The forest giants rose around her, their mossy trunks familiar and comforting. She felt disloyal to her beloved forest to say it, but she quite enjoyed being on the road instead of wending her way through the undergrowth. It wasn't just that it made for faster progress. It was also that she enjoyed being able to look up at the sky and be reminded of the endless expanse that stretched on above the canopy.

When she reached her grandparents' gate, she was surprised to find two of their burliest workers stationed at the entrance. The men greeted her cheerfully, and waved her through, but Rosa still felt uneasy as she traversed the long carriageway.

The manor came into sight, and Rosa hurried inside. She followed the men's direction to a familiar location at the back of the building. Her heart lifted when she stepped into the conservatory. It was a beautiful space, all paneled glass and sunlight, with lush foliage sprouting from every side. This was another place she'd spent many hours during childhood, helping her grandmother prune and water and tend. If the library was Grampy's personal hobby, the conservatory was Granny's.

"Granny," she said, stooping to kiss the older woman's wrinkled cheek.

"Rosa, my dear!" Her grandmother greeted her warmly, putting down her pruning shears. "Come to gloat over your ball, have you? Well, well, let's hear it."

Rosa laughed. "That's it, Granny, I was a huge hit. I even brought foreign princes vying for my hand."

"Eh?" Granny said, startled, and Rosa laughed again.

"I'm only joking. I mean, the Medullan prince was there, but he wasn't vying for my hand. Very few of the guests were up to such nonsense, I'm thankful to say. Prince Emmett was there to meet with my stepfather regarding the magic in the forest."

Granny grunted. "Bunch of royals, sitting on their thrones, making decisions about our lives as if they have any clue about the ways of the forest."

"To be fair, apparently Prince Emmett was quick to disagree with any suggestion of evacuating the forest." The words slipped out, and Rosa gave her head a little shake. First covering for him, now defending him...why did she feel any loyalty whatsoever to the foreign prince who was basically a stranger?

The thought sobered her, and she decided impulsively to unburden herself of one secret. Her grandmother had always felt like her safest confidante.

"Granny, can I tell you something that I'd rather you don't repeat to anyone?"

"You know you can," said her grandmother comfortably, picking up a watering can. "I carry no tales."

"Well, the ball isn't the first time I met Prince Emmett," Rosa said. "Remember last time I came, how I said I'd run into a stranger not far from your estate, looking lost and like he'd spent a rough night in the forest?"

"I remember," Granny said. "Your grandfather said he must have been pretty tough if he'd survived a night out there without incident." Her eyes widened as she caught up with Rosa's meaning. "Are you saying that was the Medullan prince?"

Rosa nodded. "And I have no idea what he was doing out here."

Granny frowned. "Do you think he's up to some kind of subterfuge? Like he's double dealing King Ryker somehow?"

"I don't think so," said Rosa, troubled. "He's irritating and stiff, but I don't think he's up to any harm. I can't give any reason for that opinion, though. It's just what my instincts tell me, I suppose."

The older woman nodded, turning back to her watering. "Always trust your instincts, Rosie, my dear. They know more than you think they do. Especially for one bred in the forest, like you. We have a sense about things."

"If you say so," said Rosa, amused. "Hopefully my *sense* isn't wrong this time, because I didn't even tell Mama and the others about seeing him in the forest."

"Hmm." Granny pursed her lips thoughtfully. "That's interesting. Now I wonder why you didn't?"

Rosa recognized that it wasn't a question so much as Granny's own musings, and she remained silent.

"Well, well, it will be what it will be," Granny said philosophically, after another moment's pondering. "But if this prince is going to roam the forest alone, he'd better be careful. Wouldn't do to have foreign royalty getting killed by wolves in our forest. That would put everyone in even more of a fuss."

"Wolves?" Rosa demanded. "I thought all the rumors were exaggerated. Why would you think wolves are a particular danger?"

"I'm afraid there's some truth to the rumors after all," said Granny soberly. "I didn't want to believe it at first, but your grandfather convinced me. He asked whether he'd ever given me reason to believe him either out of his mind or a liar, and I had to acknowledge he hadn't."

Rosa's lips twitched at her grandmother's regretful tone. Anyone would suppose she wished her husband to be mad or dishonest.

"So I had no choice but to believe his own account," Granny went on.

"Hold on!" Rosa laid a hand on her grandmother's arm. "Grampy saw these wolves himself? Is he all right?"

Granny nodded, her expression sober. "He's fine. But one of the boys sustained a nasty bite. He was lucky some of the others were close by, including your grandfather. They came running when he screamed, and the creature ran away. There were about a dozen of them, you see. But your grandfather got a pretty good look at the wolf that attacked. It was unnaturally large, he said, and it was hours before sunset."

"Is the worker all right?"

"He will be," said Granny bracingly. "The wound will heal fine, but he's pretty spooked. All the men are, to tell the truth."

"I'm not surprised," said Rosa, concerned. "When was this?"

"Some days back," said her grandmother, shrugging. "A week, maybe. That reminds me," she said, giving a decisive pat to Rosa's hand, where it still rested on her arm. "You shouldn't wander the forest alone until we catch the creature."

"What?" Rosa protested. "Not you too, Granny. In all those sightings, there's been one confirmed attack for all your workers. What are the chances that I'd fall afoul of the animal in any of the few occasions I'm in the forest?"

"Low or not, still too high a chance to risk it," Granny said firmly. "Your grandfather will walk you home, with a few of the men for good measure."

No amount of argument would shift her grandmother from this course, and it was in a subdued frame of mind that Rosa walked home a short time later. It wasn't that she minded her grandfather's company. She was always happy to spend time with him. But the idea of being barred her forest outings was disheartening, to say the least. Besides which, as much as she was desperate not to admit it to herself let alone anyone else, something was changing. She'd barely been in the forest an hour when she started to feel a strange pressure in her chest. It was only light, not even enough to be considered discomfort, but it terrified her. Was the magic truly as out of control as Leonhard claimed? She tried to tell herself that it was just heaviness of heart over her grandmother's pronouncement, but she couldn't quite believe it.

Her grandfather, apparently not quite as averse to the city as his wife, insisted on walking her all the way to the castle. He said he wanted to say hello to her mother, whom he hadn't seen in months, but Rosa suspected he was also motivated by making sure she went home.

The unfortunate effect of his desire to connect with her mother was that there was no way to avoid the queen learning of Rosa's outing. Her grandmother would have been more sympathetic to her desire for subterfuge, but Rosa didn't even try asking her grandfather to cover up her movements. He was too open a man—deception didn't suit him.

When Queen Ada received the pair, she greeted her former father-in-law warmly, but Rosa could see in the thin line of her mother's mouth that she would be in for it later. The fact that her grandfather expressed his concern regarding the oversized wolf he'd seen wasn't going to help.

Sure enough, when the older man left, her mother chastised Rosa once again for sneaking out of the city. After checking that they were alone, of course, given they were standing in one of the covered walkways that ran alongside the castle.

"I know, Mama," Rosa said morosely, in response to her mother's scolding. "But you can take comfort from the fact that it sounds like it'll be the last time in a while. Even Granny and Grampy seem to think I should stay safely within the city walls at the moment."

"I'm delighted to hear that we're in such agreement," said

her mother briskly. "Now, on to more pressing matters. I was thinking of inviting Prince Emmett to join the family for a luncheon tomorrow, and I—"

"Mama, no," said Rosa firmly. "I know the sight of me talking to a foreign prince sent your thoughts into a fantasy, but it bears no resemblance to reality, truly."

Her mother frowned. "Rosa, I'm trying to be reasonable, and to listen to your preferences. You said Lord Ian is out of the question—very well, I accept that. I won't attempt to force any further interactions with him. But I need you to at least try. Prince Emmett is a more eligible prospect even than I had imagined. His decision to spend the season in Lernvale is an opportunity we simply cannot waste."

Rosa groaned. "I don't share your view, Mama. I wish you would trust me to handle my own affairs in this area."

"Well, I don't," said her mother frankly. "You rate your own value too low to be trusted to select an appropriate partner."

Rosa pursed her lips. She felt that the reverse was true—she valued herself too highly to take part in the matchmaking charade her mother was trying to orchestrate. But she didn't think saying so would help the conversation. Otto wandered up at that moment, and Rosa decided it would be best to deflect her mother's attention.

"You just missed my grandfather, Otto," she said cheerfully.

"Oh, that's a shame," said Otto. "I hope he's well?"

"Don't you like Prince Emmett, Rosa?" the queen interrupted. Apparently the older woman wasn't to be so easily sidetracked. "He seemed to have excellent manners and bearing to me."

"To be frank, Mama, no, I don't," said Rosa. "He's too stiff and serious for me, and I don't think he liked me much either."

"Nonsense," said the queen, put out. "He asked you to dance, didn't he?"

"Because you backed him into a corner," said Rosa, exasperated.

Her mother frowned, looking unconvinced. "Well, what about Otto's friend, then?" she persisted. "The one you were speaking to for so long last night? He'll inherit an earldom one day, after all."

"He's just a friend, Mama," said Rosa patiently, over Otto's noise of protest. "He'd as soon marry a she-wolf from the forest as—"

Otto cleared his throat more loudly, and Rosa fell silent, confused.

"I'm not disagreeing with you," Otto said, voice lowered, "but perhaps we should suspend this conversation for the moment."

Rosa followed his gaze over her own shoulder to see a man striding toward them from the direction her grandfather had disappeared. "Leonhard," she muttered, with an irritated grunt.

"Good afternoon," Queen Ada greeted the advisor graciously.

"Your Majesty." Leonhard bowed to the queen, then turned to Otto. "Your Highness...es."

Rosa was sure she'd been added begrudgingly, but she didn't mind. Leonhard's reluctance to acknowledge her status was the least of her objections to the man.

"Good afternoon, Leonhard," she said, her chin lifting a little.

"Good afternoon," he responded, surprising her by addressing himself to her instead of one of the others. "I just passed a man on his way out of the castle. Was that your grandfather?"

"That's right," said Rosa, wondering how he knew her grandfather on sight.

"Did he come to discuss the evacuation?" Leonhard asked. "I'm aware that he and your grandmother exert great influence on the forest community. Their support would be invaluable."

"I think you mean *proposed* evacuation," said Rosa coldly. The hint of eagerness in Leonhard's voice irked her. "And no, he didn't come to discuss that. Any discussion on that topic with my grandparents would be short and uninteresting. I can guarantee that they will *never* agree to leave Ilgal."

Leonhard's eyes narrowed, his irritation showing for a moment before he managed to school his features. Taking a breath, he dipped his head toward Rosa in a gesture that didn't feel at all respectful.

"It seems I misunderstood the purpose of his visit. Thank you for the information, Your Highness."

Taking leave of the queen and prince, Leonhard turned and strode away, back the way he'd come.

"Insufferable," Rosa muttered, glaring at his back.

"If you want people to respect your position more, you need to behave according to your status," her mother told her firmly.

"I don't care about him not having respect for my position as princess," Rosa protested. "In fact, his unspoken opinion that it's absurd to give me the title is the only area in which we agree. I think he's insufferable because he's determined to push my grandparents out of Ilgal, along with all the rest of the forest community. He should know better if he was born and raised in the forest himself, as he claims. And he positively *scorned* my input at the Council of Nobles, so he clearly gives no weight to my own forest upbringing, either."

"I thought we agreed that your contribution in that council meeting was ill-advised," her mother reminded her. She glanced after the advisor. "You can't afford to alienate everyone, Rosa. Especially if you're going to spurn every eligible noble. You could do considerably worse than Leonhard. His family aren't from the nobility, but they're very influential. As is he, in his advisory role. Besides which, there's singing blood in the family."

"Mama!" Rosa gasped. "You can't be serious! I could *never* consider Leonhard as a suitor!"

"Surely not, Mama," Otto agreed, sounding faintly revolted. "He's no good for Rosa. He must be forty, or close to!"

"Not an insurmountable barrier," the queen said.

"The fact that he's insufferable is," said Rosa firmly. "And it's irrelevant, because he finds me just as repulsive, I'm sure."

"Well, you said you agreed on one thing, and as I've said before, it only takes one," her mother pointed out. "Perhaps you might both come to change your views of one another in time. All I'm saying is don't close every door, Rosa, or you'll find yourself walking into a wall."

"I would rather walk into a thousand walls than marry Leonhard," said Rosa flatly.

"Well, no one is forcing you." The queen's voice was waspish. "But I do wish you would make my work a little easier." She sighed. "I'd best set about preparations for the next gala. I'll cast a wider net this time, since the last event's attendees were so unimpressive."

She swept away, leaving Rosa and Otto to exchange helpless glances. Otto looked sympathetic, and Rosa turned her mother's determination off with a laugh. Inside, however, she found none of it amusing. In spite of the talk of not being forced, the revelation that even Leonhard was considered an acceptable option in her mother's eyes had rattled Rosa.

She'd always been determined to choose her own future, but that possibility was feeling shakier than ever.

CHAPTER SEVEN

Emmett

"Thank you for your time."

Emmett tried not to let his frustration show as he watched the villager walk out of the antechamber where the prince had spent most of the day. When the man was gone, however, Emmett let his head drop onto the table in front of him, indulging in a low groan.

It was all useless. He'd interviewed a dozen people today, and no one had any information regarding suspicious use of magic in Ilgal. No one had heard rumors of strange behavior from the few elves still in the area—either excess harvesting or uneven harvesting that might suggest they were trying to increase a certain area's concentration of magic. No one had seen any singers at work in the forest recently, either. It seemed most had moved away because the quantity of magic was overwhelming for those born with the ability to sense and channel magic.

The only thing of note which all of them had reported was that the pressure in the forest was growing more uncomfortable by the day. Those who could avoid going under the trees for long stretches invariably did so.

"Anything of use, Your Majesty? If I may be so bold as to ask."

Emmett raised his head to see his steward hovering in the doorway.

"I'm afraid not," he said, as he waved the man in. "Either no one knows anything of relevance, or no one is willing to share it."

"King Ryker will be disappointed," said the steward.

Emmett smiled wryly. "I don't think His Majesty expected much from my inquiries." He sighed. "Neither did I, to be honest."

He tapped his fingers on the table, reflecting on the depressing truth of the statement. His discussions with the Terenan king had provided the perfect excuse for conducting interviews with the locals. But of course, his true purpose in asking about the use of magic in the area had nothing to do with his desire to help King Ryker combat the magic's growth. He was trying to ascertain the true nature of the magic he'd been exposed to. His questions had been directed to that end, and he could only be grateful that none of the villagers had seemed to realize they were odd for his stated purpose.

In any event, what he'd told the steward was perfectly true. He'd heard nothing useful. It didn't help that he was now following a trail that was four years old, and no doubt accordingly cold.

He drew a deep breath, telling himself not to give in to discouragement. There were plenty more people he could speak to. He would continue his inquiries tomorrow.

"Your Highness?"

The steward's genteel cough brought Emmett's attention back to him.

"I'm sorry," he told the silver-haired man. "Did you need something?"

"Just to inform you that this arrived for you a short time ago, Your Highness."

With a bow, the steward presented him with a sealed billet. Emmett ripped it open, noting the Terenan royal seal with a frown. Was it possible King Ryker had made a breakthrough so quickly?

But just as the previous time, the letter wasn't from the king but the queen. Emmett stared unseeingly at the elegantly written invitation from Queen Ada. Another ball? Ordinarily he'd be surprised to learn of another event in such a short time. But since attending the last ball, he'd heard the rumors circulating around the region regarding the season's many planned festivities. Queen Ada was trying to find her daughter a husband, and Princess Rosa wasn't proving very malleable.

Was that why Emmett had been invited? Because he was so eminently eligible?

A smile curled his lips as he pictured Princess Rosa's eyes shooting sparks at him. The queen was wasting her time if she thought her daughter considered Emmett in any way eligible. He would be wisest to refuse the invitation, if only to avoid raising any false hopes in Queen Ada's mind.

Besides which, the ball was only three days away. Although the moon was far from full, if the previous moon's experience was an indication, he should expect the nightly transformations to begin only a night or two after the projected ball. That was cutting it closer than was sensible, in case the transformations started earlier than expected.

And yet...

Emmett was surprised by the strength of his desire to attend. In fact, once he'd entertained the idea, he found himself unable to banish it. He wanted to go. He had to go. He gave his head a little shake. He couldn't explain why he wanted to attend so much, and he certainly couldn't explain his internal insistence.

He usually had excellent self-discipline, and he was no stranger to denying himself the course he would prefer in favor of the course duty demanded.

Somehow all of these very sensible thoughts did nothing to slow the movement of his hand as he penned a response, accepting the invitation. Within an hour, it was on its way via courier. There was no taking it back now. Politeness demanded he attend as promised.

Congratulations, he told his wayward self in irritation. *You've succeeded in making your desire and your duty line up. Are you happy?*

He shouldn't be, he knew. He should be disappointed in himself for being so self-serving. And yet, he found himself looking forward to the event with expectation.

The recklessness that had led him to accept the invitation was still with him a few days later as his carriage once again passed under the archway where Terenford's southern gates were flung wide.

Perhaps that was why, although Queen Ada had invited him, he made straight for Princess Rosa across the polished floor. She was in conversation with her stepbrother, who greeted Emmett with a flattering level of warmth. A flash of annoyance went through Emmett as Otto prattled on, distracting him from engaging Princess Rosa in conversation.

His internal growl was silenced by lancing guilt. Otto didn't deserve his ire. He remembered calling the younger prince foolish and annoying in conversation with his brother Farrin. He'd done Otto an injustice. The Terenan prince was grown now, and in addition to demonstrating his intelligence, he'd shown Emmett nothing but friendliness. Was Emmett going to respond to that with hostility and contempt? When had he become so...savage?

The thought, while perhaps overblown, was enough to

sober Emmett back onto his best behavior. He did his best to respond with warmth to Otto's friendliness, and to keep his eyes from straying to the prince's companion.

Eventually, however, Otto's attention was claimed by a nobleman who seemed a close friend, and Emmett could shift his gaze to the princess without being rude.

"Don't look at *me*," she said, her eyes a little too mischievous to match the cold tone she was trying to adopt. "I don't have an endless wealth of friendly small talk. That's Otto's role in our royal family."

Emmett raised an eyebrow, reflecting once again that Prince Otto didn't deserve to be belittled, either by him or by Princess Rosa. Perhaps the princess took his meaning, because she offered a rueful smile.

"I don't mean that as an insult to Otto, you know. He has plenty of sensible things to say. The diplomatic chitchat is part of his court training, not his personality." She cast a dark look toward her stepbrother, who was now several paces away, in conversation with a small knot of his friends. "I'm just irked with him, abandoning me like that. How will I keep from dancing with a parade of near-strangers now? Hovering close to Otto is the best protection I have in a ballroom. It's one of my very favorite features of having a brother."

Emmett smiled in spite of himself. "Am I one of these wild creatures you need protection from?" The words were bitter on his tongue. Why had he said that? It was far too close to the truth to be safe small talk.

Princess Rosa eyed him. "I haven't decided yet," she said bluntly.

Emmett met her gaze, neither blinking as they considered one another. It was strange given that none of their few interactions had been especially positive, but there was something about being in Princess Rosa's presence. Something...solid.

There could be no doubt in Emmett's mind that she was his equal, both in intelligence and strength of will. It was more than an even balance of strength, however. When he came up against Princess Rosa, it was as though he'd met his likeness.

Illogical thought. The pair were nothing alike, and Princess Rosa clearly felt that way as strongly as Emmett did.

"My brother used to serve a similar function for me," Emmett said, returning to the previous topic of conversation in an attempt to diffuse the sudden intensity in the air. "Farrin. Although he came to my rescue at balls at his own expense—usually the young noblewomen would make eyes at him instead of me, thus sparing me some of the tedium of dancing."

"Tedium?" Princess Rosa looked amused. "That's not a very gallant description. I would have thought that as a crown prince, your duty would require you to dance often at these types of functions."

"It does," Emmett acknowledged.

She studied him curiously. "And I was under the impression that you were one to perform your duties rigidly."

"I certainly hope so," Emmett said. Seized again by recklessness, he added, "That doesn't mean I enjoy it." Chastising himself for the impolite honesty, he glanced down to see Princess Rosa watching him with great interest.

"Does that mean that when you danced with me it was an unenjoyable duty?" she asked. She clearly knew the question bordered on impudent, but she just as clearly didn't care. It was strangely liberating.

"It was definitely a duty," said Emmett, matching her frank, clinical tone. "I suppose I'll keep my own counsel as to whether it was unenjoyable."

Princess Rosa grinned. "*Keep my own counsel.* I like that. Since entering royal life, I've often been frustrated with the stiff formality and diplomatic answers. But I must say, you use it so masterfully, I almost start to see the appeal."

A smile slipped through Emmett's guard. He couldn't decide if Princess Rosa made him act unlike himself, or if something about the princess just brought out a part of him that was very real, but too often dormant.

Like the wolf sleeping inside him right now.

Where had that thought come from? Emmett's hands were shaking all of a sudden, and, rattled, he glanced down at them. He half expected to see fur and claws, but everything remained as it should be—strong, capable, human hands. His signet ring glinted at him from the smallest finger on his left hand, mocking him with a reminder of the collected prince he was supposed to be. In recent times, he could feel the wolf intruding on his human mind more and more, and he was becoming afraid his true self would be fully subsumed. He folded his hands across his chest, willing them to be still.

"Prince Emmett?" Princess Rosa sounded uncertain for the first time since he'd met her. "Are you well?"

"Perfectly well, thank you," said Emmett, his voice cool as he avoided her gaze, instead glancing out across the crowded ballroom.

"Well." She sounded like she wasn't sure whether to be amused or offended. "The haughty air is as effective as ever, but somehow less palatable when it's being used so effectively against *me*."

Again Emmett couldn't help but smile, something about the princess breaking down his barriers.

"My apologies," he said lightly. "I didn't mean to be rude."

"No," Princess Rosa agreed. "I have a feeling if you really wanted to be rude, I'd know it, Prince Emmett."

"There's no need for titles between royals," Emmett said, unsure what prompted him to say it. "You can call me Emmett."

"Can I?" The princess gave a dramatic sigh. "I suppose politeness dictates that I invite you to call me Rosa, doesn't it?"

"Not at all," contradicted Emmett.

She chuckled. "Well, my sense of decency does. To be honest, I'd prefer never to have the title attached to my name, so dropping it is no great ask." Her eyes slid past Emmett, and she let out a little sigh. "And here's my other favorite suitor," she muttered, apparently to herself.

Emmett followed her gaze to see a lithe, dark-haired man entering the ballroom.

He raised an eyebrow. "A little old for you, isn't he?"

"Of course he is," said Rosa. "And to tell the truth, the age gap is the least of our incompatibilities." She seemed to realize what she'd said, and hastened to add, "It was only a joke, of course. He's no more a suitor than you are. Which is to say, not at all." She cleared her throat. "I'm not helping my argument that diplomacy of speech is unnecessary, am I?"

Emmett gave a perfunctory smile, his eyes still fixed on the stranger across the room. For no reason he could define, the idea of him as Rosa's suitor had set up Emmett's hackles.

His metaphorical hackles, of course.

"Who is he?" he asked.

"His name is Leonhard," said Rosa, and Emmett frowned at the name, which he'd heard before.

"The advisor who's ready to evacuate Ilgal?" he asked.

Rosa nodded, and Emmett made a disparaging noise in his throat. "Funny, isn't it? How fools walk around looking like anyone else."

Rosa gave a delighted laugh, and Emmett's expression softened in response. But before he could turn to the princess, Leonhard's eyes raked across the room, meeting Emmett's. He didn't look unnerved to find the prince watching him. On the contrary, his expression brightened, and he moved across the room with purpose.

"Now you've done it," Rosa informed Emmett humorously. "Time to pull out that royally trained small talk again."

There was no time to respond—Leonhard was within hearing range now.

"Princess Rosa," the advisor greeted her, only the faintest hint of disgruntlement emerging with the title. "You look well."

Rosa's lips twitched, as if she was entertained by the glaring omission rather than offended that Leonhard had found a way *not* to tell her she looked beautiful in her ballgown.

"Good evening, Leonhard," she said, her cool tone not quite impolite. "I *am* well, as always."

Leonhard waited a moment, his eyes flicking meaningfully toward Emmett, but Rosa made no move to perform the introduction he clearly coveted.

"Please, allow me to introduce myself," he said to Emmett, imperfectly concealing his irritation with the princess. "My name is Leonhard, advisor to King Ryker."

Emmett inclined his head, his expression giving no encouragement.

"Am I correct in understanding you to be Prince Emmett of Medulle?" Leonhard persisted.

"You are," said Emmett.

The advisor bowed. "Your Highness, I am delighted to have the honor of making your acquaintance."

"Stealing your acquaintance, more like," murmured Rosa, and Emmett felt his lips twitch.

If Leonhard heard the muttered aside, he ignored it. "I have been informed by His Majesty that you've traveled to this region for the purpose of assisting with the crisis in Ilgal," he went on. "His Majesty has done me the honor of entrusting me with oversight of this task, and I would welcome the opportunity to speak with you."

Emmett considered the other man, surprised by his description of his role. King Ryker had called Leonhard the leading expert, it was true. But that wasn't the same as giving him oversight of the task of rescuing Ilgal. Emmett glanced at Rosa. Her face was creased in a frown—she looked like she wanted to contradict Leonhard but wasn't sure enough of her facts to do so.

"That is one of my purposes in coming to the region, certainly," Emmett said mildly. "I am pleased to work with King Ryker to address our shared problem. I have of course already met with the king regarding the matter. What specifically did you wish to discuss with me?"

"Perhaps King Ryker has already raised my recommendation with you, Your Highness," said Leonhard. "I hope you will be an ally in persuading the king that evacuating the forest is the only realistic solution remaining to us."

"I'm afraid you'll be disappointed, sir," said Emmett flatly. "I am far from agreeing with you. Evacuating Ilgal seems dire and premature. I consider it the very last resort, and I certainly don't believe we've exhausted all other options. In fact, I would go as far as to say that an evacuation would constitute failure of our efforts rather than success, given it is the very outcome we are trying to avoid."

Leonhard clearly wasn't happy with this response, but Emmett didn't care much about the advisor's reaction. He was much more interested in the satisfaction that emanated from Rosa beside him. He wasn't even looking at her, and he could just about feel her smug expression.

"I commend your desire to serve those who live in the forest, Your Highness," said Leonhard, his voice anything but commending. "But our ultimate aim is the same. The safety of

Ilgal's human residents must be our paramount consideration."

Emmett frowned. He didn't rush to answer, wisdom telling him he should first wrestle with the defensiveness rising angrily within him. On the surface, there was nothing wrong with Leonhard's words. Logic, along with his sense of duty, told him he should feel the same way. And yet, it didn't sit right at all. He found himself surprisingly vehement in his disagreement with every sentiment the Terenan advisor expressed.

"It seems, sir, we will have to agree to disagree," he said, once he was able to moderate his tone enough for politeness. He turned his head ever so slightly, in a subtle signal of dismissal that Leonhard obviously understood.

Looking as though his lips were closed over a slice of lemon, the older man gave a jerky bow before striding away.

"For a court advisor, he doesn't hide his emotions very well, does he?" Rosa said.

Emmett looked down to see her eyes fixed on Leonhard's retreating back, their expression positively gleeful.

"Nor do you," he informed her, unable to keep the hint of a laugh from his voice.

She grinned up at him. "I don't try to. I never thought I'd say it, Prince Emmett—oh, all right, Emmett, then," she amended at a look from him, "but please accept my admiration. That was beautifully handled. He'll be smarting from that for days."

Emmett grunted in acknowledgment of the compliment, but his thoughts were back on the advisor's words.

"How can he really think a full evacuation is a proportionate step? Unless he knows something the rest of us don't, his reasoning is absurd."

Would King Ryker really listen to that man? He stopped himself from asking Rosa, knowing it would be inappropriate for her to comment unofficially on her stepfather's position.

"Does he hate magic?" he asked instead. "I've encountered the odd person in Medulle who can't stand anything to do with it, despises singers, that kind of thing. That might explain why he'd rather abandon a magic-ridden region completely than try to repair it."

Rosa frowned. "I doubt that's it. He's not a singer himself, but I believe others in his immediate family are. I don't think he's against singers."

"That's right, King Ryker mentioned that," Emmett remembered. He frowned. "I wonder what his relationship with his family is like, and whether they support his proposal."

He let out a sigh. That was all King Ryker's issue, not his. He had enough to contend with. He glanced down at Rosa, seeing that she looked troubled. The expression didn't suit her, and Emmett was seized by a sudden desire to lighten her burdens. It made no sense, but it wouldn't be denied.

"I meant what I said," he told her. "We haven't exhausted all avenues. Not even close. In my opinion, we're a long way from the necessity of evacuating the forest."

"Do you really think so?" Rosa asked, a hint of entreaty in her eyes as they met his. They were an arresting feature in her pale face, no doubt about it.

"Definitely," Emmett assured her. He glanced around to ensure no one was in their immediate vicinity. "We haven't been keen to make it widely known, but since the alliance between my brother and Selvana, we're exploring a process for reclaiming the ground there."

Rosa's eyes widened. "Is it working?"

"Too soon to know," Emmett said. "And the process is certainly not without risks. But you hardly need me to tell you that if the magic in Selvana can be diffused enough to make the lethal ground inhabitable again, easing the pressure in Ilgal should be simple in comparison."

Rosa's face lit up, and Emmett felt a flash of unease at having disclosed more than he probably should. But he couldn't bring himself to regret it, not when she looked so relieved.

"Why hasn't your father mentioned this to my stepfather before now?" she asked eagerly.

Emmett hesitated. "The experiment is in its very earliest stages. We have no idea if it will work, or how dangerous it might be," he hedged. He didn't say the more compelling reason, which was that his father had very little interest in the fate of Ilgal. So little of the forest fell within Medulle's borders.

The unease was growing now, his stomach tied in such knots he felt ill. Rosa was still watching him with glowing eyes, excited by the hint of a solution to a crisis that obviously concerned her. Her dark hair had begun to come out of its elaborate style, draping around her pale face. He could no longer see the green he'd noticed in her eyes last time, but they were no less striking for the lack. Her straight nose drew attention down to her full lips, and with her head tilted back to look up at him, the line of her chin was even more defined. Emmett found his eyes drawn down to her collarbone, everything about her form conveying the elegance of a princess, whatever she tried to claim about her status.

Emmett's hands were shaking more furiously now, and an exhilarating recklessness swept over him. He lifted a hand, fully intending to ask Rosa to dance, in spite of her earlier comments on the pastime. Fortunately, his eyes flicked to his own hand before Rosa noticed the gesture, saving him from disaster.

Barely stifling a gasp, Emmett pulled his hand back, concealing it inside his doublet as casually as he could. This couldn't be happening. He'd barely felt the onset.

But there was no denying the evidence of his eyes. The gray hair sprouting on the back of his hand didn't belong to a human. Certainly not a twenty-three-year-old one. For a horrible moment Emmett stood frozen, his eyes still riveted on Rosa's face as her expression changed from eagerness to confusion. He could swear he even saw a flicker of fear. Instinctive, probably unconscious...but definitely there. And he realized with horror that he *had* felt the change coming on. It had made its presence felt in his recklessness, in the way all his usual barriers deserted him in the presence of the princess.

"Good evening," he said shortly, wincing a little at how deep and growly his voice sounded. "I must return to Lernvale. Please thank your mother for her hospitality."

Rosa's brow furrowed, and she was clearly on the point of protesting at the sudden departure. Emmett didn't give her a chance to. He turned on his heel and strode from the room, forcing his gait to remain steady and human with a supreme effort of will. He could feel the change creeping over him now, and he knew he had only a limited window before it claimed him. He needed to be out of the city by then, certainly far from this magnificent and crowded ballroom.

Why had he come? He berated himself as he hurried toward the entrance of the castle, raging at his own weakness. He'd known there was a risk, and he'd ignored it. It was inexcusable. He was barely in control of himself when he reached the carriageway outside the castle. A servant must have run ahead, because his own carriage was pulling up as he emerged.

The temptation to climb into it was overwhelming, but that would mean inevitable exposure once he reached Lernvale. He wasn't that desperate yet.

"You've been summoned by mistake," he grunted at the coachman. "King Ryker is making other arrangements for my travel. You can return to Lernvale. Expect me in the morning."

The coachman let out a protest, clearly bewildered, but Emmett turned away from him. He didn't go back through the castle's main entrance, however. Instead, he slipped into the shadows of a small decorative garden, his lope becoming decidedly canine as he hurried around the inside of the wall. The forest was close. He could sense it. He just needed to reach it without being seen.

Hair now covered much of Emmett's body under his clothes, but the transformation hadn't truly happened yet. When it did, it would be sudden and complete. He'd been hoping to reach the forest first, but when it came just inside the castle wall, it turned out to be for the best.

With a slash of agony, the magic passed through Emmett's body. His skin and clothing disappeared, replaced with another form entirely. As quickly as it had come, the pain was gone. He found himself at the wall, his nose twitching in the direction of the forest beyond. He could smell five different types of trees, and his whole being longed for the freedom of the unpeopled space. The wall before him was insurmountable for a human, but he was big, and his legs were strong. He didn't doubt himself, just crouched low before springing upward.

He didn't clear the barrier cleanly, but he hadn't expected to. His front paws found the top of the wall, his back legs scrabbling against the stone as they pushed him up and over. A moment of rapid falling, then he landed softly on the other side, streaking off into the trees without a second's hesitation.

Emmett felt his whole canine form relax as he delved deeper between the trunks. All he wanted to do was run, run, run. He was barely aware of any thoughts beyond the impulse—the desperate need—to be in motion. He found himself moving in a specific direction, and his human mind struggled to reassert control. Where was he going?

Suddenly the area was familiar, and Emmett let out a whine that originated from his human thoughts. He could never have found the place again in his usual form, but as a wolf, he'd sniffed his way straight there. This was the spot where he'd first encountered Rosa, immediately after returning to his human form one dawn.

Why was his wolf self eager to linger around this area? Had he done it before, without even knowing it? Using every ounce of willpower he possessed, Emmett forced his sleek, powerful form to obey his human mind, turning his head southward. If his body was determined to run, he'd let it run. But at least he could run in the direction of home, and leave Rosa and everyone she cared about well enough alone.

CHAPTER EIGHT

Rosa

Rosa felt subdued the morning after the ball, and it was nothing to do with lack of sleep. She couldn't stop thinking about her conversation with Emmett and his strange behavior. From all she could tell, he had indeed left the city immediately after striding out of the ballroom, not even taking his leave of the rest of his hosts. It was bizarre behavior from the proper prince, and she couldn't explain it. Had she offended him in some way? He hadn't seemed sensitive —not nearly as sensitive as she'd expected him to be. Besides, while she'd been impolite at the start of their conversation, by the end they were on much better terms. She'd had no need to fake friendliness when he told her that the Medullans were working on a solution for the Selvanan wild magic. She'd been almost ready to hug him.

An image flashed through her mind at the thought. Tall, closely cropped dark hair, a straight nose, a severe chin sporting the hint of a beard. Dark, intense eyes.

To her own annoyance, Rosa found her cheeks heating. No, she couldn't imagine herself flinging her arms around that broad-shouldered, muscular figure for a friendly hug, the way she might do to Otto when he delivered good news.

But she had been more inclined to look favorably on him, no denying it. She wasn't sure what to make of Emmett, but she stood by her statement that his love of the forest made him likable, if nothing else did. And perhaps there were other qualities as well.

Not that she would ever let her mother hear her say it.

Rosa's mind passed over her conversation with Emmett yet again, trying to understand what had prompted his abrupt departure. She couldn't guess, but she did find herself dwelling on his words regarding Leonhard. It hadn't occurred to Rosa to ask what the advisor's relationship with his family was like. Was it possible his view was influenced in some way by the fact that he'd been raised among singers? If she could demonstrate that he was biased in his advice, perhaps she could convince her stepfather to dismiss his suggestion of evacuation.

With that in mind, Rosa left her suite, where she'd been moping. She walked with purpose, hoping to clear the area before her lady-in-waiting caught wind of the fact that she'd left her rooms. She hadn't left the royal wing yet when she heard quick footsteps behind her, however. Heart sinking, she turned to see who was hurrying to catch up with her.

"Otto!" she said, pleased. "I'm so glad it's you and not one of my minders."

Her stepbrother had greeted her with a smile, but it turned rueful at her words. "What are you up to, Rosa? Don't tell me you're sneaking off into the forest when even your grandparents don't want you to go?"

"Not at present," said Rosa airily, still walking quickly to get clear of the area most likely to be haunted by her various unwanted chaperones. "I'm off on a different errand entirely, actually. I'm going to make some discreet inquiries about Leonhard."

Otto looked at her skeptically. "Discreet? That doesn't sound like you."

Rosa laughed. "Well, I'll make inquiries, at any rate. I want to speak with his family, but I don't know where to find them."

"I can probably help with that," Otto said slowly. "I know more than you think about all Father's key advisors. I'm fairly sure Leonhard's family live in the city. But why do you want to talk to them? If you go digging around, it'll get back to him. I don't see how antagonizing him further will help anyone's cause."

"My aim isn't to antagonize," Rosa assured him. "And it's not just idle curiosity. I'm wondering if he has some prejudice that might be skewing his advice. He claims the top priority is the safety of Ilgal's residents, and although I don't agree with his methods, I can at least respect his aim. But that's assuming he's been honest. I want to make sure his motives are what he says they are."

"Sounds like the kinds of questions sure to get people's backs up," Otto said frankly.

Thinking the older prince's opinion might carry more weight than her own, Rosa recounted what Emmett had said the night before. Sure enough, Otto's expression went from skeptical to thoughtful.

"I suppose it's worth having all the information." He glanced at Rosa. "Better for me to ask around than you, though. I don't know where Leonhard's family lives, but I know who to ask to find out. I'll meet you in the gardens in half an hour?"

Rosa gladly accepted the offered help. Half an hour wasn't long to wait if it meant she would avoid accidentally stirring up trouble. When Otto found her in the gardens as promised, he gave her a quick nod.

"It's not far," he informed her, as the pair headed out the castle gates. Rosa tried not to be resentful that there was no need for subterfuge when she was with her stepbrother. The guards had no hesitation in letting the prince through, without showing the smallest interest in his destination. Of course, he had two of his own guards trailing behind him, but it truly didn't seem to bother Otto, so Rosa tried not to let it get to her.

"They live near the Academy of Song," Otto said. "I knew his parents were both singers, but I didn't realize how senior they were. Apparently they both teach at the academy in their areas of specialty, and are generally highly regarded."

"So they're both singers," Rosa commented. "I wonder what that would be like, to be raised in a household where both parents could manipulate magic. And in the forest, too! There's certainly a plentiful supply there. Although I've heard that when there's too much magic, sometimes it makes it harder to wield rather than easier."

"I've heard that, too," Otto agreed. "This is the district." For a few minutes they walked in silence, taking note of the affluence of the neighborhood. "It looks like they made a good call, moving to the city from the forest."

"Living in a fancy house isn't the only type of happiness," Rosa said sharply. "Or any type of happiness, necessarily."

Otto raised his hands. "I meant no offense. I know you love your grandmother's forest cottage, but I admit," he gestured around them, "this life looks pretty good from where I'm standing."

Rosa's lips twitched at the description of her grandparents' manor, all her irritation leaking away as Otto unintentionally pointed out her absurdity. Her family might live in the forest, but their house was as grand as any in this district. She'd been basing her comments on a false distinction.

"This is the house, Your Highness." The words came from one of Otto's guards, and Rosa regarded him with interest.

Apparently they had uses other than shadowing their charges and unbearably restricting their lives. She'd never considered making one a confidante in any of her schemes. Probably because unlike Otto, her schemes were all diametrically opposed to the role of a guard.

"Thank you," Otto said, approaching the front door of the two-story mansion. He glanced at Rosa. "We're not expected, of course, so it's all pretty irregular. Maybe let me do the talking."

She gestured to indicate her willingness, and Otto knocked on the door. After a moment, it was opened by a middle-aged servant who went from irritated to astonished to tongue-tied in the space of a moment.

"Your—Your Highnesses," she stuttered. "What an honor to —I mean, can I be of service in some—"

"I hope so," said Otto in a cheerful voice, rescuing her from her stammering. "We were hoping to speak to the master and mistress of the house. Are they in?"

"More's the pity they're not, Your Highness," the servant said, her face radiating a level of distress disproportionate to the minor setback. "They're at the academy, and expecting to be there all day, but I can certainly send someone to fetch—"

"No need to do that," said Otto smoothly. Rosa understood. They didn't especially want the whole Academy of Song notified of their inquiries. "It's not an urgent matter."

"Miss Phoebe is in," the servant said hopefully. "The youngest daughter of the house. She lives here as well. I'm sure she'd be honored to assist you if it's in her power."

"Ah." Otto looked at Rosa, who shrugged as if to say, *why not?* "Thank you."

The servant ushered them all inside, her eyes awed as she

took in the guards and their gleaming weapons. She showed them to a large and comfortable sitting room, then disappeared. The woman in question arrived only moments before the most lavish refreshments Rosa had ever seen outside the castle. These people certainly did well for themselves.

"Your Highnesses." Phoebe dropped into a passable curtsy. She was an adult, but considerably younger than Leonhard. "I'm incredibly honored to host you in my home. My parents will be dismayed to have been absent when you called."

"No matter," said Otto lightly. "We weren't expected, and therefore had no expectation of being received with any fanfare. It's most impolite of us to come uninvited, really."

The young woman hastened to disclaim, and Rosa leaned forward, hoping to shorten the inevitable niceties.

"Do you have other siblings, Phoebe? Leonhard we know, of course, given he serves under my stepfather in the castle."

She nodded, looking bemused. "There are five of us. Leonhard is the second-born, and I'm the fifth."

Otto was raising a cup of tea to his lips, and Phoebe broke off to address him. "I beg your pardon, Your Highness, but I think it will be scalding. Our kitchen is used to making it hotter than normal, as we all like to modify our own to suit. Please, allow me."

She raised her voice in a quiet song, the melody simple and sweet. Rosa listened with fascination, watching the spiraling steam dissipate over Otto's cup. She'd never seen magic used for such an everyday purpose before.

"Thank you," said Otto, once Phoebe was finished. He took a sip, and smiled. "Perfect."

"It's clear you inherited your parents' gift," Rosa commented.

Phoebe smiled. "Indeed. Inherited is the word for it, I suppose, but I certainly don't take it for granted. None of us do.

Having a singer for a parent increases the likelihood of a child being born able to sing, but not by as much as you'd think. Two parents even more so, but even then...it's just as common for children of singers to be born without magic as with it. We consider ourselves very fortunate—and unusual—to have all inherited it."

Rosa and Otto exchanged a confused look, and Phoebe hastened to correct herself.

"All of us except Leonhard, I mean, of course. I just didn't mention him because...well, as you said, you already know him well, given he works in the castle. An admirable achievement," she added quickly.

Otto smiled politely, but Rosa gave no response, thinking the other woman's words over. So Leonhard wasn't just born to two singers—he was the only one of five siblings who didn't inherit the ability. It was interesting. In any other family, a commoner becoming a key advisor to the king would be an incredible achievement, which the rest of the family would likely boast of to anyone who'd listen. Apparently in Leonhard's family, it was so insignificant his family all but forgot him. Reluctantly, Rosa felt a twinge of sympathy for him.

"Were you born in the forest, Phoebe?" she asked. "Leonhard told me he was."

Phoebe shook her head. "Leonhard is almost ten years older than I am. He was born in the forest, but I was born shortly after the family moved here. I've only ever known city life." She gave a disarming smile. "My brother assures me I'm missing out, but I confess I could never relate to his admiration for the forest. It scares me a little."

"Even though there's so much magic to fuel your ability?" Otto asked.

She shrugged. "That's part of what makes it so frightening, Your Highness. The quantity of magic is...overwhelming. Magic is plentiful enough in the city, without the other risks inherent in forest life."

"So does that mean you support his controversial recommendation?" Rosa asked bluntly. Otto gave her a look, but she ignored this reminder to be subtle. She wasn't good at subtle. "To be honest, I thought it seemed over the top."

"Oh, well..." Phoebe gave a pained little laugh. "I try to stay out of any of his projects which are...controversial, as you put it. But Leonhard's always had strong ideas. He's been talking about the idea of Teren subsuming Medulle's part of Ilgal so long that he's given up expecting a response from any of us, I think."

"What?" Otto and Rosa spoke in unison, and Phoebe fell instantly silent.

"Leonhard thinks the section of Ilgal that falls within Medulle's borders should be part of Teren?" Otto asked.

Phoebe looked frightened now. "I beg your pardon...I...I mistook. I thought you asked about it...I thought you would be aware of his recommendations, and...forgive me if I caused offense."

Rosa frowned. "That's not part of any recommendations I've heard of. When I spoke of his controversial plan, I meant evacuating the forest."

"Evacuating the forest?" Phoebe repeated. "Forgive me, but... I didn't think that was controversial. I thought it was settled."

"You've been misinformed," Otto said grimly.

That was putting it mildly in Rosa's opinion. And there could be no doubt who had misinformed her. Rosa could tell that Otto was ready to leave so he could process the new information in private, and she spoke quickly, making the most of the opportunity.

"So Leonhard resents magic, does he? Being the only one in the family without it must have made him hate it. Is that why he wants to seal it off in the forest?"

"No, of course not!" Phoebe's astonishment seemed as genuine as her distress. "No, Your Highness, that truly isn't so. I mean, I know it can't have been easy for him in this household. But he values magic, truly he does. He's made it his life's study, and is never hesitant about us using it."

"Thank you, ma'am, you have no need to explain anything to us," said Otto, the firmness in his voice meant for Rosa, not Phoebe. "You've done nothing wrong, and nor has your family. We merely wished for more perspective on your brother's recommendation, as we consider all options in addressing the challenges facing our forest-dwelling residents."

"Of course, Your Highness." Phoebe stood as Otto did, dipping into a curtsy. "I only hope I've been of some assistance."

Recognizing that the moment for inquiry was past, Rosa took her leave as well, following Otto out onto the street.

"Well," she said, once they'd left the mansion behind. "That was enlightening."

"It certainly was," Otto agreed grimly. "And not in the way I expected at all."

"I confess, I didn't suspect Leonhard of harboring plans to expand Teren's borders," Rosa commented. "He doesn't seem the type. What would he gain from it, after all?"

Otto shook his head slowly. "I don't know. But I hope he lets it go. The whole idea is a distraction from the issue that really needs resolving." He considered the matter. "She said he's been talking about it for a long time. I suppose it's possible it's some youthful fancy he's never actually intended to act on."

"It didn't sound that way," said Rosa skeptically. She glanced at Otto. "We wouldn't actually ever try that, would we? Pushing our borders, taking Medulle's land?"

"I can't imagine Father supporting the idea," said Otto. "I suppose it's possible that if the forest becomes fully overrun, Medulle might not want it anymore. They wouldn't be losing too much territory. But even then, I'm not sure Father would be inclined to try changing any borders."

"Besides which," Rosa added, a thought occurring to her, "Emmett would never let that happen."

"*Emmett*, is it?" Otto ribbed.

Rosa ignored him. "Emmett is fond of the forest, remember? He would push back against any suggestion of ceding the land to Teren. The idea would never get any momentum."

Otto didn't immediately answer, and a glance at him showed that he was uncomfortable.

"What?" Rosa asked.

Otto rolled his shoulder. "I don't know that Prince Emmett would have much say in the matter." He must have seen that she was bewildered, because he clarified. "Father keeps a close eye on all our neighbors. All the kingdoms do it. Our information is that Emmett doesn't have his father's full confidence. As he's grown older, he's been given less authority, not more."

Rosa stared at him. "But why? He's so outrageously responsible!"

Otto shrugged. "I was surprised, too. At first, I thought maybe it was incorrect information. But I have noticed him taking care in how he speaks since he arrived here. When thanking Father for information, he said he'd pass it on to his father, not that he'd consider it himself. In fact, he hasn't said anything suggesting that he has authority to actually make decisions regarding the crisis."

Rosa frowned, more troubled by this information than she should be.

"All of that is for your ears alone," Otto said warningly.

She nodded. "I understand. I'll keep it to myself." In fact, she had no desire whatsoever to spread word of Emmett's unofficial demotion. Was that why he was in Lernvale, instead of in his own capital? Had he been exiled there? But why? What offense could the steady, upright prince possibly have committed that would lead his parents to send him away?

After walking in silence for several minutes, Rosa forced her mind back to the question at hand.

"Well, if nothing else, it's apparently true that Leonhard is from the forest. I was surprised to hear his sister talk as though he loves the forest. He's never given me that impression. He talks so coldly about the idea of evacuating Ilgal, as if he has no concept of the grief it would cause. And why would he even *want* Medulle's portion of the forest, if his plan is to evacuate the whole thing anyway?"

"It doesn't quite add up, does it?" Otto agreed.

It certainly didn't, and the more Rosa thought about it, the more it troubled her. She and Otto parted ways at the castle, and she didn't even ask him whether he was going to report the conversation to his father. Every time she thought about Leonhard wanting Teren to claim the Medullan portion of the forest, she felt a heavy sense of foreboding. It was all tied up somehow with the evacuation idea, she was sure of it. She just couldn't figure out how it fit together.

And, most frustrating of all, the ones most affected had no voice, no way of even knowing what was going on.

The thought decided Rosa. She knew no one approved of her going into the forest right now, but she wasn't afraid. Other than the faint pressure she'd felt last time, she'd never had an alarming experience in there. She was even beginning to suspect that Leonhard was intentionally stoking the gossip, to speed up his plans. But those who lived in the forest wouldn't be so easily manipulated. They would know the true state of affairs in Ilgal, and would be able to restore her perspective on it all.

Besides, they deserved to know what was being plotted against their homes.

Not pausing to think through the wisdom of pushing her

mother and stepfather's trust so soon after her last jaunt, Rosa hurried toward the royal stables. Her minders still thought she was with Otto, and she needed to act quickly before they realized she wasn't. She would be sensible, so no one could accuse her of recklessness. She'd ride, and stick to the road.

CHAPTER NINE

Rosa

The head groom wasn't in the stables when Rosa arrived, which was perfect. She had no difficulty cajoling a younger stablehand to saddle up Otto's personal horse for her. The stallion was her favorite mount.

"You're not scared of the woods, are you, Bullion?" she crooned to the horse, as they rode through the city's western gate and onto the forest road. "You don't mind taking me to Granny's house, do you?"

The horse gave no reply, seeming perfectly ready to enter the trees at her direction. It wasn't even the lunch hour yet, and she would make good time on horseback. She'd make it to her grandparents' and back hours before dark.

She tried to hum to herself as she rode, but her heart wasn't in it. Not only did she feel burdened from all she'd learned, she was once again plagued by the hint of pressure in her chest. She couldn't ignore it or deny it. It hadn't been there a month ago, and now it was. The magic really was growing stronger, and quickly.

The journey to the forest manor was uneventful, but Rosa's mood didn't lift when she arrived. The property's gate was more heavily guarded than ever, and worse, for the first time in her memory, neither grandparent was happy to see her.

"What are you doing here, Rosa?" Granny demanded. "It's not safe for you to be wandering the forest alone! We told you not to take the risk."

"Are you all right, Rosie?" her grandfather asked, his manner more gentle but his concern just as evident. "Did you come because you're in trouble?"

"No, I'm not in trouble," said Rosa quickly. "It's you I'm worried about."

Her grandmother waved her into the house, casting a swift glance around as she did so. Grampy stayed close to her as well, neither raising the topic again until Rosa was settled with a hot cup of tea and a scone.

"Now what's all this?" Granny asked bluntly. "We're old and tough. Why are you worrying about us?"

Rosa tried to explain her concerns about the evacuation, but Granny just waved an impatient hand.

"That's nothing new. We've been fighting that plan for a while now. It's no call for you to be tripping around like this, tempting the wolves to come for you."

"I'm hardly tripping around," Rosa protested. "I rode and everything. I think Bullion could outrun a wolf."

"Not the wolf we've been seeing," said Granny flatly. "It's the biggest one I ever saw."

"What do you mean, you've been seeing it?" Rosa demanded.

"I mean just that," said her grandmother, her expression grim. "We've had a few scares since we last saw you. It hangs about our property."

Grampy nodded. "It came out of nowhere when I was arriving home yesterday. Lunged out of the trees and snapped at me as I rode through the gate." He shook his head. "We have some enchantments on the perimeter—"

"That we paid dearly for," his wife interjected in a mutter.

"—but they'll wear off soon," Grampy finished patiently, as if he hadn't been interrupted. "And they're not absolute. There are limitations."

"Like the gaping hole in the defenses on the north western edge of the property," Granny said. Her tone turned brisk. "We'll need to buy more talismans."

"How are we going to do that?" Grampy protested. "The elves have retreated into the depths of the forest, remember? Haven't seen one around here for months." He shook his head at Rosa. "There are rumors their leader's even put some kind of ban on trading with the humans in Ilgal. I don't think we'll be getting our hands on new talismans anytime soon."

"Then we'll find a singer we can hire," said Granny optimistically. "One way or another, we need to strengthen the defenses. The creatures are targeting us. I know it sounds absurd, but there's no other way to put it." She waved a hand to stop Rosa's attempt to press for details. "In any event, that's not your problem to solve. You mustn't come roaming through the woods again, Rosa. Your grandfather will see you home."

"No he won't," said Rosa emphatically. "Not if you're being targeted. I have my horse—I'll be fine. I'll stay on the path, and ride straight home."

Grampy looked unconvinced, but Granny just sighed, not in the habit of curtailing Rosa's movements. "Very well. See that you do, my dear."

"I promise," Rosa said.

She'd barely been there half an hour, and she was longing for the chance to have a proper rest with her grandparents, away from the eyes that always watched in a castle. But she didn't argue. She could tell that her presence would cause her grand-parents anxiety rather than pleasure.

Her grandfather walked her to their small stable, where poor Bullion had barely finished being unsaddled.

"Sorry, old fellow, it's back on the road," Rosa told the horse penitently.

Her grandfather insisted on saddling Bullion himself, and Rosa watched without seeing, her brow creased in concern.

"Are you safe out here, Grampy?" she asked after a moment. "The last thing I want is to see you all driven from your home, but...I couldn't bear it if anything happened to you."

"We'll be all right," said Grampy prosaically. "We're safe enough on our property, unless the wolves were eavesdropping when your grandmother talked about the hole in our protections." He gave a light chuckle, although Rosa didn't find the topic in the least amusing. "We're not taking any foolish risks." He gave her a stern look. "And it's time you stopped doing the same, Rosie."

Rosa nodded, chastened. "I understand." She hesitated. "Grampy, there was more I wanted to tell you. Otto and I spoke to someone this morning. She's the sister of Leonhard, the advisor telling my stepfather to evacuate you all." Quickly, she recounted the gist of their conversation with Phoebe.

"Hm." Grampy considered her words. "I can't make head nor tail of all the scheming over borders. To be honest, I don't know that it would affect us much either way."

Rosa nodded. She supposed that was true.

"It's interesting that he's from a family of singers, though," Grampy went on. "I didn't know that." He scowled. "You'd think he'd be offering to use his connections to help us strengthen our protections, rather than trying to drive us all out."

"You wouldn't think that if you knew him," Rosa said dryly. "In spite of his grand words about safety, I don't think Leonhard cares much about people. Other than himself, of course." She frowned. "I just wish I knew what his motivations were."

She eyed her grandfather, remembering how eagerly Leonhard had spoken of the older couple's influence when last Grampy had come to the castle. She decided not to mention that, but she felt uneasy over how visible her grandparents were. She would prefer them not to attract the notice of someone like Leonhard, especially when she didn't understand what game the advisor was playing.

Her grandfather helped her up into the saddle, patting her leg in a fatherly way. "Be careful, now."

Rosa nodded, but didn't urge Bullion forward. She drew a deep breath, hating how constricted the movement felt.

"Grampy, there's something else I wanted to ask you."

"Mm?"

Rosa bit her lip. "Are you...are you feeling any pressure? In here, I mean?" She gestured to her chest.

Her grandfather didn't speak, but the look on his face was answer enough.

"Oh, Grampy," she said, her throat suddenly thick.

He patted her leg again. "I'm all right, Rosie." He glanced toward the house. "Don't ask your grandmother about it. It upsets her." He gave a disarming smile. "And I've never liked seeing her upset."

"You're a good man, Grampy," Rosa told him.

He declaimed in his usual modest way, slapping Bullion's rump in a manner the royal steed was certainly not accustomed to. Nevertheless, the horse moved forward compliantly, and soon Rosa was off the property, heading toward the capital.

Rosa's thoughts stayed with her grandparents, only half watching the familiar road. The pressure in her chest, although light, was constant. And it certainly did nothing to ease her rising concerns. The most alarming revelation of the day was that her grandparents had experienced enough near misses with these huge wolves to feel targeted.

Was it possible they *were* being targeted? Terrifying, illogical thought. An idea danced at the edge of her mind, but she couldn't quite pin it down. She couldn't seem to get any of her thoughts straight, in fact. Her unease was building, and it took her longer than it should have to realize that it wasn't just her thoughts that were unsettling her—it was her instincts, as well.

Her first clue was when Bullion flattened his ears, shying sideways a little on the road. It was unusual for the confident stallion to display discomfort, and it put Rosa instantly on edge. She pulled him into line with a strong hand, then clucked at him, encouraging him to increase his speed. Soon they were cantering along the road, as quickly as the terrain would allow. Her grandparents' property was far behind them now, but Rosa's unease hadn't lessened.

A flash of movement caught her eye, and she whipped her head to the side, trying to see through the tree trunks. Had that been a patch of gray? Impossible to tell at the speed her mount was moving.

"Easy, Bullion," she murmured, as the horse once again showed signs of fear.

They'd slowed slightly, and this time Rosa was sure she saw it. Gray fur, and—when she turned her head to peer carefully through the trees—a pair of glowing eyes.

Terror shot through her, and it was all she could do to keep her head. Bullion obviously sensed her fear, however, because he bolted. Rosa clung on for dear life, her breath coming in gasps as the road flew by beneath them. The speed wasn't even the most terrifying aspect of the situation, because she could still see a blurry, gray shape—much too large for a wolf— keeping pace with them among the tree trunks.

"Get us home, boy," Rosa told Bullion, trying to keep her

voice steady. "Get us back to the city." She looked ahead, her heart lifting as she saw that the light was growing. They were almost out of the forest.

A moment later, she regretted taking her eyes from their silent pursuer. Sudden movement gave her barely a second's notice before a huge gray wolf burst out of the tree line, making straight for them. Rosa screamed, and Bullion reared. She laid herself flat against his neck, gripping his mane with everything she had, and clamping her legs against his side. If she was thrown, she didn't have a chance.

In the chaos, she didn't get a very good look at the creature attacking them. She could tell it was too big for a wolf, but it was still smaller than Bullion. The wolf shied away from the horse's flailing hooves, and the next moment, Bullion had reconnected with the road and taken off at a gallop.

Rosa was still miraculously clinging on, and she spared herself only one glance behind. The wolf was following them, its pace alarmingly fast. But the trees ended just ahead, and then they'd be in sight of the city's western gate. The archers would take the creature down if it strayed close to the wall.

Obviously the wolf couldn't know this, but its instincts clearly told it to stay within the forest. It began to slow quite suddenly, and when Rosa glanced back again, as the road entered the band of cleared land near the wall, it was ducking back into the trees.

She let out a shaky breath, her fear crashing over her with even more intensity now the danger was past. Turning her attention to Bullion, she managed to gradually slow the careening horse, so that by the time they reached the city gate, they were in a fit state to be let through.

"There was a huge wolf," she gasped to the guards on duty, gesturing wildly backward. "It chased us as far as the tree line."

"Princess Rosa?" The closest guard looked horrified, but she waved away his concern impatiently.

"I'm fine. And you won't catch the creature now. It's run back into the forest. I'm just telling you to be cautious. I'll take the report straight to the king."

Without waiting for a reply, she pushed on through the city, reaching the castle in minutes. After relinquishing Bullion to a groom, she paused in the entranceway, breathing deeply and trying to restore her equilibrium. She was more shaken by the near miss than she cared to admit.

"Rosa!" The bright greeting rang across the space. Apparently a minute to regroup was too much to expect on this occasion. "There you are, I was wondering where you'd gotten to when you didn't join me for luncheon." Her mother's voice was cheerful, meaning she had no idea where Rosa had been. "I've had an excellent idea."

"Have you, Mama?" Rosa asked faintly, running a hand nervously over her braid.

Her mother took her arm, steering her across the entranceway and toward a more private part of the castle. "I heard today that the sunflower fields are especially glorious this year. And we haven't been yet."

"The sunflower fields?" Rosa asked, unable to grasp the relevance of the attraction for which the area just east of Terenford was famous.

"That's right," her mother said encouragingly. "I'm going to organize an expedition. Just our family."

"Oh. That sounds...nice." Rosa felt like she was in a dream, her eyes once again seeing those terrifying flashes of gray which clashed strangely with the talk of sunflowers filling her ears.

"And I thought we could invite Prince Emmett," her mother added, her casual tone unconvincing.

"Mama." Rosa came out of her dreamlike state at that,

turning to frown at her mother. "I told you, your hopes there are unfounded."

"Yes, I remember," said the queen, eyeing her daughter with unruffled calm. "You told me not to invite him to a luncheon with the family. So instead I invited him to another ball. At which he made straight for you the moment he arrived, and did nothing but talk to you until the moment he left. A conversation which put you in excellent spirits. And after he left, you were morose for the rest of the evening."

"I take offense at that," said Rosa. She tried valiantly to keep her tone cool, even as her traitorous cheeks heated. "I was morose the whole evening—both before *and* after my conversation with Prince Emmett."

She was inclined to be pleased with herself for learning from Otto's reaction and remembering this time to use Emmett's title. But the queen just smiled maddeningly.

"I'm your mother, Rosa. Do you think I don't know you at all? Give me a little credit."

"Really, Mama, you have the wrong idea," Rosa said desperately.

She wanted to tell her mother that she'd only been happy when talking to Emmett because he'd given her hope about reclaiming Ilgal. But she didn't think she should disclose what he'd said—it had clearly been information Medulle wished to keep quiet. Not to mention...she wasn't entirely sure that was the only reason she'd been happy.

But she certainly couldn't admit *that* to her mother.

"Mama, never mind the sunflowers. There's something I need to tell you. And the others."

Her mother's enthusiastic expression dimmed, but she nodded. "All right. Otto is with your stepfather in a last-minute meeting with some representatives of the Artisans' Guild, but they'll probably be out any minute."

Rosa followed her mother's lead toward the part of the castle where King Ryker usually met with his advisors. They were fortunate to encounter the king and prince just as they were leaving a meeting room.

"—seemed a reasonable compromise to me," Otto was saying, his casual air telling Rosa that the representatives had already left.

"Yes, I think that should resolve the matter," King Ryker agreed. His eyes fell on his wife and stepdaughter, and he smiled. "Ada, Rosa. What a pleasant surprise."

"Rosa wants to talk to us, Ryker," the queen said, her mild voice fooling no one.

"Of course." The king glanced around, then gestured them back into the meeting room.

Rosa led the way stoically. It was as good a spot as any.

"What's going on, Rosa?" her stepfather answered, once they were all inside.

Rosa drew a deep breath, looking at her mother's tense frame. For a moment, she was tempted to make up something else. She'd gotten away with it so far. Perhaps they wouldn't discover where she'd been if she just said nothing.

She pushed the thought down guiltily. This situation was beyond her own freedom. Straightening her back, she faced them all.

"I went to my grandparents' house this morning."

"What?" The exclamation came from her mother, but Otto looked just as startled. The king just looked resigned.

"But you were with me this morning," Otto said blankly. "We parted ways not two hours ago."

"Probably about that long," Rosa agreed. "I went straight there, to tell them what we'd learned. And they sent me straight back. They didn't want me traveling out there."

"And neither do we," the queen said, incensed. "You knew

perfectly well that we're all aligned on this matter, Rosa. What were you thinking?"

"I took a horse," Rosa said, her voice pleading. "And I stayed on the path the whole time. I did try to be more careful than usual."

"Bullion, no doubt," said Otto, more long-suffering than annoyed.

"Rosa, do you want the magic to crush you?" the queen demanded. "Or to be killed by a wolf?"

"The magic isn't far enough advanced to crush anyone," Rosa said placatingly. "But..." She swallowed. "But I did see a wolf. It chased Bullion and me, and we were lucky we were at the edge of the forest."

Her mother's eyes widened in horror, and Rosa couldn't help wincing.

"I know it sounds bad," she said. "I won't deny it was frightening. But I really am fine. And so is Bullion," she added hastily, for Otto's benefit. She met her stepfather's eyes. "The wolf was huge. Much bigger than a normal wolf. And my grandparents told me they've had a few near misses themselves. Apparently the creatures are hanging around their property, although why, I can't imagine."

"It's the biggest concentration of people for miles," said the king grimly. "That's reason enough, I daresay. Wolves are predators, after all."

Otto looked confused at this description of the *forest cottage*, but no one stopped to explain.

"If giant wolves are chasing travelers only a stone's throw from the city gates, the situation is graver than I thought," King Ryker said, his voice heavy. "Perhaps Leonhard is right. Perhaps we have reached the point of evacuation."

"No!" Rosa protested. "I'm sure that's not the only solution. There has to be another way."

"And there might be," her stepfather said. "But we may have to pursue it after seeing all the residents of Ilgal into safe shelter."

"They'll never come," said Rosa desperately. "Most of them would rather die defending their property from the wolves than relinquish it without a fight. I know my grandparents would."

"That's foolish beyond permission," said her mother tersely. "There's no need for anyone to sacrifice their lives."

"Mama, you know how many generations Granny's family has been on that property," Rosa said earnestly. "And she's not the only one. There's no way they'll leave willingly. We can't cut them off from the forest. It would kill them."

Her mother's face didn't soften, and her stepfather looked grave but unyielding. Rosa looked appealingly at Otto.

"Surely you agree with me, Otto."

"Often," he said soberly. "But this time, I'm not so sure." His eyes met hers, a hint of pleading in their depths. "I don't want to punish those who love the forest. I just want them to be safe. Including you, Rosa. Especially you. You're my family, and I don't know how to convince you to stop taking risks with your life. If the forest is evacuated, no one will be putting themselves at risk."

Remorse washed over Rosa at the concern she caused all her family.

"I never meant to distress you," she said softly. "I'm sorry I went into the forest today when you told me not to. But..." She made a hopeless gesture. "I'm convinced evacuation isn't the answer. The only one who really wants that is Leonhard. And I can't shake the feeling that he has an ulterior motive. If that's been his aim all along, we'd be playing right into his hands by doing it prematurely."

Otto gave her a look. "That's a little dramatic, Rosa. I agree that what we learned about him this morning gives cause for further thought, but that doesn't make him some kind of mastermind."

"I agree," said King Ryker. "Otto told me about your conversation, and it sounds to me like the talk of expanding our borders was some childish fancy, probably abandoned long ago. Leonhard has never mentioned anything of the kind to me."

"If it's not that, it's something else, then, because he's up to something," Rosa insisted. "I can feel it. He has a grudge against my grandparents, too." The thought that had tickled her mind in the forest returned to her. "They said they feel targeted by these wolves. What if he's controlling them somehow? Leonhard has a motive for going after my grandparents. They're very influential with the other forest residents. If they were driven from their home, even killed behind the supposed safety of its walls, it would seriously weaken opposition to the evacuation idea."

"Rosa," said Otto, his voice pained. "That's a stretch."

"Is it?" Rosa demanded. "Do you know for certain that there's no magic that can control animals? Maybe make them bigger and more savage? His whole family are singers—maybe they're helping him somehow."

"That's not the impression I had from his sister," Otto said. "She seemed barely familiar with his plans to do with the forest, and certainly not invested in them."

"But he has three other siblings," Rosa pushed stubbornly. "And two parents."

"Leonhard's family are well-respected and senior members of the song community," said King Ryker firmly. "I have no reason to suspect them of any kind of scheme. And I once again agree with Otto. There's no evidence whatsoever to suggest that anyone is controlling these wolves, or sending them after your grandparents intentionally."

"But—" Rosa started, but her mother cut her off.

"Leave it be, Rosa. Your stepfather has all the information. Now you must step back and trust his wisdom."

Rosa bit her lip. Her mother was right, of course. If she didn't want the burdens of royal life, she couldn't expect the power that came with it. But that didn't make it any easier to step back and let things run their course.

"I don't take the decision lightly," said the king. "But I won't deny that evacuation is becoming a more likely eventuality."

Rosa opened her mouth to protest again, then held it in with a supreme effort. Arguing wasn't going to help anything. She'd given her opinion, and it wasn't enough to change the king's mind. Her mother certainly didn't agree with her, and even Otto was wavering. She had no allies in the castle, and she was barred from reaching her family in the forest.

What could she do? Who could she turn to for help to prevent this disastrous course?

"Also, Rosa, although it gives me no pleasure, I'll have to be more explicit regarding your movements. We've given you a great deal of license, and refrained from strictly limiting you, but it's become a serious safety concern. I must forbid you to go to your grandparents' house without express permission from your mother or myself. I hope you understand."

He turned to her mother on the words, leaving Rosa in no doubt that whether or not she understood, it wouldn't change the outcome. Unhindered by anyone, she slipped from the room, feeling a desperate need to be in motion. She strode blindly through the castle, reaching the gardens without thinking about it. But pacing the covered walkways brought no relief. More than ever she felt trapped, and she had no idea where to turn.

Whatever her stepfather said, he didn't really understand. None of them could truly appreciate what the forest meant to those born and raised in it. They didn't comprehend the lifestyle of those who made Ilgal their home, and didn't grasp how it would destroy them to be ripped from it. If she was any judge, none of them would ever forgive their king for failing to prevent the loss of their home. And she didn't know how to explain it to them, because every time she opened her mouth, she seemed to say the wrong thing. They knew she was too close to the issue. They'd never believe her opinion was balanced and reliable.

Who would back her up?

A face flashed into her mind, with a serious jawline and dark eyes. She didn't immediately banish the thought. Was it possible Emmett would be an ally on this matter? He'd been firmly against the idea of evacuation when they'd spoken the other night. And his opinion would carry more weight with her stepfather and Otto. She should act quickly if she wanted to change the king's mind before he took steps that would forever blacken him in the image of the forest dwellers.

Rosa once again pictured Emmett's face, and a strange recklessness swept over her. She hesitated, guilt warring with the recklessness as a plan grew in her mind. She knew she probably shouldn't. She knew it was foolish, and her mother would be upset. Her stepfather had likely intended for her to stay within the city. But he hadn't actually forbidden her to leave. He'd just said she couldn't go to her grandparents' house. And this might be her last chance—it was too soon for any new instructions to have reached the guards at the gates. If she wanted to go, she needed to do it now.

Reckless or not, Rosa knew better than to venture back into the forest. And she also took no pleasure from causing her mother worry. Her first stop was the queen's suite, where she scratched out an explanatory note, which she left on her mother's writing desk.

Next she went back to the stables. The same underling re-saddled Bullion for her, not managing to hide his bewilderment.

The poor horse could probably do with more of a rest after his scare, but time was limited. Before another half an hour had passed, Rosa had slipped the net, leaving the city by the southern road this time, and thundering toward West River and the Medullan border beyond.

CHAPTER TEN

Emmett

Emmett flexed his hands in front of his eyes, studying his fingernails in alarm. It wasn't just his imagination. They were rougher than they had been the day before. Even a little pointed. It was subtle enough that he had hope no one else would notice. But he could tell.

He felt absolutely haggard. The previous night's transformation had been rough, and not just because of his mortification over how it had begun. How much had Rosa seen? What did she suspect? Surely she wouldn't guess the truth—it was too absurd, who would guess it? But she must have found his behavior strange. Not to mention abysmally rude. What explanation would she dream up in her mind?

It was better not to know, probably. Emmett would be wisest to put her from his mind. He shouldn't accept any more invitations from Queen Ada. He needed to keep his distance, and not just because he didn't want Rosa to see too much. It was also that he felt increasingly less able to trust himself. His usually rigid self-discipline was wavering more and more as the wolf crept into his human mind. But never was it so hard to find it as when he was with Rosa. He had no idea why she had that effect on him. Perhaps it was because she was a child of the forest. Something about her called out to the wolf within, which was also a creature of Ilgal.

A rap at the door made Emmett start, and he lowered his hands quickly, busying them with parchment on his desk so as not to draw attention to their changing appearance.

"Enter," he called curtly.

His steward pushed the door open, bowing. "Your Highness, several villagers have come in response to your summons."

"Thank you," said Emmett, keeping his face neutral. Inside, he was groaning. More interviews, no doubt each as pointless as the last.

"If I may be bold, Your Highness," the steward went on tentatively. "Ought I perhaps to send them away? Your Highness doesn't look entirely well. Perhaps it's too much exertion after the ball last night."

"No, I'm fine," Emmett said quickly. The steward was right, of course, but he couldn't let anyone see how much his affliction was draining away his strength. He needed to keep going as normal. "Thank you for your concern, but I'll meet with those who've come."

Emmett stood, following the older man from the room. He truly did feel weary, a deep exhaustion that went beyond the fact that he'd barely slept the night before. It was as though he could feel the prediction of the healer-singer his parents had hired coming true. His human life was draining away from him, and eventually his body would succumb. The only question was whether he would die, or simply become the wolf permanently. He knew which option he would prefer.

The steward was wrong about one thing—the ball the night before had nothing to do with his current state. He'd run for hours in his wolf form, not taking the most direct route through the forest. The wolf had fought him constantly, trying to turn around and go back to the area with which it seemed obsessed. The area where he'd met Rosa.

All the while Emmett's human mind had been forcing his body southward, determined to reach his own castle before he could do something he'd regret. The result had been a circuitous journey, and he'd only reached the band of cleared grass a short time before dawn, ready to collapse at the trees' edge. The moment his body returned to its proper form, he'd slunk through a side gate in the wall, one he left intentionally unlocked. The worst of it was, no one had questioned him about why his carriage had returned without him, only to have him mysteriously appear in his bed in the morning, disheveled and sleeping like the dead. There could be no surer sign that everyone in the castle knew something was going on. Something dire. He'd noticed servants starting to whisper as he passed. All the more reason to keep up appearances as much as possible, slow the inevitable spread of the rumors.

Emmett's eyes glazed over as he followed the steward, gripped by unpleasant memories from the night before. Rosa's confused face was the first of them, but certainly not the worst. The memory of his time as a wolf was a confusing mix of vivid clarity and hazy confusion. He'd never be able to retrace his route now he was human again, for example. But remembered sensations kept coming to him in flashes. The feel of the wind in his fur as he sprinted between the trees. The clear white light of the moon slanting between branches. The smell of prey.

That last one made Emmett shudder. It took an effort of will to prevent his human nose from twitching in remembered response. The wolf was so excellent at smelling out food. He always resisted, of course. The wolf might know, but how could his human mind be sure what kind of creature he was pursuing? What if he thought he was chasing down a deer, only to emerge in the path of some poor human?

Cold rushed over him as he remembered the one time he'd followed that instinct. It was back in the early days, when he was still struggling to comprehend the changes coming over him. He'd killed a rabbit, and consumed it with an eagerness that still repulsed him to remember. In a way it was foolish to feel so ashamed over that incident. He ate rabbit regularly in his human form without hesitation. But as a human, he ate to sustain himself. It wasn't the food part that was so horrifying to remember. It was the hunting. He could still recall the intensity of the wolf's drive. His own mind had played host to instincts that appalled him—the savage joy in hunting, in killing, was something that his normal self couldn't relate to. The savagery was beyond even a normal wolf, he was sure. It was the twisted result of the magic.

When he'd come to on that long-ago morning, he'd told himself never again. He wouldn't hunt or eat in his wolf form. His self-control simply had to be stronger than the wolf. A standard that was growing harder to meet with time.

Emmett stepped into the now-familiar antechamber to see half a dozen villagers waiting. Their expressions ranged from nervousness to excitement as they all bobbed into bows and curtsies.

"Thank you for coming," he told them, his hands tucked carefully behind his back. "I'll speak with each of you individually."

The first villager had nothing of relevance to say, either regarding the growth of the wild magic or Emmett's more subtle questions about magical activity in the region. He seemed most interested in talking about the rumors of giant wolves, and the fact that the legends of generations gone by were now coming to life before them. It was a topic Emmett had no inclination to discuss.

The second villager, however, had the distinction of saying something Emmett hadn't yet heard from anyone else.

"I haven't seen anything suspicious in the forest, Your Highness," the woman said frankly. "But that's because I haven't been wandering around much. I've been keeping mainly to my own village, like most of us. We're in the forest, aye, but our clearing is well protected. We don't stray out of it except in groups these days, and always with some of our men armed and ready to defend. Truth be told, it's probably more cautious than we need to be. I've seen more wolves than usual in recent months, but they looked normal enough to me, and were quick to take off when they saw the size of our group. If these so-called giant wolves near Terenford are affecting us out here, it's probably only by scaring the regular wolves out of their usual areas so that more of them find their way to the Medullan part of the forest."

Emmett nodded, trying to keep his mind on their conversation when it wanted to wander back to fruitless speculation regarding what Rosa had made of his behavior the night before.

"But there was something a bit odd in the markets the other day."

"What was that?" Emmett asked, sitting up straighter.

"Well, it was only odd because it reminded me," she said matter-of-factly. "My sister had a similar story from years back, and it struck me as odd at the time."

"What did?" Emmett pressed, impatient.

"Well, the other day, I was at market, and I heard a woman from the next village over asking for aconitum."

Emmett stiffened in his seat. He'd heard the name before, from his brother Farrin. It was the last thing he expected the woman to bring up.

"It's a plant," she explained helpfully, oblivious to his

thoughts. "But it struck me as odd because no one calls it that in the forest, and this woman was one of us, sure enough."

"What's it called in the forest?" Emmett asked.

"Wolfsbane," said the woman lightly.

Emmett stilled, his attention fully caught. Was it possible Farrin had been right? Emmett should have followed this line of inquiry from the start if so.

"No one had any, of course," the woman went on, deflating his hopes. "*If* it ever existed, it died out a long time ago. Most think it's an old wives' tale, since the stories claim it was more than just a natural repellant—they say it had magical properties to keep wolves at bay, and who's heard of a magical plant? I've never seen one, even with the magic in Ilgal supposedly so wild. But that's not the point. I just thought it was odd that she called it by that fancy name, like she'd been reading from one of them books up at the academy or something." The woman snorted. "I know for a fact she can't read no more than I can. So I questioned her on it."

"What did she say?" Emmett asked.

"Well, she didn't say it right out, but I weaseled it out of her," the woman said with satisfaction. "She wasn't asking on her own behalf. Apparently there's some man who's been asking for wolfsbane for years. Says he'll pay a handsome price. It's just like my sister said, you see. She remembers a man asking about it in the market years back. He was laughed out of the place, coming with his fancy words but believing in children's stories. I wondered if it was the same man."

"Who was this man?" Emmett asked eagerly.

The woman shrugged, looking bemused. "No idea. It was my sister who saw him, not me. And she moved to Port Dulla a couple years back, when she got married."

Emmett sighed. Not likely to find answers in that direction. Still, it was an intriguing piece of information that someone had been searching for the fabled aconitum plant years ago. Was it before or after he became a wolf? Probably after, he reflected. He'd tried to be careful, but there had clearly been sightings anyway. The sheer size of him would be enough to make most people eager to ward him off their properties if possible.

"Thank you for the information," he told the young woman. "And you said you haven't seen anything suspicious in the forest?"

"I haven't," she confirmed. "But I probably wouldn't, would I, Your Highness?"

"What do you mean?" Emmett asked.

She waved vaguely out the window. "Have you been out there lately? Ilgal is enormous. We have our established villages, and our regular routes between them. If anything odd was going on in those areas, we'd see it. But there's so much of the forest outside those routes. If someone was up to something they shouldn't be, they'd have plenty of space to do it far away from prying eyes. And any knowledge of the forest would tell them which areas to avoid if they didn't want to be seen."

Emmett frowned thoughtfully. She was right. He'd been thinking that if magic was being gathered illegally within the forest, someone must have seen something. But he hadn't been thinking like a forester. He'd been approaching it as though the communities were evenly scattered across Ilgal, when of course that wasn't the case. They clustered together for safety and ease of trade.

"Thank you," he told the woman sincerely. "You've been very helpful."

"It's my honor, Your Highness," she said, rising in a businesslike manner. "I'll send in the next one, shall I?"

The rest of the villagers had nothing of particular note to add. On being asked, they all agreed that it would be very easy for someone to find a part of the forest to engage in illicit activities unseen. Emmett even tried asking them about wolfsbane, only to be met with indulgent amusement. Clearly no one in the forest believed it existed. A conclusion Farrin had reached in his own research.

He'd just dismissed the last villager when the man paused, turning back from the door.

"May I ask something, Your Highness?"

"Certainly," Emmett said, trying not to let his weariness show. It was well into the afternoon by now, and he was exhausted.

"Is it true the forest might be evacuated?" The villager must have seen the storm on Emmett's brow, because he hastened to clarify. "I'm not complaining, Your Highness. I know others feel strongly, but I can see the wisdom in it."

"Can you?" Emmett asked flatly. "You must be the first forest-dweller I've heard say so."

The man smiled awkwardly. "Yes, opinion is pretty strongly against it. But I'm not from the forest originally. I moved here a year ago, and if I'm honest, I've been thinking about moving back to the coast for months. If we're all to be asked to leave, I'd rather do so earlier, when I might be able to sell my belongings to those still staying."

"If you wish to move back to the coast, you should certainly do so," said Emmett, his voice cool. "There is nothing preventing you. But there are no imminent plans to evacuate the forest, and I am in agreement with the general view on the matter."

The man bowed clumsily, seeming to realize he'd offended the prince. He scurried from the room, leaving Emmett to his dark thoughts.

They were darker than the occasion warranted, he had the decency to admit that. He couldn't explain the anger—almost fury—that had risen up in him when the man spoke so positively about evacuating the forest. Emmett didn't like the idea, but that didn't mean he should be angry at anyone who did. Was it just the effect of the wolf, once again heightening his emotions and reducing his self-control? A depressing thought.

Unwelcome, the memory of that long-ago hunt once again surfaced. An icy chill went over Emmett as a new thought occurred to him. Was his reaction more sinister than just a heightening of his human mind's disapproval of the evacuation plan? Could his determination to keep people in Ilgal be the wolf's hunting instinct at work? Did the part of his mind under attack by the wolf look ahead to the day when the creature would have full control, wishing to ensure a plentiful supply of prey remained within reach?

The thought was too horrific to contemplate. Emmett ran both hands through his hair, dark terror threatening to overwhelm him. He tugged a little too hard as he pulled his hands away, and he felt a few strands of hair pull loose. He opened his fist, staring numbly at the dark hair...with one strand of gray.

He was twenty-three years old. He had no business having gray hair, no matter how much stress he'd been under. This wasn't the natural result of aging. It was another sign of the wolf gaining ground.

The door flew open, causing Emmett to jump slightly in his seat. He looked up, ready to chastise the steward for forgetting to knock, and his mouth fell open when he saw instead a very different face.

"Farrin!" Emmett surged to his feet, finding to his embarrassment that he was near tears. The sight of his brother drove away the last of his already-weakening self-control, and he strode across the room, throwing an arm around the younger man's shoulder and squeezing much too hard. "Farrin, how are you here? You're supposed to be in Selvana."

"Bianca sent me back," Farrin said cheerfully. "As you'd know if you were in the capital. I sent a letter weeks ago."

"Got sick of you, did she?" Emmett asked, tousling his brother's hair in a way Farrin had hated when they were children.

"Not yet," Farrin laughed. He moved across the room, his slight limp more pronounced than usual. "Mind if I sit? I only sailed in a couple days ago, and the ride from Port Dulla just about did me in."

"Of course." Emmett joined him. "Why did you race straight here the moment you landed, and why are you in Medulle at all?"

"I raced straight here because I was told you live here now, and I wanted to see you. As for the second question, I'm in Medulle to collect the first group of volunteers from the Academy of Song in Port Dulla."

Emmett straightened in his seat. "It's starting? The attempt to reclaim the ground in Selvana?"

Farrin nodded, looking eager. "And we've had more volunteers than I dared hope for. I really think this could work, Emmett."

"If it does, it will be a huge relief for the people of Ilgal," said Emmett, hope trickling in.

"Yes, true," said Farrin. He spoke as if he hadn't thought of this potential application of their plan to get singers to vent magic from the toxic Selvanan ground. Emmett barely refrained from rolling his eyes. "If it works in Selvana, we might be able to find singers willing to try it in Ilgal, to slow the growth of the magic before it reaches crisis point."

"It's already reached crisis point," Emmett informed him. "We need to act soon, Farrin."

Farrin looked troubled. "It might not be so easy, Em. I called the singers coming to Selvana volunteers, but Father is paying their way. It's part of the alliance agreement. And many of them are coming because they're excited to discover a new kingdom.

Getting enough singers to agree to come to Ilgal might not be as easy."

"Nor will convincing Father to fund it," sighed Emmett, acknowledging the point. "If only he took our relationship with Teren as seriously as our relationship with Selvana." He looked up quickly. "Not that I begrudge the alliance with Bianca's kingdom, of course."

"I understand." Farrin waved off his reassurance. "I'm sure Father values good relationship with Teren. But there's no reason to think that relationship is in danger, is there? Selvana was cut off, and—as far as anyone knew—hostile until very recently. Of course Father is delighted to have an edge over all the other kingdoms. Selvana has many commodities not found anywhere else. We stand to gain a great deal from our trade agreement."

"Speaking of commodities unique to Selvana, you'll never believe what a villager mentioned in an interview today," Emmett said, distracted at once.

"What?" Farrin asked.

"Aconitum."

"What?" Farrin shot upright in his chair, his eyes astonished. "Someone found it?"

"No, no, of course not," Emmett said. "The locals all say it's a myth. The reason it came up was that she thought it was strange someone was asking around about it. The locals don't call it aconitum. They call it wolfsbane."

"I know that," said Farrin shortly. "I spent half a year chasing down any rumor of it here in Medulle before I sailed for Selvana in search of it. I just was careful to avoid using the common name unless it was necessary. Even in Selvana I didn't give it that name. Describing the flower was enough to convince me no one had seen it. I was afraid if I called it wolfsbane, everyone would guess why I wanted it, and I would have revealed what you'd become."

Emmett grunted.

"My point being," Farrin's voice had a scolding edge now, "how did you come to be so clumsy as to ask around for it after I took such care to keep your secret hidden?"

"I didn't," said Emmett. "The woman brought it up. The man asking around about it wasn't me. I don't know who it was."

Farrin frowned. "Is it possible they just wanted it to try to ward wolves off their property? The rumors of increased wolf attacks have reached even the capital, you know."

"The same thought occurred to me," Emmett agreed. "Although I don't think the recent increase in sightings is the cause, because apparently this man has been asking after it for years."

Farrin considered this for a moment, then shrugged. "Well, good luck to him. I have good reason to think he won't find it."

He reached around, pulling a satchel onto his lap. Emmett hadn't even noticed he was wearing it.

"It's quite the coincidence that you mention aconitum," Farrin said. "That's actually one of the main reasons I came straight here. I have something for you. Something I accidentally left behind in Selvana the first time I came back, a move I admit was idiotic."

Emmett was intrigued, but he had no chance to ask, because at that moment, they heard voices in the corridor.

"Oh, yes," Farrin said quickly, giving his brother a sheepish grin. "I forgot to say that Mother also came with me."

"Mother's here?" Emmett sat straighter, trying to tame his hair with a few frantic swipes. If he'd known the queen was coming, he'd have tried to look less disheveled.

"Lost cause," Farrin muttered.

There was no time for Emmett to do more than shoot his

brother a dark look before the door swung open and Queen Sula appeared in the doorway.

"Mother," said Emmett, trying to inject warmth into his voice as he rose. He strode across the room to take her hand, smiling. "You're very welcome."

"I doubt I am," she said, her gaze indulgent as it passed between her sons. "You two were always fond of your secret chats. But you'll have to interrupt it long enough to let your mother look you over, I'm afraid."

Both sons protested as expected, but she ignored them. Her eyes were too shrewd as they passed over Emmett's form.

"You look exhausted, Emmett." A glance behind her showed that the door was closed, the steward having withdrawn. "It's getting worse, isn't it?"

Her eyes traveled down to the hand still holding hers. Emmett tried to withdraw it, but he wasn't quick enough. Her little intake of breath told him she'd seen at once what he'd managed to hide from everyone else so far.

"I see it is," she said softly.

"What are you talking about?" Farrin asked, moving forward with concern on his face. His eyes followed hers, widening at the sight of Emmett's slightly sharpened fingernails. Emmett could hardly keep his face straight as his brother's gaze met his. "It's intruding into your human form?"

Emmett nodded reluctantly. "It's starting earlier and lasting longer, as well. The full moon is almost a week away, and last night I transformed."

For a moment, no one found anything to say.

"It's good I'm here," said Farrin, his brisk tone forced. "I can help with your investigations. I'll follow up the lead regarding the aconitum, and—"

"Aconitum?" The queen's voice was sharp. "That mythical

plant you chased all the way to Selvana, almost getting yourself killed in the process?"

"We don't know for certain it's mythical," said Farrin defensively. "And I didn't get myself killed in the end, so no harm done."

The queen's expression was forbidding, and Emmett couldn't help intervening.

"Farrin."

His rebuke made his brother fall silent, looking chastened. Emmett said no more. There was nothing to be gained from saying it, but Farrin should know better. He'd been sobered and changed through his own hard experiences in Selvana. But he'd still never be able to fully understand the agony his family had suffered when they thought him dead for two whole years. It wasn't something to make light of.

"As I was saying, we don't know the plant is mythical. The record I found at that musty old library at the old academy building in Port Dulla convinced me that it did exist once. Whether it's still around, or has gone extinct, I can't say with confidence." He met Emmett's eyes. "That's what I brought for you. The original record. It went all the way to Selvana and back with me. And if you read it, I really think you'll agree that it's a credible account, not a fable."

"And the plant is supposed to be able to heal Emmett of his affliction?" Queen Sula asked skeptically.

"Well, the original plant was supposed to repel wolves," Farrin said. "Quite naturally—its smell was repulsive to them. It was rare, though. It was apparently imported from Selvana and sold as protection from wolves, but it didn't grow well without care, not being native to these parts. So it wasn't as though it was spreading wild in the forest. The record claims that a singer cultivated it and then *crossbred* it with magic, for want of a better word. There were legends of giant wolves in the forest then, as well."

"Yes, that's come up a few times when speaking to locals," Emmett said. "They grew up on those stories from generations past, and now they feel they're living them again."

Farrin nodded. "The record calls them 'abominations' and 'creatures of magic', so I don't think they were just large wolves. The aim of the singer who cultivated the aconitum was to enhance the plant's natural properties and make it able to render the magic on these creatures ineffective." He shrugged. "When I read that account, of course I thought immediately of Emmett's situation. I wondered if the magic of Ilgal had transformed someone into a wolf before now. And given the legends died out, it's reasonable to think that wolf might have been turned back. I thought if I found it in Selvana, and brought it back here, it might be possible to recreate the cultivation that enhanced its magical properties."

"So many *ifs* and guesses," said their mother. "On this speculation, you were willing to throw away your life?" The queen was clearly still on edge from Farrin's earlier flippant words.

"Anything was worth trying, Mother," Farrin said quietly. "I'm to blame for the situation Emmett is in, and I'll do anything in my power to help him."

"Nonsense," said Emmett sharply. "We've been over this before, Farrin. You're not to blame. I agree the aconitum was always a slim hope, but I will certainly pursue it."

"If Farrin's been doing so for years without success, it seems a futile use of your time," said Queen Sula sadly. "And although it breaks my heart to say it, Emmett, your time appears to be increasingly running out."

She did indeed look heartbroken, and Farrin's face had little color left. Emmett lifted a hand as if to grasp his mother's shoulder in comfort, but let it drop. He had no comfort to offer her.

"That being the case, our other plans have become urgent," the queen said, pulling herself together.

"Other plans?" Farrin repeated, his hopeful expression painful to see. "Are you pursuing another potential remedy?"

"Unfortunately not," said the queen, her eyes still on Emmett. "Emmett, we must look to the future."

Emmett grimaced. "Mother, I'm far too tired for this argument. I spent the night running wild in the forest, remember?"

"In the forest?" his mother repeated, aghast. "I thought it had been agreed years ago that you weren't allowed to set foot in the forest."

"I can't help it," Emmett told her, his shoulders drooping in defeat. "When I'm in that form, I have to move. It's as simple as that. If I'm in motion, I can keep the instincts at bay. If I tried to sit still, perhaps lie quietly in my bed the whole night, I'm sure I would lose control. And there's nowhere I can run free like that except the forest. After all, it's not as though I'm in danger," he added with brutal frankness. "By far the most dangerous thing in the forest is me."

His mother's lips were white, and it took her a moment to find her voice again. "All of this only serves to emphasize my point," she said at last. "Emmett, you must take a wife and father an heir."

"Whoa." Farrin looked quickly between his mother and his brother, taking in Emmett's hardened expression. "Mother, should Emmett really be rushing into marriage right now?"

"Of course he should," said the queen impatiently. "The escalation of his condition is alarming, even in the weeks since I've seen him. Emmett, if you delay much longer, it might be too late for you to father a—"

"Mother, stop," said Emmett, barely able to keep his anger in check. He couldn't let the wolf rise up within him, not with his mother and brother present. "The thought of forcing a wife into having a child with what I now am is repulsive to me. I simply cannot concede it."

"There's no question of forcing," the queen said, frustrated. "I tell you, any girl in the kingdom would be happy to—"

"There's no girl in the kingdom I would be happy to marry, however," Emmett said shortly. His anger was heightened by embarrassment at the unbidden thought in his mind, regarding a girl not in the kingdom of Medulle. What did Rosa have to do with any of this? Nothing, of course.

"Emmett, you must be reasonable," his mother started. "You can't just pretend that—"

A rap on the door made them all pause, the queen falling silent at once.

"Enter," called Emmett curtly. This antechamber had become a thoroughfare.

The steward walked in, his especially stately demeanor telling Emmett he disapproved, although of what, Emmett couldn't imagine.

"Your Highness, you have a visitor."

"Another one?" Emmett asked flippantly. "Did Father decide to ride over for a cozy chat?"

"The visitor, I regret to say, is not His Majesty," said the steward, stiffer than ever. "It is..." His eyes passed to the queen, and he hesitated.

"Who?" Emmett demanded, his patience worn much too thin for games.

The steward cleared his throat. "It is a young woman, Your Highness. She declined to give her name, but was very insistent that she see you."

CHAPTER ELEVEN

Emmett

"A young woman?" Emmett demanded, nonplussed.

The steward inclined his head in confirmation. "She arrived alone and on horseback. I informed her that she was not expected, but she is proving difficult to persuade."

"One of the villagers I just interviewed?" Emmett asked.

The man shook his head. "She is too well dressed for a villager," he informed Emmett. "I would guess her to be the daughter of a noble, Your Highness. Although, as I said, she is unaccompanied." His pursed lips told Emmett exactly what he thought of this brazen behavior.

A stifled noise from Farrin reminded Emmett of his company. His brother looked taken aback, but also like he was trying to hide laughter. The queen, on the other hand, looked offended.

"Well," she said. "Is this why you've been so resistant to all my prompting on the matter? I must say, Emmett, I didn't suspect you of carrying on clandestine dalliances." She frowned. "But if the girl truly is a nobleman's daughter, why keep it a secret? Why can you not marry *her*? We're past the point of being particular."

"Mother," said Emmett, his voice strangled. "Of course I haven't been carrying on dalliances. I have no more idea who this girl is than you do. Maybe she's heard of my investigations, and has some information to share." He gestured to the steward. "Show her in, please." Once the man was gone, he sent an indignant look at his relatives. "I have nothing to hide from either of you."

When the door opened once again a short time later, however, Emmett was ready to recant. As it happened, he would very much like to have hidden his reaction to the new arrival's identity from his mother and brother. Farrin, at least, was watching him with shrewd interest, and would be sure to see too much.

"Rosa!" Emmett cried, hurrying forward. His gaze took in Rosa's tousled hair and disordered cloak. She was wearing the red one again. She certainly seemed to love it. "What in the world are you doing here? Are you well? Is there some disaster?"

"Not yet," said Rosa quickly. "Although I'm afraid we're on the point of one." Her cheeks heated slightly as her eyes passed to Emmett's companions. "I beg your pardon, I didn't realize you were entertaining."

The steward cleared his throat disapprovingly from behind her. "I did inform you, ma'am, that His Highness was unavailable."

"Yes, but that's what you say when someone just doesn't want to be bothered with visitors," said Rosa fairly. "I know how these things work. And I wasn't inclined to give Emmett the option of not being bothered talking to me."

Emmett's lips twitched in spite of his best efforts.

"Thank you, that will be all," he said to the steward, who bowed himself out with obvious reluctance.

"Rosa, please allow me to introduce you to my mother, Queen Sula, and my brother, Prince Farrin."

"I'm delighted to meet you both," said Rosa.

Emmett saw that his mother, who'd been watching Rosa with a coolly assessing eye, warmed slightly at the depth and elegance of the curtsy into which the younger woman sank.

Farrin's eyes, meanwhile, were sparkling.

"Mother, Farrin," said Emmett, bracing himself for the inevitable. "This is Princess Rosa of Teren."

Queen Sula let out a squeak that she inexpertly tried to turn into a cough. "Princess Rosa?" she repeated. "The stepdaughter of King Ryker?"

"I'm afraid so," said Rosa, her cheerful tone robbing the words of any criticism of her stepfather.

"I've been invited by Queen Ada to a few social events at the castle in Terenford since my arrival," said Emmett in a dampening tone meant to curb the excitement growing visibly on his mother's face.

He glanced at his brother. Farrin was now grinning openly.

"How delightful," said Queen Sula warmly. "My dear, I'm thrilled at this unexpected chance to make your acquaintance. I've wished for the opportunity to meet you and your mother since the marriage. Somehow the years have slipped past without it occurring."

"Happens all too easily," Rosa agreed pleasantly. "Would you believe, the first time I saw Prince Emmett, I didn't even know who he was?"

Her eyes met Emmett's, a definite challenge in their depths. His jaw set, remembering their first encounter with mortifying clarity. He'd wondered whether she'd told King Ryker of that meeting in the forest. If so, the king had kept it to himself. He knew Rosa owed him no obligation that would keep her lips closed on the subject. But what did she gain from ribbing him about it in present company? Why was she so determined to be infuriating?

And how was it possible for her to be infuriating and captivating at the same time?

"You would have no reason to recognize him, of course," said Queen Sula graciously, oblivious to their silent interchange. "But I'm pleased that you have reason to do so now. My dear, I've only just arrived in Lernvale, and I regret that I'm not yet settled enough to give you a proper welcome. I would be delighted if you would walk with me as the servants show me to my rooms."

"Uh, I..." Rosa floundered, her eyes flying to Emmett's as if seeking help. Still irked by her sly reference to his forest wanderings, Emmett just raised an eyebrow. If she remembered that occasion so well, surely she remembered telling him she didn't need his rescue in any situation.

The next moment, Queen Sula had swept the unfortunate young princess out of the room with her, leaving Emmett alone again with his brother.

"Well," said Farrin, his mild tone deceiving no one. "It seems you've been holding out on me, Emmett."

"Don't be absurd," said Emmett shortly. "You have the wrong idea entirely, you and Mother both."

"All right," said Farrin amicably, wise enough to drop the matter. Emmett doubted his mother would show the same forbearance.

"Come on," said Emmett tersely. "Let's go into the gardens. I need to walk."

"You have a need to be in motion, do you?" Farrin said with a chuckle, following him to the door. "The wolf in you coming out?"

"Yes, actually." Emmett's reply was short, and it sobered Farrin at once.

"I'm sorry, Em, I—"

"Don't worry about it," said Emmett, waving the apology away. "You don't need to apologize. It's just...hard. I don't feel like myself half the time."

Farrin frowned. "You still seem like yourself, for what it's worth. Not you at your best, perhaps. You when you're tired and overworked." He gave his brother a look. "Which is a lot of the time, let's be honest. You've always pushed yourself too hard to fulfill your duty to the kingdom."

Emmett gave a harsh laugh which sounded uncomfortably like a bark. "That's the opposite of what I've done," he said.

They'd reached the gardens now, and when the castle was out of hearing range, Farrin turned the conversation.

"Mother's pretty determined to get a grandchild from you, isn't she?"

Emmett shuddered. "Can you even imagine it? What if the child was...afflicted? How can we be sure that wouldn't happen?"

"A grand-cub?" Farrin suggested.

Emmett gave him a look, and his twitching lips turned down into a serious expression. "Sorry."

"No." Emmett gave a reluctant laugh. "It is too ridiculous not to laugh, you're right."

There was a moment of silence, then Farrin stopped, putting his hand on his brother's arm to bring him to a standstill as well.

"Emmett, it's not entirely ridiculous. Racing to produce an heir without knowing the consequences is," he clarified quickly. "But...letting someone in, that's not a bad idea. I know it's terrifying. I was in less trouble than this when I met Bianca, and I still found it near impossible to let her past my defenses. But when I did, everything became much easier. For both of us. I know you, and I know you think you have to carry all your burdens alone. You think your choice is between remaining alone and deceiving some poor girl by marrying her but keeping her in the dark. Those aren't the only options. You could actually share your burden with someone. Maybe the right woman would make it easier to bear—perhaps even help find a solution." He glanced suggestively toward the out-of-sight castle. "I know you don't want to hear it, and I'm not trying to push you, but that girl seemed plenty strong enough to handle your secrets."

"Farrin..." Emmett's voice came out strangled. "My burdens are too big for Rosa, or anyone else, to be expected to shoulder. And you really do have it wrong. She doesn't even like me. I'm confident she finds the idea of any romantic entanglement with me repulsive just on my human merits—let alone how she'd feel about marrying me—producing a *child* with me—if she knew the truth."

"If you really think she finds you repulsive then you're blind or a fool," said Farrin shortly. "But I won't argue with you about that. One thing I will argue though, with every breath I have. I'm your brother, and I'm stronger than you think. You have to let me help you. It's not optional."

"Believe me, I know you're strong enough, Farrin," said Emmett seriously. "You're stronger than I am. That's not the issue. My affliction almost killed you once before. I could never live with myself if it destroyed you as well as me. But that doesn't mean you won't be called upon to help me," he added quickly, as Farrin opened his mouth to protest. "Unfortunately, I can't see any other way. I've thought it through, and I think the only viable solution for Medulle is for your second-born to inherit. Obviously your eldest will one day rule Selvana, and I'm sure it's not what you'd choose, to have your family scattered. But—"

"Emmett, stop," said Farrin, distressed. "I won't talk about contingency plans for your death. I wasn't talking about helping the kingdom." He reached into his rucksack, extracting the folded parchment and shoving it into Emmett's hands. "I want to help *you*. There's a solution, Emmett, there has to be. And we'll find it together."

"A solution to what?"

The feminine voice made them both jump, and Emmett's eyes widened in horror at the sight of Rosa emerging from a bush just behind Farrin. He shoved the parchment hastily into his pocket, his mind racing back over the conversation.

"How long were you standing there?" he demanded.

"I wasn't standing here," said Rosa calmly. "I was walking, following your voices. I heard very little, but your reaction tells me that I missed something scintillating indeed. I'm very disappointed I didn't walk more quickly."

"It's always nice to have something to work on," said Farrin, looking amused.

Rosa eyed him. "You sound like the governess on whom I was inflicted for a year after Mama became queen." Her face broke into a sudden grin. "You don't look like her, though." She turned back to Emmett, the smile hardening into a look of accusation. "You're a snake for abandoning me like that, I'll have you know." She tossed one braid over her shoulder. "But I'm very magnanimous, so I'll let it pass."

"So gracious," Farrin muttered.

His patience wearing thin, Emmett gave Rosa's arm a tug, starting to walk away from the castle and its listening ears, toward the edge of the garden that sat just inside the castle's outer wall. Farrin followed.

"Why are you here, Rosa?" Emmett demanded, once the three of them were in motion. "What would bring you riding here all alone like a common village wench?"

"You *both* sound like my governess," said Rosa, her voice awed. "A family likeness, apparently." Her eyes passed to Farrin. "What are you helping find a solution for? The crisis in the forest? Because that's why I'm here, too."

"What do you mean?" Emmett asked sharply. "Has something happened?"

"Not yet, but it's about to," said Rosa grimly. "The king is weakening on the evacuation proposal. He's seriously considering it, and I think it could happen soon."

"That would be a disaster," said Emmett. "And difficult to come back from."

"I agree," said Rosa. "No one in the castle will listen to me, and I thought they might take your opinion more seriously."

Emmett raised a helpless hand, then remembered his nails, and hurried to fold his arms behind him again. "What can I do? I've given my opinion. Most of Ilgal falls in King Ryker's territory. It's up to him how he handles his own kingdom."

"That's another reason I need your help," Rosa said quickly. "Otto and I spoke to Leonhard's sister this morning." She glanced at the sky, muttering an aside. "Hard to believe it was only this morning. This has been quite a day."

Emmett followed her gaze, realizing for the first time how far advanced the afternoon was. It was almost evening. He would need to retire soon. He couldn't afford to be in Rosa's company when his transformation set in, not again.

"Anyway, she said a lot of things that made me uneasy. I really think he's up to something, but I don't know what. Apparently he's had this scheme for a long time to see all of Ilgal become part of Teren."

Emmett's forehead creased in a frown as he thought this information over. Farrin made a noise of disapproval beside him, and Rosa hastened to explain.

"My stepfather has no part in any idea like that. It's purely from Leonhard's own head, and as far as I know, he hasn't even tried to act on it. But it makes me nervous. I don't know what he's up to, and I don't want any part of his plans to succeed." Her eyes met Emmett's, the pleading in their depths impossible to resist. "You can't yield to his ambitions, Emmett. I don't know what will come of it, but it can't be good. Don't let him take any more ground."

"Of course Medulle won't cede land to Teren," said Emmett firmly. "The forest might be beset, but it's still part of our kingdom. We have no desire to disown it."

Rosa seemed to relax, and Emmett felt his heart lighten minutely at the sight. He glanced ahead, realizing what part of the garden they'd reached.

"Wait." He put out a hand, wrapping his fingers around Rosa's arm. She came to a stop too. "I forgot that this part of the gardens is supposed to be closed off. The wall is unstable, and we're waiting for a delivery from the quarry to repair it. We shouldn't go any further."

"All right," said Rosa, not seeming quite as self-possessed as usual. Her eyes flicked to Emmett's hand on her arm.

He removed it quickly, once again remembering the state of his fingernails, and Rosa cleared her throat.

"About Leonhard, Emmett. There's another thing. I went to my grandparents' today, and they've been having a lot of scares with these big wolves in their area."

"You went into the forest?" Emmett demanded. "You didn't go alone, did you?"

"I don't see how that's any of your business," said Rosa, clearly irked. The tension of the moment before was gone. Or rather, it had changed into a different type of tension entirely. "Anyway, they think they're being targeted. The wolves seem to hang about their property. And I know that Leonhard is aware of their influence in the forest community. I think he might be controlling the wolves somehow, sending them after my grandparents."

Emmett shifted uncomfortably. "I really don't think so."

"I know it sounds crazy," said Rosa, her tone defensive. "But magic might make it possible. He comes from a family of singers."

"It doesn't sound crazy," said Emmett reassuringly. "It's a reasonable question to ask. But...I really don't think it can be the case."

"Why not?" Rosa demanded, although she looked a little mollified.

Emmett ran a hand through his hair. What could he possibly say? He had good reason for knowing the giant wolf wasn't being controlled by Leonhard. But he couldn't exactly tell her that the wolf was him, and that he hung around her grandparents' property because that's where he'd first met her, and his wolf self was obsessed with reliving the moment for some reason. He wished he could reassure her that her grandparents had nothing to fear from the wolf, but he couldn't do so without revealing far too much.

Looking to redirect the conversation, Emmett glanced around for Farrin. To his dismay, his brother was some way ahead. He must have moved on to give them space, and not heard Emmett's warning about the wall.

"Farrin!" Emmett called. He strode forward, his eyes scanning the wall against which Farrin was leaning. It looked old and worn. Was this the dangerous section?

Alarmed, he saw Farrin turn toward him, pushing off the wall behind him. The stone above him began to shift, but Emmett barely saw it. He hadn't waited to observe the outcome —he was already sprinting toward his brother.

Rosa gave a cry of warning behind him, but he didn't pause. Without even a shout, he threw himself at the younger prince, shoving Farrin out of the way. Pain lanced up his arm as he toppled onto the grass, practically on top of his brother, but it took him a while to make sense of what he felt. A huge chunk of stone was lying on the grass next to him. It must have hit his arm on the way down. The limb was responsive to movement, but the pain was still considerable.

"Emmett! You stubborn fool, stop doing that!" Farrin's voice was panicked. "One day it'll get you killed, and then what am I supposed to do?"

There was another cry from Rosa, and both princes looked up to see the section of wall above wavering. Farrin grabbed Emmett's good arm, trying to tug him, but Emmett was already surging to his feet. He charged forward, putting his shoulder into Farrin's chest and forcing them both backward away from the wall. A few more large chunks of rock fell harmlessly onto the grass, and then all was still.

"Emmett, you'll destroy your arm!" Farrin cried reproachfully.

Emmett followed his brother's gaze down. Pain radiated out from the injury, which was already beginning to bruise, and Emmett realized that he'd pushed his brother with the shoulder attached to his injured arm. Everything ached, but it was nothing serious.

"I'm all right," he assured Farrin. "You were right under it, Farrin, it could have fallen on your head."

"Are you sure you're all right?" Rosa had hurried to his side, her dark hair a disordered frame around a face that was even paler than usual. "That looked bad."

"I'm fine," Emmett assured her. Her face didn't relax, and he felt his forehead crease in confusion. Why did she seem so rattled by the accident? She'd been nowhere near the falling stone.

"I need to go," she said suddenly, glancing again at the sky. "I told myself that if I rode hard, I could get here and back home before dark, but it took longer than I thought. My family will be furious with me as it is." She mustered a weak smile. "Thank you for your assurances regarding the border. I hope you might consider my suggestion more. I really think my step-father will give a lot of weight to your opinion regarding the evacuation."

"Rosa," Emmett protested. "You can't ride home alone now. The ride will take hours!"

"I'll be fine," she said airily, her voice a little too high and not very convincing. "I'm afraid the poor horse I brought has been worked too hard today, though. He's Otto's stallion, and the head groom will throw me into a pit if I do him any damage. If he can spend the night in your stables, someone can come to retrieve him tomorrow. Would it be possible for me to borrow a horse?"

"You're not borrowing a horse," said Emmett shortly, cradling his injured arm with his good hand. "I'll take you home in a carriage."

"That's not necessary," Rosa started to say, but Farrin beat her to it.

"Don't be ridiculous, Emmett, you're in no fit state."

"I told you, I'm fi—"

"Emmett." Farrin cut his brother off, his eyes full of meaning. "You're in no fit state."

Emmett hesitated, realizing his own foolishness. The sun would be setting in an hour. Of course he couldn't take Rosa home. But he wanted to, so badly. He wanted to finish their conversation, but he was also terrified for her safety, traveling alone after dark. This area of the forest used to be fairly safe, but in recent times wolf packs had been seen more commonly. He had a horrible feeling they'd been driven from their usual territory by his own presence, as the villager had guessed earlier. Try as he might, he couldn't seem to keep his wolf self away from the area near Rosa's home. He was drawn there as irresistibly as he was being drawn now.

For a moment, he wrestled with himself, trying to regain his control. He half believed that if Farrin hadn't been there, he would have given in to his impulses and accompanied Rosa, in spite of the disaster that would inevitably follow.

But he couldn't do that. It would be a catastrophe from which he could never recover. His sense reasserted itself, and he deflated in Farrin's grip. His brother was right. He was in no state.

"Let's get you to the physician," said Farrin, recognizing that the battle was won. "Get that arm seen to." He smiled at Rosa, and Emmett felt a stab of completely irrational jealousy. "Give me half an hour, and I'll be ready, Princess Rosa. I'll see you safely home."

Rosa said nothing, still not seeming quite her usual self. Emmett could barely meet her eye as his brother hauled him away, up the steps to the castle. She must think he'd lost his mind.

In spite of Farrin's confident words, having Emmett's arm treated wasn't so simple. The castle in Lernvale was so often unoccupied that they didn't keep a physician permanently in residence. The steward, made aware of the situation, informed them regretfully that one would have to be sent for.

"There's no point, Farrin," Emmett muttered, as the steward gave hurried instructions to an underling regarding the unstable wall. "By the time a physician comes, I won't be able to be treated."

Farrin frowned. "I don't like it."

"My arm will be fine," Emmett said impatiently. His mind on more important matters, he called the steward over. "Please have a carriage prepared for Princess Rosa to return to Terenford."

"Princess...Rosa?" The steward's face was pale.

"That's right," said Emmett. "She's waiting in the garden for Prince Farrin to escort her safely to her family. They should have armed guards to accompany them as well."

"But..." The steward swallowed. "If you're referring to the

young woman in the red cloak, she's already left, Your Highness."

"What?" Emmett said sharply. "What are you talking about?"

"She...she approached the stables ten minutes ago," the steward said. "She asked for a steed to be prepared for her, and for the one she came on to be stabled overnight. The head groom sent a message asking if the loan of a horse was authorized."

"And what did you say?" Emmett demanded.

"I...I thought it a small price to pay for her departure, Your Highness," said the steward pleadingly. "I thought she would be sure to bring the horse back if she wished to reclaim her own mount, which I understand to be of high quality. I told the groom to saddle the young roan."

"The young roan?" Emmett repeated, horrified. "That's the most skittish horse in the stables! How could you think it was appropriate for a foreign princess to ride?"

"I didn't know she was a princess, Your Highness," the steward said miserably. "I was never informed of her identity. I thought—"

"Never mind what you thought," snarled Emmett, already in motion toward the door. "I'm going after her."

"Emmett!" Farrin called, jogging to keep up. "It's almost dark! You can't go now."

"You don't understand, Farrin," said Emmett. "It's not safe out there. Even assuming she follows the road, it'll take her through the forest for a considerable distance before turning northward. Wolves are common in this area these days. And that horse will throw her and bolt if so much as a rabbit skitters across her path."

"So let me go!" Farrin insisted.

"Maybe you didn't hear me," said Emmett, hearing the growl

in his words but refusing to think about what it meant. "It's dangerous. You're not risking your neck for my mistakes. Not again."

They'd reached the stables, and Emmett barked out an order for his most reliable horse to be saddled. Farrin called for a horse as well, but Emmett was quick to override his command.

"Anyone who lets my brother take a horse out of this building is fired," he told the shocked stable. "Farrin, stay here and make sure Mother is looked after."

Without waiting to listen either to Farrin's protests or to the voice of reason screaming in his mind in a desperate attempt to curb his growing recklessness, Emmett swung into the saddle. Within moments, he was riding out of the gate and onto the forest road.

CHAPTER TWELVE

Rosa

Rosa urged her mount onward with a moan. She considered herself a good rider, but she'd never ridden such a difficult horse before. The creature pranced across the road, only occasionally responsive to her direction, its pace erratic.

At this rate, she'd be lucky to get home by midnight.

She glanced around her, trying to tell herself that she wasn't spooked by the long shadows cast on the road. The sun hadn't yet set, but it couldn't be too far off. She dragged her eyes from the undergrowth, which already looked as dark as night.

Think about something else, she told herself firmly.

Obediently, her thoughts turned back to the prince she'd just left behind. She'd been able to see the moment she arrived how foolish her impulsive ride had been. What magic did she think Emmett could work to change her stepfather's mind? At least he hadn't dismissed her request out of hand.

And it had been interesting to meet Prince Farrin. A frown crossed Rosa's lips as she thought about the final scene she'd witnessed between Emmett and his brother, when Prince Farrin had told Emmett he was in no state to accompany her. There had been a silent conversation going on, separate from the one she could hear. And she had no idea what the younger prince's eyes had been saying. Did he think there was something between her and Emmett? Perhaps he disapproved, and wanted to talk his brother down.

Her cheeks heated with the thought. Best not to dwell on that.

She thought instead about the other royal she'd just met, and winced. Unlike with Prince Farrin, Rosa had no difficulty deciphering the messages the older woman left unsaid. Queen Sula certainly hadn't disapproved of her presence in Emmett's life. On the contrary, she'd been friendly. Much too friendly. She had, in fact, treated Rosa exactly how Rosa's mother kept treating Emmett.

Heaven help them both if the two queens ever met. Their combined scheming might be a force too strong for even Rosa's stubbornness and Emmett's unyielding nature to overcome.

It was very unfortunate timing, all things considered, Rosa reflected. Why did the queen and younger prince have to appear right at the moment she'd ridden to Lernvale to speak with Emmett? Now the queen would have false expectations. Not to mention Rosa had presented a less than elegant appearance. She hadn't expected anyone but Emmett and a handful of servants to see. Her mother would be mortified if she ever got wind of the fact that Queen Sula and Prince Farrin had witnessed Rosa's brazen behavior.

A rustle in the bush made Rosa start. She was still spooked from her near miss earlier in the day. She hadn't intended to enter the forest again anytime soon. Truth be told, she hadn't realized that the road south to Lernvale entered the forest so long before reaching the castle.

"Not far now," she told her mount in a soothing voice that

only made the animal prance nervously. "Soon we'll be out from between the trees."

Her words were drowned out by a sudden howl, and a shiver of true fear went over Rosa. That had been a wolf. She was sure of it.

Apparently, so was the mount she was riding. The horse skittered across the road, shying away from the sound. Then another howl came, this one on the opposite side, and the horse lost its head completely.

Bolting, it carried Rosa straight into the trees. She tried valiantly to steer it back toward the road, but she knew at once that it was useless. She could only cling on in terror as the horse crashed through the brush. When the terrified roan cleared a fallen tree, even that feat became impossible. Rosa tumbled straight off it into the undergrowth.

Thankfully she was unhurt, but as she scrambled to her feet, she had to acknowledge that her situation was still disastrous. The horse, poor creature, was already out of sight, so there was no likelihood of remounting it. And it had carried her far enough from the road that she was now surrounded by trees on all sides. Rosa swallowed nervously, picking her way back toward the road. At least, she thought she was going toward the road. But after several minutes, she began to fear she'd gone in the wrong direction. Should she turn around and retrace her steps? Or would that take her deeper into the forest?

Fighting down panic, she drew in a deep breath. She'd been foolish to ride off like she had. She should have overcome her embarrassment and taken the offered escort. This was what came of her pride and determination not to need anyone's rescue. But there was no sense dwelling on her own stupidity. She had to focus on getting out of this mess alive. Peering around her, she decided that she had been going the right way all along. She just needed to push on a little further.

A long, haunting howl froze her in her tracks, making her blood freeze. That had been much too close. Rosa's breaths were coming faster now, and she broke into a run. She had to reach the road. Surely they wouldn't follow her there. Would they?

They didn't have to. The road was still hidden behind the trunks when a flash of gray brought Rosa's head whipping up. A wolf was standing in her path. It was a regular sized one, but no less terrifying. A rustle behind her made her whip around, and she saw two more prowling toward her from a different direction. She was being surrounded.

Her eyes darted around, looking for a means of escape. But even if she found a hole in the circle, there was no way she could outrun a wolf pack. Her eyes landed on a tree within arm's reach, and she didn't stop to think. She hurled herself toward it, scratching her knuckles as she scrambled up it, pulling herself from branch to branch. The wolves snarled, leaping after her, but they weren't quick enough. She was a child of the forest, and she could scale a tree with lightning speed. Soon she was on a high branch, breathing in pants as she stared down at four growling wolves.

Just then, Rosa heard the sound of approaching hooves. The road must be close after all! And whoever was riding past was doing so at a fast gallop.

"HELP!" she shouted as loudly as she could. "In here! In the trees! WOLVES!"

The hoofbeats faltered, and hope swelled in Rosa's heart. Had they heard her?

"In here!" she cried again. The next moment, there was a sound of breaking branches, and a magnificent horse burst into the space immediately below her perch. To Rosa's immense relief, the wolves scattered before the creature and its rider.

"Rosa!" cried a familiar voice.

Rosa's mouth fell open, and she clutched the nearest branch, allowing herself to crane her neck for a better look.

"Emmett? What are you doing here?"

"What do you think I'm doing here?" he demanded furiously. "What are *you* doing here? Why did you ride off like that? Do you *want* to get eaten by wolves?"

"Not especially," said Rosa testily. Her elation at the rescue was wearing off, her limbs shaking as the reality of her second near miss in one day set in. "I wasn't going to get eaten," she said, knowing her flare of temper was unreasonable, but not able to hold herself in check. "They can't climb trees."

"Oh, in that case, you were fine," said Emmett sarcastically. "I could have sworn I heard you screaming for help through the trees, but I must be mistaken. I suppose I should have left you there and kept riding."

"I wasn't screaming," said Rosa, mortified. Any desire to be reasonable was fleeing fast. "And yes, you should have. I'm perfectly capable of waiting out a pack of wolves. It wouldn't be the first time I'd slept in a tree."

"Not the first, but the last," said Emmett tersely. Rosa frowned, trying to make out his features through the gathering gloom. He looked like he was in pain. "Come on, Rosa."

"Come on, what?" she asked.

"Get out of the tree." Emmett's voice was a growl now.

To Rosa's surprise, a trickle of fear shot up her back, some instinct telling her to stay safely aloft. Ashamed, she forced herself to do the opposite, climbing stiffly to the branch below. She wasn't afraid of Emmett, no matter how sternly he spoke to her. That was absurd.

"I am getting out of the tree," she said loftily. "But there's no need to take that tone. Just because you consider yourself the world's rescuer doesn't mean you can tell me what I need to do."

"Why are you so infuriating?" Emmett growled.

Rosa didn't look at him, too focused on her passage downward, but she narrowed her eyes at the branch she was navigating.

"It's because we've spent too much time together," she informed him brutally. "I'm learning your ways."

She knew her behavior was absurd, her words twisted by the belated effects of her fear. But she didn't much care, not while Emmett continued to growl at her. When she finally reached the ground, she turned to face him, only to find he'd slid from the horse, so that the animal was between the two of them.

"Emmett?" she asked uncertainly.

"Unfortunately, I'm too unwell to see you home," he said, his voice stiff and disapproving. "And given the hour, I don't think it's wise for you to turn back to Lernvale. Take my horse. He's fast and reliable and will get you home safely. You're almost out of the forest."

Rosa stared at what little she could see of Emmett, confused. She didn't believe for a moment that Emmett was too unwell to accompany her, and it seemed very unlike him to suddenly relinquish his determination to do his duty and indulge his overprotective instincts. Not that she was complaining. If he didn't want to come with her, she wasn't going to force him.

"What about you?" she demanded.

"I'll go after the other horse," he said, the words clipped and tight, as if he was in pain. Perhaps the injury to his arm had been worse than she realized. "I assume the foolish creature bolted when the wolves appeared."

"It did," Rosa confirmed. "And that was a while ago. You'll never catch it now. And if you're not well, you shouldn't be wandering around the forest looking for a horse. I won't take your mount and leave you with nothing."

"Enough talk," said Emmett. The tone wasn't at all angry, and yet the words somehow still sounded like a snarl.

Before Rosa knew what he was about, the prince strode around the horse's head. She had no time to look up into his face. She'd barely registered his proximity when he seized her around the waist and threw her up into the saddle.

Rosa let out a gasp, both from the sudden motion, and from the heat of Emmett's hands through her gown. She was still trying to get her balance when Emmett gave the creature a solid slap, issuing a command in that same husky voice.

"Wait!" Rosa craned around, trying to catch Emmett's eye through the fading light, but the horse was already in motion. Within seconds, it burst onto the road, and Rosa had little choice but to settle in as it thundered eastward.

The ride home was miserable, and felt twice as long as the ride to Lernvale had done. It was fully dark by the time they emerged from the trees, and Rosa was soon chilled to the bone. She half expected to encounter a Terenan escort on the road. She wouldn't have been surprised if her mother had reacted to her note by immediately sending a carriage after her to retrieve her whether she liked it or not. But no escort appeared on the mostly deserted road. Rosa had plenty of time to regret her various hasty decisions and unfair retorts as Emmett's enormous steed carried her back to Terenford. It was a good thing she was an experienced rider, or such a big horse might have been too much for her.

As they moved northward, Rosa's mind circled anxiously around Emmett's situation. What was going on with him? Why had he been so determined to send her away? Was he truly sick? From the little she'd seen of him, he'd looked very much the worse for wear. Was he safely back in his own castle by now, or was he wandering the forest alone, vulnerable to the wolf pack he'd so narrowly saved her from?

Because now that her temper had cooled, she fully acknowledged that he had saved her. Much as she hadn't wanted to admit it, she'd been terrified before he came, and elated beyond words when he appeared.

She let out a groan, leaning down into the horse's mane. Was she imagining it, or did the creature smell like Emmett? Rosa sat up straight again, scolding herself. Yes, he'd rescued her, and yes, she was grateful. She'd tell him as much when she next saw him, and apologize for her rude reception of his help. That didn't mean she had to get soppy and sentimental in the meantime.

When Rosa finally rode through the gates of Terenford, she was so weary it was all she could do to stay in the saddle. She tumbled into the courtyard outside the royal stables, mustering enough energy to instruct the approaching groom to take special care of the horse. Emmett would come to claim it the next day, she told herself. He would bring Bullion and come for his horse. And she'd be able to assure herself that he was safe, and thank him for his intervention.

On that optimistic thought, she moved wearily into the castle, wanting nothing but bed. But first she needed to speak to her mother, and assure her that she'd returned home safely.

When Rosa knocked on her mother's receiving room, the door was flung immediately open. She blinked in surprise at the sight of not only her mother, but her stepfather and stepbrother clustered around the fire. Their anxious expressions smoothed instantly to relief at sight of her, and her mother raced forward with a little cry.

"Rosa, you're alive!"

"Of course I'm alive," said Rosa. "I'm sorry if I made you worry, Mama. To be honest, I thought it would be a shorter ride, and I'd be back before now, but it's not so late, is it? I thought I heard the clock chime nine when I passed through market square."

"The lateness of the hour is not the issue," said her mother irately, her relieved expression already gone in favor of irritation. "Rosa, how could you do it to me? To all of us? We've been beside ourselves."

"I am disappointed, Rosa," her stepfather said gravely. "I made it clear you weren't to return to your grandparents' house, and I know they said the same. Returning there against everyone's wishes was foolish. And when the guards sent to bring you safely home found no trace of you, we feared the worst."

"I didn't go to my grandparents' house," said Rosa, the color draining from her face as she comprehended what she'd put them all through. "I'm reckless, but not that reckless. Mama, didn't you get my note?"

"Note?" her mother repeated faintly. "What note?"

Rosa drew a shaky breath, fresh guilt piling on top of what she already felt regarding the day's misadventures. "The one telling you that I know you'll be angry, and I hope you'll forgive me, but I was going for one last unsanctioned trip before saying goodbye to my freedom. I told you I wasn't going into the forest, but I wasn't completely right about that. I mean, I did ride to Lernvale as the note said, but it turns out that road passes through the forest for a short way right before reaching the castle. I didn't realize that."

"Lernvale?" her mother repeated in astonishment. "Where did you leave this note?"

"In your writing desk," said Rosa, gesturing toward the window. "Right there."

"My writing desk?" The queen sounded exasperated. "Rosa, why would you leave it there? I never sit there. No one found it."

"I don't know," said Rosa helplessly. "It seemed a logical place. I used your writing paper."

Otto had already crossed the room, his eyes scanning the note quickly. His expression, which had been painfully strained, was returning to the long-suffering exasperation Rosa was used to from him.

"I'm truly sorry, Mama," said Rosa. She turned to the others. "All of you. I didn't mean to cause you so much worry, but I should have realized that's what would happen. I didn't think, and I'm sorry."

"I'm just glad you're in one piece," said Otto frankly.

"But why did you go to Lernvale?" demanded Queen Ada.

"I wanted to speak to Emmett," said Rosa. "Prince Emmett, I mean," she corrected hurriedly, but the damage was already done. Her mother's eyes had gone from harassed to enraptured in record time.

"About what?" King Ryker asked, not so easily sidetracked.

Rosa faced him. "About the evacuation idea," she said. "I hoped he would support me. I hoped that together we could convince you not to proceed with it."

"Together," murmured her mother, as if the word was the sweetest one she'd ever heard.

"Mama, don't get ideas," Rosa begged, knowing it was futile.

"I'm your mother, Rosa," the queen said shortly. "I'll get whatever ideas I like." Her brow puckered. "Speaking of which, what must people have thought of you, paying an unaccompanied visit like that? Rosa, it's too much!"

"It's not like it was some clandestine rendezvous, Mama," Rosa said quickly. "Queen Sula and Prince Farrin were visiting Prince Emmett, so they were there too."

"They were?" The queen brightened at once. "Are they staying long?"

"I don't know," said Rosa, nonplussed.

The queen gave a knowing nod. "So no time to waste, then. I'd best send out invites first thing. I'm sure the queen and younger prince would be delighted to join us."

"What? Mama—"

Rosa broke off, recognizing that she'd already lost her mother's attention. She turned back to the others. Otto was shaking his head, looking half amused, half rueful. Even her stepfather looked taken aback at how quickly his wife had gone from justified outrage to excited matchmaking.

Well, Rosa wasn't one to judge. Her emotions had taken her on bizarre and illogical wanderings that night. Her mother's earlier anger and subsequent elation were probably both heightened by the intensity of the fear she'd been feeling in Rosa's absence. Rosa had responded much the same way when Emmett found her in the tree, although in her case it had been in reverse.

The thought made her pause, remembering Emmett's anger. Had that been fueled by fear as well? Had he also had strong emotions regarding Rosa's safety which had hindered his ability to keep his equilibrium?

Better not to explore that thought too much.

Except, as soon as she banished it, another thought swept in to take its place. Rosa's own fear even earlier in the evening, when Emmett had leaped in front of falling stone to protect his brother. Rosa had been rattled by the strength of her reaction. She'd been nothing short of horrified at the thought of Emmett being hurt, and even seeing the minor nature of the damage hadn't made the feeling dissipate as quickly as it should have. Even Farrin had responded similarly. He'd expressed anger with Emmett for putting himself in harm's way for Farrin's sake.

Just like Rosa had done.

Her thoughts flowed on from that moment to the one in the forest. Contrary creature that she was, Rosa had been irked by Emmett swooping in to the rescue, even while she'd been grateful to be saved from the wolves. Poor Emmett. All he got was anger and reproach, even when he was selflessly protecting others.

When Rosa finally reached her bed, she still couldn't shake those two memories. She found herself reliving her earliest encounters with Emmett as well. She'd been so offended by his attempt to help her in the forest that first day, when she wasn't in the least in need of help. She'd also assumed he approached her in the ballroom in order to rescue her from insufferable suitors, although he'd seemed confused when she accused him of that.

Now she knew him better, the simple truth was undeniable. She'd been unfair to him. She had assumed he was someone who liked to be the rescuer because it tickled his pride and sense of importance. She'd thought he came to her aid because he considered himself strong and her weak, because she was a woman, or alone, or younger than him. She'd thought it was a failing of his, a sign of an overinflated ego.

But she'd misjudged him. When he'd leaped to save his brother, it hadn't been a considered decision born of pride. It had been an instinct, and not a self-serving one. He didn't think his brother was weak or foolish. That much had been evident from the interactions she'd witnessed between them. Emmett just had a deep protective instinct. That wasn't to say the application was never misguided. But at his core, he was driven by the desire to protect others from harm, and it was an entirely selfless one.

And for this she'd punished him since the moment they met.

For some reason, in spite of the exhaustion of the day, Rosa took a long time to drift into sleep.

When she woke the next morning, everything was sore. Her hands and arms were scratched from climbing the tree, her posterior was bruised from so many hours in the saddle, and her head ached from lack of sleep.

But she was alive, and safely home, and her family had

forgiven her more quickly than she deserved. Determined not to mope, Rosa dressed quickly and made her way toward the dining hall. Her route took her past her stepfather's study, and she slowed her steps as she approached, recognizing the voice drifting out. The guards on either side of the door eyed her eavesdropping disapprovingly, but she ignored them. If the matter was actually confidential, the door would be closed. Leonhard must have weaseled his way into an informal visit by appearing uninvited.

"—must surely agree that it's deeply concerning to hear of these increased sightings on the Medullan side of the border as well. And, much as I hesitate to say it, it doesn't seem as though King Johannes takes much interest in addressing the problem."

"If you're going to suggest that Teren should incorporate that part of Ilgal currently within Medulle's borders, you needn't waste your breath, Leonhard," King Ryker said. He spoke more tersely than Rosa had ever heard him be with the advisor. "I'm aware that you harbor such ideas, and I have no interest in them. I am satisfied with the current borders of my kingdom."

"Your Majesty mistakes," stammered Leonhard, clearly taken aback. "I didn't mean to suggest...that is, of course Your Majesty has no desire to take another kingdom's..." He trailed off, then tried again. "That wasn't what I was saying, Your Majesty, but I must confess that hearing *you* say it makes me wonder whether—"

"Don't wonder it any further," said the king. "Land doesn't change hands without conflict, and I have no interest in conflict with Medulle."

Rosa stepped forward, deliberately putting herself in the pair's line of sight. Leonhard's eyes flew to her, startled, and Rosa allowed herself a smirk. She couldn't remember the last time she'd felt so gleeful. She had no doubt Leonhard had a careful strategy in mind, and that today was to be the first, very gentle attempt to plant a seed in the king's mind. He probably hadn't intended to mention shifting the border. Just to create concern over what would happen to that part of Ilgal under Medulle's control, and how it would affect Teren. But Rosa had forestalled him by outing his ultimate goal, allowing the king to recognize his tactics from the beginning.

It was immensely satisfying.

She also realized that she'd underestimated her stepfather in thinking he'd need Emmett's influence to resist any persuasions Leonhard might attempt in that direction. He'd handled the advisor decisively all on his own.

Leonhard took in her expression, his eyes narrowing in anger. King Ryker must have noticed it, because his eyes slid to the doorway, and his expression shifted.

"Rosa," he said. "Good morning."

Leonhard took his leave, barely acknowledged by either royal as he swept from the room. Rosa approached her stepfather, smiling a little hesitantly. She wasn't sure how much trouble she was still in.

"Good morning."

To her surprise, her stepfather said nothing about the day before. He considered her with his eyes for a long moment before speaking at all.

"Rosa, I know you don't like Leonhard. I understand that his proposals have set you against him, perhaps irrevocably. But you should take more care. There's nothing to be gained by acquiring enemies."

Rosa smiled grimly. "Thank you for the advice, but you forget that I'm not in your shoes. I have nothing to gain from keeping his favor. To speak frankly, I already consider Leonhard my enemy. I don't mind in the least having the state of affairs between us openly acknowledged."

The king sighed. "A little diplomacy wouldn't do you any harm, Rosa."

"You're probably right," said Rosa, plastering on a smile. "Thank you for being so patient with me."

It was rare for her stepfather to express any criticism of Rosa. She'd noted how careful he was not to do it ever since her mother married him. So it was in a chastened frame of mind that she left his study and made her way toward breakfast.

CHAPTER THIRTEEN

Emmett

It was in a weary and bedraggled state that Emmett climbed into his bed shortly after dawn. Another miserable night as a wolf had passed, but at least this time he'd stuck close to Lernvale. He was almost completely sure of it.

His hands were still not quite right, and his voice still sounded like a growl, but he was human again. And he was fully back in his right mind. If only that brought more relief. His last thought as he succumbed to sleep at last was of Rosa, trapped in a tree and screaming for help.

His sleep was far from restful.

When he woke, the morning was well advanced. Again, none of the servants commented on his behavior the night before, or how late he'd slept. They were all acting as though everything was completely normal, and Emmett found it more frustrating than confused questions would have been. Had his mother been in the servants' ears? What had she told them?

He tried to shake off both his suspicious thoughts and his surliness. It wasn't like him to be resentful of what others might be thinking of him. But with his head pounding and his bruised arm aching, it was hard to emerge from his irritable mood.

The moment he entered the room where his mother and brother were talking, the queen started ordering food for his refreshment.

"No thank you, Mother," said Emmett quickly.

"Don't be absurd, you must be starving at this hour," she said.

Sighing, Emmett tried again. "No, really, I don't want—"

"Emmett, you must eat something, or you'll simply—"

"I don't like any of what they'll bring," Emmett snapped, cutting her off with a rudeness he instantly regretted.

The queen just studied him in silence for a moment, before turning to the servant who was hovering anxiously.

"Very well. We will eat a more substantial luncheon today. Have the cook prepare some venison, please."

Emmett sank back into a chair, grateful and chastened. Venison sounded good enough to make his nose twitch. He prevented it from doing so. He intended to apologize to his mother as soon as the servant was gone, but she didn't give him a chance.

"Emmett, I'm so glad you've joined us," she said briskly. "We were just discussing your situation. Clearly it's worsened."

"Mother, the poor man's just woken up," said Farrin. He frowned at Emmett. "How's your arm? We can call the physician now without any fear, I assume."

"My arm is fine," said Emmett, waving it for effect. "It's a little bruised, but nothing serious."

"I don't think you should be the judge of that," Farrin said, his frown deepening.

Emmett shifted in his seat, another sigh escaping him. "And I don't think we'd be wise to have a physician examine me. There are plenty of things he might find that we'd prefer to remain hidden."

Farrin bit his lip, but it was the queen who spoke.

"We will defer to your judgment on that, Emmett. But about the other matter, we really must discuss it."

"My worsening condition?" Emmett asked warily.

"The urgency created by your worsening condition," his mother elaborated. "Emmett, you must overcome this foolish reluctance to take a wife. Princess Rosa seemed perfectly lovely to me, and she's eligible! Extremely so."

"Mother," groaned Emmett. "Please, don't start with that."

"If you refuse to think of the future, I must do so, Emmett, little as I relish it," she said tightly. "An alliance with Teren would be an excellent thing for Medulle, as well."

"Formal alliances take time to orchestrate, Mother," Emmett said impatiently. "Time I likely don't have."

"You don't know that," said his mother stubbornly.

"There's no way Teren would ally itself with me in my state." Emmett's teeth were gritted now.

"They don't need to know all the details," his mother said maddeningly. "We just need to—"

"Trap their princess and their kingdom," Emmett spat out.

"Em." Farrin's voice was quiet. "Calm down."

Emmett looked down at his brother, wondering when he'd stood up. He had no memory of doing it, but he was on his feet now, and his mother looked alarmed. Emmett tried to pull himself back into line, but emotions were coursing so powerfully through him that he couldn't be still. Anger was the dominant one.

"This is all irrelevant, Mother, because Princess Rosa has no interest in me," he said tightly. "Nor I in her." The addition was said even more tensely, and Emmett found himself pacing the room.

"Well, then." The queen sounded put out. "There are other options, of course. I think I will proceed with the idea I mentioned to you before you left Port Dulla. I'll host an event here, in Lernvale, and invite eligible parties both from the region and the capital. I'm sure many won't object to traveling."

"Mother," growled Emmett, hearing the wolfishness of the sound, but unable to help it.

"Of course we will host it as far from the full moon as the cycle allows," his mother assured him. "There will be no danger. And for the sake of politeness, I think we should invite the Terenan royal family. Just because you say Princess Rosa has no interest in you doesn't mean we should exclude her from consideration. Especially since—"

"Mother, NO!" Emmett's words were more roar than growl this time, and the queen fell silent at once, her expression shocked. "We're not doing that," said Emmett angrily. "I told you already that I'm not marrying anyone while I'm in this state." His chest was heaving as he paced across the room, and it was only the look in his brother's eyes that stopped his tongue.

Clenching his fists and drawing a deep breath, Emmett forced himself to stop walking. He saw Farrin's concern and his mother's horror, and shame washed over him instantly. The desire to rage and yell was still within him, but he wrestled it down, refusing to let it take control again.

"I'm sorry, Mother," he said quietly. "Although I meant what I said about hosting an event, I should not have raised my voice. The truth is..." He swallowed, hating the admission. "The truth is that my temper is very short these days. It's something I find difficult to control, which was never the case before."

"No, it wasn't," his mother agreed, still taken aback. "Thank you for your apology, Emmett. If you are so set against the idea of hosting an event, I'll leave it for now. But this conversation is not finished." She rose. "I will see you both at luncheon."

With that, she swept gracefully from the room. Emmett had a sneaking suspicion that she was going to nurse her rattled nerves in private, but he tried not to dwell on it. The desire to prevent his parents from witnessing his descent into the monster was one of the reasons he'd wanted to leave the capital.

"You all right, Em?" There was no judgment in Farrin's soft voice.

Emmett dropped into an armchair with a groan, burying his face in his hands. "Of course I'm not."

"You don't seem your normal self," Farrin observed, his tone prompting Emmett to elaborate.

Emmett dropped his hands, looking up heavily. "I don't feel it either. What I said to Mother was true. My temper is short these days."

He hesitated, unable to bring himself to share his other thought. But privately, he was afraid there was another reason for his overreaction to his mother's words. He couldn't be sure his feelings about Rosa's poor opinion of him came from the wolf, not his true self. Having to repeatedly assure his mother of the Terenan princess's lack of interest was trying his composure in a different way from all the rest.

"The deterioration in my temper is as clear a progression as the change in my gait, or my eating habits," he said instead. "I can feel it, Farrin. All the time."

"Feel what?" Farrin leaned forward, his arms on his knees and his expression full of concern as he met his brother's eye.

"The wolf." The words came out a whisper. "I can feel it inside me, wanting to swallow me whole. Even when I'm human, it's there. My inhibition is lower, my anger is closer to the surface. I feel reckless, and barely in control. I don't feel like myself at all. At least, not the self I used to be. That person is harder to find."

"Emmett." Farrin's voice was hollow. He stood, coming to stand behind Emmett's chair and laying a reassuring hand on his shoulder. "I'm sorry. We're going to find a way out of this. If I'd realized time was so short, I'd have come sooner."

Emmett shook his head. "You couldn't have come sooner, Farrin. You shouldn't even be here now. You have a new kingdom and new responsibilities, and they're what brought you to Medulle this time. You can't afford to get pulled down into my troubles."

"Nonsense," said Farrin sharply. "You're my brother, Emmett, and everything else can wait. I know for a fact that Bianca would agree if she were here to be asked about it."

Emmett said nothing. He appreciated his brother's support, and he wasn't going to push Farrin to hurry away if he was determined to stay. But Emmett couldn't see what his brother could really do.

"What happened last night?" Farrin asked, sounding hesitant. "You rode out of here in a state—did you find Princess Rosa?"

Emmett nodded, swallowing a lump that seemed determined to rise in his throat. "She was in a tree, surrounded by a pack of wolves."

"What?!" Farrin's eyes were wide with alarm. It was a pale echo of the remembered fear Emmett felt. When he'd heard her scream—but it was better not to think about that.

"She got down all right," Emmett assured his brother. "And I sent her home on my horse. By that time I was in no state to see her anywhere. I was lucky to get her in the saddle and out of sight before I fully became the wolf. It was a pretty near thing."

"I hope she managed all right," Farrin commented. "That's a big horse, and presumably had your saddle on it."

Emmett cracked a smile, the expression feeling out of place. "From what I saw, I don't think she would have had too much trouble. She didn't hesitate for a moment when mounting into the saddle. Something tells me she doesn't ride with a lady's saddle usually."

Farrin smiled. "Good for her." His tone turned rueful.

"Apparently that skittish roan found its way home in the early hours of the morning."

Emmett snorted. "That's good, I suppose. I didn't think the creature had it in him, honestly."

"Did you get a chance to look over the record I brought?" Farrin asked, abruptly changing the topic.

Emmett nodded. "I wish now that I'd paid more attention anytime the villagers mentioned those old legends. It'll be worth asking more questions about that, to try to ascertain if it could be an old account of the same affliction. I'll have to be careful, though. I don't want to risk anyone guessing the truth."

"Do you think the servants suspect?" Farrin asked.

"They suspect something, without question," Emmett said. "Whether they suspect that I spend my absent nights running the forest as a giant wolf...that's harder to say. It seems unlikely, because although they act conspiratorial at times, none of them seem afraid of me."

"I'll see what I can find out," said Farrin briskly. "I know the right questions to ask. I'll go swipe some pastries from the kitchen and weasel information out of the kitchen maids without them realizing I'm doing it. And tomorrow I'll wander into the closest village, pretend I'm there to check out the market wares for novelty's sake, and see what I can discover."

"I can do that today, while you're asking around here," said Emmett quickly.

Farrin shook his head. "I think it's best if you lie low, Emmett. Your arm needs to heal, and it will be less suspicious if I ask questions."

Emmett wanted to protest, but truthfully he was so weary he didn't really object to sinking back into the armchair he'd just vacated. He fell into an uneasy doze from which a servant had to rouse him for luncheon.

After the meal, Farrin disappeared again, and the queen

tried to work on Emmett regarding the idea of hosting an event. She didn't say as much, and Emmett had no doubt she thought she was being subtle. But he knew what her comments and questions were getting at, and it was all he could do to remain polite. But he forced himself to keep his temper in check, determined not to expose her once again to the wolf within.

Farrin came and found him when the afternoon was wearing on, looking disheartened.

"Find out anything useful?" Emmett asked.

"Not really," Farrin sighed. "Many of the servants are locals, so you'd think they would know the legends. But although they all vaguely recall grandparents telling scary wolf stories, all anyone wants to talk about is the current wolf sightings."

"What about me, though?" Emmett demanded. "Do they have any suspicions about me?"

"Uh..." Farrin's face was contorted strangely, like he was trying to look natural and failing horribly. "They do, but...it's nothing of relevance."

"What do you mean?" Emmett demanded. "What are they saying?"

"I don't think anyone's guessed the truth," said Farrin soothingly. "Or anything close to it."

"Farrin," Emmett growled, letting the wolf's rumble out just a bit. "What are you not telling me?"

Farrin sighed. "Well, I think everyone was mystified and intrigued when you first came here. But it sounds like rumors have been spreading for some time now, and..."

"And what?!" Emmett demanded, his already sparse patience fleeing.

"The general consensus is that you and Princess Rosa are undertaking some kind of clandestine connection," said Farrin in a matter-of-fact tone. "Apparently they think you must have met on previous visits, and that's why you used to come so often.

Her visit yesterday set the castle in an absolute bustle. All under the surface, of course."

For a moment Emmett was silent, his mouth opening and closing like a fish. "I never met Rosa until the start of this current stay," he managed at last.

"I believe you," Farrin assured him. "But apparently the princess has a reputation for being unconventional and hard to handle. They say she sneaks off into the forest all the time, and the king and queen don't really do much to prevent it." He shrugged. "I guess everyone thinks they now know what she's been doing on those outings."

Emmett let out a long, low groan. Had his presence in the neighborhood destroyed Rosa's reputation? Why had she come riding out to Lernvale yesterday so shamelessly? What was he supposed to do to fix this?

Rosa's face popped into his vision, arrayed in her finery on the occasion of their second meeting, at the ball. He could remember her haughty expression perfectly, as well as her irritated words.

If you're expecting me to thank you, you'll be disappointed. I didn't need you to rescue me in the forest the other day, and I didn't need you to rescue me just now. I'm perfectly capable of handling myself both on my grandparents' land and in my stepfather's ballroom.

Well, he had his answer as to what Rosa would say he should do to fix it. Nothing at all. But Emmett wasn't entirely sure he was satisfied with that.

"And they really think our supposed rendezvous can explain all my unusual behavior?" he asked Farrin, incredulous.

His brother looked like he was trying to stifle a grin now. "They think you're out of sorts because you're suffering from the pangs of frustrated love."

"This is absurd," Emmett burst out. "You heard Mother

earlier. Rosa's mother is at least as bad. If we were trying to start something, why would we be clandestine about it?"

"How should I know?" Farrin asked. "Maybe the secrets make it more exciting."

Emmett gave him a look. "Does that sound like me?"

"Don't ask me to explain it," said Farrin, in a sanctimonious voice. "You're the one sneaking about in the forest."

Emmett seized a cushion off a nearby settee and tossed it at his brother's head. Farrin ducked, grinning openly now.

"Honestly, a pair of grown men."

They both turned at the voice to see Queen Sula entering the room. In spite of her scolding words, she looked to be in excellent spirits. Emmett watched in surprise as she turned her beaming face on him. Apparently he was forgiven for his outburst earlier.

"Emmett, on reflection, I've decided that you're right. Hosting an event here would be too difficult given all the circumstances."

"Oh," said Emmett, taken aback. "I'm pleased we agree, Mother."

"Indeed." She gave a gracious nod. "On the topic of social engagements, I have excellent news."

"Oh?" Emmett said again, his tone entirely different.

"Queen Ada has invited us all to join the Terenan royal family for an outing tomorrow."

"Mother," Emmett said warningly.

"You can't possibly object this time, Emmett," his mother informed him sternly. "It's a luncheon event, which means there will be no risk whatsoever of it running into the evening. We're to visit the sunflower fields, which are apparently a great attraction to the east of Terenford."

"Mother, it's a bad idea," Emmett said firmly. He turned to his brother. "Farrin, back me up."

"Don't look to me for help," said Farrin. "I'd love to see the sunflower fields." His lips twitched. "I'm sure they're the jewel of the kingdom. Them, or...something else."

A growl was building deep in Emmett's throat, but his mother gave him no opportunity to berate his faithless brother.

"At least one of my sons is obliging. There's no use arguing about it, Emmett. I've already sent a reply with the messenger, accepting the invitation on behalf of all of us."

She swept from the room with the words, leaving Emmett nothing to do but complain to his unrepentant brother. At Farrin's urging, he retired to bed almost immediately, in preparation for what would be another sleepless night. His body was only too ready to sink into a few hours of much-needed slumber.

That night Emmett's mind struggled frighteningly to overcome the wolf. He was able to resist hunting an unsuspecting fox, but he couldn't keep himself from running across the Terenan border and toward the area he usually haunted. Following his nose, he even found his way to the gate of a property. He was fairly sure it was Rosa's grandparents'. Even though the gate was shut against the night, it was still guarded, the men on either side of it looking tense and alert. Emmett hung back in the shadows, not sure whether the guard closest to him had seen him, or was just staring into the undergrowth. With an effort, Emmett turned himself away, padding on silent paws until he was far enough from the gate to start running again.

Running, running, but never able to outrun the wolf. Only by constant motion could he keep his savage instincts at bay for the hours it would take to return to his own form.

When Emmett crept wearily across the clearing, he was surprised to see the side gate swing open for him. Farrin waited there, and his brother's silent presence almost undid Emmett. If he hadn't been too exhausted for such displays, he thought he might have sobbed like a child as Farrin saw him safely all the way to his suite.

"Try to go straight to sleep," Farrin said quietly as he slipped out the door. "Mother will have you awake in a few hours to leave for these sunflower fields."

Emmett had no difficulty obeying. The moment his head hit the pillow, he surrendered immediately to sleep.

CHAPTER FOURTEEN

Emmett

Emmett didn't feel nearly rested enough when he was woken less than three hours later by a servant vigorously pulling back his curtains. The man's knowing glance at the groggy prince made Emmett squirm. Did he think Emmett had been meeting his sweetheart in the woods in the middle of the night? It was humiliating and shameful. He'd almost rather people knew the truth.

His mind flashed suddenly back to the night before, trees whipping past at a dizzying speed, the smell of prey in his nostrils, a true howl building irresistibly in his throat.

On second thought...it was better that they believe him unscrupulous than they discover he turned into a giant, senseless wolf from time to time.

Not senseless, he told himself firmly as he rose and tried to make himself presentable. Not yet.

His mother had ordered breakfast to be brought to his room, and less than an hour after waking, he found himself being chivvied out of the building. The journey across the border to Teren was uneventful. Queen Sula traveled in a carriage, but the princes both chose to ride. The messenger who'd brought the invitation the day before had been accompanied by a groom riding Emmett's horse. The same groom had ridden back to Terenford on the horse Rosa had left behind. Emmett had seen the creature before it departed. It was a beautiful and well-proportioned stallion. Emmett had no difficulty believing that it belonged to Teren's crown prince. If only the steward had gotten a better look at it the other day, he would surely have realized Rosa was no low-ranked noble's daughter.

Somewhat to all of their surprise, they had not been directed to meet their hosts at the castle in Terenford. The message had specifically invited them to meet the family at the sunflower fields. They therefore followed West River eastward once they'd crossed it, bypassing the capital altogether.

After another hour of riding at the carriage's slower pace, the attraction came into view, and Farrin let out a low whistle from where he was riding beside his brother.

"What a sight. I had no idea these fields were so large."

Emmett nodded his agreement. The sunflower fields stretched out further than he could see. They were obviously meticulously cared for, and contrary to his expectations, it wasn't just one uniform field. The sunflowers were arranged in different patterns, one field boasting a spiral of thick, leafy plants, another diagonal rows that increased in height. The tallest sunflowers were higher than Emmett's head.

The two brothers were admiring the view when someone officious-looking bustled forward to greet the carriage carrying their mother. The princes dismounted, handing their horses off to the grooms who'd ridden with them. They were about to join their mother at the carriage when voices reached them, wafting out from among the nearby sunflowers.

"...thought it would be overwhelming to have so many in one place, but it's very well planned, isn't it? Bright and cheerful."

"I agree."

Emmett stilled, drawn irresistibly to the first voice. He'd lost all interest in joining his mother, instead waiting impatiently for the speakers to emerge from the row of sunflowers. He was aware of Farrin watching him, but he ignored whatever smug thoughts his brother was sending his way.

"I admit, it was a good idea of Mama's to—"

The words cut off as Rosa and Otto came into view, the princess instantly freezing as her eyes flew to Emmett.

"What are you doing here?" she demanded, not in the least politely.

"Rosa," said Otto, pained. He nodded his head to Emmett. "Prince Emmett, what a pleasant surprise. And Prince Farrin. It's been a long time, but I'm delighted to see you again!"

"Surprise?" Emmett asked stupidly, over the top of Farrin's friendly reply. "I thought we were invited."

"Invi—" Rosa's word cut off into a growl that rivaled Emmett's. "I knew Mama was up to something. Didn't I say it, Otto?"

"You did," Otto agreed amicably. "Wouldn't shut up about it half the way here."

Emmett had to resist the urge to raise a hand to his thumping head as the realization washed over him. They truly had been invited by Queen Ada, of course. His mother wouldn't make something like that up. But the Terenan queen clearly hadn't informed her daughter of the invitation. Emmett had been unable to think of a reason for them to meet at the fields rather than the castle, but now he understood. Queen Ada must have thought Rosa would refuse to come if she knew Emmett was joining them.

For some reason, that thought was bitterly depressing.

Perhaps fortunately, Emmett was saved from replying to this unpromising greeting as the proprietor of the sunflower fields approached. After being welcomed with tedious pomp and flattery, they were taken on a tour of the attraction, one rich with more detail than Emmett could ever wish to know about sunflowers.

"Sorry for Rosa's rudeness earlier," Otto said, sidling up alongside Emmett as the guide droned on. "She doesn't mean it, you know. She just likes being dramatic."

"I hadn't noticed," Emmett said, his tone expressionless.

"Sorry for Emmett's stiffness," Farrin chimed in cheekily, echoing Otto's words. "He doesn't mean it. He was just born without humor."

A snort from behind them revealed that Rosa had heard the exchange, and Emmett let out a long-suffering sigh as both Otto and Farrin chuckled at their own wit.

"You're all shameless," he informed the other three.

"That's the best way to be," Rosa chimed in. "Because then you can't be shamed for silly things like climbing trees and breaching etiquette."

"In Emmett's defense," Farrin piped up, "he used to climb trees constantly when we were children. Whenever we visited Ilgal, at least. He was a better climber than me, although I suspect I've overtaken him during my years in Selvana." He nudged his brother's shoulder. "He can't be accused of breaching etiquette much, though."

"Watch yourself, little brother," said Emmett ominously. "You think you're free to tease me, but now that you've married a ruling queen, you're a monarch, well before I ever will be. You might find you have to pay a bit more attention to etiquette yourself."

Farrin sighed. "All too true, I'm afraid," he acknowledged. His face softened. "But what can I say? Bianca is worth every second of it."

"That's very romantic of you," Rosa said, sounding more

amused than touched. "You and Otto would get on well. He's a hopeless romantic at heart, aren't you, Otto?"

"Thank you, Rosa," Otto said dryly. "Just the dignified image I was trying to present."

Farrin laughed, deftly swapping places with Emmett so that he was walking beside the Terenan prince. It wasn't lost on Emmett that this rearrangement left him side by side with Rosa. Farrin was shameless indeed, the schemer.

"Princess Rosa," Farrin said, glancing back at the pair, "I heard that you were born in the forest, is that true?"

"It is," said Rosa. "I lived there for much of my childhood. And my paternal grandparents have a property there, so I still visit the forest regularly. Although not as regularly as I'd like."

"Do you wish you still lived there?" Farrin asked curiously.

"Sometimes," said Rosa, making no attempt to be diplomatic. Emmett appreciated her directness.

"What would you do if you lived there?" he asked, curious in spite of himself.

"What do you mean?" Rosa seemed confused.

Emmett shrugged. "Well, you lived there as a child, with your parents I assume. But you were a child. Now you're an adult. If you wish to live in the forest, does that mean you have some interest in the timber industry? Or perhaps some other forest-based trade?"

"No," Rosa admitted. "I know my grandparents are adept with timber, but I can't honestly say that I have any desire to make a living that way."

"Perhaps you would enjoy village life," Emmett suggested. "In one of the small forest communities. There are plenty of occupations in a thriving village."

"There are," Rosa agreed slowly. "Although...well, I never lived in a village. My parents had a small property near my grandparents'. I don't know that village life would really appeal to me." She aimed a playful kick at Otto which didn't actually make contact. "Now that my fancy castle has ruined me for life without luxuries."

Otto chuckled. "I knew you'd come round eventually. Prince Emmett makes a good point, though. What would you actually do with yourself if you lived in the forest now? I'd never thought about that."

Rosa said nothing. It was abundantly clear to Emmett that she'd never actually thought about it, either, and from her expression, he didn't think she relished that realization.

"Prince Otto, I think you're forgetting an obvious other option," said Farrin cheekily. "Princess Rosa might have a sweetheart out there in the forest, whom she wishes to marry, to make his home her own."

"Don't be ridiculous," scoffed Rosa. "Loving the forest doesn't mean I have to love the forest boys. Most of them can't see anything of the world past the closest tree trunk, they're so caught up in their village life."

Her words were met with silence, no one speaking the obvious conclusion of all these observations. It seemed that although Rosa cherished her childhood memories in the forest, her adult self didn't see any specific place for herself in Ilgal. The thought made Emmett feel hopeful, and as soon as he identified the emotion, he tried to silence it.

You don't have a future at all, he reminded himself grimly. *Let alone a future with Rosa.*

Besides, Rosa didn't look too happy with the conversation. Likely she wasn't ready to acknowledge what the others had unintentionally pointed out.

"You said you visit the forest often," Farrin said, his air too casual, "but I suppose you can't at present. What with the rumors of giant wolves and such."

Emmett frowned at his brother. Why would he steer the

conversation that way?

"Well, I was until very recently," Rosa sighed. "But I'm not allowed to now."

"And thank goodness," Otto said emphatically. "I thought it was dangerous from the start. Especially since you insist on wearing that bright red cloak everywhere, Rosa. It's like this huge sign announcing your presence to any wolf in the vicinity."

"Actually, wolves can't really see red," Emmett commented unthinkingly. "It's one of the colors they don't really make out."

"Really?" Rosa sounded fascinated. "I didn't know that. How do you?"

Emmett held in a wince as Farrin stared at him, silently asking him what was wrong with him.

"Read it somewhere," he mumbled.

"Well, I'm glad my cloak isn't a danger, but I have to admit Otto has a point," Rosa sighed. "In light of the fact that I encountered one of these giant wolves myself recently."

"You did?" Farrin and Emmett spoke in unison as Emmett felt all the color drain from his face.

"Do you mean the other night, near Lernvale?" he demanded. "Those were surely regular wolves."

Rosa shook her head. "No, this was earlier. But it doesn't matter, I'm fine."

Emmett said nothing, frozen in horror. He'd actually run into Rosa while he was in wolf form? There were whole patches he didn't remember, but surely he would have remembered that! Was it possible she'd seen a normal wolf in the darkness, and had let fear and rumors make it grow in her mind?

"Honestly, up until I saw it, I thought it was all just scaremongering," she said frankly, as if in response to Emmett's thoughts. "My grandmother's always said these legends have been around forever, and I never thought there was any truth to them."

"Did she?" Farrin asked, his casual air definitely forced now. "What were the old legends?"

"I don't really remember," said Rosa dismissively. "Something about giant wolves of especial savagery. I always scorned the stories as a child. Said they were silly tales made up to scare away the city folk."

"It worked." Otto raised a hand, drawing a chuckle from the rest of them.

"Why especially savage, I wonder?" Farrin asked thoughtfully.

Rosa frowned in an effort of memory. "There was a reason. Granny said something about them being tortured men. So evil they turned into wolves, or something like that. I think they were supposed to be able to turn back and forth at will, which made them more terrifying. They could hide among the villagers that way."

"Oh, I remember hearing something about that," said Farrin, hiding his reaction to this information better than Emmett was. "It was tied to the full moon, wasn't it?"

"The full moon?" Rosa repeated, seeming bewildered. "I don't think so. I don't remember anything about that."

"Oh," said Farrin lightly. "I must have been confusing it with another legend." He sent Emmett the ghost of a shrug, as if to say, *no answers there.*

Emmett responded with a silent glare. It was time to drop this line of questioning before Rosa started putting pieces together.

"Are you all right, Emmett?" He looked down, surprised to see Rosa watching him. "You don't look well."

"That's not very polite," Otto protested.

"I'm fine," said Emmett calmly. "I just didn't sleep well last night."

"That's something an old person would say," Rosa informed him brutally. "You're too young for a bad night's sleep."

Before he knew what she was about, she leaned so close she was almost touching him. Emmett was so distracted by her nearness, and by the floral smell that wafted out from her hair, he was taken completely by surprise when she reached out one shapely hand and plucked a hair from his head.

"Ow!" he protested, lifting his own hand to the mistreated spot. "What did you do that for?"

"A gray hair!" Rosa announced, clearly surprised. "You are old after all."

"Rosa," moaned Otto.

"What old *hair* you have, I should have said," Rosa corrected herself, a mischievous twinkle in her eye. "Perhaps it's aged ahead of the rest of you."

"Perhaps," said Emmett stonily. Inside he was mortified, but he knew it was essential that he show no sign of his alarm. "The stress of being royal, I suppose."

"That's probably it," Rosa agreed. She dropped her hand, her fingers brushing Emmett's arm on the way down. "Although that doesn't explain what hairy arms you have. They also seem to have aged beyond you."

"Arms the better for him to strangle you with if you don't stop with these abominably rude comments, Rosa," Otto scolded her, seeming genuinely embarrassed. "Prince Emmett, I apologize for my sister's—"

"Well, what a fascinating tour." Queen Sula's bright voice broke mercifully into this exchange, giving the younger group the cue that the guide had finally finished speaking. "This is truly an incredible wonder of both nature and planning, Queen Ada. I'm delighted to have been given this opportunity to enjoy it."

"You're too kind, Queen Sula." The Terenan queen

responded with the same gracious warmth. "Not as delighted as I am to have you all join us. These fields are indeed a jewel on our map."

Beside Emmett, Rosa made a noise in her throat as her mother spoke about the sunflower fields.

"You'd think she planted and cultivated them herself," Rosa muttered.

"Out of charity with your mother, are you?" Emmett asked, not caring that the question was intrusive.

"You know I am," said Rosa darkly. "And when we're alone, I'll be telling her so in no uncertain terms."

"Given your self-acknowledged shamelessness, I'm amazed you're refraining from doing so in public," Emmett said.

"It's your mother's presence that stops me," Rosa said frankly. "I can't bring myself to shatter her image of me as a well-behaved, eligible princess. It seems valuable to her for some reason."

Her last sentence was spoken in a challenging tone, and Emmett raised an eyebrow.

"Are you expecting me to deny or defend? If you think you're the only one who's been dragged here by the orchestrations of their mother, then you're not as perceptive as I thought you were."

"They're as bad as each other," said Rosa, with a little huff. She narrowed her eyes at Emmett for a moment before her expression turned suddenly conspiratorial. "So we're fellow victims, are we? Should we make a run for it?"

Emmett laughed reluctantly. It was frustrating how he couldn't help being warmed by her cheeky manner. It would be so much better for his peace of mind if he could find her impertinent rather than captivating. He didn't answer her question, instead staring down into her eyes, the moment rapidly growing more charged.

"Why is it so offensive, though?" he asked abruptly. "Your mother inviting me here, I mean. Is my company so repulsive?"

"I...no, I didn't mean...I never said..." Rosa was clearly caught off guard by the direct attack, and Emmett was a little disappointed when she was rescued from her stuttering by her mother.

"Prince Emmett, allow me to greet you properly." Queen Ada had swooped down upon them, Queen Sula at her side. "We're so pleased you were free to join us today, aren't we, Rosa?"

Rosa opened and closed her mouth a few times, her poise not fully recovered from the moment before. Queen Ada, however, seemed well pleased with this discomposed response.

"Indeed," she said, as if Rosa had agreed with her aloud. She turned to the other queen. "I find myself in need of a rest, Queen Sula. I'm afraid I feel my age in this warm weather."

"As do I," Emmett's mother agreed promptly. She gave him a smile so pointed, it may as well have been a command. "But don't let us keep you young folk from exploring further."

"Of course," Queen Ada agreed promptly. "There's more to see than just sunflowers, you know. The hedge sculptures in the next field are very cleverly designed."

With that, the two queens swept off, chatting happily with one another. They were in such excellent harmony, Emmett was half surprised not to see them linking arms, like young girls excitedly discussing their first ball.

Rosa let out a low groan, and silently, Emmett had to agree. The blatant orchestrating of the older women was embarrassing, there was no getting around it.

"I thought my mother by herself was bad, but together they're genuinely terrifying," Rosa said hollowly.

Emmett couldn't help laughing. "I agree. Come on." He jerked his head in the opposite direction from their mothers. "If we linger here, they'll come and scold us more."

"I suppose you're right," Rosa said. "But I don't have any interest in hedge sculptures. The sunflowers appeal much more."

Emmett followed her compliantly, finding it hard to take in the golden display around him. The girl at his side was much more engaging.

"You obviously got home safely the other night," Emmett said, when they were fully surrounded by the stalks. These sunflowers were about waist height, and he could see Otto and Farrin chatting cheerfully in a row not far away.

"I did," said Rosa shortly.

"I'm glad," Emmett responded gravely. "I was concerned. The wolves must have given you quite a scare."

Rosa gave him a measuring glance. "You lost sleep over my safety, did you? I'm inclined to tease you for your protective instincts, but it would be out of place this time. I was rude to you when you found me, and I promised myself I would apologize when next we met. I'm grateful that you came to my aid. I was in some trouble, and I don't deny it."

Emmett didn't respond at once, surprised and touched by her words. "I don't deserve thanks," he said gruffly. "It was my fault you were in that fix. You should never have been given that useless horse. And I should never have let you go off alone." A scowl crossed his face. "Although we did tell you not to go alone, of course."

Rosa narrowed her eyes, her penitent mood passing. "I didn't realize I needed your permission to go home. Going alone wouldn't have been a problem if not for that horse which was, as you say, useless."

Emmett rolled his eyes. "Of course you don't take any responsibility. Why would you? You only rode off alone to a different kingdom, barging into my castle, then sneaking off the moment my back was turned. Then ran afoul of a pack of wolves and needed me to come after you, in spite of the fact that you *apparently* don't need to be rescued."

He knew the words were impolite and poorly thought through, but he couldn't seem to care. He could feel the recklessness rising in him, every nerve on high alert. The wolf was surely crouching within him, ready to consume as soon as his guard was down, but he wasn't conscious of it. It was emotion that had him in its grip—whether good or bad, Rosa's presence always seemed to bring out the strongest of emotions in him.

"Fine words," Rosa said, swelling with indignation. "Coming from the one who lives to rescue everyone else from problems they didn't know they had, but felt no qualms about sending me off alone after a wolf attack while he wandered the forest looking for a worthless horse. Not entirely consistent, are you?"

"I never claimed to be consistent." Emmett's voice was edging toward the growl, his anger fueled by the fact that she was right. He'd hated having to send her off alone, but what else could he have done? It was out of his control, and he felt an unreasoning rage at having her throw it in his face. "But at least I'm not shameless and proud of it," he spat.

Rosa's eyes were as hard as flint now, and her words came hard and fast. "I don't know how you can talk about pride. A crown prince whose mother is determined to marry him off to the least princess-like princess in Providore, just because I'm vaguely eligible. How poor does she think your chances are of landing a suitable bride? I know why my mother is eager for me to marry and stop giving her sleepless nights. What's your excuse?"

"I'm dying," said Emmett bluntly. Inside, he was churning with a maelstrom of emotions, and in his effort to keep it all concealed, his voice was flat and inexpressive.

Rosa reeled back, looking as stunned as if he'd slapped her. "What nonsense is this? Is that your idea of a joke?"

"It's not a joke," said Emmett. "I'm unwell, and my time is growing shorter. My mother wishes me to marry before it's too late."

"How…" Rosa seemed to be struggling to find her voice. "How long do you have?"

"I don't know," said Emmett, still speaking in that horribly unemotional voice. "Perhaps a few years, perhaps only months. You might be lucky, I might be out of your hair in a matter of weeks for all I know. I'm sure you'll be thrilled."

Rosa had gone pale, her breaths coming unsteadily even as her voice was still angry. "What kind of a person says something like that?"

She glanced around, as if to appeal to an audience, but they were alone. In fact, they'd wandered so far they were now in the section of sunflowers that towered over their heads. They were surrounded by a green and yellow forest, no others in sight.

Rosa drew in a breath. "Just because I find you insufferable doesn't mean I want you dead."

"Strong praise," said Emmett, well past the point of reason now. He'd immediately regretted his stark admission, but there was no taking it back. He couldn't remember the last time he felt so mortified, and his control, so often shaky these days, seemed to have fled him completely. "It seems my mother's hopes are well founded after all. I'm flattered."

"Don't be absurd," said Rosa, clearly incensed by his tone. "Find someone else to marry you and produce babies as soon as humanly possible. I have no interest in doing it."

"Good!" said Emmett. The word was definitely a growl now, and he'd stepped toward her without even realizing it. "Marrying you is the last thing I want to do with what little time I have left!"

"Good!" Rosa echoed, also moving forward. She seemed as little in control as he was. "Then we're agreed."

"Perfectly," Emmett grunted, leaning forward. His face was inches from hers now, and they were both breathing hard.

"Absolutely," Rosa said, that glint of green showing in her eyes again.

Emmett had no idea who moved first, but all at once the gap between them was closed. Emmett's arms wrapped around Rosa as their lips crashed together, the embrace as passionate as the argument had been. Her mouth was hot against his, her lithe form full of tense energy in his arms. The first moment of shocked realization at what they'd done had passed, and still they were locked together, their lips moving and their hands pulling each other closer.

Emmett's mind was roaring in a jumble of approval and horror, and all at once control reasserted itself. With a gasp, he pulled back, releasing Rosa and stumbling into the nearest row of sunflowers. She looked as shocked as he felt, and for a long moment they just stared at each other.

"I..." Emmett swallowed, then gave a stiff bow. "Forgive me."

Without another word, he turned and strode away into the sunflowers. Rosa didn't try to call him back.

Emmett paced blindly down the row, his thoughts too chaotic to untangle. He was rattled beyond measure by what had just occurred, by what he'd just done. He didn't think he'd ever done anything so reckless in his life, with one glaring exception. But that wasn't what scared him. What frightened him was that it had felt *so good* to abandon his rigid responsibility and let his desires and emotions drive him. *She* had felt so good in his arms.

Was that the wolf taking over? Was the creature threatening to consume Rosa as well as him? Emmett could only hope desperately that he was strong enough to hold it at bay.

Because he could never live with himself if he let the wolf touch any part of Rosa.

CHAPTER FIFTEEN

Rosa

Rosa stared after Emmett, barely seeing his tall, muscular form. In a moment, he'd turned sideways and walked through to the next row, the sunflower plants blocking him from her view.

She was alone in a field, mercifully hidden from prying eyes by leafy green stalks and yellow petals. Rosa raised two shaky hands to cover her face.

What had just happened? Was she dreaming? Did she and Emmett just...

And what had he told her? Surely it couldn't be true that he was dying. Rumors had circulated for years that he spent time away from his capital because he was sickly. But she'd been inclined to disregard that as false gossip once she'd met him because he didn't come across as an invalid. She'd noticed several times that he looked like he hadn't slept well, but it couldn't possibly be serious enough to be fatal.

She didn't believe her denial for a moment. Emmett wouldn't make up a story like that. It was unthinkable. It must be true. It certainly helped explain both his exile to Lernvale and Queen Sula's eagerness to promote a match between him and Rosa.

Anger flared within her for a moment. Even assuming there was any possibility of it happening, was the queen proposing to go ahead with the marriage without telling Rosa the truth? Did she think Rosa would wish to be a widowed mother at nineteen or twenty?

But that anger couldn't last. Not in the face of Emmett's words. He'd made it very clear he had no intention of marrying on a tight timeframe. And then he'd....

She couldn't get lost in that memory, not here. Not when her mother was lurking around the next sunflower stalk, and Otto was strolling cheerfully about. She couldn't afford to remember how it had felt to press her lips to Emmett's, how strong his arms had been around her, how rapidly his chest had risen and fallen under her hand. He certainly hadn't seemed sick in that moment.

She lowered her hands with a groan, too overwhelmed to unravel her various reactions. She felt embarrassment, and anger was certainly still there. How dare he say such cutting things to her and then kiss her with such passion, out of nowhere? And then walk off without a word?

In honesty, she had to acknowledge other emotions as well. A thrill was still running through her, and it wasn't altogether unpleasant. But she'd be wise not to dwell on it.

Rosa stood for several minutes before she felt collected enough to emerge. Given the mortified way Emmett had walked away, she half expected to see that he'd already departed for the return journey to Lernvale. But his tall, stiff figure caught her eyes the moment she stepped free of the sunflowers. He seemed to have been captured in conversation by her mother, and even with his back to Rosa, he looked every bit as awkward as she felt. Rosa turned, determined not to approach him for both their sakes. Unfortunately, her mother had different plans.

"Rosa, there you are! Come and join us." Queen Ada sounded positively gleeful. Clearly she was delighted with how her outing was progressing. Rosa's heart sank as she moved reluctantly to meet her mother. It was horrifying to realize how dire the situation really was. Perhaps there had been some truth to the queen's claim that she could recognize the signs of attraction in her daughter, but in all other ways, her mother was completely oblivious to the undercurrents around her. She had no idea that the prince she was plotting for her daughter to marry might be dead in a matter of months.

Weeks, possibly, Emmett had claimed. Rosa's gaze was drawn to the prince, and a cold rush went over her at the lifeless way his eyes met hers. It was all too horrible.

"Rosa." Her mother regained her attention. "I'm just trying to convince our visitors to join us for dinner tonight."

"I'm afraid we really can't do that, Your Majesty," Emmett said, his tone clipped. "But you're very gracious."

Rosa could see his discomfort, and she didn't blame him in the least. After what had just passed between them, he must be as reluctant to be pushed together again as she was. She desperately needed space to clear her head. At present it was a tangled mess.

"Prince Emmett, you must let me insist," Queen Ada said. "You'll all be weary after your journey, and to send you straight home would be unthinkable. At least return with us for refreshments. Terenford is barely out of your way, and you're most welcome. Aren't they Rosa?"

"Welcome," repeated Rosa vaguely. "Yes, very welcome." She hardly knew what she was saying, all her attention focused on trying not to let her eyes stray to Emmett's face or her thoughts stray to the distressing revelation he'd just made.

"Well, afternoon refreshments we could surely manage," Queen Sula interjected.

"Mother." Both Emmett and Farrin seemed uneasy about the plan, but Rosa had no thought to spare for why the younger prince would be reluctant.

She could think of nothing to say that would discourage the scheme without being revealing, and before she knew it, she was being bundled into a carriage with her stepbrother, her mother joining Queen Sula in another while the two Medullan princes rode.

"I should have ridden," said Otto enviously, peering out the window at the others. "I feel a fool in here."

"Yes," said Rosa mechanically. "A fool...should have ridden."

Otto pulled his gaze from the window, looking at her in bewilderment.

"Are you all right, Rosa? You're acting very strange."

"Am I?" Rosa gave her head a shake. "I'm sorry. I just..."

She hesitated, debating whether to tell Otto about what had passed in the sunflower field—Emmett's shocking announcement, that was. There was no way she'd tell Otto that they'd somehow argued themselves into a kiss so passionate the memory made her feel slightly light-headed. She thought she'd sooner take on the wolf pack again than share that detail with her stepbrother.

"I was just caught off guard," she finished lamely, deciding to keep her peace on the other information as well.

"So was I," Otto assured her. "I didn't know Mama had a scheme up her sleeve. But it wasn't so unpleasant, was it? I haven't seen Farrin for years, and it was incredible hearing about Selvana. I'd love to go there one day. Did you know he can survive on the deadly ground because of his royal blood, even though he's not a *Selvanan* royal? It's fascinating! Apparently the scholars at the Medullan Academy of Song can't even adequately explain it. That might mean we could survive there, Rosa! It might even mean the pressure in Ilgal would never kill us, even if it grew out of control." He paused, considering. "Actually, you're not royal by blood, are you? I wonder if that would make a difference, given the protection is apparently in the royal blood."

Rosa let him prattle on, taking none of it in. It didn't matter. Nothing mattered except the memory of Emmett's lips on hers, and the reality of what he'd revealed. She couldn't even figure out how she felt about it. Was she devastated on her own behalf, or just on his? It was hard to untangle.

When they reached the castle, Rosa alighted swiftly, hoping to escape into the building before the riders finished handing over their mounts. For once, her mother seemed to have the same idea as her, and Rosa submitted in relief as the queen swept her up the stairs and into her suite. Her gratitude quickly faded, however, when it became clear that her mother's sole purpose was to bully her into a fancier and more becoming gown.

"Mama, they're not staying for dinner," Rosa protested. Her mother was directing a maid to draw out a pale blue dress with fabric flowers sewn onto the bodice and soft, sheer skirts that swished delightfully when Rosa moved. She knew this because it was one of her favorite gowns, but it was more suited to a ball, or at least a formal dinner, than to afternoon refreshments.

"It's a shame, I agree, but we must make the most of things," her mother said briskly.

She supervised with unyielding precision as Rosa was hustled into the gown by her maids, then directed them to pull Rosa's hair back into a bun that looked deceptively loose. In fact it was rigidly styled, fixed with dozens of pins. Even the tendrils of hair curling so innocently around Rosa's face were anything but accidental.

When the queen finally announced her ready, Rosa expressed the sarcastic view that the guests had probably already eaten their refreshments and left.

"No need to sound so hopeful," her mother scolded her. "You go ahead, Rosa, I'll freshen up quickly and join you."

Miserably, Rosa made her way down to the parlor where her mother had directed her. She knew from her looking glass that she was looking her best, but it brought her no comfort. What would Emmett think she was trying to communicate? Would he be discerning enough to realize that her mother was the one trying to catch his eye, not her?

From what little she'd observed of Emmett's mother, he would probably be perfectly aware of what was happening. It should make her feel relief, but all she could muster was pity. Emmett hadn't needed any convincing to believe that she didn't want to be selected as his bride. Her words had been harsh and rude, but although he'd responded hotly, she'd seen no sign of surprise or uncertainty. And why would he be surprised? She'd given him no reason to think she looked on him with even common politeness.

She didn't want him to think she hated him. She didn't want him to dwindle into an early death under the impression that he was unappealing. Why it bothered her so much, she couldn't tell. But it did.

When she entered the parlor, her eyes flew at once to Emmett. He was clearly ill-at-ease, and again she couldn't blame him. But she had no chance to speak to him. Her stepfather hadn't been free to come to the sunflower fields, but he'd joined the group now, and was welcoming Queen Sula and her sons with appropriate warmth. Farrin was saying everything he should, but Emmett seemed barely able to string two words together. Rosa could tell at a glance that her stepfather had noticed, and was wondering what had come over the formerly confident prince.

Emmett's demeanor was so unlike his usual self-possession, it pained Rosa to see it. It may not have been intentional, but she was the one who'd done that to him. She approached as gracefully as she could, aware of the way Emmett's eyes followed her across the room but unable to read their expression.

"Rosa," her stepfather greeted her as she drew near. "You look lovely."

"Thank you," said Rosa, uncomfortable. She wished she hadn't let her mother push her into changing clothes. "Did your inspection go well?"

"Very well," the king said gravely. "I've just been hearing about the sunflower fields. It seems I missed a delightful outing."

Rosa smiled tightly, unable to feign appropriate interest in the small talk. Gathering her courage, she moved toward Emmett, who stood off to the side. To her chagrin, he tensed visibly at her approach.

"I'm not here to create more embarrassment for either of us," she said quietly. "I know you don't want to talk to me, or even to be here. I just..." She swallowed, searching for the words. "I was thinking about it all the way home, and I'm ashamed of how I responded to...what you told me. I want another chance."

Emmett just stared at her out of those unsettlingly intense eyes.

"First of all, I'm sorry," Rosa said sincerely. "For your...situation."

He still said nothing, although his features softened slightly. Rosa had the sense he regretted telling her about his illness, so she didn't blame him for not hastening to thank her for her response.

"Secondly..." Rosa drew a breath, struggling even more to find the right words for the rest of what she wanted to say. "Well, you seemed to think your mother's plans were ridiculous. Maybe even impossible. And maybe you're right, I don't know the details of your affliction. But I just wanted to say that you wouldn't be ridiculous to want love and companionship. You wouldn't be *wrong* to want it."

He was clearly unconvinced, so Rosa hurried on. "You said you might have years. My father died young, suddenly and tragically. I'm sure if I could ask him, he would say it was worth marrying my mother and having the time they had, even if it was cut short."

"The relevant question is rather what your mother would say," Emmett responded, his voice a soft rumble that didn't carry to the rest of the group.

Rosa took a moment to answer. His meaning was clear—he hesitated to take a wife not based on his own inclinations but out of consideration for any woman persuaded into being a bride only to be quickly widowed. By now it shouldn't come as a surprise to her to know that his motivations weren't selfish. They were, of course, focused on protecting others. Perhaps whether they wanted it or not.

"I think she would say the same," Rosa answered him at last. "She loved my father sincerely. And obviously she's glad I exist." The ghost of her usual impish smile crossed her face. "Most of the time."

Apparently Emmett was in no state to appreciate her humor. "I see. Are you making a proposal, Princess Rosa?" the prince asked sardonically.

"What? No," Rosa said, flustered. "I wasn't—that's not what I'm saying, and you know it."

Mercifully, her mother entered the room at that moment, providing a distraction that broke up all conversations. Otto moved across the room to join them, and refreshments were served shortly afterwards. Rosa slunk away from Emmett, faintly resentful that her attempt to soften her harsh words back at the sunflower fields had only left her feeling even more mortified.

She wasn't forced to endure her embarrassment for long. Within the hour, the Medullan trio were insisting that it was time for them to head for home.

"Are you sure you don't wish to stay and dine with us?" Rosa's mother asked Queen Sula. The Terenan and Medullan queens appeared to have become fast friends over the course of the afternoon. Or at least fast allies in a common matrimonial purpose. Rosa's insides curled at the thought, still too confused and embarrassed to identify her own emotions on the topic.

"You're very kind, but we really must be going," Queen Sula said, with the perfect blend of regret and immovability. Most royals were such excellent diplomats, Rosa reflected.

Neither of the Medullan princes showed any desire to linger, and within a short time of the queen's pronouncement, they were out of the castle and on their way south to Lernvale.

"Well." Queen Ada seemed a little put out. "It seems their refusal of dinner wasn't just politeness. I thought for certain they would stay once we had them here in the castle."

"Likely they wish to reach their own castle before dark, love," said the king reasonably. "Understandable, given the dangers of the forest at present."

"But it's hours until sunset," the queen said impatiently.

Rosa's attempt to slip from the room was thwarted, her mother's sharp eyes catching the movement. She wanted nothing more than privacy to mull over the day's outrageous events, but it seemed the queen's campaign wasn't finished for the day. Under the guise of discussing the visit to the sunflower fields, she spent the next hour promoting Emmett to Rosa with much less subtlety than she thought she was showing. She didn't even seem to notice that Rosa hadn't yet berated her for her subterfuge in inviting the Medullans on the outing. Otto appeared to have noticed though, judging by the concern with which he watched his stepsister. He knew something was troubling her, and while that would usually be comforting, on this occasion it was merely stressful, given she didn't intend to tell him any part of what had set her on edge.

By the time they were called to dinner, Rosa's nerves were so frayed, she thought she might burst into tears if someone so much as poked her. Her intention was to eat her food as quickly as possible with the aim of being finally alone in her room, but even that mission was disrupted. They hadn't yet finished the meal when a servant entered the room, stopping at the king's side and asking if he would receive a messenger. The man in question was the servant of an earl who had a manor in Terenford, and the matter was apparently urgent.

"Yes, send him in," the king said. The family waited with interest until a weedy man entered, bowing very formally to each of them.

"You have an urgent message for me?" King Ryker asked. "From your master?"

"Yes, Your Majesty." The man bowed again. "He sent me ahead to inform you that while traveling back to Terenford this evening from business in Medulle, we encountered a damaged carriage containing Her Majesty Queen Sula of Medulle, and had the honor of assisting her and her sons."

"Oh dear!" Queen Ada cried in dismay. "Their carriage broke down? And I believe Queen Sula doesn't ride! How far out of Terenford were they?"

"They were about halfway between Terenford and Lernvale, which I understand to have been their destination, Your Majesty," said the servant, with yet another bow.

"Are they stranded still?" King Ryker asked.

"No, Your Majesty," the servant assured him. "My Lord was traveling in his own carriage, and was able to offer Her Majesty a seat as he continued his journey to Terenford. They are presently on their way here."

"Of course they should come here," agreed Queen Ada briskly. "I'll have beds prepared at once."

Rosa held in a groan. It took all her self-control not to lay her head flat on her plate of pheasant. It seemed she would be denied her evening of solitude after all, because there was no way her mother would let her get away with disappearing rather than entertaining the Medullan royals. But she couldn't face Emmett again, she just couldn't. Not without some space to collect herself.

As anticipated, Queen Ada was insistent that all members of the family be present to greet the returning guests, in spite of the fact that darkness had fallen well before their arrival. Rosa was still in the blue gown, feeling more foolish than she could ever remember feeling in her life. The servant who'd brought them the message was there as well, running forward to assist his master as soon as the earl alighted.

The earl himself offered his hand to Queen Sula, who emerged from the carriage looking as dignified as ever. A moment later, Prince Farrin rode into the courtyard and dismounted alongside the stationary carriage. Rosa found herself craning her neck for a view of the other prince, but to her bewilderment, Emmett didn't appear. She scolded herself for the sinking disappointment in her stomach. Hadn't she just been bemoaning the fact that she had to see him again so soon?

"But where's Prince Emmett?" Queen Ada demanded after greetings and commiserations had been exchanged. She sounded almost as disappointed as Rosa felt.

"He'll be home by now, I imagine," said Queen Sula. "I'm

afraid we'd already sent him ahead to Lernvale for assistance when His Lordship arrived so opportunely. We sent one of the guards after him to carry the news of our rescue, so that he won't unnecessarily dispatch another group."

As the queen gave this airy speech, Rosa's eyes happened to fall on the weedy servant who'd given them the news of the breakdown. His brow furrowed at the queen's words, his gaze flying to her in a moment of bewilderment which he quickly smoothed back into the habitual unruffled look of an experienced servant.

What had that meant? Rosa locked the information away, determined to discover what was behind the reaction. Several minutes later, when the queen and Prince Farrin had been chivvied inside, she saw her opening. Under guise of admiring the horses still harnessed to the carriage, she approached the servant.

"Beautiful creatures, aren't they?" she said in her friendliest voice.

The servant looked behind him, apparently struggling to accept that she could be speaking to him. Rosa turned, meeting his eyes and giving him a dazzling smile. "You've done us all a great service tonight."

"I have, Your Highness?" he asked, seeming wary. "Only doing as instructed."

"Oh yes," said Rosa, still in that overly sweet voice. "We're so pleased to be able to assist Queen Sula and her sons. Or rather, her son."

The servant shifted uneasily, perhaps sensing where the conversation was going, and Rosa abruptly dropped her artificial manner.

"Hang it," she said, ignoring the servant's evident surprise at the ungenteel expression. "I'm not good at diplomacy and sweet talking. I'll just be plain with you. I saw your reaction when

Queen Sula said that Prince Emmett had ridden back to Lernvale before you got there. Why were you surprised?"

"I wasn't, Your Highness," the servant said, shifting uncomfortably. "You must have been mistaken."

"I wasn't," Rosa echoed. "And you don't need to be afraid to tell me the truth. You're not in any trouble." Perhaps reprehensibly, she added on a sudden inspiration, "Although you might be if you continue lying to a princess."

"I...I don't wish to lie, Your Highness," the servant stammered. "Only, it's not my place to speak of others' affairs."

"I won't tell anyone," Rosa assured him. "And I won't think any the less of either you or Prince Emmett. I just need the truth. It's for everyone's safety."

The man swallowed, his eyes darting around nervously. They were alone in the courtyard, no one else in hearing range.

"Well, I was surprised," he admitted. "I was riding ahead of my master's carriage, and I could have sworn there were two young men speaking with the queen next to the damaged carriage. It was close to sunset, but there was still light enough to see. Very alike, they looked. And I didn't see either of them riding toward Lernvale."

"What *did* you see?" Rosa pressed.

He rolled his shoulders, clearly uncomfortable with the conversation. "I don't mean to tell tales."

"I know," Rosa told him reassuringly. "It truly is all right to tell me."

"Well, he slipped off into the forest," said the man. "The road runs right alongside the edge of Ilgal in that section. He just sort of...walked into the trees."

"On foot?" Rosa asked, alarm spiking. "And alone?"

The man nodded. "They did indeed send someone toward Lernvale, like the queen said. It was after they'd been offered a place in my master's carriage. But it wasn't the prince. It was a servant, although from what I could tell, he rode off on the prince's own horse."

The horse he'd abandoned in order to disappear into the forest on foot, Rosa reflected. She frowned. Something strange was definitely going on here. And she couldn't make any sense of it. She knew Emmett loved the forest—his one likable quality after all, although in the interests of honesty she might have to add his kissing abilities to that list. Her cheeks heated at the thought, and she told herself sternly to stop getting distracted from the mystery at hand. Emmett loving the forest was one thing. Wandering about alone in it near dark was something else entirely. Even she had always contained her visits to daylight.

And yet, wandering alone in the forest was nothing new for Emmett, was it? Rosa's memory landed on their very first meeting, before even they were introduced in her stepfather's ballroom. He'd been in the forest alone then, and given it was soon after dawn and he was a long way from his own castle, he must have been traveling through the forest in the darkness. Not to mention the more recent occasion, when he'd rescued her from that wolf pack. She'd been sure he would insist on accompanying her home, or more likely taking her back to Lernvale and bundling her into a carriage for the journey. But he'd done neither of those things. Instead, he'd given her his horse and inexplicably taken off into the forest, alone, on foot, as darkness fell. And the reason he'd given for his conduct had made no sense to Rosa at the time.

Just like he'd given his horse to a servant tonight, and disappeared in a similar manner. What excuse had he given this time? What had he told his mother and brother to make them accept such a course?

But that didn't make sense, did it? The queen had lied for her son—she'd told the Terenans that Emmett had been sent back to Lernvale by horse before the rescuers arrived, information which she must know to be false. Whatever he was up to, his mother and brother were party to it.

Could it relate to his illness? Was he perhaps trying to hide his deterioration? But surely if he was that unwell, walking through the forest alone at night would be an even worse idea. It would take him hours to reach Lernvale that way.

Rosa bit her lip, thinking it over. She was afraid for Emmett, but that was only one motivation. She needed answers. She could try confronting Queen Sula or Prince Farrin, but she doubted they would tell her the truth. Besides which, she'd promised the servant she wouldn't tell anyone what he'd revealed about the queen's lie.

You also told your family you were genuinely sorry for sneaking away and scaring them last time, a reproachful voice said in her mind.

She winced, knowing that she was about to go against that sentiment. But she would be more careful this time. They would never know she'd been away from the castle.

"Could you take me to the place?" she asked the servant. "I mean, could you find the exact spot again, on the road?"

"Perhaps," the servant said uneasily. "But it will all look different in daylight tomorrow. It might be hard to—"

"Not tomorrow," Rosa interrupted. "Now."

The man looked aghast. "But Your Highness, it's not safe. It's dark, and surely your guards won't allow you to travel near the forest at this hour."

Rosa studied him, wondering whether to try to use her princess status to gain his cooperation, as she'd done earlier. But she decided against it. It would be unkind to embroil him in her misdemeanors. If they were discovered, he would be sure to get into trouble. Besides which, she wasn't confident she could convince him, in which case the more she tried, the deeper she would be digging herself in.

"You're right," she said. "They wouldn't like it. Perhaps they'll agree to take me tomorrow, as you said." She gave him what she hoped was a disarming smile. "Do you think you could describe the place to me? So I can tell them where I wish to go? I won't reveal your involvement, I promise."

"Of course, Your Highness," the servant said, clearly relieved at her capitulation. "It was right next to a mile marker, I remember. I tied my horse to it while I conversed with the Medullan servants. I think I remember the number. At any rate, it was about halfway to Lernvale, not far past the point where a creek bends around close to the road on the western side."

He gave a bit more description, and Rosa dismissed him with her thanks and her promise of discretion. It was enough to give her a decent chance of finding it, she decided. She hurried inside, to find her family discussing the dramatic events with interest. It seemed Queen Sula and Prince Farrin had already retired to their allotted suites, with many thanks to their impromptu hosts.

Rosa narrowed her eyes. So they'd rushed away before they could be questioned too closely about events, had they? Unsurprising, given what she'd just learned. But if they thought she'd swallow their excuses as readily as her family, they were sorely mistaken.

CHAPTER SIXTEEN

Rosa

Rosa claimed weariness, retreating to her own rooms as quickly as she could without rousing suspicion. Even that took much longer than she would have liked, her mother and Otto being eager to discuss the accident, and make plans for their guests the following morning. But finally, she was able to slip away. When her maid arrived to assist her to undress, she submitted with gratitude to having her hair deconstructed and brushed, but then told the girl that she would put herself to bed as she wished for privacy after an exhausting day.

The maid complied without comment. It wasn't an unusual request for Rosa, and most of the castle staff had long since accustomed themselves to the new princess's reluctance to accept all the trappings of her status. Rosa waited until the maid had finished preparing the room and withdrawn. She was unlikely to be bothered again that night, but she left a note under her pillow just in case, informing her family where she'd gone and that she would be back shortly. Hopefully no one would find it, because hopefully they wouldn't notice her missing.

Donning her red cloak, Rosa swiftly twisted her hair into two loose braids. The night was mild, and the light cloak should be enough. Perhaps she would be wiser to change her gown, but she was impatient to be off. If she wanted to return in time to avoid being caught, she couldn't afford to delay. After the chaos of the day, the hour was already much further advanced than she would like.

Climbing out her window was the work of a moment, and she had no difficulty weaving her way undetected through the dark gardens. She'd done it many times before. She knew she wouldn't be able to get away with taking Bullion from the royal stables in the middle of the night, however, so she made instead for another, much smaller stable partway across the city. The private stable was maintained by her grandparents, who did enough business in the capital to make it worth keeping a couple of horses there. The stable wasn't closely guarded like the royal one, and the creatures were familiar with Rosa, so it presented no great difficulty to saddle one and lead it out onto the street.

Soon she was riding southward, the wind in her hair and guilt and elation warring in her heart. She knew her family would disapprove—even her grandparents would frown on this irresponsible flight. But she always felt such a sense of freedom when she left the city, especially, it had to be admitted, if she did so without leave.

It wasn't as though she was going to wander deep into the forest, she argued with herself, trying to assuage her guilt. She would stay close to the road, and keep her horse with her in case she needed to flee. This was no skittish creature like the one she'd borrowed from Lernvale. It was a reliable, familiar mount.

The road was deserted, flying by beneath the horse's hooves without incident. It took Rosa an hour and a half to reach the place indicated by the servant. In the end, she hadn't needed his careful instructions. The damaged carriage had been left there, presumably to be collected in the morning. It had probably been sitting for years in the carriage house at the uninhabited castle at Lernvale, rarely used. It was no wonder it hadn't responded well to the longer journey.

Rosa dismounted, keeping hold of the horse's halter as she examined the scene. The night was clear, and the moon was full, providing decent light to see by. But there had been such a scurry of movement around the carriage, it didn't seem likely she'd discover any useful information there. She wasn't a trained tracker, after all.

Walking the horse beside her, she moved toward the trees. Under the branches, it was much harder to see anything, but she thought she could see depressions in the undergrowth that could be caused by someone walking through there.

Or some*thing*. There was just as much chance it could mark the passage of an animal as a human. Rosa remembered the huge wolf that had chased her and Bullion, and a shiver went over her. Had she been mad to come out here?

But the horse seemed relaxed, and that reassured her. Following the tracks to the best of her poor ability, she moved further through the undergrowth. The forest was thin at this point, so near the road, and not nearly as menacing. Rosa couldn't even feel the pressure in her chest. Nevertheless, she had no intention of going far. She kept the road in view at all times. Even in her familiar part of the forest, she knew the risk she took any time she stepped off the path. Out here, in a section unknown to her, she would be a fool to lose sight of the road.

A little way in, she encountered a severely trampled patch of earth, and felt vindicated. It seemed she had been following tracks, after all. She expected them to veer south, toward Lernvale, but instead they appeared to be heading north. Rosa tried to follow them, but the light was getting worse, and there was no obvious continuation of the prints, if prints they were. Plus she could barely make out the road. It was already difficult to lead her horse between the thickening trunks. She was forced to acknowledge that she could go no deeper.

She felt disheartened as she led her horse back to the silent, moonlit road. What had she hoped to find out here? The tracks seemed to confirm the servant's story, but she'd never really doubted the man, so what did that achieve? Did she think Emmett would be sitting just past the ruined carriage, waiting between the trees to give her answers?

Her mind flashed vividly to the last time they'd been alone together, cut off from the rest of the world by leafy stalks rather than moss-covered trees. Had some part of her been hoping for another rendezvous?

Brazen though her mother sometimes thought her, Rosa herself was shocked by that thought. Surely she hadn't been harboring that hope deep down. She just wanted to find out what Emmett was up to.

Either way, she wasn't likely to learn more by hovering around the site. If she'd been there earlier, and willing to go deeper into the forest...

But there was no use bemoaning that. Resigning herself, Rosa remounted, directing her horse slowly along the road, back toward Terenford. She kept her eyes on the forest as she went, trying to spot any clues between the trees. She wasn't surprised to see nothing of value.

In this manner, the journey home was slower than the one going out. Both Rosa and her horse were exhausted after a night without sleep, and at times she could almost have drifted off in the saddle. As she neared the river, Terenford a dark mass on its other side, Rosa was uneasy to see the first hints that the sky was lightening. Her maids weren't in the habit of waking her at dawn, but if she wanted her outing to remain undetected, she would do well to hurry.

Mindful of the need to cover her tracks, Rosa didn't make for the main gate, although it was closest. As soon as she'd crossed the river, she turned left and followed it west until she hit the tree line. Moving just far enough into the forest to be out of sight of anyone on the castle wall, she traveled north, intending to enter the city by the small western forest gate.

The going was even slower among the trees, and it was with an anxious eye that Rosa saw dawn creeping over the forest. She couldn't see much beyond the forest, but she did see the gray walls of the castle loom into sight. She was almost home.

She urged her horse forward, the poor, weary creature picking its way through the undergrowth at a walk. As the surroundings became more familiar, Rosa turned her head, looking in the direction of her grandparents' house, even though she knew it was much too far away for her to see it.

What she did see caused her heart to perform some kind of backflip, and not the pleasant kind. Just as her eyes caught a flash of gray, the horse shied sideways, giving an uneasy snort.

"Steady," Rosa murmured to her steed, laying a soothing hand on the horse's mane. At least, she meant it to be soothing. Given her hand was shaking, it probably didn't have the desired effect.

The horse came to a stop in the midst of a thick patch of undergrowth, stamping uncertainly. Her knuckles white against the reins, Rosa searched the gloom of the dawn, willing herself to have been mistaken. Something shifted in the shadows, her ears catching the rustle of the undergrowth this time. Rosa knew she should flee, but she couldn't seem to move or make a sound. She was frozen in cold horror as an enormous wolf, every bit as large as the one she'd seen before, ambled wearily out from between two trees.

The fear that it was hunting her faded—the creature didn't appear to have seen her. Should they run, trust that they could clear the forest before it caught them? Or stay perfectly still, in hope it continued past?

Rosa's panicked mind was no closer to a decision when the wolf turned its head, its unnervingly glowing eyes settling on her and its body freezing. Before Rosa could move, or scream, or descend further into panic, something bizarre happened.

The wolf suddenly curled over in pain, an agonized howl escaping its lips. Rosa watched in fascinated horror as the creature convulsed on the ground, shaking so violently it seemed like it was changing shape.

Hold on...Rosa's eyes widened as the form before her lengthened, the gray fur receding and the limbs shifting to something entirely different. Before she could comprehend any of what she was seeing, it was over. Before her shocked eyes crouched not a wolf, but a man. A familiar man. One no longer convulsing in pain, but still hunched over as if wishing to hide his face. Not that there was any hope of Rosa failing to identify him.

"Emmett?" she whispered, her voice coming out strangled.

Reluctantly, he raised his head. There was so much shame and misery in the eyes that met hers that Rosa's breath caught in her throat. For a long moment, Emmett remained crouched. Then he seemed to steel himself, squaring his shoulders and pushing to his feet. He didn't approach her, just meeting her eyes with a steadiness that said clearly that he didn't intend to shy away from any of it.

As she gazed down at him from her horse, Rosa's heart swelled with a perplexing tangle of pity and admiration. He looked disheveled, like he had when they'd first met in this very forest. But he still bore himself with the quiet dignity she'd come to expect from him. He was dressed in the same blue tunic and dark breeches he'd worn when they'd kissed in the sunflower fields the day before—could that truly have been only the day before?—and he looked every bit the prince, in spite of everything.

"Rosa," he said, the name almost a groan. "You must have many questions."

Rosa swallowed, her hands clenching and unclenching over the horse's reins. At least the creature had calmed as soon as Emmett resumed human form. That was somewhat comforting.

"So many that I can't identify a single one," she said faintly. "I...I don't know what to say."

A wry smile curled Emmett's lips. "That must be a first."

Rosa stared at him in disbelief. He looked almost...relieved. As though her discovery of his secret had lifted a burden.

Perhaps it had. But his haunted eyes told her it wasn't the relief of someone who believed their troubles were past. More like someone who now knew the date of their execution, and found the prospect easier to face than the uncertainty that had preceded it.

The thought reminded her of their conversation in the sunflower fields, and Rosa finally understood.

"This is what you meant, isn't it?" she asked. "Your illness, the one that's killing you. This is it."

"This is it," Emmett agreed, his voice deep and steady. "It's claiming me at an increasing rate."

"So...so the rumors of the giant wolves terrorizing the forest...those are you?"

"Yes," Emmett acknowledged, still calm. "Although it's never been my intention to terrorize."

"What *is* your intention in turning into a giant wolf?" Rosa demanded, somehow more exasperated because he was so calm.

"I don't do it on purpose," said Emmett, with a flicker of irritation. "I can't control it."

Rosa bit her lip, a chill racing over her at the reality of the situation. If he couldn't control it...that was bad.

"You said it's getting worse. What will happen when it fully claims you?"

Emmett let out a long, slow sigh. "Whether it will kill me or turn me permanently into the wolf, I can't know. I don't think anyone knows. There are legends, but they aren't detailed enough to help me. I've been searching for years, and I haven't been able to find any credible information."

"Years?" Rosa asked numbly.

He nodded. "It's been more than four years since I accidentally unleashed magic on myself."

Rosa frowned. "But I never heard rumors of wolf sightings until much more recently. Less than a year, surely."

Emmett shrugged. "I suppose I wasn't seen in the early years, or at least not often. I..." He swallowed, then tried again. "Like I said, it's getting worse. It's getting harder to control...even to remember..." He trailed off, obviously finding it very difficult to admit to not being in control.

That figured.

"So you can control yourself?" Rosa pressed hopefully. "You're in your right mind when you transform?"

"Of course I can," said Emmett, a little too quickly. "I know who I am, and I've never hurt another human. I'm almost completely sure of it."

"Almost?" Rosa repeated, alarmed. He sounded like he was trying to convince himself as much as her. "What about all the reports of wolf attacks?"

"You know how rumors are," he said defensively. "A sighting can quickly become an attack in the telling."

Rosa frowned, ire rising as she remembered her own terrifying experience. "So when you lunged at me and my horse that time, you weren't attacking us? It sure looked like it."

Emmett's face drained of color, and for a long moment he said nothing.

"You don't remember, do you?" Rosa asked slowly. "You said it's becoming harder to recall it. How can you be sure you haven't hurt anyone?"

"I haven't," Emmett said, his voice pleading now. "I didn't attack you. I can't have. Are you sure that's what happened?"

Rosa's frown deepened in an effort of memory. She'd been certain the wolf was coming for her and Bullion, but when she actually replayed the incident in her mind she couldn't be confident. She'd seen the creature, and both she and her horse had panicked. When it came out of the trees, Bullion had reared, and it had shied back. It had certainly pursued them, but had she just been assuming it was doing so in order to attack? Had it actually been Emmett all along, trying to make contact in some warped wolf way?

"I...I don't know," she said reluctantly. "I can't be sure. But if you can't even remember the incident, I don't see how you can be sure that you *haven't* attacked anyone."

Emmett remained silent, his expression so anguished Rosa had to look away.

"My grandparents," she said suddenly, her head whipping back. "Why are you targeting them? Are they in danger from you?"

"They're not," Emmett said, holding his hands up placatingly. "I swear. I'm not targeting them."

"They say otherwise," Rosa challenged. "They claim that the giant wolves are often hanging about their property."

"That's true," Emmett said miserably. "I...I do find myself here a great deal."

"Why?" Rosa demanded. "This is so far from your castle. Why are you even on our side of the border?"

"The border means nothing to a wolf," said Emmett wryly. "I

told you I have my right mind when I'm a wolf, and it's true, I swear. But my own mind is constantly battling with the creature, fighting to retain control. I find the best way to keep that control is to be in motion. When I'm a wolf, I run, almost constantly. And I don't try too hard to control where I go. If the wolf is in control of that, and I'm in control of everything else, that's good enough."

"And the wolf takes you to my grandparents' house?" Rosa demanded, bewildered. "Why would it do that?"

"Not to their house, necessarily," he said, hedging. "Just...just to this area. The wolf seems drawn back here." He must have seen she was still confused, because he drew a steadying breath before adding, "Where we first met."

Rosa stilled, her mind completely blank of a response. She had no idea what to make of his words, and she wasn't ready to grapple with them in any event. Sensing her restlessness, her horse began to stamp, getting itself clear of the dense patch of undergrowth and turning its head toward the nearby castle. Birds were singing in the trees now. If she had any hope of reaching her room undetected, she needed to leave.

"Please."

Emmett's voice startled her with its closeness. She looked down to find that he'd approached her, laying one hand on the horse's flank as if to delay it. The steed seemed content under his touch. As for Rosa, she couldn't muster a single word, captured in the intensity of the dark eyes looking up into hers, pleading, longing, anguished and alone.

"I know I don't have any right to ask anything of you," the prince said softly, "but please don't tell anyone. We've fought so hard for so long to keep word from getting out. Even the servants at the castle don't know."

"They don't notice you sneaking out to run in the forest for hours on end?" Rosa asked skeptically, finding her voice at last, even if it came out a little gruff.

"They...have their own theories about that." For some reason, Emmett wouldn't meet her eye as he said it.

"You said *we*," Rosa pressed, finding it a little easier to breathe now those compelling eyes weren't holding her in their grip. "You said, '*we've* fought so hard' to keep the secret. Who else knows?"

"My family have known from the start," Emmett told her. "My parents and my brother. I believe Farrin has told his wife as well."

Rosa relaxed slightly. If the king and queen of Medulle knew, the burden of the secret didn't feel as great on her own shoulders. Still, she didn't like the idea of not telling her family. Emmett claimed he wasn't a danger, but it didn't sound like he could really be sure he posed no threat to either them or their kingdom.

As the silence drew out, Emmett let out a bitter huff. "Of course you'll tell them all," he said, the murmured words more bitter than resentful. "I didn't really expect you to have so much faith in me."

The reproach, unreasonable as it might be, cut Rosa to the core. She'd been unjust to Emmett since the beginning, and she'd been brought to acknowledge it before now. He didn't deserve any of this, and she could see that it was destroying him in more ways than one. She didn't know the details of how he'd been attacked by this magic, but she believed him when he said it had been an accident. She'd certainly done her share of foolish things, and was simply lucky none of them had resulted in catastrophic consequences.

She did have faith in him. And more than that, she admired him. Even knowing what she'd just learned, even against the sense that warned her she'd be wisest to distance herself from him, she found herself drawn to him instead. Standing there, hair tousled and chin dark with the scruffiness of a man who hadn't yet shaved, he was just as attractive as he'd been in the ballroom in his formal garb. Perhaps more so. She found her eyes roaming over his face, her mind once again pulling her back to a sunlit field of yellow and green...

"What is it?" Emmett asked dully. "Do you see the wolf still?"

"No," Rosa told him, pleased to find her usual equilibrium restored. "I just see you."

Feeling daring, she reached across, one hand making contact with his face. He started at the touch, then stilled, closing his eyes as she ran her fingers down the scratchy surface of his jawline. His frame was so tense she longed to touch his shoulders as well, to smooth out the hardness in his tight muscles. But perhaps the gesture was enough because he let out a long, shaky breath, seeming to release a fraction of the stiff responsibility he'd shown as he faced his unwelcome witness.

"I can't even see me anymore," he whispered, his eyes still closed. His breath was warm on Rosa's fingers, and a small shiver went through her. She let her hand trail up the side of his face, running her fingers through his hair and restoring some semblance of order to it.

"I can," she insisted. "It took me a while to see you properly, but once I did, I couldn't stop seeing it."

Emmett opened his eyes, their expression heavy with a different kind of tension as he met Rosa's gaze. She swallowed, knowing as clearly as if he'd said it that he was thinking of their passionate, unplanned kiss just as she was. But she wasn't trying to make a declaration. She didn't even know what she felt, let alone being sure what she wanted to tell him about her feelings.

"I can even relate," she said, her voice becoming more casual as she withdrew her hand.

Emmett gave a rueful smile, accepting the change in tone

without resistance. "Been turning into a huge, savage beast a lot lately, have you?" he asked.

Rosa laughed, although the sound was a little strained. "That's probably putting it too strongly, but my mother would say you're not that far off." She smiled sadly at him. "I was referring to what you said about needing to stay in motion in order to stay in control. I...I understand that. Even though I've never been cursed. I've done a lot of stupid things—many of them recent—because when I'm troubled, or frustrated, the one thing I *can't* do is nothing. It feels like I'm physically incapable of it. When I feel trapped, it's like I *have* to get free, or I'll explode. I have to be in motion."

"That is just how it feels," Emmett said, sounding surprised. "It's an excellent description. I never used to feel that way before. I didn't realize some people lived in that state." He met her eyes, another wry smile on his face. "It's insupportable, I don't know how you stand it."

"Not very graciously," laughed Rosa. "That's the point. And I don't think people live that way who are settled, and content with their lot. But ever since Mama married my stepfather— even before that, when we moved to the city—I've found it hard to sit still. I keep sneaking out and doing foolish things, no matter how unlikely my outings are to bear any fruit." She gave him a meaningful look. "Like slipping out in the middle of the night to see if you really did return to Lernvale, or if you wandered off into the forest."

Emmett looked startled at that. "You've been out all night? Looking for me? Rosa, it isn't safe! Anything might have happened to you."

She raised an eyebrow. "I thought you said you were in control."

"I wasn't referring to myself," said Emmett with dignity. "There are plenty of other dangers in the forest."

"Hm." Rosa eyed him, almost inclined to be amused. The feeling was relieving after the tension of all that had come before. "Fortunately I have a huge and savage wolf on my side out here in the forest. If anything else comes for me, I'm sure you'll protect me, won't you Emmett? It's in your nature. You can't help yourself."

"It's not a laughing matter," Emmett scolded her. "It might be in my nature, but it's not in the wolf's. I'd prefer not to put it to the test. So please, for the sake of my sanity, get back inside your castle's walls where you're not likely to get eaten by anything."

"You've forgotten about my mother," said Rosa frankly. She peered through the trees above, trying to see the sky. "But you're right, I do need to go." She sighed. "I suppose there's no time to return this horse to my grandparents' city stables and still make it to my room before I'm missed."

"I'll take the horse," said Emmett firmly. "No one will recognize me in my current state. Tell me where the stables are, and then you can go straight back into your rooms."

Rosa had to laugh again. "You really can't help yourself." She narrowed her eyes in mock scrutiny. "But why are you helping me?"

"We're helping each other," said Emmett firmly. His expression became vulnerable. "At least...I hope we are."

"We are," Rosa said, her voice soft again. Whether it was wise, she couldn't tell, but she simply couldn't bring herself to betray him. "I won't tell your secret, Emmett. I promise."

Emmett's eyes were so full of gratitude—and something warmer—that Rosa found herself blushing as she met them. Her face heated even more when Emmett abruptly placed his hands on her waist. She let out a little gasp as he lifted her smoothly from the saddle, placing her on her feet on the forest floor.

They were so close now, it would be so easy to reach out her hand and feel the firm muscles of his chest. But she refrained. For the first time in the conversation, she found herself looking *up* into his eyes, only to see him gazing steadily down at her. The silence between them was thick enough to slice, in spite of the birdsong around them, and the scurrying noises of creatures in the undergrowth. It was impossible not to remember the one time they'd been closer still, when he'd enfolded her in his arms and they'd kissed as though tomorrow wouldn't come. And perhaps, for Emmett, it wouldn't. The thought, uncomfortable enough when she'd first learned of his situation, was now like a knife in her ribs.

"Tell me where the stables are," Emmett said, his voice low and throaty. Another shiver went over Rosa, one that had nothing to do with danger or wolves or cold.

Her words not as coherent as usual, she gave him the directions, all the while painfully conscious of his nearness, the warmth that radiated from his form, the intent way he gave her his full attention.

"I'll find it," he assured her, taking charge of the reins. "But I'll watch you safely inside the castle wall first. I'm assuming you have a clandestine way in."

Rosa grinned. "It seems you've seen me as clearly as I've seen you."

She'd meant the comment to be lighthearted, but Emmett's expression remained serious as he searched her eyes. She had the sense he was still trying to fully understand the earlier comment she'd just referenced. She couldn't help him there. She still wasn't at all sure what she'd meant.

"Stay safe, Rosa," he said at last, stepping back and releasing her from the tension that had held her in thrall. "And thank you for your promise. It means more than you can possibly know."

Rosa couldn't find a single word to reply. Neither her

common nor royal life had given her the tools to respond to a situation as complex as this one. So she didn't try. With a tight smile and a soothing murmur to the horse, she turned and slipped away through the trees toward the castle, her mind filled with awareness of the man whose eyes were on her every step of the way.

CHAPTER SEVENTEEN

Rosa

By a miracle of luck, Rosa managed to reach her own room undetected. She knew she couldn't have done it without Emmett's assistance, and she wasn't sure what to think about it all. Once, she would have been sure that in this situation he would have ratted her out to her family, for her own safety. But she'd obviously misjudged him in those early days.

He'd passed it off as an exchange of assistance, but she wasn't fooled. He'd offered to take her horse back before she promised to keep his secret. He had hours of walking before he could reach his own castle as it was, and he must be utterly exhausted. No wonder he looked so rundown half the time she saw him. How often did he change into a wolf? Did he have control over the timing of the transformation, or just over his actions when he'd transformed? How long did he stay in that state, and what conditions brought it on?

There were so many questions she didn't ask. She'd been too caught up in the emotion of the revelation, and in her fears for everyone's safety. It was only once she was in her bed, her pounding head making the much-needed sleep hard to reach, that they all burst on her at once. Why hadn't she asked for more information?

The sun had well and truly risen now, but no maids had yet appeared. Then it hit Rosa. There was someone else she could ask for information. She'd promised Emmett not to tell anyone his secret, but if his family already knew, then speaking to Prince Farrin surely didn't breach that promise. Queen Sula and her younger son had stayed the night in Terenford. She would find a way to pull the Medullan prince aside after breakfast.

With the thought, Rosa felt some of the tension leave her. Unfortunately for her plan, that tension had been the only thing keeping her exhausted mind awake. She found herself drifting into sleep within moments, not waking until hours later to find her lady-in-waiting pulling back the curtains with much tutting and disapproval.

"I don't know what your maids are thinking, letting you sleep so late, Your Highness. They claim you didn't stir when they came in, but that's no excuse to let it go so long. It's almost noon!"

"Almost noon?" Rosa struggled upright, her groggy mind struggling to latch on to anything. "But I need to go to breakfast. I need to speak with Prince Farrin."

"Breakfast has long since passed you by," the older woman said, pursing her lips. "As have the Medullan queen and prince. They left two hours ago to return to Lernvale."

Rosa fell back with a groan, putting her hands over her face to block out the harsh sunlight the other woman had let into the room.

"Then why do I have to be awake?"

"Because you're a princess, not a slovenly tavern wench," the lady-in-waiting said tartly.

Rosa sat up slowly, wincing at the many muscles still sore from spending a night on horseback.

"That's incredibly unjust," she informed her companion. "Tavern wenches are anything but slovenly. If they sleep until noon, it's because they've been up all night, working in a job neither you nor I would wish to take off their hands."

The lady-in-waiting sniffed. "And what does a princess know of such matters?"

"*This* princess knows a great deal more than you think," Rosa told her, stretching her limbs as she moved toward a nearby chair and the day gown laid across it. She must have been sleeping very deeply if her maids had dealt with her discarded blue gown and laid out fresh clothes all without rousing her. "When we first moved to the city, Mama and I could only afford to rent this tiny place right next to a tavern. I used to be up half the night listening to the din, and I learned a great deal."

"I've no doubt," the other woman said quickly, cutting off this promising start. "All of which I'm sure you'd do well to forget now your station has been elevated."

"I'm not sure I agree," said Rosa, considering the matter. "I think rulers are probably better placed to serve the people they lead if they have more understanding of the reality of the lives of common folk. My experiences are an asset, one princesses rarely have."

The older woman looked taken aback by this measured response, and truthfully, Rosa felt a little that way herself. She couldn't remember ever before contemplating what she could offer in her role at the castle, or how her unusual background might make her a better royal rather than a worse one. She'd always been too focused on insisting that she wasn't a real royal and never would be.

The thought soon faded, however, to be replaced with the much more pressing issue of Emmett's condition. Rosa found herself reliving every part of their encounter. To her private embarrassment, it was hard to remember all the details of what he'd said. Her mind wanted instead to focus on how his face had felt under her fingers, the way he'd relaxed into her touch as if it was a balm he desperately needed, how effortlessly he'd lifted her down from her horse. A tiny smirk curled her lips. He hadn't even seemed scandalized that she was riding astride, using a man's saddle purloined from her grandparents' stables. Whatever their first impressions of one another, it was becoming increasingly clear that neither party found the other disagreeable.

What would come of that change, she couldn't say. She sobered, the smile sliding from her face as one of her maids worked on her hair. Perhaps nothing could come of it. Emmett might not have long enough.

No. Rosa stood abruptly, startling the maid and drawing a disapproving cluck from her lady-in-waiting.

"Thank you, but you can leave my hair," she informed the baffled maid. "I'll just braid it myself. I'm in a hurry."

"Just for something different, Your Highness," said the lady-in-waiting in a long-suffering tone.

Rosa couldn't help smiling. "But this time it really is important. I'm going to visit my grandparents."

The older woman swelled visibly. "If you think, Your Highness, that you're going to sneak off into that nasty, dangerous forest again under my watch, then you—"

"The forest isn't nasty or dangerous," Rosa retorted hotly, as she braided her hair with deft fingers. She paused, adding in fairness, "Well, it is dangerous, but not as dangerous as you think it is. Anyway, I'm not sneaking off anywhere. I'm going to do things properly this time."

Head held high, she stalked from the room, making for her mother's suite.

"The queen isn't in there, Your Highness," said her lady-in-waiting, following her with dogged determination. "She's enjoying luncheon with His Majesty and His Highness. Your absence from the table prompted her to send me looking for you."

"Excellent," said Rosa, pleased. "I'm famished."

She descended on the private dining hall with gusto, to exclamations of greeting from her family.

"Rosa, you were just sleeping late," said Otto comfortably. "We were beginning to think you'd snuck out again."

It was on the tip of Rosa's tongue to admit that she had, but she curbed the impulse given her mother and stepfather were present. She would tell Otto all about it later. The thought made her pause, however. She couldn't tell him all about it because she'd promised not to reveal the main point of interest. She wasn't in the habit of keeping secrets from her stepbrother, but given she couldn't tell him the whole story, perhaps she'd be wisest to say nothing at all. Especially if she wanted his support on her next proposal.

"Mama," she said, once she'd shoveled some food down. "I want to visit Granny and Grampy."

"Rosa." Her mother's voice was sharp, but the king intervened before she could scold her daughter.

"Hear her out, Ada. I notice that she's telling us rather than trying to slip away unnoticed. I, for one, would like to encourage that kind of openness."

"Thank you," said Rosa to her stepfather. "I know I've been irresponsible in the past, but I really do want to do it right. I know you won't approve, Mama, but I have good reasons for wanting to visit them." She bit her lip. "I can't tell you all the details, because it involves someone else's confidence. But I think they might have information that could help us with our Ilgal crisis."

Her mother had perked up at the mention of confidences, and her stepfather at the mention of the Ilgal situation.

Rosa knew that neither of them had any idea what she was talking about. No doubt the queen thought she and Emmett had exchanged secrets in the sunflower field, a promising step in their blossoming connection. Well, they'd certainly had an exchange of some kind, one that would probably scandalize and delight her mother in equal measure. But Rosa was miserably aware that the secret Emmett had imparted wasn't at all romantic in nature.

And the king clearly believed her to be speaking of the growing magic in the forest, as she'd hoped he would. She didn't intend to tell him that the crisis she meant was the wolf situation.

The truth that she didn't intend to tell them was that she had decided to rescue Emmett. She knew he'd been trying for years without success, but she refused to be deterred. She wasn't going to let him die, or become a mindless beast doomed to roam the forest until death took him or the villagers hunted him down. She was going to find a way to undo the magic that had him in its grip.

And after all, why shouldn't she have more success than he had? Emmett might love the forest, but he wasn't a child of Ilgal like she was. He didn't have the experience or the resources she could claim. And judging by the fact that the calamity hadn't been shared in every corner of the forest along with a desperate plea for answers and a solution, it seemed to her that his parents had made the mistake of hampering their attempts to fix it in their desperation to keep it secret. There must be plenty of stones left unturned, and Rosa happened to know just where to start.

Because although Emmett hadn't said as much, she had instantly assumed that the magic in question came from the forest. It must, given the rumors that had dogged Ilgal for generations regarding giant wolves. She suddenly remembered the conversation in the sunflower fields, when all the young royals had been together. Prince Farrin had been very curious about the legends regarding the wolves. He'd said something about the full moon, too. Did that relate to Emmett somehow? How could she have been oblivious to the fact that there was something behind his random questions?

She frowned as she remembered what she'd said on that occasion. She'd told them that her grandmother grew up on legends of giant, savage wolves which were actually men, and could transform back and forth at will. She'd been absolutely blind not to have even an inkling of what was going on with Emmett.

In any event, all the information pointed to the likelihood that whatever affliction was affecting Emmett was the same one that the ancestors of the current forest dwellers had seen in generations past. And if there were records that could tell them what had happened back then, she knew which forest-bound library they'd be found in.

With an effort, she pulled her mind back to her family. Her mother and stepfather had engaged in a private conference after her last words, but they were now turning back to her.

"We don't wish to restrict you unnecessarily, Rosa," the king said kindly. "But we haven't asked you to stay out of the forest for no reason. There's a great deal of danger at present."

"I know," she said. "I'm not unaware of the dangers, I promise. But I really do need to see my grandmother."

"Perhaps a message could be sent requesting her to come to the castle," suggested the queen.

Rosa shook her head. "I need to look through her library," she said. "I think there might be records there that could help us."

"Library?" Otto repeated, bewildered. "How big is this cottage that there's a library?"

Rosa grinned at him. "I think it might be time you came with me to see Granny's forest cottage, Otto."

"That's an excellent idea," said the king unexpectedly. "I had been intending to do a forest visit myself within the next few days, to reassure the people that we have not forgotten or abandoned them. Tensions have been high since I announced that preparations will begin for evacuation. If you're willing, Otto, you can go in my place."

Rosa bit her lip. Alarm had washed over her at the progress regarding the evacuation plan, but she didn't want to change her stepfather's mind if he was inclined to let her go. She still thought evacuation was a terrible idea, but Emmett's crisis had taken precedence in her mind. Once he was free, she assured herself firmly, they'd find a solution for the forest together.

"I'd be glad to assist, Father," said Otto staunchly, his usual hesitance about the forest admirably hidden.

"Are you sure, Ryker?" Rosa's mother didn't seem as ready to comply.

The king nodded reassuringly. "The magic isn't yet at a level that should be dangerous for a single visit. And they won't be going alone. I'll send two squadrons of guards with them. Not even a pack of wolves could be a threat to them with that much protection, and of course no pack would approach. They'd be sensible enough to find easier prey."

The reference to Rosa and Otto as potential prey didn't seem to ease the queen's anxiety, but she didn't try to stand in the way of the king's plan.

"Rosa," she said seriously. "This isn't the time for one of your games. I want you to promise me that you won't leave the road, or speak to anyone you don't know."

Rosa couldn't help laughing, which her mother didn't appreciate.

"I'm serious, Rosa!"

"I know, Mama, I'm sorry," she said penitently. "And I promise. If it makes you feel better, I don't even want to leave the road, and I agree that it's a very reasonable restriction. It was the other part that made me laugh. It made me feel five years old again. You used to say exactly that to me when I was a small child, do you remember? You'd let me walk from our house to Granny's, but only if I promised to stay on the road and not to speak to anyone I didn't know."

Her mother smiled, the hint of reminiscence in her eye unusual given they were speaking of their forest-dwelling days. "Yes, I remember. Your father told me not to worry so much, that you'd be fine, but I spent many an anxious hour convinced that you hadn't kept your promise."

Rosa noticed her stepfather and Otto exchange a look, both likely surprised to hear this rare mention by the queen of her first husband. But Rosa ignored them, delighted to have her mother join in for once in sharing memories of that happy time.

"Well, you were both right, Mama," she said, her cheeks dimpling in a smile. "I was fine, just as Papa said I'd be. But..." She winced in apology. "I also didn't always keep my promise. I used to wander off to pick wildflowers for Granny and nuts for Grampy. I knew it was naughty, but the whole area was so familiar to me, I could never really believe it was dangerous."

"I knew it," her mother said, without heat. "You were always difficult to tame, Rosa."

Rosa chuckled. "I suspect I always will be, Mother. So show some compassion for the poor noblemen you're trying to marry me off to, and stop trying to push them into a stress-filled life."

Her mother didn't respond as Rosa expected to this sally. She said nothing, just smiling at her daughter in a knowing way that made Rosa's cheeks heat and her heart beat uncomfortably quickly. It didn't bode well, and she decided not to dwell on it, hastening instead to expand the conversation to again include the others.

Thankfully for Rosa's impatient nature, Otto had finished his meal and was ready to begin preparations. Content for once to let someone else organize her movements, Rosa sat back and waited while Otto coordinated with the royal guard. It took the better part of two hours, but eventually they were riding out of the city, Rosa mounted on a lesser steed due to Otto claiming his own horse for once.

"I can hardly believe I'm going into the forest with you after all this time," Otto told her cheerfully.

"I can hardly believe it's *taken* all this time," she retorted. She flashed him a grin. "Perhaps you'll feel the magic of the place and fall in love."

Otto grinned back. "I doubt it."

Half an hour later, his grin had turned to a grimace. They were well into the forest by now, traveling at such a fast pace that Rosa expected to reach her grandparents' gate within minutes. Clearly the head guard wanted to keep the group moving, limiting the time when the crown prince was exposed to the dangers of the open forest. Rosa wanted to roll her eyes. Even if every rumor was true—which was far from the case— the idea of there being significant danger on the well-tended, often-trafficked main road, surrounded by two squadrons of guards, was laughable.

"You were right," said Otto, making a face at her as he massaged his chest. "I do feel the magic. But I wouldn't quite describe myself as in love."

Rosa sighed. "I know. I feel it, too. I never used to. It's only very recently that it became a problem."

"The deterioration really is alarmingly rapid, isn't it?" Otto asked soberly. "I hope you're right that your grandparents have some new answers."

"Actually…" Rosa bit her lip, guilt washing over her at keeping her stepbrother in the dark. It was different from her mother and stepfather, somehow. "The records I'm hoping to find don't relate to the magic. They're about the wolves."

"Wolves?" Otto asked, frowning.

A call sounded from the front, and Rosa looked up to see the familiar burnished metal wolf perched on the open gate to one side of the road, and a smile crossed her face.

"Where does that road lead?" Otto asked curiously. "It looks like the entrance to some big estate, but I didn't think there was anything like that out here."

Rosa laughed aloud, refusing to do more than shake her head when he questioned her. It was entertaining to witness Otto's confusion when the guards in front—who'd stopped to speak with the pair of her grandparents' workers who were stationed there—turned in at the gate. But it was nothing to the satisfaction of seeing Otto's mouth fall open in astonishment when the grand manor house came into view.

"Otto," said Rosa solemnly, her eyes dancing, "welcome to Granny's forest cottage."

"You little vixen," said Otto, his indignation already evaporating into his usual good humor. "You've been lying to me all this time."

"Not lying to you," contradicted Rosa. "Just omitting information and not correcting you when you drew incorrect conclusions."

"Hm." Otto gave her a sideways look that was too shrewd for her liking. "I have a feeling you do a lot of that. Especially when it comes to a certain Medullan prince, perhaps?"

Rosa opened her mouth in outrage, but truthfully she was too stunned by Otto's perceptiveness to think of an appropriate retort. Fortunately for her peace of mind, her grandparents appeared at that moment and provided a welcome distraction.

"Rosie, my dear, we didn't look to see you anytime soon!" said her grandfather, acting as naturally as if there weren't two dozen guards ranged across his carriageway. Granny wasn't as forbearing, eyeing them with blunt disapproval.

"I'm afraid it's not a social visit, Grampy," Rosa said, as he helped her dismount. The experience was wildly different from the last time a man had lifted her down from a horse. She embraced her grandfather. "We're here to visit your library. You know Otto, of course."

"Of course we do," said Granny, bustling up. She subjected the young prince to her silent scrutiny, then gave a brisk nod. "You're a good lad, and very welcome to visit with Rosa, of course."

"Thank you," said Otto, clearly enchanted by a mode of address which Rosa could tell had won her Granny no favor in the head guard's eyes.

The elderly couple swept the two of them inside, Granny waving away the housekeeper's offers of refreshment with impatience.

"They're not weaklings who'll fade away if not fed every two hours, look at them. Healthiest young things you've ever seen. Now leave us be."

The housekeeper gave a huff as she stalked off, and Rosa couldn't help chuckling. "She's getting us refreshments anyway," she informed Otto. "She rarely listens to what my grandmother tells her."

"Most useless housekeeper imaginable," grumbled Granny, leading the way to the library.

"The household couldn't possibly function without her," Rosa explained helpfully to Otto, who looked hopelessly bewildered.

"Now, what are you looking for, Rosie?" Grampy asked, once the four of them were alone in the large, shelf-filled room.

"I want to know more about the old legends," Rosa said promptly. "The ones you used to hear as a child, Granny, about giant wolves."

CHAPTER EIGHTEEN

Rosa

Rosa's grandmother frowned. "The old stories about giant wolves? I don't know if we have any written records about those. They were bedtime stories, things my father would tell us to scare us into behaving right."

"Sounds like a delightful way to be lulled to sleep," Otto commented.

Granny grinned at him. "He wasn't what you'd call soft around the edges, my father. But then, nor am I, thanks to him, and I'm not complaining. The forest will eat the soft alive."

"Who's telling scary stories now, Granny?" Rosa asked. "Are you sure you don't have written records?"

"There's a book of children's stories somewhere," said Grampy helpfully. "I'll have a look."

He went to ferret around in the records, and Rosa turned to her grandmother.

"If it's not written down, we'll have to rely on your memory, Granny."

"It's not what it used to be." The mutter came from the housekeeper as she appeared behind their hostess, bearing a tray with tea.

"My memory is as good as the day I was born," said Granny in outrage. "Now out, you!" The housekeeper withdrew with a smirk of victory at having goaded her mistress into a self-incriminating answer.

"The cheek of that woman," Granny grumbled, and Rosa laughed again, as much at Otto's expression as at her grandmother's words.

"Never mind the housekeeper, Granny. Tell us what you can remember about the stories."

"Ah well, they changed a bit each time, didn't they?" Granny said skeptically. "So I doubt there's much truth in any of them. But it's like I told you when you were little. There were men who could turn into wolves, but giant ones. They were vicious, and terrorized the villages."

"Do you really think the big wolves roaming the forest could be humans under an enchantment?" Otto asked gravely.

The elderly woman eyed him for a moment, then let her shoulders slump a little. "I don't know. I would have said that was nonsense a short time ago, but now I don't know what to think. I've seen one of the beasts myself, and it's not a natural wolf, that's certain."

Rosa bit her lip, not liking where the conversation was going. She didn't want to reveal Emmett's secret by accident.

"How did they get turned to wolves in the first place?" she asked. "In the old legends, I mean."

Granny narrowed her eyes in an effort of memory. "The forest did it," she said. "The magic in the forest. It had a quality to it that changed people."

"Experts at the Academy of Song do claim that different regions produce magic with different...flavors, for want of a better word," Otto interjected.

"And Ilgal produces wolf-flavored magic?" Rosa said sardonically. "Come on, that's ridiculous. How could the magic just launch at someone and turn them into a wolf?"

"Oh, it couldn't, of course," said Granny. "Not even the bedtime stories claimed that. It had to be done on purpose, gathered and manipulated by someone."

Rosa frowned, remembering Emmett saying that he'd unleashed magic on himself accidentally. "Manipulated by whom? Singers?"

The old woman shrugged. "Or elves, maybe. I don't know."

"Here it is." Grampy re-entered the conversation, a book of children's stories gripped in his hand. He and Otto bent their heads over it, flicking through the pages as Rosa continued to interrogate Granny.

"Why were the wolves vicious? Just because the type of people who would want to turn into wolves were already vicious?"

"How should I know?" laughed Granny. "My father wasn't the type of storyteller to spend a lot of time focusing on the state of the human heart. He just wanted to scare us into staying on the path."

"But you always made a point of saying the wolves were vicious, or savage, or something along those lines," Rosa insisted. "Every time."

Granny sighed. "Did I?" She closed her eyes, trying to stretch her mind back across the years. "There was something about the men being evil. What did my father used to say? The magic of Ilgal wasn't meant to be used that way...that kind of magic corrupts the human who uses it. Something like that."

Rosa frowned, her heart thudding uncomfortably in her chest. Was that what was happening to Emmett? Was he being... corrupted? It almost sounded worse than dying. The thought of honest, upright, inflexible, stiff, maddeningly noble Emmett being corrupted was unbearable.

"How could it be reversed?" she asked, unable to keep a hint of desperation from her voice. "How could the magic be undone?"

Her grandmother frowned, scratching her chin. "Don't think it could. I don't remember anything about that in the stories, anyhow."

"But the stories disappeared for generations, only just resurfacing now," Rosa protested. "They must have dealt with the giant wolves somehow."

"They did," said Granny prosaically. "Same way we're going to deal with them. They hunted them all."

"It's not in here," said Otto, sounding disappointed. "No stories about giant wolves. Is there another book of children's stories?"

Grampy shook his head regretfully. "Just this one."

"Hold on," said Rosa, staring at her grandmother. "What do you mean the same way you're going to deal with them?"

"The hunt's already started," Granny told her in satisfaction. "No luck last night, but the group is assembling as we speak."

"Granny, no," said Rosa, alarm sweeping over her. "You can't hunt the wolves!"

"What are you talking about?" Granny protested. "Of course we can."

"But what if they really are humans, like the stories say?" Rosa said, her hands suddenly clammy at the thought of Emmett being hunted by a group of armed forest workers.

"Oh, Rosa, they're bedtime stories," Granny said impatiently. "There's some magic at work, no doubt, but it's a far cry from that to claiming that the wolves are humans in disguise."

Rosa opened her mouth, then closed it. What could she say? How could she argue her case without risking Emmett's secret?

"Granny, I know you're frightened. But...I think it's possible the wolves aren't as big a danger as we've thought. I know everyone says they're savage, but have they ever really attacked anyone? You know how easily sightings get reported as attacks when it comes to trying to spin a good tale."

"Tell that to our boy whose leg is still bandaged," Granny snorted. "The wolf went right for him, no question. And he's not the only one."

Rosa swallowed, horror washing over her. She'd forgotten all about the worker who'd been bitten. So Emmett hadn't always managed to keep control, and he likely didn't even remember it. It was too horrifying.

"We'll catch them," Granny said confidently. "A group of elves came through here last week, offering talismans and the like. We purchased some very potent ones. They'll identify any creature larger than a badger, and put us on their trail. Only magic can defend against it, so unless they make it inside our protective enchantments, they'll have nowhere to hide." She scoffed. "And they won't make it in here. Place is too well guarded."

"You keep saying *we*," Rosa said, alarmed. "Are you joining the hunt, Granny?"

"Course I am," she said impatiently.

"You know," Grampy said thoughtfully, shutting the children's storybook with a snap. "I'm *sure* I read an account of those wolf-men somewhere."

"You're just thinking of the tales I told you," Granny said.

"No." Grampy shook his head slowly. "I definitely read it. Here in this library. It wasn't a story book. It was technical. Talked about the magical theory behind it all, that sort of thing. I didn't take much note because it made no sense to me, not being a singer and all."

"Where was it?" Rosa asked eagerly. If there was a remedy, surely it would be in a record of magical theory, not a book of children's stories.

"I could have sworn it was over here," Grampy said. "But I've already looked, and couldn't see it."

"Let's look again," said Rosa eagerly.

Granny shook her head, giving them up as a bad case as they hurried across the room. "Too much time poring over books is bad for the mind," she told Otto wisely. The prince was too polite to walk away while she spoke to him, so he stayed with her near the door as she prattled on. "Fresh air and growing things, that's the better way to unwind. I never had the patience my husband has for all this writing. I prefer my plants. They're less obnoxious and opinionated than records written by a bunch of scholars who've never felt the wind in their hair or suffered so much as a splinter."

"Your plants?" Otto asked curiously, his eyes flying to Rosa across the room.

"Now you've done it," Rosa informed him. "No getting out of it now."

"Ah, you haven't seen my plants, have you?" Granny asked brightly. "Come on, lad, I'll show you the conservatory. Much more pleasant than this musty old room."

"Oi," called Grampy at this parting shot toward his beloved library. But there was no real heat in the reproach.

He and Rosa searched for almost two hours, Rosa becoming increasingly frustrated as they turned up nothing. Grampy seemed confident on where the record should be, but there was simply no sign of it.

"Perhaps it was misplaced in the audit," the housekeeper commented, as she deposited another tray of unsanctioned refreshments. "I'm sure a few records were missing after that."

"Audit?" Rosa asked in confusion.

She nodded. "The castle conducted an audit on the records years back. Routine, the auditor called it, but I can't remember hearing of any other time they did it, and I've been here four decades. Anyway, the records were a mess afterward. Took us weeks to get them all back in their right places."

"That's right," said Grampy. "I'd forgotten that. It was years ago. As many as ten, do you think?"

The housekeeper frowned. "I wouldn't have thought as long as that, but hard to be sure. Time all blends together after a while, doesn't it?"

"It certainly does," Grampy said amicably, apparently feeling none of the frustration still gripping Rosa at their fruitless search.

"The castle ordered the audit, you said?" she pressed the housekeeper.

The older woman nodded. "That's right. And very officious they were about it too." She paused, seeming to recollect to whom she was speaking. "Meaning no offense."

"None taken," Rosa said absently. She turned to her grandfather. "If it's possible the records were misplaced, they could be anywhere. Should we look in a different section?"

At that moment, however, one of the guards appeared in the doorway to inform Rosa that it was time to leave.

"Can't I just have half an hour more?" she pleaded.

He shook his head. "I'm sorry, Your Highness, but our orders are not to keep you out near dark under any circumstances."

Rosa sighed, recognizing that it was useless to argue.

"I'll keep looking, Rosie," Grampy assured her, giving her a squeeze. "If it's here, I'll find it."

"Tomorrow," Granny clarified, reappearing with Otto in tow. He looked like he'd just been told everything anyone could ever want to know about plants. "Tonight you're already spoken for. The hunt awaits us."

Rosa stiffened. She'd forgotten about the hunt. But she was given no more chance to protest, the guards bearing her and Otto out of the manor with irresistible force. Their horses were already saddled and waiting, and before she knew it, they were riding out of the gate.

"Did you find what you were looking for, Rosa?" Otto asked, once they were on the forest road.

She shook her head, a lump rising in her throat. Things were even worse than she'd thought. She was no closer to helping Emmett, and her own grandparents were out hunting him. She just wished she'd been able to tell them that the wolf wasn't a real danger.

She just wished she was able to believe it herself.

"What's going on, Rosa?" Otto asked, his gaze once again shrewd.

She just shook her head again, struggling to keep her emotions at bay. She couldn't tell him the truth, and she didn't have the capacity or the desire to make something up.

Several minutes passed in silence, but eventually Rosa pulled herself together.

"What about you? Did you enjoy seeing Granny's conservatory?"

"It is impressive," he said diplomatically. He flashed her a grin. "I probably could have done without such a detailed tour."

Rosa laughed. "She certainly loves her plants."

"I can understand why," Otto said, amenable as always. "The hothouse was especially impressive. I've never seen one like it. Not exactly pleasant, though. I don't know how she stands to spend hours gardening in there."

"Hothouse?" Rosa asked. "Oh, you mean that little room at the back, where she keeps it artificially all hot and steamy? Yes, I never liked going in there. I always came out feeling sticky."

"So did I," Otto acknowledged. "But she had some very unusual flowers in there."

Rosa nodded. "Ones that usually grow only in tropical climates, I know. She prides herself on her ability to keep anything alive." She grinned. "That included me in some of my more reckless childhood stages."

Otto smiled, but whatever answer he gave regarding her grandmother, Rosa didn't hear it. Her attention was fully caught by the sudden flash of movement she'd seen in the forest. Her hand slipped on the reins, causing her horse to shy a little. Or was it shying because of whatever creature was watching them through the tree trunks?

Rosa squinted, trying to catch sight of it. She could have sworn she saw gray, and whatever it was, it was following them, keeping an eye on their party. She swallowed, then told herself not to be afraid. Emmett had said that by allowing the wolf to come to the area where it wanted to be, he was able to maintain control of himself. She had even less reason than the previous time to assume the wolf was trying to attack. It was making no move to approach the party.

What should she do? If it was a regular wolf, she'd be taking a risk to approach it. But not a great risk. It would surely run away at sight of the size of their party rather than attack. And if it was Emmett, as she suspected...

Rosa swallowed. She'd personally seen the hunting party assembled in the carriageway as she left her grandparents' house. These were strong, hardy men and women who'd worked in the forest all their lives, and were familiar with both trapping and hunting. Most wielded axes, and they meant business. If this was Emmett, the risk of doing nothing was far too great.

"We need to stop!" she called out, pulling her horse to a halt.

The guards around her pulled up as well, looking confused. The head guard rode down from the front of the group, his expression concerned.

"Is all well, Your Highness?"

"I need to relieve myself," Rosa informed him. "I'm afraid it can't wait."

"Rosa," muttered Otto. "Of all the ridiculous—"

"I was hurried away in such a rush, I had no chance back at Granny's place," she told him with dignity.

The head guard looked uncomfortable, having been the one to tell her she had to come immediately.

"It will only take a moment," she said briskly, swinging down from the saddle.

"Your Highness, I will accompany—"

"Accompany me?" she cut the guard off, with her best scandalized princess expression. "To relieve myself?"

He shifted uncomfortably. "It's a matter of safety, Your Highness. I meant no—"

"I shall be perfectly safe," she told him. "I'll only go as far off the road as modesty requires."

Several guards around them were shifting on their mounts now, some looking awkward and some trying not to laugh. Rosa ignored them. She didn't care what they thought of her. But she was squirming a little at her own words. They reminded her too much of the promise she'd made to her mother, not to leave the road. A promise she was about to break.

But what am I supposed to do? she pleaded with her conscience. *Emmett's life is in danger, and no one but me can warn him.*

Not pausing to give either the guards or her guilt a chance to talk her out of it, Rosa seized her skirts and hurried between the trees. She wended her way far enough in to be able to hide behind a trunk, moving in the direction she'd last seen the gray form.

"Are you there?" she called softly, gripping her skirts tightly in her nerves. "I saw you—I know you are. Can you understand me?"

For a moment there was no response, then a huge, gray shape slunk out of the gathering gloom. It really was enormous, and its eyes glowed faintly. Rosa stared wide-eyed at the huge wolf, trying not to give in to the instinctive fear that was telling her to panic, to scream, to flee.

It's Emmett, she told herself. *He's in control. He'd never hurt you. You can trust him.*

Her frantically hammering heart didn't seem to have gotten the message, but she forced herself to stay in place.

"You have to get out of here," she told him, willing her voice to be steady. "They're hunting you, and they'll kill you if they catch you. You have to leave. Cross the border to Medulle. I don't think they'll chase you that far."

The wolf's tail flicked back and forth, the creature regarding her with just as much intensity as the human Emmett did, although it felt entirely different in wolf form. It made Rosa's skin crawl, the urge to flee rising up again.

It's not his fault, she reminded herself reproachfully. *He can't help it. He doesn't want to be a monster. Just talk to him, make him understand.*

The memory of her words to her mother flashed through her mind again. She'd already broken her promise to stay on the road. Now she was breaking her promise not to speak to someone she didn't know.

But I do know him! she argued with herself. *It's Emmett. And I can't let him be killed.*

She closed her eyes, willing her mind to picture the man she was so drawn to instead of the wolf he currently was. Tall, muscular figure, dark eyes, serious jawline...The image steadied her. The wolf was frightening, but Emmett was safe. He could be trusted.

His words came back to her, bitter but not reproachful. *I*

didn't really expect you to have so much faith in me. She wouldn't prove his fears justified.

She opened her eyes, and although the wolf looked as terrifying as ever, it had made no move to come closer, shown no aggression. It watched her with human intelligence, waiting for her to speak. Surely that was evidence enough that Emmett was in control.

"Can you leave?" she asked him anxiously. "Or is that not an option?" She remembered him saying that the wolf seemed determined to bring him here, to her grandparents' territory. "Run away if you can," she told him seriously. "You must have seen the guards with me through the trees. I'll be safe until I get to the castle. Get as far away as you can. And if you can't..."

She hesitated, some part of her screaming not to break the confidence she was about to expose. She would never forgive herself if harm came to her grandparents. But those grandparents were the very ones unwittingly trying to murder the man she...well, the man she was determined to save, and that thought was too horrific to contemplate.

"If you can't get away cleanly, the only place you'll be safe from their seeking talisman is inside my grandparents' property," she said. "There's a weakness in the boundary." She remembered the words her grandmother had said so lightly on a previous visit. "A hole in the defenses on the north western edge of the property. You could get inside and hide near the edge. The hunt will die down by midnight, I'm sure. If you hide out until they give up, then you can flee."

The wolf gave no indication of understanding her, and Rosa could no longer deny her body's determination to put distance between herself and the predator. Swallowing nervously, she backed away, watched by the slightly glowing eyes of the unnatural wolf. Emmett made no move to stop her, and as soon as she'd put a few tree trunks between them, Rosa turned and ran, only just reminding herself to be composed before exiting the trees.

The head guard was waiting, tension leaking from his frame as she emerged unscathed. In moments, Rosa was back on her horse and the group was once again on the move.

"Are you all right?" Otto asked, looking her over in concern. "You're very pale. Did something happen out there?"

"I'm fine," said Rosa, taking a deep breath.

Her nerves were settling now she was away from the monstrous form poor Emmett had become. She'd done the right thing, surely. That hadn't been an out-of-control savage beast, likely to attack on sight. It had listened to her as intelligently as a human, and she had no doubt the man had the beast firmly in hand. Her conscience squirmed at the knowledge that she'd betrayed a weakness in her grandparents' security to the very beast they were trying to protect themselves from. But they didn't know what she did. And it wasn't as though they were at risk. They were both out on the hunt, and the rest of their household should be safe enough. The day's work would be done by now, and everyone inside the buildings. And Rosa knew that even if Emmett did get onto the property in his wolf form, he wouldn't be able to enter the house. The buildings had enchantments which prevented any creatures other than humans from crossing the threshold. It was a risk, but a calculated one.

Not a risk your grandparents were given any say in, her inner critic reminded her. The truth of the statement was undeniable, but Rosa had no response. She'd made a choice to trust Emmett even in his wolf form, and while some might think her out of her mind, they didn't know the prince like she did. What was done was done, and she couldn't change it even if she wanted to. She could only hope that everyone she cared about would still be in one piece come morning.

The rest of the ride passed without incident, and they reached the castle comfortably before dark. Their arrival was anticipated, and dinner awaited them. After her disrupted night the night before, Rosa was rapidly fading. She was only too glad to be bundled off to bed early by her lady-in-waiting, who seemed personally affronted by the fact that the monarchs had granted her charge's request to venture into the forest.

Rosa slept fitfully, her dreams full of howling wolves and dark, anguished, human eyes. She woke earlier than was usual for her, and hastened to track down her father's steward before breakfast.

"Your Highness," he said, bowing with a stiffness that told her he was impatient to return to whatever task she'd interrupted. "May I be of assistance?"

"I hope so," Rosa told him. "Do you know if it's normal for the castle to audit the records collections in private residences?"

The steward frowned in thought. "It's not a matter of routine, but I wouldn't say it was abnormal, Your Highness. Such audits occur from time to time if there is reason to think that information of value to the kingdom is in danger of being lost due to lack of care or some other cause."

Rosa felt her forehead crease as she thought of her grandfather's meticulously kept library.

"Who orders them?"

"Sometimes the king, sometimes the Council of Nobles."

Rosa nodded slowly. "I'm looking for information on an audit that was conducted on my grandparents' records within the last decade. Do you know anything about it?"

The steward looked faintly amused. "Within the last decade? Not very precise information, Your Highness. But records are kept of such audits, of course. Usually kept for ten years, I believe, so if you're correct in your timeline, they should still be accessible."

"Where can I find these records?" Rosa asked eagerly.

"In the castle's sealed records room," the steward told her. "You'll need authority from His Majesty to access them."

Then authority from His Majesty she would get.

"Thank you," she told the steward, hurrying away. Her stepfather usually breakfasted early, and she'd be wise to catch him before the business of the day swallowed him alive, likely not spitting him out again until dinnertime.

But she was already too late. Only her mother was at the breakfast table, the king having already eaten and departed. Disconsolately, Rosa picked at her food, unable to muster any enthusiasm for it. Even Otto was nowhere to be seen. In fact, she still hadn't spoken to her stepbrother two hours later, and her impatience was growing unmanageable. She was seriously considering trying to break her way into the sealed records room when she heard running footsteps approaching the covered walkway she was pacing.

She turned to see Otto jogging up, his face grave.

"Otto!" she cried. "Where have you been all morning?"

"Father had me join the dawn patrol on the walls," said Otto shortly. "The current situation in the forest provides a good chance to see the guards in action." He seized her arm, his eyes searching her face. "Are you all right, Rosa? Have you heard? Don't do anything rash."

"Heard what?" Rosa asked, her heart in her throat. Was it Emmett? Was he...had he been...

"Your grandparents," Otto said, the words falling like lead into her stomach. "A messenger from their place came through the gates not long ago. Apparently the rest of the household aren't far behind. They're seeking refuge in the capital. Their property was breached last night, by one of those giant wolves."

Rosa swallowed three times before she could get any words out. "Are they all right? Was anyone hurt?"

"They're fine," said Otto reassuringly.

Rosa shook her head, not believing him. "Don't soften it for me, Otto, tell me the truth! I know my grandparents—nothing short of full-scale catastrophe would drive them from their home."

Otto squeezed her arm, where his hand still rested. "I didn't explain properly. Your grandparents didn't leave. They sent the rest of the household away as a precaution because their security is no longer certain. But the messenger said that your grandmother refuses to leave the property, and your grandfather refuses to leave her."

Rosa raised a shaky hand to her eyes. That sounded about right. "But they're all right?"

"Of course they are," said Otto. "They're the toughest people in Ilgal." He gave a dry chuckle. "Your grandmother is blind with rage at the creature's audacity, according to reports, but otherwise fine."

"And everyone else?" Rosa asked faintly. "What happened?"

Otto let her go, running a hand through his hair. "A few of the servants were outside last night, one emptying the ashes from the fire and the others bringing in wood, when the creature came at them from the darkness. They all got the scare of their lives, and one was bitten, but it's not serious. The others helped her get back inside. The creature tried to claw its way in through the door and some windows, but it couldn't get inside the actual buildings."

"Because they have enchantments on them," Rosa whispered, the words falling from numb lips. She'd used that fact to justify her breach of her grandparents' trust, but she hadn't actually thought the extra protection would be needed. She hadn't really believed Emmett would try to hurt them. "No creature other than humans can get in."

"That's a relief," said Otto. "And probably explains why they waited until light to evacuate the servants. Even then they took a risk. The creature was skulking in the shadows last they saw, and they don't even know for certain whether it ever left their property." He frowned. "The real question is how it got in. No one seems to know that."

"I do." The words were the merest whisper as Rosa buried her face in her hands.

"What was that?" Otto asked, confused. "Rosa, are you all right?"

"This is my fault, Otto," she said hollowly. "Completely my fault. I'm a fool. An absolute *fool*!"

She could have screamed the last word, so frustrated was she with herself, so furious with Emmett. Otto looked utterly bewildered, but she didn't give him the chance to ask for an explanation.

"I need to go to them," she said.

"No way." There was no compromise in Otto's voice. "Why do you think I came to find you immediately? I'm not going to let you do anything rash, Rosa. There's no way you'll be allowed to go to your grandparents' property now we know there's a wolf roaming around inside it."

"He—*it* has probably left by now," Rosa said. "But if it hasn't, that's all the more reason for me to go. My grandparents are there, Otto! And they're in danger because of me!"

Their argument was cut short by the sound of approaching footsteps. Rosa swung around to see a servant hurrying toward them.

The man bowed to them both, then addressed his words to Rosa. "Your Highness, you have a visitor. Prince Emmett of Medulle has arrived at the castle and requested to speak with you."

Fury filled Rosa, fueled by her shame at her own reprehensible part in the previous night's disaster. At least they knew the creature was no longer lurking on her grandparents' property.

No, it was waiting in her mother's parlor, dressed in the deceptive finery of a prince.

Through the haze of her anger she saw the hint of a smirk on the servant's face. He thought he knew the nature of the visit, but Rosa knew better. Romance had nothing to do with it.

Emmett had come to beg her forgiveness for his loss of control, and she had no intention of granting it.

She was going to throw him to the wolves.

"Show me to him," she growled.

CHAPTER NINETEEN

Emmett

After he returned Rosa's horse to a very confused stablehand, Emmett had intended to return to the forest and walk back to Lernvale. But the morning was advancing, and he was just so exhausted. Taking the chance that no one would recognize him, he secured a place in a public coach heading south into Medulle. The journey, while far from comfortable as he was squashed between a middle-aged farmer and a snuffling child, gave him plenty of time for thought. In the space of one brief morning, his world had been turned upside down.

Rosa knew. She knew everything.

Well, not everything. There were so many details he hadn't told her, so many questions she hadn't asked. But she knew the main thing. She knew about the wolf. And she hadn't fled from him or exposed him. She'd even let him come near. He could still feel the warmth of her fingers on his face. It didn't feel real, any of it. And yet, he'd never felt so alive.

He could hardly believe she'd spent the night looking for him. It was equal parts touching and terrifying. Had she made it back to her room undiscovered? He wanted to believe her word, but it was hard not to worry about what she'd do with the information he'd just given her. She had the power to seriously damage Medulle's interests if she chose. But when he'd told her the terrible truth and she'd looked so unflinchingly into his eyes, he hadn't seen any thought of kingdoms and politics there. She'd seen only him.

And while he wasn't entirely sure what that meant, he did know he'd felt something he hadn't felt in a long time. Something suspiciously like hope.

The walk from the main road to the castle was only an hour, and he didn't even have to complete the whole thing. He was only halfway there when a carriage bearing the Terenan royal crest pulled up and Farrin jumped out.

"Emmett," he said, his voice quiet for the sake of the coachman, but relief evident on his face. "You're all right. Get in."

Emmett clambered gratefully into the carriage, greeting his mother before letting his head drop back against the seat. He was too weary even to be embarrassed by the distress on her face.

"So that carriage took you back to Terenford, did it?" he asked. "And you spent the night there."

"Yes, we did, but what about you?" Farrin asked. "Were you safe? Have you slept at all?"

"As safe as I ever am in that state," Emmett said through a yawn. "And no, I haven't slept."

"We'll be back at the castle soon," said Farrin reassuringly. "I'll get you to your room."

"I'm not a child, Farrin," said Emmett, amused by his little brother's coddling. "I can walk myself there."

But he didn't really protest when Farrin helped him to his room, shooing away the hovering servants. Emmett collapsed gratefully onto his bed, not even the memory of Rosa's breathlessness as she looked up into his eyes enough to keep him from sinking into sleep.

When he woke, a servant was bustling about his room, and the light streaming through the window suggested he'd missed lunch. He ignored the servant's sly looks as he rose from his bed. The rumor had no doubt spread about the bizarre method of his return to the castle, and the servant was probably thinking he was exhausted from a secret rendezvous in the forest.

A small smile curved his lips as he thought of his encounter with Rosa. Rumors sometimes had a grain of truth.

But the expression quickly melted away. After all, it was no laughing matter that Rosa had found him out. She was the first one in four years.

He found his brother in the castle's main study, a room their father had used when they visited Lernvale as children, and which Emmett had adopted more recently. Farrin was focused on his task as he scratched out a letter, and Emmett hovered in the doorway for a moment so as not to interrupt him.

After a moment, Farrin leaned back, spotting the older prince and putting down his quill with a smile. "Emmett. You're awake. How are you feeling?"

"I'm all right," said Emmett, strolling in and taking the seat across from Farrin's. "Still alive, at least for now."

Farrin frowned at that, but Emmett didn't wait for him to speak. He nodded toward the letter.

"Is that going to the capital? Business regarding the first expedition of singers to Selvana?"

"It is going to Port Dulla," confirmed Farrin. "The first expedition was due to leave in a few days, but I expect they'll be delayed."

"Why?" Emmett asked, then slapped a hand to his forehead as he realized. "Because you're supposed to be on it, aren't you?

And I'm keeping you here. Farrin, you need to return to Port Dulla."

"I'm not going anywhere," said Farrin calmly. "The expedition will have to wait. A few weeks won't make any great difference, not after generations." He pulled the parchment toward himself, a self-conscious smile crossing his face. "To tell you the truth, this letter isn't business. It's to Bianca. I've given instructions for a small supply ship to return with an update for Bianca, and I'm hoping this letter can be included."

"Do you miss her?" Emmett asked.

"Like crazy," Farrin acknowledged unashamedly. "I wasn't entirely sure about coming at all, but we thought things would go more smoothly if I was present for the departure of the first expedition at least. I just never planned to be away for this long." He gave Emmett a crooked grin. "None of which makes a difference to what I'm doing here. It just explains why you caught me writing my wife soppy love notes."

"Nothing soppy about it," said Emmett. "I've seen you and Bianca. You'd be mad not to appreciate what you have."

"I do appreciate it," Farrin assured him.

He leaned back in the chair, reminding Emmett strangely of their father in that very seat. When had Farrin grown up so much? It felt at times like everyone else's lives were moving forward, leaving him behind, stuck in place because of his affliction.

"And," Farrin added, "while you might have, I haven't given up on seeing you find the same thing."

Emmett let out a groan, deciding it was time to be candid. He had very little left to lose, after all. "If you're talking about Rosa, I think the chances of her wishing to marry me—always slim—are now nonexistent. She saw me transform back this morning. She knows what I am."

"What?" Farrin bolted upright in his seat. "Princess Rosa knows? How have you left it this long before telling me that?"

Emmett just shrugged.

"What's she going to do with the information?" Farrin demanded.

"I think...nothing," said Emmett slowly. "As unbelievable as that sounds. She promised she'd keep my secret, and I think I believe her."

"Hm." Farrin looked very thoughtful, but the worry line between his brows hadn't eased.

"It worries me too," Emmett admitted, with a smile. "But there's nothing to be done about it now."

"I know you can't change what happened," Farrin said. "But that doesn't mean there's nothing to be done. Was she shocked? Angry? Eager to get away from you as quickly as possible?"

"Shocked, yes," said Emmett. "But the others...not really. I know it sounds bizarre," he added hastily. "But it really is true."

"It doesn't sound bizarre," said Farrin impatiently. "It sounds like the response of someone with a good heart who's head over heels for you, as anyone but you can tell Princess Rosa is. But it's still a lot to leave her with. I think you should talk to her once she's had a chance to take it all in, offer to answer questions and explain anything she wants to know. That's the best way to keep her from driving herself mad with speculations, and possibly convincing herself she needs to expose you after all."

"Do you think so?" Emmett perked up, more elated than he should have been at having an excuse to seek Rosa out again. He glanced out the window, remembering that it was already afternoon. "I'd better wait until tomorrow, perhaps. Then I won't be arriving close to twilight, and she will have had more time to cool off."

"Excellent idea," Farrin agreed. "I think you should go to bed as early as you can this afternoon, get some more sleep before nightfall. You don't want to be a wreck when you arrive to speak with her."

Emmett followed his brother's suggestion, and also did his utmost to convince his wolf self to stay close to Lernvale that night. That way, when morning dawned, he would be able to make himself presentable and set off at once for Terenford by more conventional means.

All of these strategies meant that when he rode through the gates of the Terenan capital late the following morning, he felt passably human, in spite of another rough and increasingly hazy night.

His nerves gave an extra spring to his step as he followed a servant into the castle. He knew Queen Ada would be delighted to learn he was there to speak with Rosa, but he was past the point of trying to manage the queen's expectations. He no longer had any clear concept of his own expectations. All he knew was that the phantom sensation of Rosa's hand in his hair had refused to dissipate in all the hours since he'd seen her.

How would she receive him? The fact that he was being received at the castle at all suggested she'd kept her promise to him, but Emmett was more interested in Rosa's reaction. Would she be as understanding, as kind as she'd been that morning in the forest? Or had time and reflection brought her to the realization of just how monstrous his affliction—and deception—was?

He was led into a small parlor, and he didn't have long to wait for Rosa to arrive. The moment she entered the room, it became clear which of the reactions Emmett could expect. His heart sank to the region of his polished boots at the absolute fury leaping at him from the princess's eyes.

"Rosa," he said, stammering a little under her glare. "I...I came to—"

"I know why you came," she spat at him. "You came to make excuses. But I'm not interested in them, Emmett. I don't care.

There's nothing you can say that would make me feel even slightly better about any of it. I made a terrible mistake in trusting you, it's true, but your betrayal is so much worse."

"Rosa, please," said Emmett, dismayed at the intensity in her voice. He'd never seen her like this. She was livid. "I never meant to betray you. I know it's distressing, I know it's a lot to process, but please let me explain better."

"I don't want your explanations!" Rosa cried, on the edge of tears now. The sight cut Emmett to the heart. "You *lied* to me, Emmett."

"When did I lie?" he demanded, starting to get angry. Why agree to meet with him if she was just going to shout, and give him no opportunity to explain himself? She was entitled to her reaction—he'd expected it immediately upon her discovery, and didn't really blame her for the fact that it had come belatedly—but surely he was also allowed to speak.

"You said you were in your right mind when it happens," said Rosa. "You said you were in control of it. Can you look me in the eye and tell me that was true?"

"I..." Heat rose up Emmett's neck, a feeling of suffocation coming with it. What could he say? He wanted it to be true, desperately. But he'd begun to doubt it himself.

"Do you even remember what happened last night?" Rosa challenged him.

"Last night?" Emmett asked. He frowned in an effort of memory. All he could come up with was a haze of motion, hour upon hour of running between the trees. "Yes, I think so. I mean, I don't remember every detail, but well enough. Why, what happened?" He started forward, half reaching for her. "Are you hurt? Were you in danger?"

"Your concern exposes you," Rosa said coldly. "If you could truly remember all that happened, you wouldn't need to ask if I'd been at risk. You'd have no cause to worry. You don't even know what you did." She seemed to swell before his eyes, tears glistening on her cheeks now. "I ignored my instincts. I lied for you, I broke my promise for you. I *trusted* you! And you betrayed me! I can never forgive you for this."

Cold, icy horror washed over Emmett, and not just because of Rosa's contempt. Was his memory failing him? What had he done? Before he'd arrived, he would have sworn that he hadn't hurt anyone—hadn't even *seen* anyone—the night before. But now, in face of Rosa's certainty, his own began to waver. Could he be wrong? So much of his recollections were blurry these days, and the previous night was no exception. Had he committed some terrible atrocity while in the grip of the wolf?

"Rosa, what happened?" he demanded. "Why are you shouting at me?"

"You know why," she snapped. "And if you don't, that's even worse." She drew a shuddering breath. "I regret the things I said to you before. I hope you know that I would never want to marry a monster, prince or not. No self-respecting girl would think a crown was worth it."

Pain flashed through Emmett, as sharp and merciless as a knife thrust. For a moment he was speechless, then anger rose to his rescue, pooling into the emptiness that had filled him at Rosa's words.

"Good," he said, his words coming fast and low. "I'm glad we've cleared that up. It's certainly my view. Perhaps you could write to my mother and tell her as much, because she seems bizarrely convinced otherwise. As for me, I never had any intention or desire to pursue you or anyone else."

"Fine, I'll do that," said Rosa, her chest heaving with emotion as she glared at him.

"Fine," said Emmett.

"Fine!" Rosa shouted, apparently unconcerned by the fact

that they were in a building inhabited by many people, and the door to the parlor could only deaden the sound so much.

For a moment they just stared at each other, the tension between them more potent than it had ever been. Then, abruptly, Rosa turned on her heel, sweeping from the room in what could only be called a blind rage.

Emmett stood alone in the middle of the room, trembling with anger and something else. Slowly awareness of his surroundings returned, and he realized he needed to move if he didn't want to be caught there by Queen Ada or Prince Otto, and forced to endure the agony of making small talk while his life crumbled around him and his heart shattered into a thousand pieces within his chest.

He flung himself from the room, dodging more than one interested eavesdropper lingering near the door. He couldn't even bring himself to care about the humiliation of Rosa's rejection. He was still too destroyed by the rejection itself. He heard whispers follow him as he rapidly escaped the castle, surprising a groom who'd only just finished removing the saddle from Emmett's horse.

"Never mind," the prince snarled, turning away from the stables and toward the city wall. He thought he heard someone hail him, but he ignored it. Without even thinking about his destination, he found himself leaving through the western gate and plunging into the forest. It felt familiar under the branches, safe and enclosed. He could run here, he could move.

He started to do just that, running with the thoughtless abandon of an animal. The undergrowth flew away beneath him at an increasing pace, his breaths coming too steadily, his energy too high.

He barely noticed the transition from two legs to four. There was no rending pain. For the first time in over four years, the transformation was seamless. And for the first time, he found himself running canine under the light of the sun.

The curse was taking him at last, and he couldn't even bring himself to care, to fight. Perhaps the wolf's oblivion would be better than the agony of being human.

CHAPTER TWENTY

Rosa

Rosa threw herself around a corner, desperate to reach her room. She half-ran into a tall figure which some part of her mind recognized, but she didn't pause to identify the person, let alone apologize. She didn't care who it was. She didn't care about anything. Her rage was sustaining her, and she stoked it desperately. She couldn't afford to let it go out and feel what would surely take its place.

She couldn't afford to acknowledge why Emmett's betrayal was so devastating. Why she felt like she'd lost someone she loved, even though neither of her grandparents had been so much as touched by the wolf.

Her heart wasn't ready for that admission. Not now any hope of a happy ending had been ripped to shreds. She couldn't have a future with a mindless beast.

He wasn't mindless, a voice whispered in her head. *He stopped and listened to your words—he understood well enough to find the weak point in the protections. And, with an excellent opportunity to attack you, he didn't do it.*

But the memory of the wolf's intelligence made it worse, not better. Was she supposed to be satisfied with being the only human Emmett didn't savage in his monstrous form?

She remembered the agony that had crossed his face when she'd called him a monster, and told him that she would never want to marry him. He'd tried to hide it, but she'd seen. She'd seen.

Agony just as acute lanced through her, and it only fueled her anger. She was furious with him, and for good reason. Was she supposed to feel pity as well? The trouble was, what she felt wasn't pity. Pity was a response to something pathetic...something, well, pitiable. And even having witnessed what he'd become, she couldn't think of Emmett as pathetic.

No, what she felt was the deep, aching grief of seeing a good man brought low through circumstances he could neither control nor escape from. It was unendurable, and she couldn't bear to give any room to the grief. The anger was a safer companion.

True to her word, Rosa swept into her own rooms, making straight for the elegant writing desk in the corner, which she rarely used. Thankfully there were no maids tending the fire or straightening her clothes. She didn't want witnesses to her unstable mood.

Yanking a fresh sheet of parchment toward her, she grabbed a quill and dipped it in the inkwell. A detached part of her mind noted that someone kept the ink fresh in spite of how infrequently she had need for it. The luxuries of castle life.

Her penmanship far from its best thanks to her shaking hand, she scrawled angrily across the page.

To Her Majesty Queen Sula of Medulle

Thank you for your <u>flattering</u> interest in me for your horrible son's bride and heir-producer, but I decline.

I have no interest in marrying a monster like your son, and if you think his crown will tempt me, you must have confused me with the type of vapid, shallow girl you would no doubt choose if his impending death didn't force you to seize the closest candidate and wring grandchildren out of her immediately. Find someone else to produce your horrifying son's cubs.

The words flowed with vicious fluency, Rosa taking great satisfaction from each falsely polite phrase. She pulled back and read the rambling tirade, the parchment shaking slightly in her grip. She gave a derisive snort when she reached the word *cubs*, the sound rough and unappealing even in her own ears. Then, all at once, Emmett's face flashed through her mind, her memory brutally accurate at recreating the pain he'd tried to shield at her harsh words.

Abruptly, Rosa lowered the letter and burst into tears. The storm of emotion that held her in its grip was so intense, she could no longer see the parchment before her. The last time she remembered crying like this was when her father had died. Hot tears fell onto her sprawling words, blurring the strokes so that they were as messy and confused as her own conflicted heart.

In this state, she didn't even hear the door open, and barely caught her stepbrother's voice as he spoke her name in concern.

Rosa jumped as Otto's hand fell on her shoulder. But there was no slowing the tears now they'd taken hold, and she just continued to sob, her palms flat on the desk on either side of the letter.

"What's that?" Otto asked sharply. "Have you received some bad news? Has someone..." His voice trailed off as he no doubt recognized Rosa's own writing. She didn't try to stop him from scanning what she'd so furiously scrawled across the now tear-spattered parchment.

"Stars above," said Otto hollowly. "Rosa, for the love of our kingdom, please tell me you're not going to send that."

Rosa made a hysterical sound, somewhere between a laugh and a hiccup. She wiped the palm of one hand across her eyes, trying to stem the flow of tears while simultaneously scrunching up the parchment with her other hand. With a shuddering gasp, she lobbed it into the smoldering fire, watching along with Otto as the paper blackened and curled until the fire had completely eaten away her angry words.

Rosa pulled in a long, slow breath, finding to her surprise that some of her rage and grief seemed to have burned away as well.

"Are you going to tell me what's going on?" Otto asked, settling on the edge of a nearby chest so he could look her in the eye.

Rosa gave him a sad smile. "No, I'm afraid I'm not. Although I would if I could, Otto, I hope you know that."

"Rosa, this isn't a joke," Otto said warningly. "I saw Emmett storming out of the castle barely five minutes after you went to speak to him. I don't think he even heard me call his name. What happened between you two?"

Rosa just shook her head, a sick feeling rising up her throat at the memory of their miserable encounter.

"Fine then, what about the letter?" Otto demanded. "What was that about Emmett's impending death?"

"I can't talk about what I wrote, Otto," Rosa said desperately. "I'm sorry. You should never have seen it. I was just letting off some steam."

Otto frowned at her, but didn't press further. His forbearance was one of the things she'd always greatly admired about him.

"I really am sorry," she told him, trying to smile. "You're the best of brothers, Otto, you really are. It's not about trust, I swear. If it were, I'd tell you everything."

Otto's expression softened, his ears going pink at the praise.

"What can I do to help?" he asked quietly. "Don't tell me you don't need help, because you're a mess."

Rosa leaned forward, resting the top of her head against his shoulder. He patted her back in a comforting way, and after a moment she was able to breathe more naturally.

"I am a mess," she agreed frankly. "And I don't know what you can do—all I know is that *I* need to do something. I can't bear to sit around here feeling depressed."

"Rosa..." Otto sounded uneasy. "I know you're worried about your grandparents, but I really don't think you should be sneaking off to the forest after everything that's—"

"No, no, of course not," Rosa said hurriedly. "I didn't mean that."

She was ashamed to realize that in her anguish over Emmett, she'd momentarily forgotten that her grandparents were still in danger. But they weren't, really. Not now that she knew the wolf was no longer on their property. And she would be no help to them in her current state.

"I've been trying to follow up on the audit my grandparents' mentioned yesterday," she explained.

"Oh, well, I suppose that's harmless enough," Otto said, relaxing. "I can cover for you if needed."

"Thank you, Otto," said Rosa warmly, pushing herself to her feet. Already she felt impatient—almost desperate—to be moving again, to be doing *something*. Inevitably, it made her think of Emmett, and what he'd told her about his need to be in motion if he wished to retain any sense of control when in his wolf form. It was painfully relatable.

You're as much a wolf as he is, a voice told her brutally. *More, by nature.* She ignored these internal strictures. She wasn't going to think about Emmett or about wolves. That was the whole purpose of her self-appointed task.

"So do you know where to start?" Otto asked, as they moved across the room.

Rosa nodded. "I already spoke to the steward, and he thinks the audit might have been ordered by the Council of Nobles. I want to check the—" She cut herself off with a groan. "Oh no, I forgot. I need the king's authority to enter the sealed records room."

"I don't," said Otto, and Rosa stopped walking.

"Don't what?"

"Don't need Father's authority to view the sealed records. I have access any time I wish."

"Of course you do," said Rosa darkly.

Otto just grinned. "Would you like me to bestow my favor upon you, sister dearest?"

She chuckled half-heartedly. "All right, I suppose you can come along."

"Very gracious of you," he said.

Otto took the lead, shooting her a sideways look as they emerged into the corridor. "Why did you call Emmett's hypothetical children cubs, though?" he asked abruptly.

Rosa gave a laugh which she quickly curbed. It was almost as hysterical as her tears had been. "Just trying to be hurtful, I suppose," she said dully. "Who knew I was such a bitter old hag?"

"You're not a bitter hag," Otto told her calmly. "But you would have been a dead princess if you'd sent that letter and Mama had gotten wind of it."

Rosa shuddered. "And she would have gotten wind of it, given how chummy she and Queen Sula have become. They're a terrifying force." As if Emmett needed more to contend with than he already faced. She ran a hand through her hair. "I was never really going to send it, though."

"I know," Otto assured her.

They fell silent, neither speaking until they reached the room containing the sealed records. The guards on the door looked a little uncertain about Rosa's presence, but neither challenged the crown prince's right to bring his stepsister with him into the restricted room.

As for the clerk within, he was so flustered by the presence of his future king that he barely seemed to notice Otto's companion. Clearly the room wasn't frequently accessed if the appearance of royalty had that effect.

"Audit records are over here, Your Highness," the clerk said, once they'd explained their errand. He practically tripped over himself in his hurry to show them across the room. "The records are very comprehensive, which makes storage an issue. They're usually kept for ten years, then burned."

"Are they categorized by date, or by the name of the person whose records were audited?" Rosa asked.

"Both, of course, Your Highness," the clerk said, bowing to her.

She had to acknowledge the place was well organized. Even without any idea of the date, once she told the clerk her grandparents' names, he produced the relevant records within moments.

"You weren't kidding about it being comprehensive," she said, her eyes widening as she flipped through the many pages of the tome. It was so big, it had been split into two volumes.

"Every record in the audited collection is listed," the clerk said, nodding. "Along with a brief explanation of its contents."

Otto let out a low whistle, presumably sharing Rosa's mental image of the size of her grandfather's library.

"That would have taken forever," she commented. "No wonder it was a memorable incident to the housekeeper, even so many years later."

"What exactly are we looking for?" Otto murmured, leaning over her shoulder for a closer look.

She lowered her voice as well. "Grampy said it was a technical book on the magical theory behind the legends of the giant wolves. They have a fair few books on magic in their collection, so I suppose the best thing would be to look for the word *wolf*."

"And hope it was in the title," Otto said skeptically. But he took the second volume when Rosa handed it to him, scanning the front page without complaint.

To Rosa's relief, the word appeared less than a third of the way through her section.

"I think this is it," she told Otto excitedly. "Look: *The Forest of Ilgal: A Case Study on the Magic Behind Legends of Shapeshifting*. And in the description it mentions the legends about giant wolves."

"That's surely the one," Otto agreed, sounding relieved as he marked his place in his own volume with one hand.

"I'm sure this is the record Grampy mentioned," Rosa said confidently. "And we definitely didn't find it yesterday." She turned to the clerk. "Where are the records mentioned? Are they stored somewhere in the castle?"

The clerk looked confused. "No, Your Highness. Records aren't acquired as part of an audit, only examined. It's only in rare cases the crown takes custody of a record, and there's a separate process for that."

"How can we find out if that occurred in this case?" Rosa asked, frowning.

"At the back of the audit account," the clerk told her. "There would be a note if an acquisition had been recommended."

Otto flipped through his volume, smoothing out the last page. "I can't see anything about any acquisitions," he said. "It just ends with, *site inspected and audit approved*, then there's a signature."

The clerk nodded. "That will be the official who ordered the audit. Often it's the king himself, on advice of the Council of Nobles."

Otto shook his head. "That's not Father's writing." He squinted. "The name isn't very neat. It's more of a scribble. I think it starts with an L."

"Let me see." An ominous feeling washed over Rosa as she shouldered her way in beside her stepbrother. A moment's examination convinced her that her suspicion was correct. "Leonhard," she breathed.

A sudden realization hit her—that was who she'd run into in the corridor when she fled from Emmett. Leonhard. Her uneasiness grew. She'd been angry, and she wasn't confident she'd kept her voice down as much as she should. Was it possible he'd overheard any of what passed between them?

"Leonhard," Otto said, sounding pleased to have the mystery solved. "Yes, that's what it says." His mind catching up, he looked sharply at Rosa. "Hold on. Does that mean he authorized the audit?"

"It does," said Rosa grimly. "And he stole the record about shapeshifting magic, I know he did."

Otto glanced at the clerk, whom Rosa realized was looking intrigued. With a quick word of thanks, the prince returned the documents and chivvied Rosa from the room.

"Rosa, you can't just throw accusations like that around," he scolded her once they were in the corridor.

"Think about it, Otto," said Rosa quickly. "He's had his eye on my grandparents for a long time. I'm still not satisfied that we understand his reasons for wanting to clear the forest. But I think his interest in them goes beyond their influence in the forest community. Maybe they have information that's a threat to him somehow."

"As far as we can tell, they don't have the information anymore, actually," Otto pointed out mildly.

Rosa didn't answer at once. She tapped one fist against the other open palm, thinking. What was Leonhard involved in?

"The date of that audit was more than seven years ago," she mused. "Long before the rumors of giant wolves started up again."

She bit her lip. Emmett had told her in the forest that he'd accidentally unleashed magic on himself four years ago. By that time, the record outlining any magical basis there might be for the shapeshifting legends had been in Leonhard's possession for a few years already. Plenty of time to decipher any truth in the legends and figure out how to replicate the magic.

"Do you think Leonhard is behind the magic?" she breathed. "Did he set it up somehow?"

She frowned. But why would he attack the crown prince of Medulle? *Had* it been an attack, or a genuine accident? She didn't know enough about the circumstances of Emmett's curse to draw accurate conclusions. And like the hotheaded fool she was, she hadn't taken the opportunity to ask him, instead yelling at him and storming away.

She let out a low groan. That was about right.

"Leonhard can't be behind the growth of the wild magic," said Otto. "That's been building for decades, and it's the same issue Selvana experienced. Besides, he's not a singer, remember?"

It took Rosa a moment to realize her error. Caught up in her theories, she'd forgotten that Otto knew nothing of the magic afflicting Emmett. And in spite of everything that had passed between herself and Emmett, she still intended to keep her promise not to expose him.

She didn't correct Otto, thankful for his convenient misunderstanding. Let him believe she was speaking of the wild magic, not the magic that had cursed Emmett.

"But what if Leonhard is lying about not being a singer?" she demanded. "He's the only one in his family who isn't...surely that's suspicious."

"You heard how his family look down on him for it," Otto told her skeptically. "You really think he would spend his entire life—even from his childhood—pretending not to be a singer so he could plot some elaborate magical exploit?"

"It seems unlikely," Rosa agreed reluctantly.

Otto's gaze passed suddenly over her shoulder, and Rosa turned to see her lady-in-waiting moving toward them in her usual stately manner.

"Your Highnesses." The woman curtsied to them both, but her words were directed to Rosa. "Her Majesty sent me to find you."

Rosa stifled a groan. In the intrigue of what she'd discovered regarding the audit, she'd momentarily forgotten why she'd been so eager to immerse herself in an activity. But it came rushing back now, and she couldn't face a confrontation with her mother about the scene she and Emmett had shared.

"Can you please tell her that I'm otherwise occupied with Otto right now?" she tried hopefully.

The lady-in-waiting's expression was unamused. "I trust I would never be called upon to carry such a disobliging message, Princess Rosa. It is entirely unnecessary. Your mother didn't ask for your presence. She merely wished me to pass on a message."

"Oh." Rosa relaxed. That wasn't so bad. "What's the message?"

"She wished me to ensure that you are within the castle, and to adjure you to stay here," the older woman said.

"Oh," Rosa repeated. "Well, I'm here. Why particularly?"

"That was not part of the message," said the older woman.

Rosa opened her mouth to retort, but Otto beat her to it.

"I would also like to know why the queen is particularly concerned," he said, his tone carrying an understated but compelling authority Rosa had never been able to replicate. "Has something happened since I left my father an hour ago?"

"It has, Your Highness," the lady-in-waiting said, thawing to Otto with deeply unjust speed. "As I understand, one of these giant wolves was sighted from the castle walls within the last hour. Very close to the forest's edge, I believe. The king has ordered a hunt."

"A hunt?" Rosa started forward, feeling the color drain from her face. "They're going to kill—the creature?"

"That's the plan, Your Highness." The older woman looked bemused by her reaction.

"Father's been talking about it for a while," Otto told her. "He knows that residents in the forest have begun doing their own hunts, and he's been thinking it would be better to coordinate on official one before someone gets hurt. And to demonstrate to everyone that the castle takes the threat seriously."

"Very wise of him, I'm sure," said the lady-in-waiting. "I believe His Majesty is overseeing the preparations himself."

Otto nodded, clearly not surprised to learn any of this. But Rosa was paralyzed with horror. Emmett had left the castle an hour ago, in a state of great distress. She'd assumed he would ride back to Lernvale, but he must instead have run to the forest. Which meant that her grandparents weren't as safe as she'd assumed, for one thing. But, more drastically, there was now a risk that Teren's king was about to unknowingly kill the crown prince of Medulle.

What should she do? Was it time to break Emmett's confidence and tell her family the truth about him? Rosa hovered in an agony of indecision until the older woman had left her and the prince alone again. She wasn't sure she could bring herself to tell everyone the truth. For all she knew, they wouldn't even believe her.

Besides, perhaps she was overreacting. Was Emmett really in such danger if he could turn human again as soon as any hunt drew near? Maybe he'd long since reached the Medullan side of the border, anyway.

"I think I'll go and speak to Father," Otto said, breaking the silence. "He might want my assistance with the hunt."

"Otto..." Rosa trailed off, still not sure of the best course. "I'm not sure the hunt is such a good idea."

Otto frowned at her. "Are you worried about your grandparents? Surely this is safer for them than the less organized hunts they were already taking part in."

"No, it's not that," said Rosa. "I don't think they'll be joining any hunt if they've sent everyone else away from the manor. They'll be settling in to defend their property."

"Then what is it?" Otto asked. "If the wolves are bold enough to come almost to the city wall, we can't leave the situation any longer. Do you have a better solution?"

Rosa bit her lip, the question cutting right to the heart of her anguish. She had no solution to Emmett's affliction. But she was determined to find one.

"Never mind," she said, deciding that the situation didn't justify revealing Emmett's secret. Not until she'd exhausted all other avenues. "Stay safe, Otto."

He nodded, then paused, looking at her with narrowed eyes. "You're not going to ask to come with me?"

Rosa shook her head. "I don't want any part in the hunt."

The prince looked suspicious. He knew her too well. "Rosa, you heard what Mama said, right? You can't go into the forest— you need to stay here where it's safe."

"I know," Rosa assured him. "Going to the forest is the last thing on my mind right now."

"Then what will you do?"

"Try to think of a better solution," Rosa said cryptically.

Otto continued to hover, evidently not convinced, but Rosa chivvied him away with her hands.

"Go, I'll be fine."

With one last skeptical look, Otto hurried away, clearly eager to be involved in whatever his father was planning.

Rosa, however, turned her sights toward a different target altogether. She was glad that Otto had worded his warning more generously than her mother had. Rosa could tell her stepbrother with a clear conscience that she didn't intend to go to the forest. Staying in the castle, on the other hand, was more than she could promise.

The tangle that had them all in its grip was only getting messier, and she could see no hope of a good outcome without breaking Emmett's curse. The Medullans had obviously failed to find an answer in more than four years, but they would have no way of knowing about the unusually large private collection of records held by her grandparents. The document mentioned in Leonhard's audit was by far the most promising lead Rosa had seen, and evidence or not, she was convinced that the advisor had stolen it.

She would need all her extensive experience in sneaking around if she had a hope of getting away with what she had in mind.

CHAPTER TWENTY-ONE

Rosa

A few hours later, Rosa could be found—or hopefully not found—easing her way into a window of Leonhard's residence. It had taken some time to discreetly discover where the advisor lived, and considerably more time to find a way in undetected. Even getting out of the castle had been harder than usual, with everyone alert on account of the wolf sighting. It helped that many of the guards had been sent to join the group gathering outside the city walls for the hunt.

The advisor's home was unsurprisingly located near the castle, in the wealthiest part of the capital. And it was large— much larger than necessary for an unmarried man who lived alone.

Well, not really alone. Rosa knew there would be servants in the house, even though her information was that Leonhard was currently in the castle. Still, the size of the house was likely to work in her favor. When she dropped from the helpfully ajar window—using all the agility she'd gained from her many excursions over the castle wall—she found herself in a small and mercifully empty parlor.

She didn't know how long Leonhard might be occupied at

the castle, but she also knew speed would be a false gain if it got her caught. She therefore tried her best to display a patience that had never come naturally as she moved stealthily from room to room, more than once having to duck into a storage space to avoid detection from a passing servant.

After a methodical search, however, she found what she was looking for. Leonhard's study.

The room was meticulously tidy, and clearly home to many documents. The fire burning in the grate told Rosa that the study was regularly used, and she would be unlikely to have long. She wasn't daunted, though. She had a feeling that finding the stolen record would be as simple as finding the storage area Leonhard considered worth locking.

Sure enough, several minutes of searching identified a locked cabinet in a secondary desk pushed against one wall. Rosa squinted at it, wondering how best to proceed. She was tempted to abandon subtlety altogether, and smash up the desk in order to reveal the locked section. She'd smuggled one of Otto's daggers for that purpose, unbeknownst to the prince. But would she be able to do it quietly enough not to draw attention from the servants?

Before Rosa had decided what to do, the unmistakable sound of the door clicking open made her turn, gasping.

A chill went down her spine at the sight of Leonhard himself, standing framed in the doorway, watching her with an expression she couldn't read.

"Princess Rosa," Leonhard said, his voice as smooth as silk. "What an honor to host you in my humble home. In my study, of all places."

Rosa drew herself up, refusing to be intimidated. Otto might not be convinced, but she was sure this man had stolen from her grandparents, and she was simply there to reclaim the stolen property. Not to mention that was likely the least of his schemes.

"I can't say I expected you," she said brazenly.

"I'm sure you didn't." Leonhard gave a chuckle, moving fully into the room and closing the door behind him with a quiet click. The sound was deeply unnerving.

In fact, the advisor's whole demeanor was off. In Rosa's experience, he was usually angry when he saw her. Probably because of seeing her. But now he seemed relaxed, satisfied. Like everything was finally going according to his plans.

She didn't like that thought.

"You appear to be contemplating my locked cabinet," Leonhard said, coming to stand alongside her. "Allow me to assist you."

He pulled a key from a hidden inner pocket, fitting it into the lock and sliding the cabinet smoothly open.

Suspicious, but ridden by her curiosity, Rosa glanced down. There, on top, was a sheaf of parchment, with the words *The Forest of Ilgal: A Case Study on the Magic Behind Legends of Shapeshifting*, written across the covering page.

Without thinking it through, Rosa seized the record, flipping it open. Her eyes sped rapidly over the first paragraph, which contained a warning to the reader. It stated somewhat dramatically that the contents were intended for academic purposes only, and any attempt to harness magic as described in the volume would corrupt the harnesser beyond redemption. Rosa's eyes flew to the opposite page, which contained a table of contents. She'd barely taken in the first few headings, her gaze catching on the unfamiliar phrase, *The Role of Aconitum*, when the paper was plucked from her hands.

"Is this what you were searching for, Princess?" Leonhard asked, flicking through the volume with a casual air. His eyes traveled to hers, and he shut the pages, perhaps realizing that she was debating whether she could wrest it off him without ripping it. "I'd be very interested to know how you concluded you would find it here."

Rosa said nothing, unwilling to give him any information he didn't already have.

"If you're here looking for answers, I gather you've heard the terrible news, then," Leonhard went on in a voice of unconvincing concern. "Distressing, isn't it?"

"News?" Rosa asked, her eyes narrowed.

"About the giant wolf." Leonhard's eyes searched hers. "The one which has all but breached the city."

Rosa frowned, caution telling her not to give any hasty answer. There was something in Leonhard's manner that made the hairs on the back of her neck stand up. His words were nothing new, nothing to cause fresh concern. But instinct told her there was more he wasn't saying, and the unspoken alarmed her. Why wasn't he berating her for breaking into his home, and rushing to report her to the king in outrage? Why did he show no discomfort at being found with the stolen record?

"All but breached the city?" she repeated, in reference to the wolf. "That's an exaggeration, by the account I heard."

Leonhard's eyes seemed amused as he watched her. "Is it? And I thought I was being delicate in my understatement."

He knows. The thought flashed terrifyingly through Rosa's mind. *He knows the wolf is Emmett.*

She had no grounds for the suspicion, but it refused to be shaken. She remembered how she'd run into Leonhard—quite literally—when she fled her argument with Emmett. Had he heard something? Had he perhaps even followed the prince?

But if he knew, why was he radiating private satisfaction? Why did his expression suggest that everything was falling into place in his favor? His reaction was almost more alarming than his discovery.

Rosa didn't dare confront him. Her hunch might well be

wrong, and if he didn't know, any attempt to broach the topic would be disastrous.

For a long, charged moment, Rosa held Leonhard's gaze. His eyes seemed to mock her, to challenge her to speak. Only the knowledge that she was on dangerous ground kept her from letting her anger show. He wasn't to be trusted, this man. She'd always found something to be off about him, but it was stronger now than it had ever been. In spite of his smooth words, the glint in his eyes was almost...savage.

"What are you doing with that record?" she demanded abruptly. "I know you've had it for years. What's your role in the appearance of these giant wolves?"

Leonhard raised one eyebrow in apparent surprise. "My role? What can you mean?"

Rosa held in a growl, unconvinced by his incredulity. "You did this," she said through gritted teeth. "You're the one who gathered the magic somehow. You used that record as a guide, and you—"

"What nonsense," Leonhard said, still maddeningly unperturbed. "But you do make a valid point. I read it only to understand the unfortunate phenomenon. But clearly in the wrong hands, this record could be dangerous. We'd best not take any risks."

And before Rosa could even make sense of the movement, he'd tossed the entire sheaf into the fire that burned just behind him. Rosa lunged forward with a cry, but Leonhard blocked her with one arm, while the other hand seized powder from a small basin on the mantel and tossed it into the fireplace. The flames flared with unnatural speed, consuming the thick sheaf within seconds before dying immediately back down.

"Handy use of magic, isn't it?" Leonhard asked pleasantly. "Much like the warning that alerts me to unauthorized access to my study. Coming from a family of singers has its uses, you know."

Somewhere in the back of her mind, Rosa wondered just how often Leonhard burned incriminating documents in order for him to have a supply of that magical powder ready. But most of her mind was consumed with the rage and despair that had gripped her at the sight of the last blackened page turning to ash.

"What are you doing?" she cried. "How dare you? If you think destroying that absolves you of your guilt, you must be mad. I saw it, and I'll tell everyone. You were the only one who had the information on how to turn a human into a giant, savage wolf!"

"Turn a human into a wolf?" Leonhard repeated, feigning shock. "Do you mean to suggest that these wolves are really humans?"

"You know they are," growled Rosa, enraged with herself for being the first to slip up in their silent dance.

"I'll tell you what I do know," Leonhard said pleasantly. "That you're wrong to claim that I'm the only one with whatever information was in that record. I have evidence that your own grandparents were the ones to acquire it. Curious, isn't it, how resistant they've been to any suggestion that these giant wolves were a problem to be feared, or that their presence necessitated any evacuation?" He gave her a bland smile. "Until recently, that is."

Rosa narrowed her eyes, furious that he was baiting her, and even more furious that it was working.

"What did you call the, uh...wolf? Giant and savage?" He tutted. "Savage, is he? I've never seen him myself, but I heard that you have."

The gloves were off now, and Rosa was struggling to keep her composure. But she couldn't be the one to say it in so many words and confirm that Emmett was the wolf. Not if there was any chance she was wrong about the meaning behind Leonhard's taunts.

"I'll make you pay for what you've done," she said, her anger stoked by having to resort to such vague responses. Even to her own ears, the words felt empty. She had no proof that Leonhard had been the one to afflict Emmett, and she couldn't even reveal his crime, since it wasn't her secret to tell.

"Yes, I thought you'd take it personally," Leonhard said, his eyes glinting again. "Given your...ah...*connection* with the situation." He stepped forward, invading Rosa's space with a sudden movement that caused her to back up against the desk. "What was he like?" Leonhard breathed, his body much too close to hers and his eyes much too intense as they bored into her own. "Was he simply terrifying? Or was there a magnetism?"

Rosa swallowed, finding it suddenly hard to draw breath. Leonhard seemed to sense her fear, because his lips curved in a smile that was almost feral. He was nothing like the polite advisor she'd seen around the castle on countless occasions. She felt like she was seeing his true self for the first time, and it was horrifying.

"You could sense it, couldn't you?" Leonhard asked, his voice rough and low. "How easily he could devour you." He reached out a hand, and to her own shame Rosa stood paralyzed by his hypnotic gaze as he lifted the end of one of her braids. "Did you have the sense to run in fear?" he asked, his face angled down enough that she drew her own back in alarm. "Or were you drawn in?"

Rosa closed her eyes, cutting off her view of the advisor's face in an effort to restore order to her chaotic thoughts. How had she been fool enough to be sucked into his mind games? Perhaps it was because his words hit too close to the truth of her reactions to Emmett. But none of that was any of the advisor's business.

"If you want to know what the wolf is like, feel free to wander the forest alone," she said coldly, once again master of herself as she opened her eyes.

Leonhard chuckled, dropping her braid and stepping back. The spell was broken, and Rosa could breathe freely again.

"It's not kind of me to tease you, is it?" he asked, his voice once more indulgent rather than obsessive. "Poor child, you must be mortified."

"I'm sure I have no idea what you mean," Rosa spat out.

A smile stretched across Leonhard's face. "And I'm sure you do. Your courtship is no secret." He shook his head, tutting again as he did so. "I shudder to think what might come of it all. One can't help but wonder whether King Ryker, fond stepfather that he is, maintains his views after such a public and humiliating slight to you."

"What views?" Rosa asked suspiciously.

"His declaration that he has no interest in conflict with Medulle," Leonhard explained, the picture of innocence.

Rosa narrowed her eyes. She remembered the comment in question. It had been in relation to the idea of territory changing hands between the two kingdoms.

"Well, thank you for your visit," Leonhard said in response to her silence. "You've helped me reach my decision."

"What decision?" Rosa's voice was wary.

"I had hesitated to reveal what I witnessed this morning," Leonhard told her. "Out of respect for royalty, you understand. But I realize now that loyalty to my own king demands that I tell him how grossly he has been deceived."

"No," Rosa said sharply, then bit her lip.

She didn't want Leonhard to tell her stepfather the truth about Emmett's condition, but even less did she want the advisor to know he'd gotten under her skin. She had the sense that was dangerous information.

"If you go to the king, how do you plan to explain what you just did?" she challenged, gesturing at the fire.

Leonhard's expression was politely puzzled. "There's nothing to explain, Your Highness. All I'm guilty of is wishing to know whether there's any magical truth behind the tales of the giant wolves. And that volume, sadly, was useless. Very little information in there."

Rosa seethed. She had no doubt that was a bald-faced lie, but of course she couldn't prove it. She'd never seen beyond the document's first page.

"What were you hoping to find?" he asked indulgently. "A cure? I hate to disappoint you, Your Highness, but I've read it through, and there is no cure."

"I don't believe you," Rosa said, wishing her voice wasn't tinged with desperation.

"Whether or not you believe me doesn't change the truth," Leonhard said comfortably. "Now, as pleasant as it has been to host you, Your Highness, I'm afraid I must bring our visit to an end. If I'm to seek an audience with King Ryker for such a somber reason, I have some preparations to make."

For a moment Rosa just glared at him, hating the smugness of his expression. Then she turned abruptly, realizing that there was nothing to be gained from prolonging the encounter. If he truly had followed Emmett from the castle and seen him transform, she couldn't stop him from recounting it to her stepfather.

The question that occupied her most as she swept from the house under the astonished gaze of several of Leonhard's servants was whether she should tell her stepfather first. Perhaps it would go better if he heard it from her.

The trouble was, although she had no doubt now that Leonhard knew, he hadn't actually said as much. He'd never mentioned Emmett's name, and she had no evidence of any part of their interaction. Perhaps he was bluffing, or trying to bait her into making a more credible revelation than he was capable of.

Hesitantly, Rosa inquired after the king when she reached the castle, only to be told by a servant that he'd already left to oversee the hunt. Whether he was venturing into the forest or just supervising from the city wall, she wasn't sure. But she didn't need to know. She hadn't yet decided whether to tell him. She asked for Otto and was told that he had departed the castle with the king. After a moment's reflection, she decided it made no sense to call him back unless she was going to tell him the truth about Emmett. And that was a question she still didn't know how to answer.

Dismissing the servant, she retreated to her rooms to pace in privacy as she wrestled with her thoughts. She'd hardly noticed the day wearing away, but it was almost dark when a knock sounded on her door.

She called eagerly for the knocker to enter, hoping that Otto had returned unasked. But instead she was confronted with a servant who bobbed a quick curtsy before relaying her message.

"Prince Farrin of Medulle is here, Your Highness," she said, her eyes alight with the gossip she'd soon be spreading in the servants' hall. "He's asked for you particularly."

"Prince Farrin?" He was the last person Rosa had been expecting. "Where is he?"

"In the green parlor, Your Highness."

Rosa nodded her thanks, moving quickly into the corridor. What could have brought Farrin here at this hour? How much did he know of everything that was going on?

When she reached the parlor where he waited, Prince Farrin was standing at a mullioned window, passing one riding glove through the other hand in a rhythmic, anxious motion.

"Prince Farrin," Rosa greeted him, and he turned so rapidly his boots squeaked on the polished floor.

"Princess Rosa," he said, striding forward to meet her. "Thank you for receiving me." He glanced behind her to check they were alone, going so far as to walk past her and close the door. "Forgive my impertinence, but I wish to speak frankly to you."

"Please do," Rosa said, gesturing for him to sit.

He declined to do so, cutting right to the chase. "I'm incredibly anxious about my brother. And I came to you because I know you've become aware of his situation. He told me as much."

"Oh." Rosa blinked rapidly, trying to figure out how to respond to this unexpected candor. Then she felt her shoulders slump, the relief of not having to keep the secret sudden and overwhelming. "Yes, I know. And I wish I had hope to offer you. I don't know why you'd think I can help you, but I can't. I don't know how to lift the curse."

For a moment Farrin regarded her shrewdly, and when he spoke, his voice was more measured. "I didn't expect you to be able to lift his curse. I just hoped you might know where he is. The last I heard, he was coming to see you. And we haven't seen him since. I expected his return hours ago."

Rosa frowned. "He did come to see me, and we..." She swallowed, self-conscious. "We argued. He left the castle in anger, and I didn't see him after that. But there was a rumor shortly afterward, that a giant wolf had been seen just outside the castle walls." She hesitated again, but there was nothing to be gained from beating about the bush. "They've organized a hunt. I believe it will begin imminently, if it hasn't already."

Prince Farrin's face had drained of color. "When was this? How long ago did he leave you?"

"Hours ago," said Rosa. "It happened late this morning."

The prince's eyes widened in horror. "This morning? He transformed during daylight?"

"I…I think so," said Rosa, unsettled. "That's my assumption from the information I've heard. Is that surprising?"

"It's never happened before," said Prince Farrin hollowly. "He only transforms at night, and not every night…only around the full moon." He sank into a chair, letting out a low groan as he brought one hand to cover his face. "Has it taken him then? Am I too late?"

"What do you mean?" Rosa demanded. "This isn't the first time he's transformed during the day. I heard reports weeks ago about wolf attacks at noon. It was one of the things that made people realize it wasn't normal wolves, because that's not their usual habit."

"That can't be," argued the prince. "It can't be that much more advanced than he said. He would have told me."

His voice lacked conviction, and Rosa understood why. They both knew that if anything could prompt Emmett to lie, it would be the desire to protect those he loved from the monstrous extent of what he'd become.

But that wasn't good enough, Rosa reminded herself firmly. By keeping silent, he'd endangered many others.

"So has he been a wolf all day?" Farrin said in a whisper. "Running through the forest, alone and hopeless?"

Rosa felt the lump rising again in her throat, and she forced it down. "I'm afraid it might be even worse than you fear," she told him. "I have some reason to think that someone saw him transform. An advisor of my stepfather's. I have no proof, but I think he knows what Emmett is."

She hovered on the edge of telling him her suspicions about Leonhard's involvement in the original magic, but she wasn't sure it was wise. She had nothing to go on but her own speculation, after all.

"Isn't there anything we can do to break the magic?" she asked instead.

Prince Farrin raised a helpless hand. "I've been trying," he said. "For years, I've been trying. But all I found was one vague record...it didn't have specifics about the magic, or how to undo it. I've lost hope that such a record exists."

"I think it did," said Rosa through numb lips. "I think I held it in my hand today. But it's gone now, burned," she added quickly, as Farrin leaped hopefully to his feet. "And I didn't see enough to help Emmett."

The light died from Prince Farrin's eyes as she explained about the record that had once been in her grandparents' library before being seized by Leonhard, and ultimately destroyed.

"He said he'd read it, and there was nothing in it about a cure," she finished. "But I don't trust his word at all. It's possible that there is a cure, and he's lying about it. And if I can just convince my stepfather to arrest him, perhaps he can be forced to say what it is."

"He must be lying," said Prince Farrin angrily. "I can't believe a record that comprehensive could exist regarding the wolf legends without at least exploring the role of aconitum."

"Aconitum," repeated Rosa, straightening. "It did talk about that! I saw the heading. But I didn't get to read what it said. I've never heard of it."

"It's a plant," said Prince Farrin, perking up. "The locals called it wolfsbane, back when it was brought here from Selvana, a long time ago. That's why I went to Selvana in the first place, to look for it. But I couldn't find it. Supposedly when it was brought here, a singer experimented with it, creating a sort of crossbreed that was used against the giant wolves of the time." He sighed. "I'd once hoped that magical strain of aconitum might have survived, but I gave up hope a long time ago of finding it growing wild here. It was never common, and it grows best in tropical climates, so I don't think any would have survived out in the forest."

"It grows...in tropical climates?" Rosa asked, her voice sounding foreign in her own ears. She could barely move, her mind fixated on Otto's comments after their last visit to her grandparents' house. "What does it look like?"

"It has pale purple leaves, with these small clusters of white flowers," Prince Farrin said, watching her closely. "Why? Don't tell me you've seen it?"

Rosa shook her head slowly. "I haven't. And I don't know if there's any of it left in Ilgal." She met his eyes, trying desperately to prevent hope from bubbling dangerously inside her. "But if there is, I know where it will be."

CHAPTER TWENTY-TWO

Rosa

Rosa glanced sideways at Farrin from under her hood. Not the red one this time. She was trying to be inconspicuous.

"What is it?" the Medullan asked. "Are you expecting trouble?"

Rosa shook her head. "No. If we find Otto, he'll cover for us wherever necessary. To be honest, I'm just surprised that you were so unflinching in helping me sneak out of the castle. Not that I mean it as a criticism," she added hastily.

Farrin gave a crooked smile. "I've heard the rumors about you, Princess Rosa. I'm sure you think you're an expert at sneaking off from royal duties, and that those born into the crown would have no clue about it. But I've done my fair share of escaping the net. Far more than my share." He grimaced. "And so has Emmett. How do you think we got ourselves exposed to this twisted magic in the first place?"

"I can't imagine," Rosa told him frankly. "And I'd love to hear that tale." Her eyes slid over his shoulder, and she gestured upward with her head. "But it'll have to wait until another time. There's Otto."

Farrin looked around, spotting the Terenan prince on the city wall above them. To Rosa's eye, her stepbrother looked tense in the dim light of dusk. But at least he was still here.

She hurried toward the nearby steps that would lead her up onto the wall, only to be stopped by a guard.

"Excuse me, miss, but I'm afraid you can't go up—Your Highness?" The guard looked suspicious as her identity dawned on him. "I beg your pardon, but...are you supposed to be out here?"

"Of course I am," said Rosa dismissively, choosing to apply her own definition of *supposed to*. "I need to speak with Prince Otto."

The guard hesitated, unconvinced. Deciding to bypass him completely, she raised her voice.

"Otto!"

Her stepbrother turned at the sound of his name, his brow furrowing as he took in the two figures standing on the flagstones below. He hurried down the steps, looking every bit as suspicious as the guard.

"Rosa, what are you doing here? You were supposed to stay in the castle."

"We need to speak to you, Otto," said Rosa, ignoring the admonition. "It's urgent."

"We?" Otto's eyes flew to Rosa's companion, surprise flitting across his face. "Prince Farrin. Is everything all right?"

"Not even close," Rosa told him. She looked toward the nearby western gate. She'd expected to see a gathered group, but there was no one beyond the usual guards. "If you're here, that means the hunt hasn't started yet, right?"

"No, they left an hour ago," said Otto, sounding none too pleased about it. "Father went with the main group, but he wished me to stay behind to take charge here."

In any other circumstance, Rosa would have commiserated

with her stepbrother on being told to wait in safety while his father assumed all the risk and experienced all the action. But as it was, she was grateful Otto was there. He was the only one she was confident would believe her without question.

Farrin, however, appeared to feel no relief. "An hour ago?" He met Rosa's eyes, and she could read the panic there.

"Can we speak privately, Otto?" she said, with a pointed look at the guard.

"Of course. Come up here."

At the prince's words, the guard stepped aside, allowing Rosa and Farrin to run lightly up the stairs in Otto's wake. The prince led them along the wall to a section of battlement out of hearing range of the guards with whom Otto had previously been standing.

"What's going on, Rosa?" he asked as soon as they'd stopped moving.

"Otto, I have to tell you something...shocking. I don't even know how to prepare you for it."

Otto gave her a wry smile. "I've had you as a sister for years now, Rosa. I'm used to shocking."

She shook her head. "Not like this. Otto, you have to call off the hunt. We can't kill that wolf."

Otto frowned. "Why?"

Rosa drew in a breath. Part of her still resisted the idea of betraying Emmett's trust, but she'd gone past the point of discretion. Besides, Leonhard knew, and he'd already threatened to tell the royal family. Better Otto heard it from her.

"Because the wolf is Emmett," she said bluntly. "And quite apart from the fact that killing the crown prince of Medulle would probably plunge our kingdom into war, I couldn't bear for it to happen." She met her stepbrother's eyes unflinchingly. "I really think it would kill me, Otto. We have to save him."

His mouth had fallen open, and for a stunned moment he simply stared at her.

"It's true," Farrin chimed in. "Emmett has been cursed for years, and we've been doing our utmost to hide it."

"I...I don't know which question to ask first," Otto said helplessly.

"I understand," Rosa said. "I felt the same way when I found out. But there will be time for questions later. First you have to call off the hunt!"

"I can't just cancel it," said Otto. "I can give the order not to send any further teams, but there are already half a dozen groups combing the forest. They're scouting the whole region, reporting back to the main force, which is led by Father."

"Then you have to reach that force," said Rosa. "You have to tell him what I just told you, and get him to send out the word to withdraw."

"Yes." Otto nodded, trying heroically to keep up with it all. "Yes, I can do that." He straightened, and Rosa could tell that some part of him was elated to have an important job, instead of waiting in safety on the city wall. "I'll take some guards, and we'll find them," he said.

He'd already started moving toward the stairs, but he paused, casting a glance back at the pair of them.

"You're sure about this?" he asked.

"Very sure," Farrin said grimly.

"And what about you?" Otto's eyes passed to Rosa, belatedly recognizing how unusual it was that she wasn't trying to come along.

"You don't need me for this," Rosa said quickly. "You'll travel faster without me, and be more likely to be believed."

Otto frowned, smart enough to realize she was holding something back. But Farrin shifted restlessly, and that seemed to give Otto his prompt. With a reassuring nod to them both, he swept toward the staircase.

"Why didn't you tell him about the aconitum?" Farrin asked, the moment Otto was out of earshot.

"Because I'm going to get it," Rosa said. "And he'd try to stop me."

"Why?" Farrin asked.

She gave him a look. "For the same reason you're an ocean away from your wife and home, ready to throw yourself in harm's way to help Emmett. Otto is my brother, and he cares about me." She let out a breath. "Much more than I deserve, honestly. But given what Emmett told me about the wolf, my grandparents' house is probably the most dangerous part of the forest right now. There's no way I'm sending Otto in there, not when someone needs to warn his father anyway."

"I hope you don't think you're leaving me behind," Farrin said flatly.

"I'm not foolish enough to think I have any right to stop you," Rosa said. "But you'll have to keep up." She gave him a tight smile. "Time to show off those sneaking out skills you mentioned earlier. Because unlike Otto, I'm definitely not allowed to ride openly out the gate."

Rosa glanced at the canopy above, although there was little point. It was so dark now under the trees that she could barely see the branches. Fortunately there was a small clearing ahead, and the moonlight that flooded into it illuminated the forest floor enough for her to pick her way through the undergrowth.

For the third time, she cast her eyes back, thinking Farrin must have fallen behind. But the Medullan prince was right there, following closely without making so much as a sound, his habitual limp pronounced.

He caught her surprise, and a wry smile twisted one side of his mouth. "Climbing over city walls under the noses of guards isn't my only skill, Princess. I spent two years living wild in the Selvanan jungle. I don't mean to offend, but Ilgal is a picnic in comparison."

Rosa said nothing, a little embarrassed that she'd expected to be more at home in the forest than the foreign prince.

Neither spoke as they crossed the clearing, the mossy ground ghostly under the light of the full moon. Once they plunged back into the undergrowth, Farrin's quiet voice sounded in the darkness.

"Why did you say that Emmett had made you think your grandparents' house was particularly dangerous?"

Rosa grimaced to herself. She didn't especially want to share this detail, but it was only fair that Farrin have all the information.

"He said that the wolf always pulls him back to the area. And he's breached the boundary of their property at least once."

"Why this area, though?" the Medullan pressed.

Rosa spoke emotionlessly. "Apparently, because it's where we first met."

Farrin had no response to this information, and for a long minute he didn't speak.

"I feel the pressure," he said at last. "In my chest. It's like what I feel whenever my feet touch the ground in Selvana, but not nearly as intense. I'm sure it wasn't like this when we were children."

"It wasn't," Rosa said, disheartened at this confirmation that what was happening to Ilgal really was the beginning of the same process Selvana had suffered. "It's been getting slowly worse for years, and the rate of deterioration has increased rapidly in the last few." She peered through the trees ahead. "We're almost at the road, and from there it's not far to the estate."

Farrin froze halfway through a nod of acknowledgment as a mournful howl split the air.

"Emmett," he whispered, his expression haunted.

Rosa stiffened, fear rippling over her. "That was close by."

She'd barely said the words when the sound of thundering hooves reached them, followed by a horn blast. The road was even closer than she'd realized, because she could hear the voices of the guards as they gave chase.

"It's one of the hunting groups," she gasped. "They're on his trail!"

Farrin's face was pale with horror. "If they catch him, they'll kill him. There's no way Otto's message has reached all the groups yet."

"Surely it won't come to that," said Rosa, willing herself to believe it. "I know he's terrified of exposure, but surely he'll turn human and reveal himself rather than let himself be *killed*."

Farrin stared at her in the darkness. "Turn human? That's not a choice he has. He can't control it. The magic takes him without permission, and releases him only when it's done with him. He won't be human again until morning."

"What?" Rosa's lips were numb. She remembered how she'd witnessed Emmett's transformation at dawn. There was so much she hadn't understood—so much she still didn't understand. But once again, there was no time to seek answers.

"Go," Rosa told Farrin. "You have to intervene."

Farrin took a step toward the sound, then hesitated. "What about you?"

"I'm going after the aconitum," Rosa said determinedly. "Find Emmett, and bring him to my grandparents' house if you can. I'll be waiting."

Farrin didn't pause to argue, his fear for his brother evident on his face. Without another word, he grabbed a nearby branch, swinging up into the tree. Rosa watched in amazement as he loped his way from tree to tree, incredibly agile and traveling much faster than he had on the ground.

She turned her face toward her grandparents' house, wishing she felt half the confidence she'd put on with her parting instructions. She didn't even know for certain that her grandmother's hothouse contained the wolfsbane, let alone whether she could get there and find it in time. And even if she did, how was it to be administered? She'd had no opportunity to read Leonhard's stolen record and find out. There was so much guesswork in this plan, but it was the only plan she had. And doing nothing wasn't an option.

She pushed on, feeling more afraid in the darkness now she was traveling alone. Had Farrin had success in catching up to the hunt, or to Emmett? The sounds of the chase had faded. Had Otto reached the king yet, and passed on the message?

Every minute felt like an hour as she hurried through the darkness, but soon enough she found herself at the entrance to her grandparents' estate. She swallowed, her eyes lingering on the burnished metal wolf on the gate as she hurried past. It felt ominous that there was no one manning the boundary, although she knew the enchantments would still be functioning.

Enchantments which had a weakness. A weakness she'd shared with Emmett and he'd then exploited to get inside the property and threaten her grandparents' safety.

Rosa let out a low moan as she hastened up the path to the manor under the silvery light cast by the full moon. She could barely even find it in herself to feel angry about that betrayal anymore. Everything that had passed since made it feel distant and unimportant. But in reality, it had only been the night before. And it was night again, and she had every reason to think that the wolf was once again in the area, hostage to who knew what savage impulses.

No, she told herself firmly, trying to suppress the shiver that rose up her spine. *He's out there being hunted by the guards, not in here terrorizing my grandparents.*

The thought brought little comfort as the manor house at last came into view. It looked different under the ghostly light, the absence of its usual bustle making it eerie. She reached the front door, wondering what time it was as she raised her hand to knock. Would her grandparents be sleeping?

Before she could actually knock, however, a sound behind her made her spin, her hands fisting nervously in her cloak. Her shoulders drooped in relief when she caught sight of the tall figure striding toward her.

"Grampy." Rosa put a hand over her heart as its frantic rhythm slowed minimally. "You scared me."

"Rosa?" Her grandfather sounded thunderous—an unusual tone for him. "What are you doing here? Did you come all this way alone, and in the dark? Rosa, what were you thinking?"

"I know, I know," Rosa said pleadingly. "I realize it's dangerous, and I swear I didn't do it pointlessly. It's important, Grampy, I need to get inside."

"I should think you do," said her grandfather, yanking the door open with one hand. "Lock the door at once, and don't open it for anyone but me, Rosie. I'll be along in a minute."

"Why, what's wrong?" Rosa asked quickly. Her eyes strayed to his other hand—she'd been too distracted to even notice at first that he had a large ax resting on his shoulder. "Where's Granny? Why are you out here?"

"She's inside," Grampy said reassuringly. "In the back room when I left her. I thought I heard something in the yard, and came to check. Just a feeling I had."

"But you should stay inside," said Rosa, alarmed. "I thought the building had an enchantment that would prevent any creature other than a human entering."

"It does," Grampy confirmed. "Thank goodness."

"Then why would you come out here and expose yourself?" Rosa demanded, still hovering in the doorway.

"Because enchantments aren't foolproof," the older man said grimly. "As we learned with the one around our boundary."

Guilt washed over Rosa, and it was on the tip of her tongue to confess her part in that incident. But confessions weren't top priority in such a moment—Grampy's safety was.

"They're better than nothing," she told him. "Please come back inside, Grampy. The sound you heard was probably just me."

"Nothing?" Grampy repeated, smiling at her. "I don't have nothing." He wiggled the deadly ax in a way that would have been comical if the situation hadn't been so dire. For all his advanced years, he didn't seem to find its weight any great strain. "And it wasn't you, Rosa. I can tell." He gestured with his chin. "Get inside with your grandmother, and I'll be along once I've checked the surrounds."

Rosa didn't like it, but it was clear she wasn't going to convince him. And after all, the best way to keep everyone safe in the long run—including her grandparents—was to find that aconitum and turn Emmett back to a human permanently.

She slipped inside, latching the door as instructed and hurrying down the corridor.

"Granny?" she called, uneasy at the silence. On reflection, she was surprised her grandmother hadn't heard the commotion at the front door and come to investigate. "Granny, are you here?"

A faint sound, like breaking glass, reached Rosa's ears, and she froze. It hadn't come from the direction of the back room, and she changed course, sprinting toward the large kitchen usually presided over by a paid cook. As she approached, she heard a familiar voice raised in an angry shout, and another smash. Except this time, it was followed by a vicious, inhuman snarl.

CHAPTER TWENTY-THREE

Rosa

"Granny!" Rosa screamed, throwing herself down the corridor and around another corner. Her heart was in her throat as she flung herself into the kitchen.

The scene that met her eyes was horrifying. Her grandmother was backed into a corner, indomitable as ever as she raised a kitchen knife in front of her. Across the room stalked the enormous wolf Rosa had seen on her last visit to the forest, the creature's eyes glowing with an inhuman light. Its paws crunched on broken glass as it stalked toward the elderly woman, and Rosa saw that the area was littered with the remnants of kitchenware which Granny must have thrown. It seemed she and Farrin had been wrong about how close the hunt was to catching Emmett. He hadn't even gone in the direction they'd guessed.

"Get away from her!" she screamed, all her mixed feelings toward Emmett fleeing in favor of anger. How dare he come after her grandmother in her own house? How had he even gotten in? The enchantments should have prevented it.

"Rosa!" Granny's face showed fear for the first time since

Rosa had entered the room, her gnarled knuckles white against the handle of the knife. "What are you doing? Get out of here!"

"Not likely." Rosa vaulted over a low bench, placing herself between her grandmother and the wolf. "Stay back," she ordered it, seizing a heavy pan from the counter and wielding it like a weapon. "If you hurt her, I'll never forgive you."

"Why are you reasoning with it?" demanded Granny, ever practical. "It can't understand you!"

"Yes he can," said Rosa. Her eyes were locked on the wolf's, and she could see the truth of her claim. The creature radiated a savagery that was gut-wrenching to behold, but there was intelligence in that gaze. Too much intelligence for a mindless beast.

The wolf let out a low growl, its hackles rising as Rosa stared it down.

Come on, Emmett, she pleaded silently. *Take control over it. Come back to me.*

But the creature in front of her showed no sign of softening. It advanced another step, its growl turning into a snarl. Rosa's hands were shaking, but she didn't back up, determined to protect her grandmother with her own life if that was what it took. No one else would pay for her foolhardy decision to trust the Medullan prince.

The kitchen looked out on a small herb garden, and the door leading to it was now between Rosa and her grandmother. In her peripheral vision, she caught a flash of movement through the window, before a thump on the door from outside made her turn her head.

That was a mistake. Seeing its opening, the wolf lunged at her, snapping its jaws. Rosa swung back around, bringing the pan up in front of her with all her strength. It caught the wolf on the nose, causing the creature to howl in rage. Rosa didn't dare take her eyes off the wolf again, but the movement and sound behind her told her that her grandmother had unlocked the door and wrenched it open. It hit the counter with a crash, and Grampy stormed into the room with a battle cry.

He raced toward Rosa, his ax raised with purpose. The wolf turned to him instead, growling furiously as Rosa sprinted to her grandmother.

"Get to safety," Grampy shouted, facing down the wolf without a tremor.

"Don't be absurd," Granny said stubbornly. "I'm not leaving without you."

Neither Rosa nor her grandfather wasted time arguing. They both knew Granny meant what she said.

"Then don't look if you don't want to see this," Grampy said grimly, planting his feet and raising the ax.

"Grampy, NO!" Rosa screamed, racing toward him and grabbing his arm. She didn't know if his confidence in his ability to kill the creature was misplaced, but either way, she couldn't let the fight happen. Letting her grandfather kill Emmett was as unthinkable as the reverse. "Please, please don't kill him!" she begged, not even sure whom she was speaking to.

Her grandfather kept his ax raised and his eyes on the wolf —which had gone quiet as if listening to the argument—but the bewilderment on his face was all for her.

"Not kill it?" Grampy repeated. "Rosa, I have to. The creature has been targeting us for weeks. If inside the manor isn't even safe anymore, we're left with no choice."

"There's another way," Rosa said desperately. "Please, you have to trust me." She looked at the wolf, which had remained still. Even the growling stopped as it seemed to await the outcome of their conversation. Encouraged, Rosa turned pleading eyes to her grandfather. "Trust me, Grampy."

"I do," he said gruffly. "But that doesn't mean I'm going to let you get torn apart by wolves."

"No one's tearing anyone apart right now," Rosa pointed out.

Moving surreptitiously as she spoke, she pushed the door to the outside closed with her foot. Reaching behind her, she locked it, all while keeping her eyes on the wolf.

"Move toward the other door," she murmured to her grandparents. "If we trap him in here, he'll be contained. You'll be able to get to safety."

"I think you mean *we* will be able to get to safety," said Grampy suspiciously.

Granny, on the other hand, wasn't accepting even that. "I'm not leaving my home," she said stubbornly.

"Yes, you are." The note of steel in Grampy's voice was so unexpected, both women stilled, looking at him in surprise. "I don't value this home more than your life, and if you do, I don't know how I could forgive you."

This uncharacteristic firmness stunned Granny into silence, for the first time in Rosa's memory. She seemed to still be trying to decide how to respond, but at least she was letting Grampy chivvy her toward the far door while she did. He walked backwards, hands still gripping the ax and eyes never leaving the wolf. Rosa started to inch backwards as well, hardly daring to hope. If she could trap Emmett in this room, she would be able to run to the hothouse and get the aconitum.

But while the wolf had watched the elderly couple's retreat without reaction, Rosa's attempted departure was apparently a step too far. Without warning, the creature lunged forward, its jaws snapping as the human trio abandoned caution.

"Run!" Rosa screamed, diving after her grandparents. She saw her grandfather half drag her grandmother across the threshold, then turn back for Rosa. But he wasn't reaching to pull her through. He was raising his ax, ready to permanently prevent the wolf from following them. Some part of Rosa's mind knew that her life quite literally depended on the decision she made next, but she couldn't afford to be overwhelmed by the gravity of it all. She'd reached the door, and without giving herself time to analyze, she grabbed the handle.

"Sorry, Grampy," she murmured into her grandfather's horrified face as she slammed the door shut and clicked the lock in one motion. She'd half expected the wolf to fall on her, but it hadn't, so she took a moment to drag a heavy chair over and barricade the door before turning slowly to face her adversary.

The wolf was crouched halfway across the room, a low growl vibrating from its chest. It watched her with those unnerving eyes, not moving a muscle.

"It's just you and me now," Rosa said, her voice shaking a little. "There's no need to attack. I can help you."

The creature made no move, its eyes intent on her face. As when she'd last spoken to it, Rosa knew it could understand her. There was no doubt that a human mind still existed behind the savage front. The question was how much control it had.

"Are you in control?" she asked. "Can you stay here and stay calm while I get the help you need?"

A low snarl issued from the wolf's mouth, and Rosa swallowed nervously. Was Emmett losing the control he seemed to have regained? Would he start attacking her again if she tried to leave? She took an experimental step backwards, and the growl rose to a snarl. She could hear her grandfather pounding on the door and calling for her, but she kept her full focus on the creature in front of her.

And as she stared into the wolf's eyes, a horrible feeling washed over her. She wanted to believe Emmett was in control when calm and the wolf was in control when attacking. But that didn't make sense. It was all too calculated for that. The eyes boring into hers were intense and terrifying, but they weren't wild. They were... predatory. And while Emmett's gaze had often taken her breath away with its intensity, it had never made her feel like prey. Even at their most overwhelmingly fervent, his eyes had always drawn her in. The eyes staring at her now weren't magnetic in any way. In spite of the obvious intelligence, they remained...savage.

Words from hours before flashed through her mind, spoken in an unnervingly eager voice from the advisor who'd abandoned his usual polished facade.

What was he like? Leonhard had asked. *Was he simply terrifying? Or was there a magnetism?*

What did Leonhard care about the effect of Emmett's wolf form on her? She'd assumed it was a clinical interest in the results of his experiment, but suddenly it occurred to her that it might be something else entirely, something much more personal.

"Leonhard?" she breathed, horror washing over her. Some part of her hoped desperately that she was wrong, but the rest of her was seeing it all slip into place, and wondering how she could have been so stupid for so long.

There was a moment of charged stillness, the only sound the continued hammering Rosa's grandfather was giving the door.

Then, its body rippling disturbingly, the wolf suddenly folded in on itself, its shape changing and its size shrinking until Rosa found herself looking at a man, crouched on the floor.

Leonhard lifted his head slowly, the rest of his body following before Rosa's horrified eyes. Clearly Leonhard didn't suffer the same restrictions Emmett did. There could be no doubt he was fully in control of the transformation. And he was obviously in control of all his actions while in wolf form, too. Rosa remembered, with a sick lurch, how closely the wolf had listened to her the first time she'd spoken to it.

"It was you," Rosa whispered through numb lips. "You who I spoke to in the forest, you who attacked this place last night. All the attacks were you. Emmett never harmed anyone." Her heart twisted in agony as she realized that he'd never done any of what she accused him of. And she'd made even him doubt the truth of his denials.

"Very good, Princess," the advisor said smoothly. "Although it took you a laughably long time to figure out the obvious." He gave a nasty laugh. "Did you really think that your stiff, weak-minded prince could be capable of what I've achieved in my true form?"

"Your true form?" Rosa repeated, her voice shaking with both anger and fear. "Just because you somehow twisted your-self into a wolf doesn't change the fact that your true self is a human, and as magic-less a human as I am."

"Silence." Leonhard went instantly from smooth to enraged, raising his hand as if to strike her.

Rosa curled her fists, ready to defend herself if necessary, but Leonhard lowered his hand again.

"Being born with magic is no indication of whether it's deserved," growled Leonhard. "I should know. My own family call themselves singers, and yet none of them truly feel the lure of magic. They chose to leave Ilgal because there was *too much* magic, as if such a thing were possible. I lost all respect for them that day."

"If you love Ilgal so much, why are you trying to evacuate it?" Rosa demanded, her mind still reeling from the revelation.

"Because humans don't deserve it," he said, his voice low and fervent. "Singers *or* non-singers. The forest needs to be reclaimed for the magic. We shouldn't be trying to lessen the flow of power. We should separate Ilgal from the rest of the continent and let magic grow as wild as it wishes to. Selvana is the true paradise."

"Selvana's ground is deadly to humans," snapped Rosa.

Leonhard's eyes glowed, looking almost like the wolf's. "Exactly. And in my true form, I am no longer human."

"So you want to clear every creature out except yourself?" Rosa asked sarcastically.

Leonhard made a dismissive noise in his throat. "Of course not. The creatures of the forest do nothing to offend it. Even the elves understand its beauty to an extent, and are not as obsessed with the presence or absence of a singing ability as humans invariably are. But they're also not so foolish as to be driven off by the strength of the magic, or the movement of a few wolves, so my activities haven't affected them. They've been wise to retreat deeper into the forest, to sections where the magic is even more plentiful than here."

"They can't feel the magic like humans can, and you never attacked them in wolf form," said Rosa scornfully. "Your arguments are nonsense, and no sensible person would follow your plan."

"And yet, Ilgal is on the point of evacuation," Leonhard said mockingly. He nodded toward the door which, by the sound of it, was now being subjected to Grampy's ax. "Even your grandparents are ready to flee. And you yourself didn't recognize me for what I am."

He scowled. "Although there I am also to blame. It took me far too long to realize what Prince Emmett had become. But how was I to know he was the one who'd unleashed my magic before it was ready? Idiotic boy, loosing an unfinished enchantment of that complexity. He's lucky he survived it at all. He clearly doesn't have the control over his condition that the completed enchantment would have given him." His eyes darkened. "That it was supposed to give *me*. Years of effort were wasted that night, and I will never forgive him for the time I've lost. It took me three more years to recreate the experiment for myself, three years I was forced to spend as a human, pandering to our weak-willed king and winning people over with tedious persuasion."

"How?" Rosa demanded, desperate for answers.

At least she knew now why Emmett had so little control over his own wolfish state—if he'd run afoul of an unfinished enchantment, who knew what it could do to him? It occurred to her that she also had her answer for how Leonhard had gotten past the defenses preventing any creatures but humans from entering the manor. It changed a great deal that, unlike Emmett, he could transform at will. He must have learned the nature of the protections, turned human to get inside the building, then transformed back.

"How did you do it, if you're not a singer?" she pressed. "Surely no singer would help you do this, and the elves know it's highly illegal for them to sell non-singer humans anything that could help them gather magic. "

Leonhard's smile sent a shiver down her spine. "You call yourself a child of Ilgal, but you know nothing of what's possible in the depths of the forest, Princess. In the city people cling to their restrictions preventing those not gifted with singing from accessing magic. Out there, where the elves are not so fastidious, the lines between singing and mining magic are blurred. When magic is this plentiful, money and connections can give access to power you can't imagine."

"And you willingly used the power to turn yourself into a monster?" Rosa demanded.

"A monster?" Leonhard's lips curved into a smile that didn't look quite human. "I am a creature of magic. Like so many others, you do not understand the true sanctity of magic. You do not have the reverence I have for it. An accident of fate—an accident I once believed a mistake—denied me the magic the rest of my family were born with. But I have learned to see my lack as a blessing. Growing up in the presence of magic, but blocked from the easy access which made my family take it for granted, I alone grew to love and treasure power for the gift it is. I alone had to work to gain access to it, and therefore I alone truly value it as it deserves." His eyes looked savage as he stared her down. "You call me a monster, Princess. But the real monsters are the humans who are capable of recognizing the sanctity of the magic and refuse to do so. I will drive each and every one of them out. Evacuation is neater, but other methods will suffice if necessary."

To Rosa's alarm, he was dropping back into a crouch, as if to transform back. She hadn't even noticed him doing it, but he'd also maneuvered himself so that he was between her and the door that her grandfather was trying to hack to pieces.

"What are you doing?" she demanded uneasily. "Stop it!"

"Much as I enjoy our conversation, Princess, I can't waste this excellent opportunity," Leonhard said. "I can't reclaim all of Ilgal in my advisory role if some of it belongs to Medulle. King Ryker himself said that land won't change hands without conflict. Now that everyone will soon know the truth about your prince, I think having you viciously killed by him in his wolf form should be sufficient reason for war. It's a cause I hoped to pursue from the moment I found out the truth about him, but I didn't dare dream you'd hand me such a perfect opportunity. I'm afraid I can't delay, however. It wouldn't do for your grandfather to make it back through that door with me still in this paltry form."

His skin was already rippling, and moments later—before Rosa had done more than cry out in protest—the wolf was once again crouched before her, ready to spring.

Rosa whirled around, looking for a weapon, but a furious howl made her stop in her tracks. It hadn't come from Leonhard —it had come from outside. The wolf beside her had frozen, and Rosa took advantage of its distraction to fling herself toward the door into the garden, fumbling with the latch as she threw it back open and tumbled out.

With a growl of fury, Leonhard leaped after her, but he wasn't as quick as the enormous shape flying out of the darkness. Rosa dove aside as a second huge wolf cleared a garden bed in one bound and landed between her and Leonhard. The creature swung its huge, gray head to face her, and Rosa found herself arrested by the intensity of those eerie, glowing eyes. It was an entirely different sensation from what she'd felt when Leonhard held her in his gaze.

"Emmett," she whispered.

The wolf lowered its snout, bumping her shoulder with its furry head. There was no whisper of doubt that he understood her, that he was in control.

Rosa screamed a warning just as a vicious snarl made Emmett whip back around. He was only just in time to leap out of the way of the other wolf's gnashing teeth, and the next moment he'd lunged at Leonhard, teeth bared. The wolves met mid-air in a terrifying tangle of fur and teeth, and Rosa once again dove out of the way. The yells from inside the house had become frantic, but she didn't re-enter the kitchen. Letting her grandfather and his ax into the fray would only put everyone involved in more danger. And it wouldn't help end this. Only one thing could do that, and she could afford no more distractions. She would reach the hothouse best via the garden anyway.

Terror rose in her throat at the sight of Emmett locked in battle with Leonhard. But there was nothing she could do to help him in this fight. She needed to trust him to take care of himself until she could end the nightmare once and for all.

Turning her back on the thrashing wolves, she threw herself into the dark, unforgiving night.

CHAPTER TWENTY-FOUR

Emmett

Emmett's mind was a mess of impressions—sound, smell, and sight blending together into one chaotic jumble. He didn't know how long he'd been running, but it had already been many hours by the time the hunt found him. Even with his unnatural wolf strength, he was flagging. He couldn't run all night this time, and he knew that if he stopped, he would die.

Would that be so bad? It would mean he could never hurt anyone else ever again.

His brother's face flashed before his eyes, then his parents'. Then, perhaps most painfully of all, Rosa's, eyes sparkling with angry tears as she'd fled from him that morning.

It was selfish to wish for death, and foolish to think that wouldn't cause pain to anyone. But he couldn't see how else this nightmare was going to end. He'd been a wolf for most of the day, his state was continuing unchecked into the night, and at no point had he felt any hint of a coming transformation. It seemed likely to him that there would be no more transformations. However long was left to him would be spent in this form, and he couldn't decide if it was mercy or cruelty that he still had his human mind.

A shout sounded behind him, and he increased his pace. He couldn't let the hunt get any closer. The instinct to attack was so strong, especially knowing his life was on the line. How could he be sure he wouldn't turn on one of the humans who were only doing their job? He forced himself to focus on the consistent thuds his huge paws made as they connected with the forest floor. The pace was frantic, but the rhythm was steady. He would let it consume his mind, try to ignore everything else. But the hunt was still gaining on him. He would have to change tactics.

Veering suddenly into the undergrowth, Emmett began to move in a wide arc, hoping to confuse his pursuers. If he swung wide enough, he might be able to travel back the way they'd come and take off in the opposite direction. The horses weren't as maneuverable in the forest as he was.

It was all his own fault, he berated himself as he ran. If he'd exerted more control over his wolf form, he would have run back to the Medullan side of the border hours ago. Why couldn't he keep himself from hanging around the area? It wasn't as though Rosa was going to be wandering around in the forest in the middle of the night, so why did he feel the need to be near her?

Rosa.

For the briefest of moments he doubted his senses, wondering if his thoughts had confused him. But he knew they hadn't. The wolf's nose was immeasurably superior to his human one, and it was never wrong, especially when the subject was so familiar to him.

He'd just crossed Rosa's trail.

Emmett swung himself around, returning to the place in question and taking off in a different direction again. He'd hoped the scent might have been old, but it was fresh. Rosa was out here somewhere, in the darkness of the forest. And according to the trail, she was traveling alone. Was she looking for him? Exposing herself to danger on his account yet again?

The frantic flight instincts prompted by being hunted faded away. They were nothing compared to the pure, unbridled panic that took Emmett over now. His lagging form found new energy, and he took off like a shot. At first he didn't even ask himself where the trail was leading, but before long he found himself plunging across the road and toward a burnished metal gate. The light of the full moon bathed the road, but it made little difference to Emmett. His wolf eyes saw excellently in the dark.

The gate stood open, but when Emmett threw himself toward it, he smashed into an invisible barrier. Some kind of magic was at work to prevent his passage. Desperate, he tried again, coming away battered and no closer to gaining entry.

Emmett stilled, pricking his ears and listening. He thought he could hear sounds of conflict carrying faintly on the air, but it was hard to tell. It could be the now-distant hunt. Fear riding him, he took off around the boundary of the property, choosing at random to go left instead of right. The property was marked with a low wooden fence, there for identification rather than to prevent entry. Every few yards, Emmett threw himself toward the property line, only to be met with the same result as he'd found at the gate.

His thoughts were muddled and confused, the wolf and the human at war, but both seemed to feel a panic that refused to ebb—on the contrary, he was growing more frantic the further he went. Soon he was bashing himself against the invisible wall with almost every step he took.

He'd gone a considerable distance along the fence line when it happened. He threw himself sideways, fully expecting to rebound, and instead fell through. He lost his balance, his flank hitting the ground on the other side of the boundary with a painful thud. But he was back on his paws in moments, scenting the ground without consciously deciding to. The wolf didn't fully understand what was happening, but it knew it was desperate to recapture the trail of its quarry.

There was no sign of Rosa, but that was hardly surprising. She'd entered through the gate, not at this spot. Emmett retained enough awareness to realize he must be at her grandparents' property, and he took off into the darkness with a loping gait. Before long a building loomed out of the gloom, and Emmett slowed his pace, sniffing the air. His ears made out muffled shouts of alarm, but none of them sounded like Rosa, and his wolf self lacked the control for altruism. Unintentionally, he'd managed to transfer his focus on Rosa into his wolf form, and even the beast seemed to feel a desperate urge to find her and protect her. But bringing it to care about anyone else was likely a feat beyond his shaky control.

Just as he caught a faint hint of the scent he was looking for, a protesting cry cut across the other sounds.

Rosa's cry.

Without Emmett's permission, his wolf self raised its head to the sky, letting out a bloodcurdling howl. The next moment he was running, sprinting even faster than he had when he'd first caught her scent. It was only seconds before Rosa came into sight, tumbling out of a door with a giant wolf hard on her heels.

Somewhere in his human mind, Emmett registered the shock of the sight. There was another wolf like him? But the wolf was in control now, and it didn't hesitate. It felt only blinding rage at the sight of Rosa under attack. Throwing himself forward, he faced off the stranger with a threatening growl.

The scent he'd been pursuing wafted to his nose, stronger

than ever, and once he was sure the other wolf's attack had been arrested, he couldn't resist turning for a moment to see her.

Rosa was staring at him in shock, but there was something else behind the expression. It wasn't the anger he'd seen the last time they'd spoken, or the revulsion he'd expected when she first learned his secret. It was trust, and relief, and...maybe something warmer. Something his wolf mind couldn't comprehend.

"Emmett." Her quiet murmur sent a shockwave through him, giving a surge of energy and power to his human mind. He wrested back a little more control from the wolf, realizing as he did so that even in his savage mind he could find no desire to hurt her.

Emmett lowered his head, nudging Rosa's shoulder as gently as he could manage. Her resulting scream was one of warning, but Emmett didn't need it. He'd heard the other wolf's snarl, and he was already in motion. Propelling himself away from Rosa, he launched himself at the growling creature, every part of him prepared to do battle to protect Rosa.

In the back of his mind he was aware of her pushing herself to her feet and running, but he didn't turn to look. Better to keep the other wolf's focus on him.

The wolf rammed its head into him, throwing Emmett off balance. His opponent took full advantage, sinking its teeth into Emmett's flank. But the pain barely registered. Emmett was still fueled by intense instincts, focused on nothing but bringing down the beast that had threatened Rosa.

He heard a splintering crash, and Rosa's voice raised in a warning. But it didn't seem to be directed at him. A man's shout responded, then Rosa yelled something to the speaker about getting himself and Granny to safety, and that she was clear. Emmett didn't try to look at any of the three humans his nose could detect. He was too focused on his own battle.

He threw the other wolf off, lunging after it with teeth bared. All the instincts he'd denied for four years of wolf transformations came pouring out. The desire to hunt, to subdue, to attack, raged with him, and he felt a savage delight in directing it toward a worthy target. The wolves were the same in size and ferocity, and although neither let up for a moment, Emmett couldn't have said who was likely to overcome. There was no end, no thought beyond the outcome...there was only the vicious battle in which they were locked.

His nose alerted him first to Rosa's return. Panic once again clouded his instincts, and he turned his head to see her standing to the side, calm and unprotected. She was alone, so she must have had success in sending her grandparents away. Probably they, like Emmett, had never dreamed she would willingly return to the scene of the wolf fight.

In her hand Rosa clutched a large white flower, not just a cutting but an entire plant with clumps of dirt hanging from the bulb. She'd obviously uprooted the whole thing.

"Stop!" she called, her voice cutting through the night. "There's no need for any of this. I can help you both. I can change you back."

Emmett stilled, his flanks heaving as his wolf eyes focused first on the flower, then on Rosa's face. Did he dare to hope? Was it possible she'd actually found aconitum?

His paws shifted under him, the wolf restless at this turn of events. Emmett pulled his mind ruthlessly back under his own control, everything in him being drawn toward the possibility of redemption.

The other wolf's response to Rosa's words couldn't have been more opposite, however. It went berserk, throwing itself toward Rosa as a feral snarl ripped from its throat. Emmett rammed himself into the other wolf's flank, but even that wouldn't have been enough if Rosa hadn't dived out of the way.

Except she dropped the flower in the process.

Emmett's eyes had barely caught the flash of white on the dark ground when the other wolf fell on it.

"Stop!" Rosa screamed. "That's the only one!"

Emmett lurched forward on the words, but not quickly enough. The other wolf had been very eager to use its teeth in the fight with Emmett, but it kept its muzzle well away from the flower this time, ripping it awkwardly to shreds with its claws. In the space of seconds, the flower was mangled and mutilated, trampled into the ground by the wolf's paws.

There was a moment of stillness as the three of them all stared at the destroyed remnants of the plant.

"Well." Rosa was the one to break the silence, her face more than usually pale. "That answers that."

Unbidden, a forlorn howl rose in Emmett's throat, carrying hollowly through the still yard. He thought he'd resigned himself to his fate, but the brief moment of hope made it unbearable.

"It's going to be all right, Emmett," Rosa said, and he realized she had tears in her eyes. She took a step toward him, and although he knew he should run, put distance between her and the danger he represented, he found himself instead leaning toward her.

Until the other wolf lunged. Only his quickened wolf instincts allowed Emmett to catch the movement early enough to intercept. The wolf, thrown off course, didn't get its teeth into Rosa, but did manage to knock her to the ground. It threw Emmett off, closing in on Rosa's prone form. It was going straight for Rosa's throat, and that realization sent Emmett into another blind rage. He was barely aware of his actions as he fell on the wolf. The sight of Rosa on the ground, her hair splayed across the dirt and her eyes wide and terrified as the wolf bared its teeth, gave Emmett an energy the previous fight had lacked. He put all his tension into one final crouch, springing on the beast just as it lunged again toward its prey.

Emmett's teeth closed around the other wolf's neck, the force of his own jaws frightening to his human mind. But for once he didn't try to wrestle for control. He let his human thoughts fade into the background so the wolf instincts could take over. He didn't want to know the details of what had to be done. He didn't want to remember after it was over. All he knew was that he had to protect Rosa at all costs, and this creature had shown itself determined to kill her.

It was over in a moment. Victorious, but still repulsed by his own savagery, Emmett pulled back, watching the creature's dying gasp. The urge to fight was gone completely. Not even the smallest part of him wanted to turn on Rosa, or anyone else. He wanted it to be over, all of it.

The night's horrors weren't done yet, however. As the life drained from the enormous wolf before him, its body began to transform. Emmett found himself looking at the lifeless form of a human. A human he recognized.

"Yes, it's Leonhard." Rosa's voice was sad and weary. She stepped up beside Emmett, her lack of fear jarring. "I feel such a fool, Emmett. It took me far too long to realize there was more than one wolf. And he wasn't only transforming at night like you were." She glanced at Emmett. "Your brother told me that you usually only transform at night, around the full moon. But Leonhard could do it at will. He's been roaming the forest causing havoc on purpose." Her eyes were penitent as she turned to him. "Every attack I blamed you for was him. I'm so sorry, Emmett. Of course you never bit anyone, or terrorized anyone. I should have known that."

Emmett, of course, could say nothing. But underneath his numb disbelief, he was aware of a heavy burden lifting. He hadn't been forgetting substantial events as he'd started to believe. He truly hadn't harmed anyone.

"He did terrible things, but I still thought I should give him a chance, with the flower," Rosa added. "I thought he should at least know he had the option to turn around, make a different choice. But it's clearly not an option he wanted."

At the mention of the flower, it was all Emmett could do not to howl again. He felt his whole form deflate, not even the wolf within him offering any fight against his longing for the rescue that had so nearly been his. He walked over to the trampled, shredded petals, sniffing dolefully at them. They were beyond reclaim, he could see that at a glance.

An unbearable grief rose inside him. He couldn't live his life doomed to be a savage animal. To never be able to communicate with those he loved, or even trust himself to be around them without fearing a lapse in control that would see them ripped to pieces. It wasn't a life he could face. His eyes traveled to Rosa, who was watching him quietly, showing none of the fear or revulsion she should. He could hardly bear to look at her.

His gaze returned to Leonhard's body, and he saw that the advisor had a knife strapped to his belt. Softly, Emmett padded forward, using his teeth as delicately as he could to draw the blade out. He trotted back to Rosa, dropping the weapon at her feet with a whine. She'd seen where this curse would take him as well as he had. She would surely understand that it would be better to kill the wolf before it had attacked anyone instead of after lives had been taken.

"Absolutely not," Rosa said flatly, just as if he'd spoken his thoughts aloud. "And frankly, I'm offended you would even suggest it." Her face softened as she looked at him, and she stepped carefully forward. When Emmett jerked backwards, she hesitated. "Is it safe for me to approach?"

Emmett paused, taking stock of himself. It seemed safe enough for the moment. Hesitantly, he dipped his head.

"Good." Rosa came forward, laying a hand on his furry head. Her touch was warm and reassuring, and he felt himself relax slightly under it. "I thought so. I could tell it was you straight away." Her voice turned repentant. "Which means I have no excuse for not realizing earlier that Leonhard *wasn't* you. Emmett, I'm so sorry. All the things I accused you of were him all along. I should have believed you."

Emmett shook his head slightly in silent protest of her self-criticism. Considering he hadn't even been sure he believed himself, how could she be blamed for doubting him?

"But we can talk about all this after," Rosa said briskly.

Emmett tilted his head quizzically. After what?

Rosa reached a hand into the dark blue cloak she wore, and Emmett stopped breathing altogether as she pulled out a clump of flowers, these ones cuttings rather than a whole plant. The flowers weren't as big as the last one, instead forming small white clusters. And, as best as Emmett could tell in the moonlight, the leaves were an unusual pale purple.

"If I've remembered Farrin's description correctly, this is the real aconitum," Rosa said. "And it's not all there is. There are a few plants growing in the hothouse. I just pulled off some flowers."

Emmett's heart was pounding in his chest now. Forcing himself to draw breath again, he let out a sneeze. The plant smelled awful. His instincts told him to stay far away from it, but he forced those instincts down, instead leaning closer.

"The other plant was a decoy," Rosa told him, sounding endearingly pleased with herself. "Or a test, more accurately. Like I said, I thought Leonhard should be given the option. And his response gave me the answer I was looking for." A smile softened her face. "So did your response." She held out the plant. "I don't know how it's supposed to work, but like I said, it's not the only plant, so we don't have to be too afraid to try. Judging by how carefully Leonhard avoided getting the fake plant in his mouth, I think the best bet is for you to just eat it."

Emmett stared at it for a long moment, terrified by the intensity of his hope. Was it really possible that the elusive plant had been in Rosa's grandmother's hothouse all along? And if this really was aconitum, was it the original kind imported from Selvana that simply acted as a deterrent to normal wolves, or the magically enhanced crossbreed that could undo the magic that had held him captive for so long?

No way to know but try.

Moving carefully so as not to alarm Rosa, he lowered his muzzle into her hand and grasped the plant between his teeth. It tasted foul, suggesting that one way or another it retained the wolf-deterring properties of legend. He swallowed it whole, making sure to consume every leaf and every petal.

The effect was instantaneous. At once, his fur began to quiver, and he felt the familiar sensation of the change. Except this time his fur didn't recede into his skin like normal—it fell out in great tufts. His claws also dropped off as his paws turned back to hands and feet. A moment later, he was standing upright under the light of the full moon, his body whole and human, and his mind more his own than it had been in four years.

"Rosa," he rasped, emotion threatening to overwhelm him. "Rosa, you did it. You freed me."

The shock on Rosa's face gave way to something much more raw. In a flurry of motion, she threw herself toward him, and the next thing Emmett knew, she was in his arms.

"Emmett!" she cried, her voice muffled where her face was pressed into his tunic. "Emmett, you're free."

Emmett's arm tightened around her, the other hand finding

its way under her chin to gently ease her face out from where she'd hidden it. Rosa responded at once, leaning back and pushing herself up on her toes.

Taking the invitation eagerly, Emmett pressed his lips to hers, his hand cupping the back of her head while the other arm crushed her against him. Rosa seized the collar of his tunic with both hands, intensifying the kiss so enthusiastically Emmett's head began to spin. For a moment, time and space were lost—there was no one else in the world, and nothing existed beyond their lips moving against each other's, and Rosa's form in his arms under the silver light of the first full moon his human eyes had seen in years.

Emmett's heart was singing with something as potent as magic, and he wanted the kiss to never end. The wolf was gone, but it seemed that when it came to Rosa, his impulses were every bit as intense as they'd ever been. Before she'd entered his life, he'd never known it was possible to feel anything so intensely. His every nerve felt twice as alive as it had any right to be. Fully returned to his own body, he was experiencing every sensation as potently as a man released into the fresh air after years trapped in a cave. And it was hard to believe that any sensation could top the experience of Rosa encased in his arms, kissing him as if her life depended on it.

Much as he wanted the moment to last forever, Rosa apparently felt differently. A moment later, she broke the kiss, gasping a little as she pulled back.

Reluctantly, Emmett let her go, although he kept his arms looped loosely around her.

"Don't get me wrong," Rosa said, sounding delightfully dazed. "I'd love to keep kissing you. But I have so... many...questions."

"I can imagine," Emmett acknowledged, his voice a low

rumble as he led her a short way across the yard, putting some distance between them and Leonhard's body.

Rosa barely seemed to notice the movement, grinning up at him with the mischief that had both maddened and captivated him since their first meeting. "The first of my questions being, is the offer of marrying you immediately and having your babies still on the table?"

CHAPTER TWENTY-FIVE

Emmett

Emmett gave a groan that was half laugh, half wordless longing.

"Rosa, I want nothing more. But even without the wolf, it's hard for me to believe I could ever be good enough to deserve you. And my life has a great deal of all the things you hate about being royal."

"I don't want you to deserve me," Rosa said dismissively. "I want you to love me."

"I love you with all my heart." Emmett had no hesitation in saying it. "More than I ever dreamed I could love someone."

"I feel the same way," said Rosa, her cheeks warming with pleasure.

Emmett rested his forehead against hers. "I can't believe you freed me, Rosa. I can't believe you found me underneath it all. I felt like the wolf was slowly swallowing me whole, and I was losing myself. But somehow you found me."

"No digging was required in order to find you," Rosa informed him. "You may have felt like you were losing yourself, but your real self was there all the time. I could see it clearly—

you were never as buried as you thought. After all, I fell in love with you even in spite of my best efforts not to."

"I think I must be the luckiest dog—or rather wolf—alive," Emmett said emphatically.

Rosa gave a delighted chuckle at this sign of his willingness to laugh about the wolf. Honestly, Emmett felt as though he could laugh about almost anything in that moment. Hours before, he'd thought his life was over, and there was nothing left but misery, violence, and a shameful death. Now he was not only free, but he'd won his heart's desire.

"I guess that's settled then," Rosa said contentedly. "My other questions can probably wait."

She leaned up hopefully, and Emmett was only too ready to comply. However, the moment his lips touched hers, a shout carried across the night, breaking the moment. He turned to see Farrin sprinting across the yard, beside himself with excitement.

"EMMETT!"

"Farrin!" Emmett released Rosa to turn toward his brother, who catapulted straight into him as if they were roughhousing children instead of grown men.

"Emmett, you're free! You're human!"

"Yes, it's over," Emmett told Farrin, who seemed to be unable to find enough of his brother's arms and back to thump in congratulations. "Rosa found the aconitum, and I ate it."

"Is it permanent, do you think?" Farrin asked.

Rosa turned anxious eyes to Emmett, clearly not having considered the question.

But Emmett gave a reassuring nod. "It's over," he repeated. "I could always feel the wolf inside—always. Now it's gone."

"Yes, I'm just hoping he doesn't become horribly dull without it," Rosa said cheerfully, her relief evident behind the joke.

Farrin gave a choking laugh that was half cry.

"Because we're going to get married of course," Rosa said comfortably, her tone making it clear she was fishing for congratulations.

Farrin readily complied. Emmett knew his brother well enough to recognize that his delight was completely genuine. His exclamations and insistence that he'd seen it coming since the moment he arrived were cut short by the appearance of a group of riders, Rosa's grandparents at their head.

"Ah yes, I'd just run into the hunt when your grandparents caught up," Farrin said. "When they said there were two wolves fighting here, I knew I had to get here before I was too late." His eyes passed around in confusion. "Speaking of which, where's the other one?"

"Over there." Emmett gestured to the unmoving form of Leonhard, and Farrin gave a low whistle.

"There's a lot to be explained," Rosa acknowledged. "But my first priority is getting back to the castle. Poor Otto is going to be very upset when he realizes we gave him the slip and came out here."

"Yes, we need to return to Terenford," Emmett agreed. "I want to speak to your mother and stepfather." The fire in Rosa's eyes matched his own as he looked down at her. "Urgently."

"All right, you two, tone it down," Farrin said indulgently, as two figures detached themselves from the approaching group and ran to Rosa.

"I'm all right, Granny, Grampy," she said quickly. "The danger is over, there are no more magically enhanced wolves."

"Rosa, why did you come back here?" Rosa's grandfather demanded. "I thought you were running for the entrance like we were, and when you didn't appear, we were frantic."

"I'm sorry I scared you," she said penitently. "It's hard to explain, but I promise I'll do it, if you come to the castle with us. For now, it's enough to know that I'm not at all hurt." She grinned up at Emmett. "My heroic prince was here to save me, after all."

"That's a bit of a change in tone from you," said her grandmother, not sounding especially impressed about it.

"Rosa is speaking in jest," Emmett assured the older woman, inclining his head respectfully in her direction. "The truth was very much the opposite, actually. She saved me in more ways than one."

"Both are true," Rosa said, linking her hand with Emmett's with a comfortable familiarity that made his heart soar.

When the hunt arrived, all was chaos for a few minutes. But eventually the Terenan soldiers were convinced to follow the directions of the Medullan princes, and order emerged as some took charge of Leonhard's body, and others took responsibility for escorting the princess back to the city. In a short time, they were all mounted—those not in the hunting party borrowing horses from the manor's stables—and riding back toward the capital.

Emmett's body was sagging with weariness, but his mind was on high alert. He kept glancing over at Rosa, warmth spreading through him every time he caught her watching him, a smile lurking at the corner of her mouth.

When they finally emerged from the forest, they created a commotion. The city gates were flung wide, and they rode through to discover a group on the point of departure.

"Looks like Otto found the king's hunting party," Farrin commented, his eyes on the two mounted figures at the front of the group.

"And brought him back to the city only to discover we'd snuck off," Rosa finished, wincing. "I'd better go explain."

She spurred her horse forward, Emmett and Farrin following close behind. The king was visibly relieved at the sight of her, and Otto half pulled her off her horse to both hug and berate her. It was clear that the royals had been extremely worried—even Queen Ada was there, although Emmett had rarely observed her leaving the castle. Hopefully when all was explained, they would understand.

"I really am sorry, Mama," Rosa was saying when Emmett dismounted beside her. "I know it was terrible of me to put you through that, and I swear I had a very good reason for it." The queen didn't look much mollified, but her face changed completely when Rosa pushed blithely on. "If it makes you feel better, I've decided to marry Emmett after all."

"What?" The queen's cry was almost a shriek, and Emmett had to stifle a laugh at his betrothed's graceless way of announcing their plans.

"With your blessing, Your Majesties," Emmett said, bowing to both Queen Ada and King Ryker.

The king eyed him. "I have a great many questions I'd like answered, Prince Emmett. And there are many details that would need to be discussed if our kingdoms are to form an alliance."

"Ryker," said Queen Ada, in the exasperated tone Emmett had usually only heard her use toward her daughter.

The king's face softened into what was almost a laugh. "But of course we would be delighted, if this is the path Rosa wishes to follow."

"It is," Rosa said, her confidence making Emmett feel so light he could have flown.

"Are you sure?" the queen asked her.

"Mama!" Rosa protested, laughing. "You've been hounding me to do exactly this all summer, and now you're trying to talk me out of it?"

"I'm not trying to talk you out of it," said Queen Ada. "I'm just making sure you understand."

"She's right," Emmett said seriously. "I'm my father's heir. I'll need to return to Port Dulla soon, and make my home there. If we marry, it would have to be your home, too. You wouldn't be able to live in the forest as you've hoped to do."

Rosa met his eyes seriously. "I know," she assured him. "I'm fully aware of all of that." She glanced toward the trees, then sent an apologetic smile toward her grandparents. "I love Ilgal. I always will. I come from the forest, and it will always be a part of me. But...I suppose I've been realizing for a while now that when I talked about returning to live in the forest, I was enamored of a concept, not a real lifestyle that I could actually live."

"You know," Farrin chimed in, "it's possible to love the forest without living there." He elbowed his brother playfully. "Emmett's done it for years. All his life, really."

"I know," said Rosa, smiling fondly up at Emmett. "It's his only likable quality."

Queen Ada made a strangled noise of protest, and Prince Otto let out a shout of laughter. Clearly there was an amusing story behind the words, and Emmett resolved to ask Rosa later. They would have all the time in the world to share their stories, after all.

"Anyway, I'm ready to do the same," Rosa said staunchly. "To love the forest without living there, that is." She leaned against Emmett. "Although maybe I can convince Emmett to visit Lernvale from time to time, to tend to the alliance, you know."

"Of course we can do that," Emmett said readily, moved by her willingness to make sacrifices in order to be with him.

She squeezed his arm. "You said back at Granny's house that your life involves lots of the things I hate about being royal." Her eyes were earnest as they met his. "But I don't hate being royal. There are things that frustrate me, but other things I like." Her eyes passed to her mother. "It's been dawning on me for a while that I could have been more understanding of why you embraced this life so wholeheartedly, Mama. I realize now how different the shackles of marrying into royal life are when you're the one who chooses it."

"I don't want marrying me to mean shackling yourself in any way," Emmett said, distressed by her choice of wording.

Rosa sent him a cheeky grin. "Then you're more generous than I am, because I fully intend to shackle you to me for life."

"That doesn't sound so bad," Emmett countered, unable to help laughing.

Rosa gave a satisfied nod. "Then you know precisely how I feel." Her expression once again turned serious. "I've been a princess for years now, Emmett. I do know what I'm getting myself into. And I think, if I stop fighting it and start embracing it, I can contribute a great deal. Including things a born and bred princess couldn't."

"That's what I've been saying for years," the queen chimed in with satisfaction.

"I completely agree," Emmett assured Rosa.

"I'm glad you two have worked it out," interjected Otto. "And I'm not in the least averse to gaining Emmett as a brother. But some of us are still waiting for answers. And lots of them."

Rosa drew a big breath, turning away from Emmett. "You're right. But we should go back to the castle. You'll want to be sitting down for this."

After some grumbling and practical maneuvering, the group began to make its slow way up the cobblestoned streets toward the castle. Farrin and Otto took the lead, chatting amicably, but Emmett lingered behind, hoping to stay at Rosa's side.

When she'd answered the questions necessary for immediate action to be taken regarding Leonhard's body, she appeared at his side, taking his arm readily.

"Ready to face the wolves?" she asked him jokingly. "So to speak."

Emmett chuckled. "I don't know if I am. I don't have nerves of such steel as you do."

"Yes you do," Rosa told him quietly. "You're the strongest person I know, Emmett."

He shook his head as they followed the rest of the group. "I wish that was true. I was so weak against the wolf so often. Especially when it came to you." She made to protest, and Emmett cut her off. "No, I need you to hear me, Rosa. I don't think you realize how much the wolf stripped away my inhibitions. Usually nothing is more important to me than duty, and yet I failed it at every turn."

"You didn't though," Rosa told him softly. "I do believe you that the wolf was eroding your control, truly I do. But thanks to your unyielding sense of duty, your idea of failing your duty at every turn is still most people's idea of taking your duty incredibly seriously."

Emmett shook his head. "It's not good enough. Not when it affected you as well. You didn't even know you were in danger. I knew I shouldn't lead you on, shouldn't involve you at all. But the temptation to give in to what I wanted was just *so* strong when it came to you. I didn't know how to fight it."

Somehow, even this information didn't seem to perturb Rosa.

"Emmett, you don't see yourself clearly at all," she informed him. "And you said yourself that you never knew you could love someone like this. It was a new experience for both of us, and you can't know it was the fault of the wolf that you found me hard to resist." She tossed a disheveled braid over her shoulder coquettishly. "Maybe I'm just irresistible."

"That's undoubtedly true," Emmett informed her, amused.

Rosa smiled back at him, although her words were perfectly serious. "I'm not denying it was bad that you were constantly under attack from the magic." She gave him a half-apologetic look. "But honestly, I can't help but feel that maybe it was a good thing that you were made vulnerable enough for your rigid focus on duty to be loosened just a little. Just enough to give you a glimpse of what you wanted, and the push to pursue it."

"But if you'd been hurt—" Emmett started, before she again cut him off.

"I was never in danger from you," she told him, the certainty in her voice absolute. "I'm telling you, Emmett, you are far too harsh on yourself. You feel like you weren't in control, but that's only according to an impossibly high standard. Trust me, I saw a real wolf tonight, so I know. Even when not in his wolf form, Leonhard was a predator in a way you could never be. In your most wolfish moments, you never made me feel hunted. You fought the magic, and you didn't let it corrupt you."

Emmett didn't know what to say. Part of him still felt he was to blame, but in face of her confidence, he was starting to wonder if she could be right. It was so incredibly liberating he was almost afraid to believe it.

"I don't know what I did to deserve you," he murmured, looping one arm around her shoulders.

"It was the kiss in the sunflower fields," Rosa informed him solemnly. "If I'd known such a serious mouth could kiss like that, I would have baited you into kissing me much earlier."

"You're baiting me right now," Emmett informed her, a wolfish growl lingering in his voice.

Rosa laughed, pausing to push up on her toes and press a quick peck to his lips. "Even princesses need to have a little fun from time to time, you know," she told him. "It's how I make sure that royal life doesn't get dreadfully dull."

Emmett grinned as she tangled her fingers with his and tugged him back into motion. He had a feeling that his life, royal or otherwise, was going to be anything but dull from here on out.

Rosa

Rosa peered eagerly out the window as the carriage bumped along.

"How long now?"

"Until we reach Port Dulla?" Emmett asked, sounding amused. "A day and a half."

Rosa shot him a look. "You know that's not what I mean. You've been going on for months about how you can't wait for me to see the sea, and now you act like you don't know why I'm so eager to reach it?"

Emmett scooted across the seat of the carriage to join her near the window. "I was only teasing you," he said. "And we'll reach the coast any minute now. The road goes along it for ages, so you'll have plenty of opportunity to admire it."

She nodded, her eyes still directed out the window. She didn't voice it aloud, but they both knew that her focus on glimpsing Emmett's beloved ocean for the first time was in part a distraction from her nerves about their arrival in Port Dulla, and the formal betrothal celebration that awaited them. It had been months since their betrothal, and although Emmett had spent almost all of that time back in the

Medullan capital, Rosa had yet to meet King Johannes or visit Port Dulla.

"Don't worry, Rosa," Emmett said, his voice gentle as he apparently read her thoughts. "They're going to love you."

"I don't know why you assume that," she said ruefully. "I'm not many people's idea of the proper princess."

"Have you forgotten how eager my mother was to set us up when she was in Lernvale?" Emmett asked.

Rosa gave him a look. "Because you were a cursed wolf whose time was rapidly expiring. Now your curse is lifted, and you're the most eligible catch on the continent. You could have anyone."

"No I couldn't because I'm already taken," said Emmett comfortably. "And don't forget that you're a princess yourself, Rosa. If eligibility is your concern, there's no reason to worry. But you hit on the main point already. My curse is broken, and you're the one who broke it. Trust me, my parents are very ready to welcome you."

Rosa shifted, seating herself beside him in the carriage. "You do make a good argument," she acknowledged. "And I shouldn't be wasting our time like this. I've missed you so much while you've been gone."

"I've missed you as well." Emmett entwined their fingers, his touch still making Rosa's heart flutter.

"And I doubt we can weasel our way into a second leg of the journey alone in a carriage," Rosa went on candidly. "I don't think Mama realizes we're the only ones in here, to tell the truth. Otto helped me bundle her into his carriage first so that she wouldn't notice."

Emmett grinned. "Otto is an excellent brother."

"He is," Rosa agreed. "But even so, I'm glad for a break from hearing about his departure plans. For someone who only recently claimed to love the luxuries of castle life too much to venture into the forest, he sure is obsessed with preparing to relocate there."

"You mean his trip into the deeper parts of Ilgal to oversee the rehabilitation process?" Emmett said. "I was going to ask about that. I thought King Ryker had been having trouble finding enough singers willing to assist in an attempt like the one they're currently undertaking in Selvana."

"He has," Rosa confirmed. "They're still scouring the kingdom for volunteers, and that's part of what Otto is going to be doing in Ilgal. He'll be looking for any singers living in the more remote regions. We figure that they're more affected by the building magic, and therefore might be more willing to help try to lift it. If they find some singers along the way, they'll hopefully also be able to perform a magical audit of sorts to figure out which areas need the most attention. He's hoping to find the elves, too, I think. I'm sure you know that the bulk of them withdrew deeper into the forest some time ago, and have been no help whatsoever in any attempt to address the magic crisis."

Emmett nodded, and Rosa paused, scowling.

"Ugh. Why am *I* talking on and on about it now?" She gave her head a little shake. "It is endearing to see how proud Otto is at being given the responsibility, though. I think in part he's trying to make up for how reluctant he used to be to come into the forest with me. It's sweet, but he doesn't need to. I don't hold any grudge there."

"But you will miss the forest," said Emmett quietly.

"Of course I will," Rosa said. "And my grandparents. And the rest of my family. "But I really am ready to build a new life with you, Emmett. I didn't want to spend the rest of my life in the castle in Terenford, and I don't really see a future for myself in the wilds of Ilgal, either."

Emmett squeezed her hand. For a few minutes there was silence, then he cleared his throat, his voice a little gruff.

"I heard that Leonhard's death was officially recorded as an animal attack."

Rosa sighed. "Yes. It's sort of true, after all. I had no part in the decision, but to be honest I'm glad you don't have to go through any kind of questioning or hearing or anything. It would just be too much after everything you've already suffered because of him."

"I would have been willing to do it if necessary," Emmett said.

"I know," Rosa assured him. "Which is why I'm glad it wasn't necessary." She stared unseeingly out the window for a moment, before letting out another sigh. "I can't believe how long it took me to see what he'd become. What he'd willingly turned himself into. The record said the magic would corrupt anyone who used it, and even you had started to have wolf-like characteristics creeping into your human form. But until that time in his study, I didn't see any sign of the wolf in him."

"I've discussed it at some length with our top singers, and I think he was more corrupted by the magic than I was, not less," Emmett said. "Perhaps not physically speaking, but within himself. He was good at hiding it for a while, but the truth is he was becoming unbalanced. Remember that he'd been a wolf for a lot less time than I had, and already he'd begun to abandon logic, and make decisions according to his more brutal instincts."

"But you were holding the wolf at bay when in human form," Rosa argued. "And like you said, you'd been afflicted longer."

"That's the crucial point," Emmett said. "Our experts believe that there was one factor responsible both for it affecting me more physically and for it affecting me less on the inside."

"What factor?"

"That, like you said, I was afflicted. I didn't intentionally expose myself to the magic like Leonhard did. I was resisting it the whole time, with all of my waning strength. He, on the other hand, was embracing it. That meant there was no need for the wolf to fight the human, which I'm sure is what caused my wolfish mannerisms and physical changes during my human periods. The wolf in Leonhard and the human in him were one and the same. There was no fight, no barrier to the wolf taking over his mind completely."

"Because he was the wolf all along," said Rosa softly. "As evidenced by his decision to become it in the first place."

Emmett nodded, and Rosa studied his face. He was truly the most honorable man she knew. It was impossible to imagine him becoming corrupted. No wonder the wolf had been forced to take over his body in order to get control. His mind and heart weren't so easily overcome.

The carriage turned a corner, and Rosa glanced out the window. A gasp of excitement escaped her, and Emmett banged on the roof of the carriage. The driver obediently pulled the vehicle to a stop, and Rosa tumbled out, Emmett close behind.

Simply put, the sight before Rosa robbed her of words. They were standing on the top of a cliff, a gusty, salty wind whipping her skirts and braids. And before her eyes stretched an immeasurably huge expanse of water. It wasn't anything like the lakes Rosa had seen. It was...alive. There was no other way to put it. Its motion, the song of the waves, the smell in the air. Something powerful moved in Rosa's chest as she gazed out at it, something not unlike the deep peace she'd always felt when under the canopy of her beloved forest.

"What do you think?" Emmett asked, slipping an arm around her back and looking out over the waves. "Pretty breathtaking, isn't it? I never know how to describe it to someone who's never seen it. And not everyone who sees it feels it. But I always have."

"I know exactly what you mean," Rosa said. "You can really see the ocean from the castle in Port Dulla?"

Emmett nodded. "You should see the ballroom. It has a wall of glass with this breathtaking view, and opens right onto the sand."

"It sounds magical," Rosa breathed. She leaned into him. "I will miss the forest, like you said. But this..." She breathed in the salty smell, the excitement of discovery and fresh adventure rising within her. "It's a good thing there's room for so many kinds of love in my heart."

"What kinds, as an example?" Emmett asked innocently.

Rosa turned to him, not deceived. "You're shameless, Prince Emmett, trying to pry a declaration of love out of a girl so brazenly."

Emmett turned to fully face her, slipping his other arm around her and holding her comfortably there. "Maybe it will be less brazen if I go first. I love you, Rosa, my reluctant but radiant princess."

Rosa grinned, delighted with this title. "And I love you, Emmett, my rigidly dutiful, intensely serious, surprisingly passionate kisser of a wolf-man."

Apparently not quite as pleased with his labels, Emmett gave a growl which Rosa cut off by pressing her lips to his, a gesture he seemed to accept as a peace offering.

After all, Rosa reflected as her prince kissed her on the top of a wind-blown, seaside cliff, there was a great deal to be said for fresh starts and new adventures. Nerves notwithstanding, she was full of excitement for the life they were only just starting together.

NOTE FROM THE AUTHOR

Thank you for reading *Song of Moonrise*. I hope you enjoyed returning to the world of Providore. I would be so grateful if you would consider leaving a review on Amazon—it would really make a difference!

If you want to read Otto's story, and learn more about the growing magic in Ilgal, check out *Song of Trails*, the next installment of *The Singer Tales*. You'll find more adventure, fantasy, mystery, and hard-won happily ever afters!

Join up to my mailing list at deborah gracewhite.com to be kept up to date on new releases, specials, and giveaways, such as bonus chapters. You'll receive some great freebies, too, including *An Expectation of Magic*, a novella which is a prequel to my completed YA fantasy series *The Vazula Chronicles*.

Plus, you'll receive *Dragon's Sight*, an 8,000 word prequel to my completed YA fantasy trilogy *The Kyona Chronicles*.

Again, thanks for entering the world of Providore! I hope to see you back again.

ALSO BY DEBORAH GRACE WHITE

The Kyona Chronicles: YA Fantasy

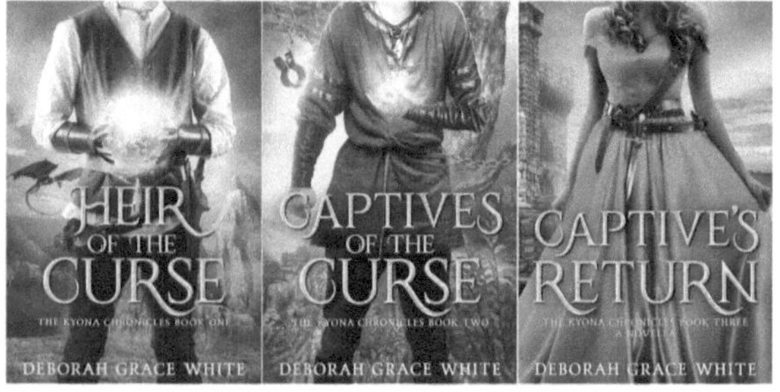

The Kyona Legacy: YA Fantasy

The Vazula Chronicles: YA Fantasy

The Kingdom Tales: Fairy Tale Retellings

The Singer Tales: Fairy Tale Retellings
(releasing throughout 2023)

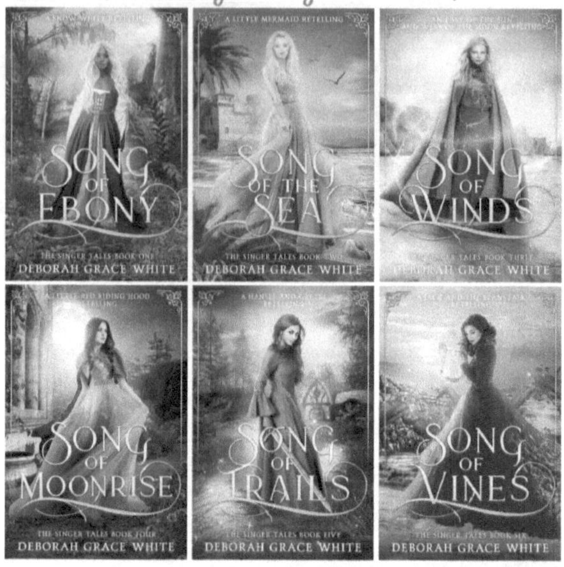

The Unlucky Prince: Fairy Tale Retelling
(Once Upon a Prince Multi-Author Series)

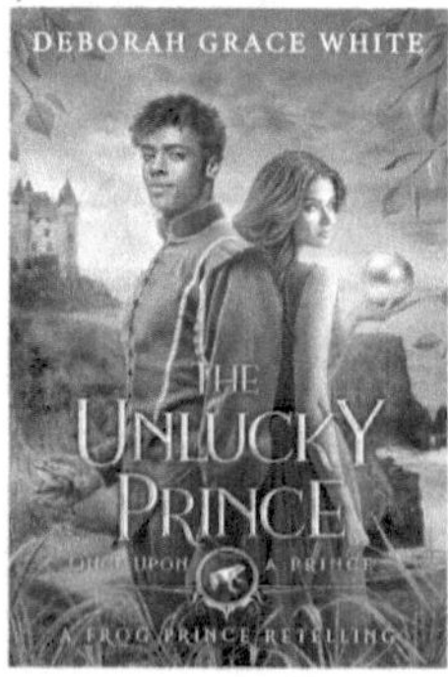

ACKNOWLEDGMENTS

Massive thank you to my awesome team for their help with *Song of Moonrise*. I was a little unsure whether I could pull off a werewolf story, and the encouragement and assistance was invaluable.

Ray, my long-suffering husband and first reader, for listening so well and providing such helpful feedback. My betas for your usual awesomeness: Mel W, Mum, Dad, and Adrian. Thanks also to Shae for the excellent job proofreading. Any remaining errors are of course my own.

Thanks to Karri for the beautiful cover that merges Rosa's character and the Little Red Riding Hood story so perfectly, and to Becca for the gorgeous map that continues to bring Providore to life.

To you, the reader, thank you for giving me the privilege of being an author.

And most importantly, to God, who can redeem us even from the darkest of places.

ABOUT THE AUTHOR

I've been a reader since I can remember, growing up on a wide range of books, from classic litera- ture to light-hearted romps. The love of reading has traveled with me unchanged across multiple continents, and carried me from my own childhood all the way to having children of my own.

But if reading is like looking through a window into a magical and beautiful world, beginning to write my own stories was like discovering that I could open that window and climb right out into fantasyland.

I cannot believe how privileged I am to actually be living that childhood dream and publishing my own novels. I do so from my hometown of Adelaide, Australia, where I live with my husband and our three little ones.

I've never outgrown my love of young adult stories, so the genre of young adult fantasy was always going to be my niche. Feel free to email me at deborah@deborahgracewhite.com and introduce yourself! Or subscribe to my mailing list at deborah gracewhite.com for free giveaways, sales, and updates.